Mick Finlay was born in Glasgow but left as a young boy, living in Canada and then England. Before becoming an academic, he ran a market stall on Portobello Road, and has worked as a tent-hand in a travelling circus, a butcher's boy, a hotel porter, and in various jobs in the NHS and social services. He teaches in a psychology department, and has published research on political violence and persuasion, verbal and non-verbal communication, and disability. He now lives in Brighton with his family.

Arrowood

and the Thames Corpses

MICK FINLAY

ONE PLACE. MANY STORIES

This novel is entirely a work of fiction. The names, characters and incidents portrayed in it are the work of the author's imagination. Any resemblance to actual persons, living or dead, events or localities is entirely coincidental.

HQ
An imprint of HarperCollins*Publishers* Ltd
1 London Bridge Street
London SE1 9GF

This paperback edition 2020

1
First published in Great Britain by
HQ, an imprint of HarperCollins*Publishers* Ltd 2020

Copyright © Mick Finlay 2020

Mick Finlay asserts the moral right to be
identified as the author of this work.
A catalogue record for this book is
available from the British Library.

ISBN: 978-0-00-8324520

MIX
Paper from
responsible sources
FSC™ C007454

This book is produced from independently certified FSC™ paper
to ensure responsible forest management.

For more information visit: www.harpercollins.co.uk/green

This book is set in 10.6/15.3 pt. Sabon

Printed and bound in Great Britain by
CPI Group (UK) Ltd, Croydon, CR0 4YY

Arrowood and the
Thames Corpses

Chapter One

We were playing cards in the parlour when the captain and his daughter arrived. It was late morning, the flies drifting around the guvnor's knuckle head in the midsummer heat. For the last few days we'd been waiting on a case from the lawyer Scrapes, but he kept delaying and the longer it went on the longer we weren't earning. Arrowood was vexed: he hadn't been sleeping too well since his sister Ettie returned from Birmingham with the baby, and he was suffering a rash under his arm. Each hour that passed worsened his temper.

'A bit of breeze, is that too much to ask?' he grumbled, throwing his cards on the table in frustration. As he pushed himself up, the back of his britches clung for a moment to the damp chair. He stuck a finger in his waistcoat pocket and hooked out a coin. 'Get me a kidney pudding will you, Barnett? You won't be hungry, I suppose. It's only eleven.'

I got to my feet. It was an errand I'd run hundreds of times before, and I knew how it went with him. Money was tight between cases. Always was. Maybe one day it'd be easier, but I wasn't holding any hope on it.

The guvnor's rooms were behind the pudding shop on Coin Street. It was hot as a foundry in there, the long black range

3

baking with all its might, pots boiling away on the top. A couple of sweaty customers stood in line waiting to get served by Albert, who seemed to be the only one in the family still working. Mrs Pudding was bent double over the counter, her face resting on a cloth. Little Albert stood wheezing on the doorstep, staring at his boots in a fug. Next to him on the pavement sat a couple of little monkeys, no more than six or seven years old, their hands out in the hope some punter might give them a bit of food.

'Lucky you come in just now, Norman,' said Albert in his usual glum voice. 'These folk were just asking for Mr Arrowood.'

The captain was solid and square-faced, about forty or fifty I supposed, his eyes shaded by a battered riverboat cap. He grasped a small packet of meat in both hands. Behind him was a girl of fourteen or fifteen, her shoulders wide and strong, her face covered in freckles. A thin bonnet, its edges dark with sweat, was tied tight over her head.

'I'm his assistant,' I said, offering each my hand. 'Come through.'

I led them back up the dusty corridor lined with sacks of sugar and flour and into the parlour. The guvnor looked at us in horror as we stepped through the door. A little groan came from the girl.

In the short time I'd been away he'd taken off his britches and shirt, and now sat at the table wearing nothing but his drawers and vest, a piece of bread and butter in his hand. His stumpy legs were white as lard, hairy here and bald there, and his drawers were stained in the most shameful way, the sagging lump between his legs like a clutch of baby mussels.

'Oh, Lord,' he muttered, grabbing his britches from the

floor and trying to shove his bloated feet through. 'Excuse me, please. I was just . . .'

As he fumbled with his shirt, the man and the freckled girl stood in the doorway, silent and still.

'This is Mr Arrowood,' I told them.

The boatman nodded, a grim look on his square face. Doing her best not to see the writhing spectacle before her, the girl's eyes travelled over the gloomy little parlour, the flies circling in the centre of the room, the bare floor, the stacks of newspaper against the walls. By the open window was a shelf holding his books on emotions and the psychology of the mind, but her eyes lingered longest on the orange cat sat like a sentry on the mantel. The man seemed to fix on the sticky tabletop with its melting packet of butter, its ragged Allinson's loaf, its wild scatter of crumbs.

'I'm so very sorry, miss,' said Arrowood, tucking in his shirt. 'I can only hope the sight of the good Lord's creation hasn't caused you any spiritual distress.'

The young woman dropped her eyes and smiled.

'Now,' he said when all was right again. 'Please have a seat. What did you want to see me about?'

'Name's Captain Moon,' said the bloke when they were sat down at the table. He twitched his head at the girl. 'This here's my daughter, Suzie. We've a problem and hoped you could help.'

The captain pulled off his cap and wiped the sweat from his brow. His eyes were small, his jaw and mouth hid beneath a bush of orange and grey hair. His suit was too thick for such a warm July, its elbows a little over-polished.

'We run a little pleasure steamer, sir. The *Gravesend Queen*. Take folk up to Gravesend every Saturday and Sunday for the pleasure gardens. Anyways, there's a fellow been damaging the boat when she's moored overnight. It'll put us out of business if it keeps on. Summer's when we make our money, see.'

'Polgreen's his name,' said Suzie. 'Ain't it, Dad?'

Moon gave a nod.

'What sort of damage have you suffered?' asked the guvnor.

'First it was rocks through the windows,' answered Moon. 'Next thing I turn up one morning and me lamps is all gone.'

'The fish guts, Dad,' said Suzie. She looked at me stood by the door, her eyes strong and hard.

'Aye. That was the first, the windows was after.' He jumped up from the chair, pacing over to the door, his hands in his pockets. 'He dumped a load of old fish guts in the saloon! Disgusting it was, like the devil himself'd spewed all over the place.'

'Where's the boat moored, Captain?'

'We had her just off the old pier by Victoria Bridge when it started. We moved her since.'

'Any other boats there?'

'Five or six, but he's careful. Nobody's seen anything.' He pointed at the guvnor's pile of books. 'You read all that?'

'They help me do my work. Are you interested in the psychology of the mind, Captain?'

'No, sir.'

'Dad went to the police but they won't do nothing,' said Suzie. 'Told us to moor her somewhere else. Hide her, like. So we move her up to Bermondsey and what happens, we turn up this morning and the awning's sliced to ribbons!'

'We paid four quid for that awning,' said Moon.

'Can't afford to get another, not right now, and the customers ain't going to be too happy with no shelter on deck,' said Suzie.

'The Old Bill told us to put the deckhand on board overnight,' Moon went on. 'But what if they scuttle her? He'd be killed. That you, is it?'

Moon was pointing at the photographic portrait of the guvnor above the little fireplace.

'Yes, indeed,' said the guvnor, a contented smile coming over his face. The photographer'd told him he looked like Moses and he couldn't help but think that maybe there was something in it. He gave the hot rash under his arm a rub.

'Very striking,' said Moon. 'Very good.'

'Thank you, Captain. Now, are you sure it's this fellow Polgreen?'

'We know it's him, sir,' said Suzie. She sat forward, her arms on the table. 'He's the only one runs a steamer on our route to Gravesend. Takes the day-trippers, same as us. He's trying to drive us out, ain't he, Dad?'

Her old man nodded.

'But you're not so sure, Captain?' asked the guvnor.

'No. Yes. Yes, I am sure.' He nodded. 'I am sure.'

'We been running up there since more 'n thirteen, fourteen year,' said Suzie. 'Tell him, Dad.'

'Used to be quite a few boats on the route afore they built the railway out that far. We was the last one left and what happens this time last year? Only this blooming foreigner Polgreen comes along with an old bucket of a boat and starts taking passengers. Same piers, same route.'

'Which piers d'you use?' asked the guvnor.

'We pick up at Old Swan Pier by London Bridge and take them to Terrace Pier in Gravesend.'

'You don't use the pier at Rosherville?'

'Too dear, Mr Arrowood. The customers don't mind walking to the pleasure gardens if it saves them a few coins. I told Polgreen Gravesend can't support two boats, but he won't listen.'

'So now we're taking half the money we took before,' cried Suzie, her face red with it all. 'We can't hardly get by, but those foreigners seem to live on half what we need.'

'Eat rats, I heard,' declared the Captain. 'Live on the boat too, like bargees.'

'He's trying to make it that bad for us we pack it in.'

'Have you actually seen Polgreen damaging your boat?' asked the guvnor.

'We ain't seen him, but it's him all right,' answered Suzie. 'Ain't it, Dad?'

Moon nodded.

'Who else works on your boat?' asked Arrowood.

'Only Belasco, the deckhand,' said Moon.

'D'you trust him?'

'He'd never harm the boat. Been with us since the start.'

Just then, the guvnor's sister Ettie called out from the bedroom upstairs. 'William! I need some help!'

Arrowood winced. 'Carry on, sir,' he said, rubbing his forehead. 'What else can you tell us?'

'I ain't so sure Polgreen's a captain neither,' said Moon. 'Don't seem to know the rules of the water.'

Now the baby started to cry. A moment later we heard the door at the top of the stairs creak open, and Ettie's feet coming down the steps.

'Oh, I'm sorry, I didn't realize,' she said, startled to see the Captain and his daughter there. She looked worn out, her face pale, her hair loose and falling over her shoulders. There were baby stains on her blouse. She wasn't used to caring for a child, wasn't the sort of woman who could be contained inside a little place like this for long, and it was getting to her.

'I'm in a consultation,' said the guvnor.

She shot me a tired smile, then nodded at our two guests.

'I won't disturb you.' She looked at the guvnor. 'The curtain's come down again, William,' she said, turning to climb the narrow staircase at the back of the parlour. 'The child won't settle.'

The guvnor raised his eyes to the ceiling, muttering to himself as the crying continued. There was only one bedroom up there, and Arrowood shared it with his sister. He pushed himself to his feet with a groan and waddled over to the mantel, where he collected his pipe. He smiled at Moon. 'Please, sir, continue.'

'When he turned up, his boat was *Barley Belle*,' said Moon. 'Then, a week after he starts taking our custom, he goes and names his boat the same as ours. *Rosherville Queen* she was then. I tried to get him to change it. The Company of Watermen tried, and the Conservancy officials, but he wouldn't do it so we had to change *our* name! Didn't want the punters confusing his old bucket with ours, did we? Our boat, what'd been there first! That's how she became the *Gravesend Queen*.'

The guvnor shook his head as he lit his pipe. 'The fellow sounds difficult. He's determined.'

Moon sighed. 'It has wore me out, Mr Arrowood. I own it.'

'Have you considered changing your destination? Hampton Court or Southend or somewhere?'

'But it's our route.'

'All those other routes got bigger boats than ours,' said Suzie. 'With food and music and such. We can't take them on. Gravesend's the only place we can go with a little old boat like ours. The punters who still like Rosherville Gardens ain't too choosey, and that's the truth of it, sir.'

'I'm sorry for you,' said the guvnor, shaking his great ox's head. 'This isn't right. Tell me, how did you hear of us? Was it the Catford Inquiry?'

'The salt thieves,' answered Moon. 'That's what we heard about.'

'Salt thieves?'

'From the barges,' said Moon. 'Deptford, was it?'

The guvnor looked at me, a puzzle in his eyes.

'That's not one of our cases,' I said.

'Perhaps you read of the Fenian case?' asked the guvnor.

'Sorry, sir,' said Moon, shaking his head. 'I ain't a reader.'

'The gas pipe affair?'

'You never caught the salt thieves?' asked Moon.

'No. You're not confusing me with Sherlock Holmes, are you?' asked the guvnor.

'Well, now I ain't sure about those cases, Mr Arrowood, but I can't see anyone confusing you with him.'

'Can we help him, sir?' I asked, seeing the guvnor starting to lose his good temper. He always thought we should be known more than we were, and it upset him to find almost nobody'd ever heard of us. The only private enquiry agent the papers ever seemed to cover was Sherlock Holmes, and just reading about the fellow's cases upset the guvnor worse than sour beer. Arrowood was an emotional fellow, and it was one of my jobs to keep him on the level. That and a bit of strong-arm business from time to time.

Upstairs, the baby's crying got quieter, till it was only a whimper. Arrowood glanced up at the ceiling and sighed.

'I'd like to do something for you, Captain,' he said. 'But I'm afraid we're about to start on an important case with a lawyer. I'm not sure we've enough time to do yours justice.'

Moon looked at the guvnor like he didn't understand.

'Why didn't you tell us that at the start?' asked Suzie, her eyes lit up. 'Is it because we never heard of your cases?'

'Of course not. I didn't know how long yours would take until you explained it.'

'But can't you do anything?'

The guvnor thought for a moment, his fingers tapping away at the table. Through the open window we could hear the hens in the yard next door.

'We can go and have a talk with this Polgreen,' he said at last. 'Mr Barnett's rather good at persuading people to stop doing things, as you might guess from his appearance.'

'Well, he's big enough,' said Moon, looking at me.

'He's more than that, Captain. He's an expert negotiator.' The guvnor winced as the wailing started again upstairs.

'We'll warn him off,' I said. 'You're sure it's him though, are you?'

'We told you,' said Suzie. 'It's him.'

The guvnor gave me the nod and rose from the chair. 'I must attend to my sister, Captain,' he said. 'Mr Barnett will deal with the arrangements. We'll visit Polgreen and call on you later this evening.'

He waddled over to the stairs and took himself up to face the fallen curtain.

'Ten shillings for half a day's work,' I said. 'In advance.'

The captain flitched when he heard the price, but he fished in his pocket and pulled out a purse. When the money was handed over, I took down his address and the mooring of Polgreen's boat. It all seemed pretty straightforward. Little did I know that I'd soon come to wish I'd never met Captain Moon, nor ever heard of the *Gravesend Queen*.

Chapter Two

After lunch, we took the train to Queenstown then walked across Battersea Park to Ransome's Dock. It was a long, deep creek, with a wide basin at the end, a foundry on one side and an ice warehouse on the other. A bloke hoiking bales of hay from a barge pointed us past a row of lighters to where Polgreen's boat was moored, a small paddle steamer, old but well kept. The funnel and paddle boxes were yellow and black, the awning bright and stripy. A saloon with windows along its length took up half the boat, with a wheelhouse at the front and a sundeck on its roof. A boy with a bare brown back stood up there polishing the brass.

'Captain Polgreen around, lad?' asked the guvnor.

'In the saloon, sir.'

A woman of middle age rose from the deck behind him, a scrubbing brush in her hand. Her face was dark as a Hindoo, and she watched us close as we climbed aboard and made our way along to the door. Inside we found an older bloke fiddling around under the drinks counter. He stood when he heard us, a heavy wrench in his hand. He was a strong fellow, a bit battered, an ugly burn running the length of one arm. Like the lad, he wore no shirt.

'What can I do for you, gentlemen?' he asked, coming out from behind the counter.

There was a heavy accent in his voice, Cornish or something I supposed. He had the same thick black hair as his son, his brow low down his sun-tanned face. He breathed heavy.

'Captain Moon's engaged us to discover who's been damaging his boat,' said the guvnor. I watched Polgreen real careful as he talked. 'He says it's you.'

'Oh, that's the game, is it? And who may you be?' He had the look of a smuggler about him, with mean, darting eyes, his whiskers stiff and tight like black gorse. Tattoos ran up and down his arms, most of them smudged and stretched out of shape.

'Mr Arrowood. This is Mr Barnett. We're private enquiry agents. So, was it you?'

'Well, he thinks it was. Accused me of it in front of my customers as well. Bloody wild, he were. Shouting at me. Cursing me. Shouldn't be in charge of a boat, that bloke. Need a calm head to steer a steamer on a river as busy at this one, and Moon ain't got one.'

The guvnor smiled and cocked his head. He laughed.

Polgreen's face fell. 'What's funny?'

The guvnor laughed some more. I did too, just like he'd taught me. Polgreen scowled. Finally, the guvnor leant in to him and whispered: 'You didn't answer my question. Did you damage his boat, Captain?'

'I didn't touch his blooming boat.'

'Did you arrange for someone else to damage it?'

'No. And I don't suppose he told you he threw all my lifebuoys in the current? And the cushions off my benches?' Polgreen looked from the guvnor to me. His knuckles were white as he gripped the wrench. 'No? Well, he did. In Gravesend, it were. He waited till I'd gone off for my lunch and he shoved my lad out the way and threw them all in the water. That's two quid, more or less. Two quid! I got the police onto him. They took him up before the beak. Got fined ten bob for it and had to pay me back.'

'Why did he attack your cushions, Captain?'

Polgreen brought his face up close and spoke real slow, like the guvnor was stupid, ''Cos he thought I'd damaged his boat.'

'He thinks you're trying to drive him out of business.'

'I am trying to drive him out of business.'

'Why'd you set up on the Gravesend run when every other boat's given up?'

'Folk from the East End still go there. Folk who can't afford to go anywhere else. Listen, Moon don't own that route. He's got no right to it.'

'He was there first,' I said.

Polgreen scratched his sun-scorched belly. 'But I want it,' he said.

The guvnor looked at him for a while. 'If it wasn't you, then who'd you think's been doing it?'

'There was a fellow asking after his boat a few week since. Asking where she was moored.'

'Did you tell him?'

'Don't know where she's moored, do I?'

'Really, sir?'

Polgreen shrugged.

'Did this fellow say anything else?' asked the guvnor.

'No.'

'What did he look like?'

Polgreen frowned. His eyes moved from the guvnor to me.

'A bit like him,' he said, twitching his head at me. 'Big, eyes far apart too. Made you queasy just to look at him. But it was dark. I didn't get a good look.'

'Clothes?' asked the guvnor.

'Checked shirt. Not so well off.'

'Hair?'

'Brown or black, and a moustache.'

'His voice?'

'London, I'd say.'

The guvnor looked at him for a while without speaking.

'Just like Mr Barnett, then,' he said at last.

'That's what I said,' answered Polgreen. 'Now, get off my boat.'

The guvnor looked over at me, twitched his eyebrows, and stepped back. I moved in, taking the bloke by the throat and pushing him back towards the bar.

'Leave off!' he growled. He didn't shout; I guessed he didn't want his family to hear. He tried to break free, but I had hold of him tight. I caught his arm as he swung his wrench at me and threw him onto the floor. Soon as he landed I had my boot and all my weight on his wrist. He groaned.

I pushed down harder. He twisted, trying to hammer on my knee with his other hand, but it just hurt him more.

'Any more damage to Moon's boat and I come back for you,' I told him.

His face was screwed up in pain. 'And I'll be waiting, you prick,' he hissed.

We walked back through Battersea Park, the guvnor tapping his stick on the path as we went. It was a fine old day. The lawns were dotted with folk enjoying the sun: couples murmuring soft to each other, old codgers nattering on benches, little gangs of kids shouting and showing off. Along the path people sold lemonade and ginger beer, ice cream and oranges, and everybody had a smile on their face.

'You didn't have to hurt him,' said the guvnor. 'Not with his lad on the roof.'

'I didn't hurt him.'

'All you needed do was threaten him.'

'A man like that'd need more than threatening,' I said. 'If it was him.'

'You don't think so?'

'Do you?'

We stepped onto the grass to get round a nanny trying to settle a little lad with a great gash in his knee. Two young ladies on bicycles came directly towards us. They didn't seem to see us, so wrapped up were they in their conversation. We stepped further from the path to get out of their way, and they passed without even a nod.

'I just don't know,' he said as we approached the little row of caged birds at the far side of the park. 'It's clear the two men have confronted each other, but Suzie was more certain it was Polgreen who'd damaged the boat than her father. Moon only confirmed her when pushed, and even then he wavered. D'you remember how he spoke? And as for Polgreen, well, it was too convenient that the fellow he says was asking about Moon's boat looked like you. I know it's difficult to invent a story on the spot, but he was almost telling us he was deceiving us. On the other hand, when he described Moon throwing his cushions in the water his anger seemed real enough. Did you see how his eyes widened, how his jaw stuck out? Everything Darwin says about anger was there.'

'It doesn't mean he didn't damage Moon's boat.'

'True, but his denial was convincing. There was no slight twitch or hesitation. Nothing. So I'm wondering why he'd invent this mystery man if he didn't have something to hide?' He grunted and shook his head, pausing a moment to examine a peacock in one of the cages. 'What did you think of Captain Moon, Barnett?'

'I liked him.'

'I also. He seems very worn down. I wish I could believe that's the end of it, but I'm afraid whatever's going on is more complicated than it seems.'

Chapter Three

We visited Moon to tell him what had happened, shook hands, and hoped that was the end of it. When we got back to Coin Street, a message from Scrapes had finally arrived asking us to start on his case. A letter had gone missing from a fellow's house, one that might have caused a scandal if ever it should get out. Took us a day to track it. A bit of easy money for a change: no freezing nights on the watch, no getting stamped in the face, just a lot of questions, a bit of walking, and a little righteous housebreaking.

It was turning into a hot summer, so I treated myself to a nice straw boater from the pawn shop, with a green and yellow band and a good brim to shade the sun. I'd had my eye on it for a while, but this was the first time I had a few spare coins to buy it. Wearing it felt like a bit of success: it made me feel a happier man.

It was the day after Scrapes' case that Captain Moon found us again, this time in Willows' coffeehouse on Blackfriars Road. We were at lunch; the guvnor had took all the Thursday papers and shoved them under his thigh so none of the other punters could get at them. He was reading them through one by one, catching up on the cases as were going on in other parts of town. All the windows were open and the door wedged ajar, but it was still hot in there with the kettles and the great vat of soup aboil on the range. We were both in our shirts, our sleeves rolled up, our chests there for all to see.

'Miss Arrowood told me you'd be here,' said Moon, lowering himself onto a stool opposite. He wore a stained canvas shirt, a blue handkerchief around his neck. His boatman's cap was on his head. 'He's been at it again.'

'You want something, mate?' asked Ma Willows, coming over to the table. Her red hands had swelled up as they always did on a hot day. She was breathing heavy.

Moon ran his tongue over his dry lips. He shook his head.

'Another for me, Rena,' said the guvnor, holding out his empty mug. 'And a bit of seed cake.'

'You got anything for that rash?' asked Rena, her nose wrinkling as she watched him itch away at his oxters.

'I've been using Whelpton's. Doesn't seem to do anything.'

'Try Elliman's Universal. That's a better one.' Her eyes fell on the jacket hanging from the back of my chair. She pointed at the patch I'd sewn on it the week before and laughed. 'Who put that bloody thing on?'

'What's wrong with it?'

'Couldn't you have got one the same colour?'

'It's almost the same.'

'You must be blind,' she said, turning to collect the mugs and bowls from the table next to us.

'I never been in this place afore,' said Moon, looking around at the food on the other tables. 'You from around here, Mr Barnett?'

'Born and raised in Bermondsey,' I told him. 'What about you?'

'From up country,' he said. 'What about you, Mr Arrowood?'

'I've been here since I was twenty,' said the guvnor. 'How about you tell us what happened, Captain?'

'Belasco and me kipped on the boat last night.' Moon's mouth was dry as flour, and his tongue made a clicking noise when he spoke. He scratched his wild orange beard. 'Been sleeping there all week. Something woke me, maybe the good Lord himself as if he hadn't I might have rose with the angels this morning. There was a little launch right up aside us, and two big blokes making ready to board.'

Moon stopped when Rena Willows came over and dumped the coffee and cake on the table. As the guvnor took a bite, she patted his shoulder and rubbed his back, looking down on his uneven hair and red scalp beneath. She seemed to appreciate the guvnor eating more than anything else in that coffeeshop; sometimes she'd put her elbows on the counter and just watch him gobble down a beef sandwich or shovel great spoonfuls of porridge down his hole. And the messier it got, the more she seemed to like it.

A rabbitman came in the shop and went to the counter. Rena gave the guvnor's neck a little tickle, then lumbered over to have a look at what the fellow had.

'Belasco gave the first one a wallop with the boathook as he tried to get aboard,' Moon went on. His eyes seemed to crackle with anger. 'We were shouting away anyways. When they saw there was two of us they pushed off and raced away downriver.'

'Did you pursue them?'

Moon shook his head, his eye on the guvnor's coffee. 'Takes too long to get the steam up. Coffee good in here, is it?'

'It is,' said the guvnor. 'Are you sure you don't want one?'

Moon shook his head. The guvnor looked over at Rena. 'Mug of ale for our friend, Rena, if you will.'

'What d'you think they were going to do?' I asked.

'Who knows? Could put me out for good if they broke in the engine room. It's a bad lot, Mr Barnett, it truly is.'

'Was it Polgreen's boat?' asked the guvnor.

'No. One of them new electric launches, about twenty-five foot. Brown. Name covered over with a blanket.'

'Can you describe the men?'

'They'd caps and scarves over their faces. I did go to the coppers again this morning. Told me to hire a guard. Seems to me they don't want to know about half the crimes in London. Not interested least happens right in front of them.'

Rena came over with the ale: Moon drank it down in one swallow.

'Cheers, mum,' he said, handing the mug back to her.

'You didn't see Polgreen, then?' asked the guvnor.

He shook his head.

'You're not as sure as Suzie that it's him, are you, Captain?' asked the guvnor. 'Why?'

It took a moment for him to reply. 'I do think it's him,' he said.

'But you're not certain. Tell us why.'

Moon shook his head. 'I am sure. Suzie and me both.'

'Well, if you want us to help we can. The other case is finished.'

'Thank you, Mr Arrowood.' Moon reached over and took the guvnor's hand, shaking it, squeezing it. 'You're a gent.'

'It'll be twenty shillings a day,' I said. 'Three days in advance.'

The guvnor cleared his throat, looking out the window. Though he was greedy for money, he never liked to bargain, never even liked to ask for payment. He saw himself as better than that. He picked up his mug and blew on the coffee. He slurped it in.

Captain Moon took off his boating cap and wiped the wet from his forehead. He looked at the guvnor. 'Any chance I could give you ten now and the rest in two day? Tickets've been down since this business started.'

'Talk to me about the money, Captain,' I said. 'I do the bookkeeping.'

'I will get it you,' he said, turning to me. 'I swear I will.'

I held his eye hard for a time.

'You got my word, Mr Barnett,' he said. 'Please. It ain't just for me, it's for Suzie too. We rely on that boat.'

'Ten now, another fifty in two day,' I said at last. 'No delay.'

Moon put his fingers in his pocket and pulled out a handful of coins. He dropped them in my hand: it was exactly ten bob.

The guvnor put down his mug. 'Now, there's no point us threatening him again, Captain,' he said. 'If it didn't work last time, there's no reason it'd work this time.'

'You going to hurt him?' asked Moon.

'That's not how we work.'

'It's the only way he's going to stop. He won't be reasoned with. I've tried hard enough.' He looked at me again. 'Just break a bone in his arm, Mr Barnett. That'd finish it.'

'Is that what your daughter'd want us to do?' asked the guvnor.

'She's young. She don't understand folk as we do.'

'Is that why you came alone this time, Captain Moon?'

Moon blinked and was silent for a few moments.

'Leave her out of this, Mr Arrowood,' he said at last.

'If you want us to help, you'll have to let us do it our way,' said the guvnor. 'Now, when's your next trip?'

'Got two Gravesend runs, one on Saturday, the other Sunday. I lay her up by London Bridge tomorrow night to get an early start Saturday, then again Saturday night for the Sunday trip.'

The guvnor raised the saucer and tipped the cake crumbs into his mouth. As he sucked on them, he looked out the window at the carriages going past, pondering.

'If he wants to drive you out of business, he'll try to stop you going out this weekend,' he said at last. 'But I don't think he'll do it tomorrow night. It's too busy by London Bridge. No, the chances are he'll get to you while you're still in the dock, and that means tonight. Since he knows you're sleeping on the boat, he'll no doubt bring more men this time.'

'Want me to move her?'

Arrowood thought again.

'No,' he said. 'If he can't find the boat we'll never get evidence it's him. We'll wait on board with you tonight. I'll bring a pistol. If Polgreen isn't with them, we'll catch one of the men. I'm sure we can get a name out of him.'

We got the new mooring off him and arranged to meet at nine that night.

Chapter Four

The light was just starting to fade when we reached St Saviour's Dock. On one side was a jumble of wharves, on the other a row of sooty warehouses rising straight from the brown milk of the Thames. The dock was still busy: barges queued down the neck of the inlet to unload grain at the New Concordia; lighters at the crooked landing stages were dumping their cargoes of tea and tapioca, straw and stone. Porters and carters lifted and winched and strained at trolleys, their chests grimy and wet from a long day's work in the sun.

The *Gravesend Queen* was moored at a little repair yard where the neck of the inlet opened into the dock's basin. It was a fair bit smaller than the pleasure steamers that worked the river these days, and an awful lot older. Still, it was a boat that was cared for: the brass rails and lights were polished, the hull painted a thick red, the funnel a deep green. Captain Moon stood on the sponson deck in his shirtsleeves, smoking his pipe and looking out of the dock to the busy Pool of London beyond, his face carved deep with worry. He didn't notice us till the guvnor called his name.

He led us up to the sundeck, where he passed around a jug of ale while we talked a bit about the river. Moon tried his best to make conversation, but something was distracting him. The spark we saw that first day was gone, and he seemed blue. The guvnor lit up a cigar; I rolled a smoke. When we were all puffing away, Moon broke the silence with a long sigh. He looked at me with a nod, his mournful eyes a mess of blood vessels. He nodded again and looked away to the river.

I stood and stretched, then rested my elbows on the balustrade and looked down into the creek. The dirty streams from Jacob's Island on one side and Horsleydown on the other opened into the dock, and the water was thick and greasy, slopping up and down the slimy bricks of the embankment walls. Around the boats floated turds and papers, dead gulls and bones. A couple of swans, too white for the dirty docks, drifted out towards the river like lost princesses.

After some time, a bloke climbed the stairs to join us. He was small and stocky, with a tattoo of crossed hammers on his arm. His eyes were too close together, and the thick tousle of brown hair on his bonce stood up straight like a hedge.

'Belasco,' said Moon, the relief clear in his voice. 'Meet Mr Arrowood and Mr Barnett.'

'These the private agents, Captain?' asked Belasco with an odd smile across his face. He took the guvnor's hand, then mine. His voice was high like a woman; his grip was strong.

Moon nodded.

Belasco looked us up and down. 'Like Sherlock Holmes only cheaper, that right?'

'Not like Sherlock Holmes at all, sir,' said the guvnor with a twitch of his nose.

'That's a shame,' said Belasco. He leant back against the balustrade, folding his arms over his chest.

'Holmes doesn't always solve his cases, you know,' said the guvnor.

'He's solved every one I ever heard about,' replied Belasco as Moon handed him the jug.

'They don't report on the ones he fails to solve. He didn't solve the case of the Stockbroker's Clerk. Or the Adventure of the Yellow Face.'

'I doubt that.'

'Watson says it himself,' said the guvnor.

Belasco seemed to lose interest. He looked at me.

'You're a big bloke. You his helper, are you?'

'Help him with his bootlaces. When he can't reach.'

Belasco grinned. 'Same with me and the captain, so he don't fall in the water.'

'Now, here's the plan,' said the guvnor, uninterested in our conversation. He brought out one of his friend Lewis's pistols from his pocket. 'We'll hide. If they come, we wait until the first one's on board then you two capture him. I'll use the pistol, order the rest to unmask.'

'What if Polgreen ain't there?' asked Belasco.

'We'll still have our prisoner. We'll make him talk then hand him over to the police.'

'Could get nasty,' said Belasco, his smile widening. I couldn't make out if he was happy or nervy.

'Are you willing to fight, my friend?' asked the guvnor.

'Blooming right I am,' answered Belasco. 'But what if the one we capture don't know who's behind it?'

'He'll know who's paying him at least,' said the guvnor. 'We'll pick up the trail there.'

'Here, you ain't kin to Belasco the prize fighter, are you?' I asked.

'My old man.' As he spoke, his arms hardened, his tanned chest puffed out. 'You heard of him, then?'

''Course. He ever taught you to fight?'

Belasco smiled. 'Reckon you'll find out tonight, mate.'

I offered him my baccy pouch.

I liked Belasco.

Captain Moon got a packet of potato and onion from the engine room, and we had dinner there on the deck. He was still blue; he'd answer your questions all right, but after that he'd dry up, looking out over the water, puffing away on his pipe.

'Where's Suzie tonight?' asked the guvnor, after a long stretch of silence. A warm drizzle had started to fall but we stayed out on the deck: it was a relief from the heat.

'At home looking after the birds,' said Moon. 'Didn't want her here if there's trouble.'

'D'you have other children?'

A long pause.

'Had three. The Lord took them, one after the other. And the wife.'

'I'm sorry,' said the guvnor, patting Moon's knee in the gloom.

The captain cleared his throat and spat over the railings into the water. A couple of bats swooped and twisted above us. 'If there is a God he's a bad 'un, that's for sure.'

Further up the dock, someone emptied a bucket into the water. A seagull cried on the roof of the boatyard shed. Moon got to his feet with a groan and walked over to the far side of the deck, where he stood alone at the balustrade, his back to us.

'He lost one as a babbie,' said Belasco real quiet. 'Weak blood. Then another, little Katie, she had typhus. The oldest, Annabel, was took away in the fire at their rooms.' We watched Moon's dark silhouette, his hands gripping the rail. Belasco whispered now: 'Mrs Moon, well she finished herself off. Couldn't take it no more. Drank down a whole jug of paraffin.'

'Oh, Lord,' murmured the guvnor.

'Suzie's the only one he got left, see, her and his bloody birds.'

As darkness fell, the wharves started to wind up. Some of the boats drifted past us back to the river. Others laid up for the night. All around we could hear the voices of the lightermen and porters having a drink. A concertina started up over the other side, and we listened as the music filled the darkness. Then Moon, alone on the other side of the deck, began to sing. His voice was deep and handsome.

> *'Oh, Reuben was no sailor*
> *Ranzo, boys, ranzo*
> *He shipped aboard a whaler*
> *Ranzo, boys, ranzo*
> *'They took him to a gangway*
> *Ranzo, boys, ranzo*
> *And gave him forty lashes*
> *Ranzo, boys, ranzo.'*

As he sang, voices began to join in from the barges and lighters moored around the dock. Soon, we three also joined in, singing out to the river and the sleeping city. Though the guvnor'd been having singing lessons over the last few months, he was the only one flat, but it didn't matter. All that mattered those few minutes was being part of that great dockside chorus.

At the end of the song the concertina went silent and the voices disappeared back into the night. Though the sky was still covered with a murky brown cloud, the rain had stopped. We had a few more swigs of the rotten ale, a few smokes, listening as hatches were shut, pisses were taken into the stinking water. After an hour or so the place was quiet.

'Come,' said the guvnor, climbing down the stairs. 'Let's get ready.'

We followed him as he inspected the main deck. The middle of the boat had a small saloon, with a walkway on either side. In front of it was the wheelhouse, and at each end of the boat were benches.

'The two of you need to be on the water side so you can seize the first fellow who comes aboard,' he said to Belasco and me. 'Best sit here, against the saloon wall. Have you something we can put over you?'

'There's what's left of the awning aft,' said Belasco.

'Fetch it, will you?'

'Might be an idea to get a weapon too, mate,' I said, pulling my neddy from my jacket.

Belasco came back a few minutes later dragging a heavy canvas sheet behind him, a scaling hammer tucked under his arm. We got down on deck with our backs to the low wall of the saloon and they covered us with the awning. Through the rips in the fabric I'd just be able to make out an invader on the bow; Belasco was to watch the stern. The guvnor and Moon went off to wait in the wheelhouse.

We sat there on the deck for a long while, listening to the

water move around, to the clink of the boats and the rats padding about on the path. After an hour or so, Belasco whispered, 'Can't keep my eyes open.'

'Nor me. What's wrong with the captain? Something happen this afternoon?'

'Sometimes he's blue. Sometimes he ain't. Just comes over him like that.'

We talked on, quiet as we could, trying to keep each other awake. He asked me where I came from. I told him about the workhouse and the court on Jacob's Island I lived in with my ma, just up the road from where we were that night. I told him how the guvnor and me met when I worked in the law courts and he was a reporter for *Lloyd's Weekly*, and about how I started helping him after we'd both lost our jobs. He told me about growing up in Wapping, about his old man, the bare-knuckle fighter Aby Belasco, about how life goes when you're the son of a champion. I didn't tell him how well I knew Wapping myself, just as I'm sure he didn't tell me about those parts of his life as needed most explaining. But I knew that if we got to know each other one day we would; we came from the same world, Belasco and me.

I asked him how he started working for Captain Moon.

'Had a job at Thames Ironworks before,' he whispered. 'There was a bit of trouble, a strike and all.'

'I remember.'

'It was a bad time, mate. Anyways, I was fitted up for thieving and out the door.'

'Fitted up by who?'

'Story for another time, Norman. But they put the word about to all the other shipbuilders, all the repair yards. I had my ma and uncle back at home, and me the only one able to work. Tried the docks too but there was nothing for me. We were close to losing our room. That's when Captain Moon took me on. Didn't know me from Adam.'

'Did he know about the thieving?'

'He knew.'

'Why'd he hire you?'

'I do not know, mate, I do not know. Perhaps he believes in giving a bloke a chance. He had the boat in the repair yard when I came in asking for work. He saw the shipwright send me packing and offered me this job there on the spot. Been working for him ever since. Thirteen or fourteen year.'

We were both tired, and the chat dried up. I must have dozed off as the next thing I knew I was woke by his hand gripping my arm.

'They're here,' he whispered.

Chapter Five

Through the holes in the canvas I could just make out a dark boat moving up alongside us. All we could hear was the slip of oars through the water, then the softest thud as its side touched ours. On its deck were five figures, scarves over their faces. I gripped my neddy and held my breath.

One of them struck a match and lit a torch. A black claw rose over the gunwale and hooked itself on the top rail. The boat tipped a bit, then a dark head rose over the side. Hands appeared, and the figure hoiked itself up and onto the deck. As it stepped toward us, another head rose over the balustrade.

Belasco leapt out from under the awning. The first bloke grunted in surprise, then turned back to his boat, scrambling to get over the rail. I flew at him and grabbed his arm but the skin was all greased up and I couldn't get a hold of him. He pulled away; I stumbled, dropping my neddy and falling to the deck as the bloke jumped over the side and into the electric launch, crashing down onto one of the men below. Yelling to rouse the guvnor, I jumped to my feet.

There was another bloke in the launch using the torch to light a rag stuffed in a bottle. Belasco was reaching over the side, cursing and shouting. He had one of them by the hair, but as he tried to pull him aboard the bloke with the bottle hurled it. It smashed against the saloon wall behind us, exploding into flames. The sky lit up, and I caught a glimpse of the men, all bare-chested, greased black and holding more bottles stuffed with rags. One of them brought down a club on Belasco's arm, while the other three lit their bottles from the torch. As one, they launched them at us.

The guvnor burst out of the wheelhouse at the same moment one of the bottles smashed on the sun-deck above. Paraffin. Another bottle flew at the saloon windows, crashing through and spraying the floor inside with fire. The last came hurtling through the air towards me. I knew at that moment I had to get out the way but I was frozen: I couldn't take my eyes off it. Then I felt myself knocked to the floor, with Belasco on top of me and the bottle of paraffin exploding in the pile of awning aside us.

'Fire!' cried Moon, ringing the bell again and again. 'Fire! Fire!'

The flames were all around us, growing and spitting. Shouts were coming from the other boats around the dock. We got to our feet to see the villains pushing the launch away with their oars, their torch doused, the deck black again. Its engines rose; its propeller ground the water; its speed picked up.

As Moon rang the bell over and over, Belasco raced over to collect buckets from the bow, tossing them to the guvnor and me. Cinders burnt all along the deck as smoke drifted from the doors and windows of the saloon.

The guvnor held a bucket, staring up at the sun-deck where the fire was lighting the sky. I shook him hard. 'Water! Now!'

We dropped the buckets in the creek, hoisting them them up by their ropes and turning to throw them onto the flames, Belasco and Moon doing the same up by the prow.

Watermen and bargees were climbing aboard from all parts of the dock, each with buckets of their own. Some went up to the sun-deck, others to the saloon, organized in silence like it was born into them. Chains of men and women and children passed buckets to each other, coddled in smoke and lit by the yellow of the flames. Orders were given, and the air was filled with the sound of shouts and curses, coughing and choking, the hiss of water on heat, the splash of buckets.

'Man down!' came a cry. A couple of women rushed past me to the prow. Through the smoke I saw them lifting Moon to his feet and putting him on a bench as he gasped and retched. While they helped him recover, I hauled up more water, chucking it onto the flames behind, the guvnor doing the same on one side, a boy wearing only a pair of shorts on the other. We worked for ten, fifteen minutes, emptying bucket after bucket, choking as the smoke ripped at our throats. My muscles ached, my eyes were blurred and flooded, yet still we hauled and chucked, hauled and chucked.

Then, slowly, it all ceased. We stood, our eyes sweeping the decks for sparks and smoulders. The air was thick with the smell of burnt wood and sewage; the decks and benches were slick and charred. I patted the boy's back and held out my last bit of toffee for him.

'Thanks, lad,' I said.

His face was streaked with wet and soot.

'Cheers, mister,' he said, his voice quite hoarse. 'Saved her, didn't we?'

He limped off past the engine house to find his family.

Those who were working nearest the flames were heaving and retching with the smoke, bent double on the seats while others poured bucket after bucket of water over them, cooling them down.

'Who was it?' asked a grizzled old fellow in only his drawers. 'Saw a launch tear off.'

'Covered the name,' answered Moon. He sat heavily on a bench, the river people all around listening. 'Covered their number too. They tried to board last night and all.'

'Anybody else have trouble?' asked the guvnor through his coughs.

Nobody had.

'Anybody see who they were?' I asked.

'They went past us,' said a well-fed woman whose fellow was clutching her arm while he retched over the side. 'Had their faces covered.'

Nobody knew anything. They stood around talking for a while, cooling down, then they shook Moon's hand and went back to their boats.

In the still night, the captain made his way around the wet, charred boat, taking in the damage. It was hard to see just what it was like in the lamplight, but it didn't look good.

'That's it, then,' he said when he sat back down on the benches with us. He coughed. 'We're finished.'

'No, Captain,' said Belasco. 'This ain't going to stop us. I'll fix her up the best I can tomorrow and we'll take her out on Saturday just as we always do. We won't be beat by that prick. He won't drive us out.'

Captain Moon didn't reply. He bent over, his elbows on his knees, and covered his face with his hands.

Chapter Six

I didn't get back to my room in the Borough till seven that morning. The sun had already been up for a few hours and I was tuckered out, the taste of smoke still in my mouth, my eyes blurred and weeping. Mr Askell, the rent collector who lived in the ground floor rooms, was in the hallway when I opened the front door. I gave him a good morning but he ignored me: he never spoke least he was asking for money.

I paid a visit to the outhouse, then climbed the stairs, wanting nothing more than to get some kip and hoping that Lilly was really gone this time. I'd only met her a few nights ago, but she'd somehow got herself attached to my bed and I wanted it back to myself. That one room was the only place I had. But soon as I opened the door I saw her there, laid out asleep on the bed, the chamber pot full to the brim on the floor. Draped over her was Mrs B's shawl.

I snatched it off her.

'I thought I told you to leave.'

She opened her eyes slow, blinked, and gave me a smile.

'Don't go on, Norm,' she murmured, shutting her eyes again. 'I'll go later.'

She turned to face the wall.

I was too tired to argue. I pulled off my boots, my stockings, my britches, and lay down next to her. For a few moments my mind turned over what had happened that night, then my eyes became heavy. Just as I started to drop off, I felt her fingers on my drawers.

I was back at Coin Street about five that afternoon. Ettie answered the door looking fed up. Her usual tight bodice was hanging loose from her skirts, the long brown hair that was always up in a knot before the baby came falling ragged down her back. There was something about Ettie that got to me, even in a state like this. I felt good just seeing her. Behind her in the parlour the child was asleep in a wooden box on the table, and by the open window sat Mrs Campbell, a friend of hers from the mission. Before Ettie went away she was one of the deaconesses working for Reverend Hebdon's lot. She was always busy at meetings, visiting the slums of Southwark and Bermondsey, helping in the women's sanctuary and teaching in the ragged school. But since she came back from her cousin's with the baby, she'd been too busy to go back, and the guvnor told me that the other ladies there had cut her off. They were too proper, that was the problem. Wouldn't have been the same where I came from, but that's the type of lady the mission attracted. Except for Mrs Campbell, it seemed.

'He's not here, Norman,' said Ettie, holding my eye in the unsettling way she always did. 'You won't believe what's happened.'

She took a telegraph from the table and handed it to me.

SIR. NEED YOUR ASSISTANCE ON URGENT CASE. MATTER OF LIFE AND DEATH. COME TO THE ANGEL, COVENTRY IMMED. S. HOLMES.

I read it again. It didn't make sense.

'Why's Holmes asking *him* for help?'

'I've no idea,' said Ettie. 'But the minute he read it he had his coat on and was out the door. Wouldn't even go upstairs for an overnight bag.'

We laughed. The guvnor'd never met Sherlock, but he'd read every story Watson had written and followed all the cases in the papers. Not because he was an admirer: the fame of Sherlock Holmes made him spit and curse. He'd pick faults in every deduction that bloke made, and had bilious attacks whenever he heard his name.

'I like your boater,' she said. 'Green and yellow suits you. But you must let me do that patch, Norman. It's the wrong shade.'

'It's not that bad. He leave any message for me?'

'You're to go to the boat by yourself. He says the visit to Polgreen will have to wait until he returns.'

I wasn't too happy to hear that. Moon and Suzie were going to a wedding party in Lewisham tonight, and the guvnor was supposed to be guarding the boat with Belasco and me. It meant it'd just be the two of us, and that wasn't enough. It was clear after last night that this case wasn't just about a bit of property damage; if we weren't careful, someone would be killed protecting the *Gravesend Queen*.

'Will you have some tea with us before you go, Norman?' asked Ettie.

I sat down at the table, glad to spend a few minutes with her. She'd been away six months or so, and I'd missed her more than I had a right to. I only wished Mrs Campbell wasn't there;

I hadn't seen Ettie on her own since she'd come back, and I had questions to ask her. She'd refused to explain to the guvnor where the baby came from, but I wondered if she might tell me. He reckoned it might be hers; she'd been away long enough for it not to be showing when she left. If that was right, he believed the father had to be Inspector Petleigh, since he'd been courting her just afore she left. I never thought she liked the inspector much, so to me it seemed more likely it was an orphan Ettie'd taken pity on, or maybe the child of a young girl who couldn't look after it. The guvnor'd asked her over and over, but she just wouldn't say. It was driving him wild, and I had a feeling that somewhere in her heart she enjoyed that just a little.

Mrs Campbell smiled. 'Are you on an interesting case, Mr Barnett? Something about a boat, I hear?'

Ettie handed out the tea while I told them about the fire the night before.

'*He looked and behold, the bush was burning, yet it was not consumed,*' said Mrs Campbell in her low, Scottish voice. 'Exodus.'

'*Each one's work will become manifest for the day will disclose it, because it will be revealed by fire and the fire will test what sort of work each one has done,*' added Ettie, a pleased sparkle in her eyes for having thought up a verse about fire in the midst of her exhaustion. 'Corinthians.'

'*Those who do evil fear the light*, Mr Barnett,' trumped Mrs Campbell. '*Be strong in the Lord and his mighty power.*'

'Yes, ma'am,' I said, taking one of the ginger nuts Ettie offered me and hoping the versing was over.

Mrs Campbell was neat and proper, her blouse and skirt not long out the shop, her boots clean and polished, and she watched me close as I ate the biscuit. Colouring, I tucked up my jacket, hiding the patch.

Ettie bent over the baby and stared at it sleeping. It clucked and raised its hand. Ettie tensed. Then the hand fell. She straightened with a sigh and went over to sit at the table.

'How is she?' I asked. Ettie still hadn't found the baby's name.

'She does what she's supposed to.' She smiled. 'Quite often. Oh! There was something else he wanted me to tell you.' She looked at Mrs Campbell. 'Please excuse me, Mary.'

'Oh, don't mind me,' answered her friend, picking up a tract as was sitting open on her lap.

Ettie cupped her hand round her mouth and whispered, 'You're to go to Lewis's shop and borrow a ...' She glanced back at Mrs Campbell, who was pretending to read the tract, then made a pistol sign with her thumb and forefinger. It made me grin; she pursed her lips, trying to stay serious, and whispered again: 'You're to shoot in the air if the men come back. Scare them off. And you're not to try to catch one, not until William's back.'

I finished off my tea and stood. 'Anything else?'

'No, but be careful, Norman.' She held my eye and I felt a sudden anger that Mrs Campbell was sitting there, her face now upturned. 'Please. Don't take any risks.'

'I've the deckhand with me. He knows how to look after himself.'

There was a knock at the door. Ettie opened it to find Reverend Hebden stood there.

He removed his fine topper and greeted us, then glanced at the infant sleeping in the box. He frowned, as if he didn't expect to see her there. His eyes fell to the floor, then rose to look at the child again.

'Sit, please,' said Ettie, pulling a chair from the table. 'Would you like some tea?'

'No, thank you. It's only a brief visit. I . . . uh . . .' He was staring in my direction like he wanted something out of me. He was a bit younger, though not a lot, with a fine, strong build. His topper was on his knee, his finger picking at the weave. 'Is your brother here?' he asked at last.

'No,' replied Ettie. She stood by the fireplace as if in alliance with me. 'You said there was a matter you wanted to discuss with us?'

'Yes, yes of course.' He lifted his glorious head and straightened his back. 'The mission's grown since you've been away, Miss Arrowood. The men's side is bringing in a few hundred more, and the school's added an extra class. Pleasant Sundays have been a great success. Mrs Campbell might have told you.'

'Yes,' said Ettie with a tired smile. 'Praise the Lord.'

'We also have some new benefactors, and they're keen to begin a medical mission.'

'That's wonderful,' said Mrs Campbell, clapping her hands together.

'You always wanted one, Reverend,' said Ettie.

'For His glory.' He looked from one woman to the other. 'I was hoping, that is the committee were hoping, that the two of you would take charge of it together. There'd be no salary at first, but when we find more subscribers we'll be able to offer you both a stipend.'

'Well,' said Mrs Campbell slowly, her eyes fixed on the tract in her hands. She seemed uncertain. 'There is such a great need.'

'You'd train the deaconesses and send them out. Ensure they had medical provisions and so on. They'd serve the area

42

north of Paradise Street in Rotherhithe to Marygold Street in Bermondsey. You both know those parts well. We could do so much good, and bring many more back to the church. I'm truly hoping you'll agree. You with your nursing experience, Ettie, and you with your way with the poor, Mary. You're my most capable ladies.'

'We're not your ladies,' said Mrs Campbell.

'No, of course. I didn't mean . . . I meant only—'

'And when did you hope this would begin?' interrupted Ettie.

'We hope to begin training the ladies in September.'

'I have a child to look after,' said Ettie sharply.

Now the Reverend was surprised. He blinked and drew his head back.

Ettie raised one eyebrow and pointed at the table. 'Or are we pretending that little thing in the box doesn't exist?'

Mrs Campbell now coloured. She brought her teacup to her lips and had a swallow. The holy man nodded, but he didn't look at the box.

'Of course not,' he said. 'I thought a wet nurse.'

'I've no money to pay for a wet nurse.'

'Perhaps one of the girls from the sanctuary?'

'Without being paid?' demanded Ettie, glaring at him. 'How dare you suggest that!'

Mrs Campbell put her cup and saucer back on the side table but missed somehow, and the cup clattered to the floor. The baby squawked.

'Ettie, I'm so sorry,' said Mrs Campbell, jumping from her seat. 'I'll get a cloth.'

The baby's little foot jerked up above the edge of the box as it started to make unhappy noises.

'Oh, not again, please, darling,' said Ettie, getting to her feet. Reverend Hebden also rose from his chair.

'Perhaps we can discuss this another time,' he said, just as the baby started to bawl.

On the way to the pier, I picked up a little pistol from Lewis's shop on Bankside. It was the same one he'd given me before, battered and silver, cold in my hand and strange in my pocket. I got a bit of bread and watercress from a woman outside St Saviour's and crossed London Bridge, through the crowds of folk chewing straw and watching the ships. It was another still, muggy evening, the sky covered with a golden cloud. I found a place to stand halfway along the bridge and watched the river as I ate, the sailing ships from all over the world anchored on both sides, their masts and rigging filling the sky in a haze of rope and wood. It was busy tonight, a line of low barges labouring upstream, the steamboats hurrying past, burping out clouds that disappeared the moment they formed. To my left the bawleys and smacks queued for Billingsgate, the seagulls flapping and crying above them. Up ahead, Tower Bridge rose like the entrance to a blue and enchanted land. The entrance to the rest of the world, I used to say to my old darling Mrs B. How she used to love coming here of a summer's night to see all the business of the Empire and the ocean laid out before us. I shoved the last of the watercress in my gob, and just as I chucked the paper over the side I fancied I heard her laugh from somewhere in the crowd. A smile came to my lips, then just as quick I remembered the cuckoo in my room. Mrs B'd forgive me, I knew it. But I had to get that woman out of my bed.

Chapter Seven

Evening was falling when I got to Old Swan Pier. It was on the other side of the bridge, right next to Fishmongers' Hall, and I sat on a crate by the steps as I waited for the *Gravesend Queen* to arrive. The pier was busy. Paddle steamers were arriving from Essex and Kent. The *Clacton Belle*, the *Koh-i-noor*, the *Oriole*, the *Glen Rosa*. Just as Suzie said, these were bigger and better boats, and I watched them dump their passengers, the children tired and complaining, the unsteady, sun-faced men, the ladies with parasols and fans.

At the top of the steps stood an old soldier playing 'God Save the Queen' on a tin whistle, blasting it out as he tried to be heard over the honks of the oompah band drifting down from Swan Lane. Beside him a crippled boy sat begging on a crate. His face was burnt and peeled, his eyes too big and one lower than the other like it had melted. Both arms were twisted and bent, held upwards across his wide chest, the hands drooping and useless. He wore a pair of torn shorts, his legs bare. A cap lay on the floor. When someone threw him a coin, he'd pick it up with his toes and drop the money in a bag as hung over his shoulder. He didn't thank them, didn't smile, just sat there gazing at the river as the children slowed to stare.

The tired families trudged up to the embankment, into the moving horde of river-people, merchants, hawkers and chancers. Among these was a little gang of dippers following a well-to-do gent who was tacking badly from the refreshment he'd had on his outing. Easy to spot for me who'd lived close to that life, but the weary day-trippers could hardly see them. The youngest was maybe six year old, a little girl wearing a ragged dress, the oldest eleven or twelve, dressed posh and in full mourning: black coat and trousers, shiny boots, a silk tie and beaver hat. The gent's family hurried ahead, keen to get to the cabs on Upper Thames Street, leaving him staggering and stranded. The lad in mourning stood a few yards ahead, pretending to search the crowd for someone, while his gang laughed and wrestled behind the gent. When the man got near, a little boy in white britches pushed one of his mates right into the gent, who stumbled forward into the older lad. In a flash the kids disappeared, dissolved into the crowd like they were never there. That was it. The gent's watch or purse would be gone.

The traffic was dying down when finally I saw the *Gravesend Queen* poke its head out from under the bridge, dodging a tug pulling a string of barges upriver. At the helm was Captain Moon, his jacket off, while Suzie stood on deck. She gave me a wave, and the boat slowed as it approached the pier, pulsing with the heavy chug of the engine. I caught the rope that Suzie threw and tied it off on a bollard. She dropped the gangway and stepped ashore.

'Have you seen Belasco?' she asked, retying my knot. Her dress was marked all over with soot, her hands black. Her hair was wild and tangled.

'He ain't with you?'

'Dad sent him home for a rest.'

Moon appeared at the rail, his pipe in his mouth. 'Where's Mr Arrowood?' he asked.

'Called away. He sends his apologies. He'll be back tomorrow.'

Moon frowned at Suzie. A bigger paddle steamer, approaching from the other direction, gave a long ring of its bell. 'Shut it,' growled Moon, glaring at it.

'Did you manage to fix up the boat?' I asked Suzie. It looked seaworthy enough to me, but there was no mistaking there'd been a fire. Charred stains ran up the side of the saloon wall, and the paint on the balustrade was black and bubbled.

'Good enough, I reckon. Been cleaning all day.'

'Could do without that wedding party tonight,' muttered Moon. 'Lewisham and all.'

The bell sounded again from the other paddle steamer.

'Move off, will you!' called out one of its deckhands. 'We got that docking!'

'Give us a bloody minute!' shouted Moon, suddenly angry. He turned back to us. 'We got to go get cleaned up, Suzie. We're already late.'

'What about Belasco?' she asked.

'He'll be along soon. Katie'll take him over.'

Suzie untied the rope from the bollard.

'You best get on, Mr Barnett.'

Moon went to the helm while we pulled up the gangway, and soon we were moving to a mooring about a hundred yards out in the river. We dropped anchor next to two barges, and Suzie tied the boat to an iron piling jutting out the water. When Moon had the engines shut down, he gave a whistle and a wherry pushed off from the pier. A woman was at the oars.

'Shame your guvnor ain't here,' he said as he climbed onto the little boat. 'You'll take some money off the fee, will you?'

'We'll give you an extra day, Captain. You sure Belasco's coming?'

'Don't worry,' said Suzie, already sitting in the boat. 'He oversleeps sometimes. His missus always makes sure he gets here.'

'Let's get off, Katie,' said Moon to the woman in the wherry. She cast oar and they set off toward the pier.

'You look after our boat, Mr Barnett,' Suzie called out. 'And look after yourself!'

'Just make sure you enjoy yourselves,' I called back.

'Oh, blimey, I wish you hadn't said that,' she cried over the water. 'There's always trouble when Dad enjoys himself!'

She had a good laugh at that.

When they were back ashore, I had a look round the boat. They'd done a fair job of cleaning it up, but there were burns on some of the benches, and the paint had been scorched off the deck. You could still smell the smoke, though maybe that wouldn't matter tomorrow when the engine was on and pumping out black steam.

When the light began to fade, I found a jar of paraffin and lit all the lamps: one at the stern, one at the bow, two on each side. I wanted them to know there were people on board. In the saloon I found a pot with a bit of cold porridge in it. I took it on deck and ate as the darkness crept up, looking out onto the grey outlines of the wharves and warehouses lining the river. The two barges we were moored next to were derelict and we formed a little bobbing island with me as the only inhabitant. If anything happened I wouldn't be able to get to the bank;

I was never a strong swimmer, and the currents this side of the bridge were lethal.

After some time, I climbed up to the sun-deck and sat there watching out for Belasco arriving at the pier. Every time I saw a boat on the move I stood, showing myself on board, feeling the river bounce and rock under my boots until the boat passed and the water settled again. The stars came out, adding to the dim twinkle from the lamps of London Bridge.

At some point I realized Belasco wasn't coming. I wasn't too happy being out there on the river knowing what those blokes were capable of, not too happy at all. But I'd be all right. I'd show them the gun, fire into the air. They wouldn't come on if they thought they'd be shot. I lit a smoke. The thing was to stay awake.

I paced the deck, examining the London skyline. On north side St Botolph's spire, the dome of St Paul's, the Monument. On the Surrey side Hibernia Wharf, the church of St Saviour's, Pickford's still working by torchlight, unloading bricks and gravel from low-slung barges, the shouts of the stevedores and bargees carrying over the water to me. Behind it would be Coin Street, where Ettie'd be sleeping with the baby in its box, I thought. And there, across London Bridge and down Borough High Street was my room, empty now, I hoped.

I lit another smoke. What was the guvnor thinking? We were in the middle of the case, for Christ's sake. He knew it was turning out a dangerous one and the minute Holmes calls he just ups and leaves. How many times had he raged about the man's infernal logic? How many times had he cursed Watson and his stories that he just couldn't believe made sense? The damn fool. Holmes always made him lose his balance. He thought it'd get him in the papers, that's why he raced off to Coventry. That's what he always wanted, all these years we'd worked together. He wanted to be known. I hurled my butt in the water, cursing him for leaving me alone. But it wasn't doing me any good getting vexed. I'd get through tonight. With Lewis's pistol, I'd get through. And where the hell was Belasco? I stamped my feet and shook my head, trying to put away these thoughts running around inside me, but I was chafed, and they kept returning.

I went back to the saloon and brought up a few bottles of beer from the bar. The bells of St Saviour's rang midnight. The moon was out now, the warehouses all shadow and glimmer. I pulled my jacket close, lit another smoke and brought the pistol out my pocket. As I held it, I remembered Ettie making the gun shape with her hand that afternoon, her face so serious. I smiled. Time passed. I must have fallen into myself a bit, as I was suddenly brought to by a loud rending noise and men shouting. Fearful the boat had been damaged, I ran to the other side.

I saw it straight away: between me and the pier was a lighter almost split in half and sinking fast. Two blokes held onto the sides, their bodies in the water, crying out. I pulled a lifebuoy from the rail and hurled it, but it didn't get halfway. Jumping down to the main deck, I rang the bell, hoping to rouse someone from the embankment. I dashed back to the gunwale, shouting for help. One half of the lighter tipped up straight, then was sucked under by the black water. It was then I saw a third head in the river, drifting away with the current. I rang the bell over and over.

Shouting now came from the piers and a police galley pushed out, its long oars chopping the river. Bells began to sound ashore too, raising the alarm. I heard the grunt of a steam engine downriver and ran to the stern, waving my arms and yelling. A little boat lit by three silver lights was coming under the bridge, heading upriver. For some moments it kept on course, then I saw it turn towards me. A fellow appeared on deck and waved. I beckoned the boat over, watching as it turned just too late to catch the lone person drifting in the current. I yelled at them, pointing, and saw the steamboat turn again, slow, too slow, then picking up speed and chasing after the bobbing head as it passed through the bridge and into the Pool.

The other half of the lighter was gone underwater now, and the two blokes wailed as they swam in the black ooze. Their arms were heavy and slow, and for every stroke they took towards the bank the current took them further downriver. The ogglers in the police galley were heaving at their oars, moving out into the stream as the two blokes were pulled by the current towards the arches of the bridge, where water jumped and foamed at the buttresses. I shouted at the coppers; the patrol boat turned to try and cut them off, but it was clear it'd never reach them fast enough.

Seconds later the two men were carried under London Bridge by the rushing tide, past the steamboat that was stopped still now, the folk on board yelling and holding torches out over the water. But the lone head had gone, disappeared into the thick water. The cries of the other two men were weak and pitiful now, like they'd just about given up.

Then, as bells rang out from every wharf and pier around, a dredger came lumbering out from Billingsgate. I watched through the arches as it moved side-on into the current like a great, drifting wall, the folk on board leaning over the side with boathooks, angling to catch the two men. Finally, just before the boat disappeared behind the arches of the bridge, they snagged them.

I fell onto a bench, a great tiredness come over me. Feared I'd fall asleep, I rose again and took up my weary march.

Chapter Eight

I walked up and down that boat all night. The bells rang the quarter hour, the half-hour, the hour. I filled the lamps with paraffin and lit them again. The tide went down, making the air heavy with mud stink, then crept up again. Sometimes a boat would drift past, and each time I tensed and gripped the gun. When the sun finally warmed the sky over the Monument, my body was heavy, my spirit in a daze. Quickly, the river got busy again, and by the time the five o'clock bell rang at Billingsgate the eel-boats and shrimpers were already bobbing on the other side of the bridge, waiting to unload. Only then did I sit down to rest.

Just after seven, Suzie and Captain Moon pulled up in the wherry and climbed aboard. Suzie was fresh, her eyes bright. She drew a carrot and a couple of rusks from her basket and handed them to me. The captain looked like he hadn't slept: his broad face was grey, his eyes yellow. His trousers were creased and stained.

'They come?' he growled, his face screwed up against the pain of the sun.

'No,' I told him. 'How was your do?'

Moon ignored me and shuffled off to the engine house.

'Too much brandy last night,' said Suzie, watching his sorry shape clutching the rail as if he'd unbalance. 'Couldn't lie down without holding on.'

'Can he take the helm like that?'

She shook her head as she lowered a bucket over the side. 'Belasco'll take over if he gets wretched.'

'He never came last night.'

'Oh, Lord. Sorry, Mr Barnett. He's never done that before.' She pulled up the rope. 'You go and rest. Have your breakfast.'

She threw the water over the deck, then pushed it back and forth with a broom. I sat up on the sun-deck and had my breakfast. Barges and lighters were queuing at the wharves on the Surrey side, while a few early steamers heavy with day-trippers headed up to Hampton Court and Windsor. I watched the piermaster carry a crate from his cabin, climb the stairs, and put it down at the pier entrance. He came back down to talk to one of the captains. A few minutes later the crippled boy limped over and sat on the crate. He let his cap fall off his head onto the floor, moving it into place with his toes. Soon after, the piermaster climbed back up the stairs. The crippled boy bent his leg up and poked about in his shoulder bag with his foot, pulling out a muffin between his toes. Without a word passing between them, the piermaster took it, nodded, and ate it as he climbed back down to the pier.

When I'd finished my own sorry meal, I lay down for a snooze, only waking when the paddles started to turn below. Suzie raised the anchor and the boat began to drift towards the pier, where there was an empty space next to a steamer twice the size of ours, its red and black funnel spitting out steam. A queue of well-dressed families waited in line to board her.

Suzie threw the rope down to a bloke who was waiting by

the bollards. As he tied off the boat, she let out the gangway and stepped down to talk to him. He was fifty or so, a pair of long pointed shoes on his feet but his britches too short, a solid round belly, a pink and green waistcoat with pictures of the hunt on it. Half his collar had come loose from his shirt.

'This is Ken, Mr Barnett,' said Suzie when I'd climbed down. 'He sells our tickets.'

'You're the private agent, are you?' asked the bloke as we shook hands. He was clean-shaven but for a long, curled moustache. He spoke loud and bold like he owned the place.

'One of them. You got many passengers today?'

'Twelve. But there's still two hour. Any bother last night?'

I shook my head.

A cry came from the other side of the boat, then a great splash.

'Dad!' yelled Suzie, turning and bounding up the gangway with us close behind. 'Dad!' she shouted again as she leapt aboard and raced through the saloon.

When we reached the other side, we found Moon sat on a bench, his mouth open, his eyes wide with fear.

'What is it, Dad?' asked Suzie, taking his shoulder.

He pointed at a thin rope tied to the balustrade, his hands wet with black ooze.

The three of us peered overboard into the thick brown water, where the rope disappeared. Suzie frowned and looked back at her old man.

'That ain't our rope,' she said. 'You pull it up?'

Moon shut his eyes and burped. He bent forward, resting his arms on his knees, moaning under his breath. His cap slipped off and fell at his feet.

'You going to be sick?' demanded Suzie, her voice harder than I'd heard it before.

Moon shook his head.

She looked over the side again. 'There's another up there,' she said, pointing towards the bow where a thicker rope stretched down the hull and into the water. She took the thin rope in her hands.

'You put that down!' barked Moon.

She stopped, staring at him, her eyes filling with tears. 'I was only—'

'Down!' he bellowed.

'Let me, Suzie,' I said, taking it from her. The rope was slick, covered all over with a stinking, tarry mud. I pulled it hand over hand until something burst out the water. It was a brownish, yellowish thing like a big egg, the rope tied through a hole in the shell.

'What the hell is that?' asked Ken.

I kept pulling. Then, as the thing rose up the boat, another one appeared in the brown water, tied a few feet further down the rope. As it broke the surface, it rolled on its side.

Suzie gasped.

I stopped pulling and stared.

It was a skull. The eye holes were plugged with black mud, the teeth little and bright. The rope ran through where the nose should be. Only now could we see that the first one was also a skull.

'Oh, Christ,' murmured Ken.

Suzie's fingers dug into my arm. 'Dad,' she whispered.

I pulled again. After a few more feet of rope another skull appeared, this one a bit bigger. I felt like I was floating somehow, that I was outside my body looking on. I paused to steady myself, then pulled again. A couple of feet later another appeared. Then another. When the first skull reached me, I lifted the little thing over the rail. It was light and cold, its jaw broke off, a brown stain covering one side of its dome.

Suzie stepped back, her hand covering her mouth. It was a child. I placed it on the deck and drew up more of the rope, feeling a cold fury fill me as skull after skull came up from the water.

Finally, I laid the last one down and stood back, the grey Thames slick pooling at our feet, the coil of filthy children's skulls like a monstrous necklace. I looked at them each in turn, wondering who they were, those little, dissolved lives. I thought of my sister, dead at five, my niece Emily whose dress caught fire when she was four and burned her black, and the twins we shared a room with, taken by the river at three. In the workhouse and the courts of Jacob's Island, little nippers were just queuing to join the angels. I turned away.

Moon's jaw trembled as he looked at the chain of skulls. His eyes were shot through with blood. His mouth hung open.

'You were here,' said Suzie to me, her voice quiet.

'Nobody came near.' I rubbed the greasy black ooze on my britches, my voice rough and cracked. 'I was awake all night. Walking up and down.'

'Well, it weren't here last night,' she said. 'I cleaned that rail.'

'You must've fallen asleep,' said Ken.

I shook my head.

'This side was next to the barges,' said Suzie. We all looked out into the river to where the *Gravesend Queen* was moored the night before. The two barges were still there, rocking gentle

57

in the wake of a tug chugging upriver. 'Ain't nobody on them overnight, is there, Dad?'

Moon didn't seem to hear. His eyes were fixed on the skulls, his trembling hands gripping the sides of his head.

'I suppose someone could've been hid in one of the cabins,' I said after a while. 'Wouldn't have taken long to tie the rope on when I was on the other side of the boat, but I'd have heard them leaving. I'd have noticed.'

'They might be still be there waiting for us to go,' said Suzie.

We watched the sleepy black barges rolling up and down with the lap of the water. Gulls stood about on the furthest one, but there was no other sign of life.

'I'll get out there and have a look,' I said. 'But first let's get the other rope up. No point in drawing this out.'

I walked alone down to the rope at the bow. There I shut my eyes and breathed in slow. I would have prayed too if I thought it'd make the rope disappear. I took in another deep breath, hardened my heart, and pulled.

It barely moved. I pulled again, this time with my whole body. It rose a few inches, no more. Whatever was on the end of this rope was heavy. I wiped the sweat from my face, cursing Belasco for not being here to help. Where was that prick? Why the hell hadn't he turned up? Suzie came over by my side. I braced and pulled again. The water below was thick and brown, bits of paper and sticks and sewage bobbing and drifting in it like workhouse soup. Suzie got her hands on the rope and we pulled again.

We pulled again.

There was something just below the surface now, a mess of bladderwrack, its tangle drawn by the current. Something blurred and yellow was below it. We pulled again. The thing broke the surface and a groan fell out of my mouth. It wasn't bladderwrack, it was hair. Long hair floating in the water.

It was a head.

A woman's head.

'Help us, Ken!' snapped Suzie.

He stepped over and took the end of the rope. We hoisted again.

The rope formed a noose around the dead woman's neck as she rose inch by inch from the water, her head tipping down, her arms hanging heavy at her side.

'Oh Lord, no,' murmured Suzie. I could feel her arms shaking on the rope behind me. We heaved again and again, the body inching its way up the gunwale, Ken grunting with each pull. The higher it got, the heavier she became.

We heaved again, but the weight was too much now and the rope slipped from my hand. Suzie and Ken couldn't keep hold either, and the body fell back into the water.

'Get help, Ken,' I told him.

He ran off. Suzie stood staring at the body floating just under the surface, her breath short and fast. Her face was rolling with sweat, her eyes pink like she had a fever.

'You go sit down,' I told her. 'Look after your old man.'

She nodded and stepped back, sitting down next to Moon. He sat hunched over, his elbows resting on his legs, watching the floor. She touched his hand but he made no response. She stood again, stepped over to the rail, wiped her hands on her dress.

'This is my boat, Mr Barnett,' she said at last.

We stood by the rope saying nothing until Ken came back with the piermaster. The four of us took up the rope and heaved.

The head broke the surface again, and we worked the body up the side of the boat, pull after pull. The woman wore a long brown nightdress, torn and tattered. When she was almost clear of the water, I saw there was something tied to her ankle. We pulled again and her foot broke the water. It was a hand. A hand tied to her ankle.

'No,' whispered Suzie. 'Please, God, not another.'

'Let it go,' said Ken with a cough. 'We need the Old Bill.'

'Keep pulling,' I grunted, wanting it over now. 'Let's get them out.'

Again we heaved at the rope. The woman's head was now level with the rail. Her hair was long and curled, soaked in the filthy water. Her face was white as goose fat, her tongue grey and poking out her mouth like a third lip. She glared at me with crimson eyes, as if it was me who'd done this to her.

We could now see the freckled arm of a second woman rising out the water. We pulled again. Her head broke from the water, her face tipped down, her hair tufted and short, her neck bruised black. The undershirt she wore was made for a man, both its sleeves torn off.

As the other three took the strain, I grabbed the first woman under the arms and pulled her sodden body on board, feeling her cold skin on my hands, her dead meat. She slid onto the deck and rested there on her back, her head tilted to the side. The water streamed out of her. The front of her nightdress was ripped, the wet fabric around it stained pink. Though the folds and ruck of the material covered most of the damage, I could see her belly'd been cut open. The second woman was bent double over the rail now, her undershirt snagged on a curl in the ironwork. Suzie, Ken and the piermaster came over to take the rope at the balustrade, where it led back into the water. I freed the second woman and she fell aboard, her head resting upon the first woman's belly. Quick as I could I pulled her torn shirt tight over her body, hoping Suzie hadn't seen the skin slashed open on her belly too, her muscles and innards purple and grey, washed and bloodless. She was smaller, three-quarter size. Her starry eyes looked up at us, an uncertain smile on her face like she'd just done a joke and wasn't sure we'd laugh.

'Help us, Mr Barnett,' said Suzie. Tears ran down her cheeks as she and Ken and the piermaster strained to keep hold of the rope. It was looped around the first woman's neck, then around her ankle and the second woman's hand, and from there fell taut into the water. We pulled again. A bald man's crown now rose from the river, a great, bruised dent across the back of his head. His ears were gone, and in their place were ragged wounds, pink and white and brown. Though he was heavy we pulled quicker: he was the last.

When his shoulders were level with the balustrade, I hauled him over and he fell in a ball, his bruised yellow head on the floor like a Mohammedan at prayer. He wore nothing but a long white shirt.

Suzie was on her knees, panting. Ken dropped onto a bench, his eyes fixed on the bodies, convulsions running through his limbs.

'I'll find a copper,' said the piermaster, his voice dull. He shuffled off through the saloon.

I held on tight to the rail, trying to catch my breath, unable to take my eyes off the three slippery bodies sleeping on the deck. They hadn't been in the water long. I'd been there when my Uncle Norbert's body was pulled from the river back when I lived on Jacob's Island, and they didn't look anything like him. I looked over at Moon, still hunched over, still refusing to look.

'Who are they, Captain?' I asked.

He made no reply.

'You've got to tell me now,' I said, the anger rising in my voice. 'What's going on? Who are those people?'

'Dad?' asked Suzie.

Moon shook his head, covering his face with his hands.

'Suzie, what do you know about this?' I asked, turning to her. 'Who are they?'

'I don't know, Mr Barnett. I swear it. I don't know anything about this.'

For some time nobody spoke.

'Look,' said Suzie, climbing to her feet. She was pointing out into the stream.

Out near last night's mooring was Polgreen's boat, its engine chugging, its paddles holding it still against the current. On its deck stood the foreigners. And they were watching us.

Chapter Nine

The father, the mother, the son, all in a row, their hands on the rail. Suzie and Moon did nothing. They just sat there on deck watching the Polgreen family watching them.

'Were they at the barges?' I asked.

Suzie shook her head. 'They come from upriver just now. Stopped when they saw us.'

Polgreen took his wife's arm and pulled her into the wheel room. The lad stood frozen, unable to take his eyes off the bodies. We heard their engines change gear; the paddles started to churn the water. The boat moved off.

'I need to check the barges,' I said. 'Ken can come with me. Suzie, pull up the gangway and don't let anyone on board until the coppers come.'

She wiped the tears from her face and nodded. 'Wait here, Dad,' she said, patting Moon's knee. 'I'll be back soon.'

The pier was even more crowded now: families were queuing for the *Koh-i-noor*, the women in frilly lace dresses and bonnets, the children running around laughing, excited to be getting on the water. The men wore boating jackets and straw hats and white britches, while a few dogs stood panting by their owners. A bloke who looked a bit like Ken went between them selling parasols and cures for seasickness.

Another shorter queue was starting to form by the *Gravesend Queen*. These were the East End day-trippers. Their bonnets were simpler, their dresses coarser and less frilled, their suits old and plain, and not a white trouser-leg to be seen. Their kids laughed and ran too, but the two sets of children kept away from each other, already knowing their place.

Ken and me got Kate, the wherry woman who'd taken Moon and Suzie the day before, to row us out to the barges. They were empty, stripped of sails and rigging, boughs and booms. The only sign of life was the gulls who'd claimed them as their shit-spattered slum. Just as we were climbing back onto the pier, the guvnor came shuffling through the crowds.

'Ah, there you are, Barnett,' he said. He was tired, a defeated look on his face. His cheek glistened with damp. Noticing my shirt and britches wet and messed with river mud, his brow wrinkled.

'You'd better go aboard and see what we just pulled out of the water,' I said.

Usually he'd ask what was going on, but seeing my face so grim he simply turned and picked his way through the queues. I followed him aboard, then waited by the gangway while he disappeared into the saloon. I rested my hands on the rail, watching the crippled boy sat on his crate at the top of the embankment stairs as he picked up a coin with his foot and dropped it in his bag. He was some kind of contortionist, that was sure. The boy pickpocket in full mourning dress came along and started to talk to him. The little dipper slapped the cripple's twisted arm. The beggar kicked out at him. They laughed like it was the best game in London.

After five minutes, the guvnor returned to my side of the boat. He looked at me, the colour gone from his face.

'What the hell are we dealing with here, Norman?'

He listened careful as I told him about the night before, asking about everything, every little detail. I knew he would, and I'd tried to repeat as much of it back to myself so I wouldn't forget. He didn't try to explain why he'd left the day before, and I didn't ask him what he'd been up to. That could wait.

'There's something more behind this, Barnett,' he said. 'Why would Polgreen commit three murders just to put Moon out of business? Easier to sink the boat.'

'It's a police case now, sir.'

He nodded, his eyes scanning the pier. Spotting Katie lounging in her wherry, he climbed down and approached her.

'Have you been here all morning, ma'am?' he asked.

'On and off,' she said sharpish. Her tattered purple hat was pulled low over her eyes. She looked bored.

'Did you see anything unusual? Anyone suspicious?'

She shook her head. 'Pier's always packed at the weekend. I just let them get on with it.'

'What about last night?'

She nodded at me. 'Saw him get aboard. Saw the Moons leave.'

'Did you see anyone else approach the boat?'

She shook her head. 'I went home soon after.'

The piermaster was coming down from Swan Lane with two coppers. I led them up the gangway to the saloon, where Moon sat next to Suzie. When I'd answered his questions, the sergeant sent his constable off to find a detective.

'You all stay in here while I inspect the boat,' he told us, and for fifteen minutes we watched him through the window as he stood looking at the bodies, wandered up and down the deck, rested his arms on the balustrade and inspected London Bridge. Then he lit his pipe and sat on a bench, staring out over the water at the wharves and warehouses of Southwark. As he was inspecting it all, the young copper returned.

'I've brought the detective, sir,' we heard him say.

'Good Christ,' said the guvnor. 'What the hell's *he* doing here?'

In the saloon window had appeared Inspector Petleigh of the Southwark Police. There was a lot of history between the guvnor and him, some of it good, some of it bad. For the moment, what with the chance he was maybe the father of Ettie's baby, he was one copper we took no pleasure in seeing.

The sergeant led him round to where the bodies lay on the bow. After they'd had a good look, Petleigh nodded, turned, and came into the saloon.

When he saw us, he groaned.

'I knew it was you two,' he said in his clipped, nervy voice. 'As soon he told me there were private agents I knew it.'

I glared at him.

'How's your wife, Petleigh?' demanded the guvnor. 'Happy? Well fed?'

'She's fine, since you ask.'

'Did you ever get that divorce you were talking about?'

'I'm not here to talk about my marriage,' snapped Petleigh, his cheeks colouring.

'What the hell *are* you doing here? This isn't your parish.'

'I've been assigned to the City Police for a few months. Both of their detectives are out of action.'

66

'Why the blazes do we always get you?' exclaimed the guvnor, throwing his hands in the air. 'We might as well give up now!'

Petleigh's eyes narrowed. He stroked his neat, waxed moustache. 'Control yourself, William. Now, tell me what you're doing here. What case are you working on?'

The guvnor glared at him.

'Well?' demanded Petleigh.

Finally, the guvnor explained it to him. As he spoke, Petleigh wrote notes in a little blue book. When he'd finished, he looked at Moon.

'So you think it's this Polgreen chap, Captain?'

Moon blinked like he was startled by the question. Then his face darkened. He looked at Suzie.

'Yes, sir,' she said when it was clear her old man wasn't about to speak.

'D'you recognize the bodies, Captain?' asked Petleigh.

Moon shook his head and sighed deep.

'He's in shock,' said the guvnor.

'Miss Moon?' asked Petleigh, looking at her with his sly eyes.

'No, sir.'

'What about the children's skulls, do they mean anything to you?'

It was hot in the saloon, and Petleigh seemed to have a kind of skin-coloured powder caked on his forehead. Little cracks were appearing in it, where wet came out and ran down to his eyebrows.

Suzie shook her head.

'Captain Moon?' asked Petleigh.

Moon was still as a statue for a moment, then he shook his head. He didn't look up.

'Dad?' asked Suzie.

Again he shook his head.

'The sergeant says the deckhand's gone missing,' said Petleigh, tapping his pencil on his teeth. 'D'you have his address?'

Suzie gave it him. He wrote it down, then looked out at the pier. 'Ah. The police surgeon's here. Please remain inside until we've finished.' He looked at the guvnor. 'All of you.'

Arrowood waited a few moments while Petleigh showed the police surgeon the bodies. Then, having lit a cigar, he got up and went out on deck, watching as the doctor did his work. After a few minutes, he came back into the saloon.

'Well, they didn't die by drowning. Both women were stabbed in the belly and chest. The man has head injuries from a blunt instrument.'

The guvnor took Moon by the shoulder. 'Captain. Listen to me.'

Moon didn't seem to hear him.

'Captain Moon!' The guvnor gave him a shake.

At last Moon looked up.

'What do those skulls mean to you, Captain?'

The black of Moon's eyes shrunk, and for a moment there was hatred in his wind-burnt face.

'Fourteen skulls. Tell me what they mean.'

Moon shook off the guvnor's hands and stood, walking to the open door facing onto the pier. There he brought out his pipe, his hand shaking. Four times he broke his match trying to light it. In a howl of despair, he wrenched the pipe from his mouth and hurled it off the boat.

Petleigh stepped back into the saloon.

'We've sent the constable for a cart,' he said. 'This is a police matter now, William. Find yourself another case. If I have further questions I'll send for you.'

'We're still engaged by the Captain to find who's been damaging the boat,' said the guvnor. 'You cannot object to that, surely?'

'You're off the case and that's final. Now, please go ashore.'

The guvnor puffed furiously on his cigar as he glared at Petleigh. 'Are you the father?' he asked at last.

'That what?'

'The father! Don't act dumb, Petleigh. Are you?'

'The father of who?'

'Just tell me.'

'What are you talking about?'

'Ettie's child! Are you?'

'What d'you mean, Ettie's child?'

For some time they glared at each other.

'What child are you talking about?' asked Petleigh again.

'That's the way you're going to play it, is it?'

'Oh, I can't be bothered with this,' said the inspector with a wave of his hand. 'Get off the boat. Now!'

'Ettie's well,' said the guvnor. 'Fine and healthy the both of them, Inspector, in case you were wondering.'

Petleigh blinked. He touched his moustache. His face loosened.

'That's good,' he said, and stamped back out on deck.

Chapter Ten

We walked down Lower Thames Street, through the mayhem of porters and wagons outside Billingsgate, past Custom House and around the great grey walls of the Tower, the guvnor wheezing and complaining about his feet all the way. After the bridge, we wound our way through St Katherine's Dock and over the basin lock. The deeper we went into Wapping, the darker it became, the high walls of the dockyards rising over the slouching buildings, shutting out the sun. As we marched down the busy high street lined with provisions shops, ship chandlers, missions and pubs, we could hear languages from all the continents of the world. I'd spent a lot of time in these streets when I was sixteen or seventeen, trying to earn a crust when my ma was laid up at home. It was a seafaring neighbourhood, and money ran through its calloused hands like water. Money I'd do just about anything to get my own hands on.

Belasco's home was on a dirt alley behind the High Street, two doors down from a pub where red-faced Russians stood sweating and swearing on the street. It wasn't such a well-off alley but not a slum either. Kids were everywhere, hanging out windows, sitting on doorsteps, running up and down after a ball of paper and string. A few old folk sat on stools, watching the nippers. Through the windows you could see women working:

sewing collars and sacks, pressing clothes, gluing matchboxes, boiling up shrimp and sheep's trotters.

The door to Belasco's building was open. Inside, the corridor was dark, the floorboards bare and dusty. Just past the staircase was another door, also open, and there was Belasco, asleep on a mattress on the floor.

We walked in. He had a poultice tied to his head with a bit of rag, dried blood crusted round his ear. His thick brown hair was hard and stuck together.

'What d'you want?' asked a woman coming out from the gloom at the back of the room.

She was maybe ten year older than Belasco, with a growth on the side of her chin and a hard look in her eye.

'Mrs Belasco?' said the guvnor. He gave a bow. 'I'm Mr Arrowood. This is Mr Barnett. We're here to see your husband.'

She nodded, the hardness in her face turning into a smile.

'I heard of you.'

'Your husband didn't arrive for work last night. We were worried.'

'And you can see why,' she said with a nod. 'Got clouted, didn't he?'

Belasco slept on.

'When?' asked the guvnor.

'On his way home yesterday afternoon. Been drinking, of course. Mate of his brung him back. Didn't Captain Moon get my message?'

'No, ma'am,' I said.

'I sent a boy. Paid the bloody rascal.'

I dropped to my knee and gave Belasco a poke. He grunted, so I poked him harder. 'Wake up, mate.'

His eyes opened. It took him a few moments to see straight, then he raised himself on an elbow.

'Norman. Mr Arrowood.'

'What happened to you?' I asked.

He sat up proper, leaning his back against the wall. I could see one of his arms was bruised and swollen. He felt the bandage on his head, wincing.

'Blimey, that hurts.'

I pulled out my box of Black Drop and tossed it to him.

'Cheers, Norman,' he said, dropping a few of the pellets in his mouth and swallowing. He spoke slow. 'I was just leaving the pub. Some bloke come up behind and coshed me.'

'What did he look like?'

'Didn't see him. I was out like a lamp. Lucky my mate came out else I don't know what else the bloke would've done. He ran off, anyways.'

'Did your friend see him?'

'Only from behind.' Belasco shook his head. 'Bughunters. They work the area. I'd had a few mugs of gin. Weren't too steady on my feet.'

Mrs Belasco brought over four mugs of tea and handed them round. There were only two chairs. A little table was piled high with lengths of cotton and half-made shirts. Another straw mattress was leant against the wall.

'Something else happened to the boat last night,' said the guvnor, having a swallow of his tea. 'Someone tied two ropes to the gunwale. One had children's skulls knotted on.'

'What?' asked Belasco.

'Children's skulls. Fourteen.'

Belasco shook his head, his face pale. His wife stared at the guvnor, her mug of tea frozen in the air just before her open mouth.

'The other rope was tied to three corpses. Two women and a man.'

'Come off it, Mr Arrowood.'

'The police are there now,' said the guvnor.

Belasco looked at him for some time. Several times he seemed about to say something, but each time he didn't. Finally, he asked, 'Suzie didn't see it, did she?'

'She saw everything.'

'So it's murder now,' said Belasco, pushing himself to his feet. 'Jesus bloody Christ.' He found his britches and pulled them on. Seeing him struggle with only one good arm, his wife went over to help him.

'The skulls must mean something,' said the guvnor. 'Can you remember anything you've seen, anything you've heard? It doesn't matter how obscure. Something the captain might have said. Or Suzie.'

Belasco shook his head. 'It don't make sense. Lord, they must be out of their minds about it. Where are they? Still on the boat?'

'Yes,' said the guvnor, slurping his tea. 'The police want to speak to you.'

'Course.' Belasco took his shirt from the floor. 'I'll go now.'

'You ain't well enough,' said his wife.

'Captain needs me.'

'Wait a moment, my friend,' said the guvnor. 'There's more to this than just driving the *Gravesend Queen* out of business. If it is Polgreen then there's something else behind it, something more personal. He wouldn't risk being hanged just to gain the

73

Gravesend run for himself. Can you remember anybody who might have a feud with the captain? Anyone at all?'

Belasco stuck his feet in his boots and bent to do up the laces. 'I been thinking about it since this thing started, but there's nobody. He talks away with me and Suzie when he's not blue, but he keeps his distance from just about everyone else. Most folk don't even notice him.'

'What d'you know of his life before he took you on?'

'He never talks about it. I only know about his wife and kids from Suzie.'

'Did you ever ask him?'

'Few times, but he don't like to look back, he says. I know he had another steamer, but that's all.'

'The name?'

'I don't know.' As he talked, Belasco struggled to get his swollen arm into his greasy shirt. His wife helped him get it on, tuck it in. He picked up some coins from the table, spooned a bit of porridge in his mouth. 'Don't even know the route. I did ask him but he always says the past's the past.'

'What about his friends?' asked the guvnor. 'D'you know any?'

'There's a fellow in Gravesend he sees when we're waiting for the return trip. Has his dinner with him. Curtis. Lives somewhere near the high street.'

The guvnor scribbled it in his notebook.

'Any others?'

'I never heard him mention anyone else.' Something came over him as he spoke and his eyes did a flutter. He clutched the doorframe. I got up to help him, leading him to my chair where he sat heavily, holding his head in his hands.

74

'What is it, darling?' asked his wife, laying her palm on his back.

'Just come over dizzy,' he mumbled. Then, real quick, he reached for the chamber pot and spewed up the tea he'd just swallowed. Then came another spurt of a different colour.

Mrs Belasco gave him a rag for his mouth. 'You'd better stay home today, mate.'

Belasco shook his head. Holding the back of the chair, he rose slowly. 'I'm all right now. Must've needed to get that out.' He leant over and kissed her.

'You be careful,' she said.

''Course,' he said. 'I've got the detectives with me, ain't I?'

Chapter Eleven

It was midday when we got back to the pier. On the boat, we found the Moons still sitting in the saloon, while Petleigh and the constable waited on deck, guarding the bodies against the gulls circling above. Belasco strode over to Suzie and gripped her arms.

'Suzie,' he murmured.

Her eyes glazed like tears were about to come. They didn't. She pulled away.

'Where was you?' she asked sharply.

He pointed to the grey bandage on his head. 'Got knocked out last night. Don't know who by.'

'You was drinking.'

Belasco looked at Moon, who sat staring out the window. 'How is he?'

'He won't talk. His nerves is gone.'

Petleigh poked his head through the door. 'Are you Mr Belasco?' he asked.

'Yes, sir.'

'Could you come over here and look at the bodies?'

We followed Belasco onto the deck, where the three corpses had been laid out on their backs. A seagull stood on the smaller woman's arm, trying to pull out a little purple sweetbread from the wound in her belly. Petleigh yelled and clapped his hands.

Vexed, the gull beat its monstrous wings and rose, hovering above the bodies and shrieking back at the copper. Then, in an instant, it twisted and shot off across the river.

The guvnor turned away, his belcher to his mouth. The tall woman still had the bit of rope round her ankle where she'd been tied to the other one. Her bloody eyes, dried out in the sun, stared dully into the blue like week-old herring. Over the deck spread her tangled hair, run through with sticks and straw, knotted with bits of black river grease. They'd closed her nightdress over her belly, giving her a bit of dignity. The guvnor coughed, then turned back. Next to the big one the little one was laid out, her undershirt ripped almost in half. This hadn't been arranged for her modesty, and we could see her belly torn open, the ragged purple muscle and pipes washed clean of blood by the river and now baking in the summer heat. Her innards seemed to be full of animal parts, sheep's ballocks and pigs' livers and bits of calves' brains. On the deck next to her lay the sweetbread the gull had been trying to pull out, a spleen or something, a thin blue tube leading back inside her. Her hands were open on the deck, the palms facing the sun and one finger sticking up queer like a prick. Her head twisted towards the other woman, her starry eyes bright, her lashes glinting with river salt.

Next to her the man lay on his back. His head was clean-shaven, smooth and yellow like he was made of butter, spoiled only by the ragged wounds where his ears should be.

'They call those butcher's earmuffs in the criminal world,' said Petleigh.

A long shirt covered the dead man down to his thighs; below that he was bare. Petleigh nudged a baby eel twitching on the floor next to him.

'We pulled that out of his backside.'

The guvnor flitched.

'D'you know these people, Mr Belasco?' he asked.

'No, Inspector.'

'Customers?'

'Can't remember ever seeing them.'

'Acquaintances of Captain Moon?'

'No, sir.'

'What did the surgeon say about the skulls?' asked Arrowood.

'Children, all different ages, died anywhere between five and a hundred years ago, he thinks.' Petleigh brought out his snuff box and had a toot. His eyes watered. He sneezed. 'Dug up from somewhere. Though why anyone would do that I do not know.'

'It's a message, for goodness' sake,' snapped the guvnor. 'A child could've worked that out.'

'I know it's a damn message, William.'

'It didn't sound like it.'

'Why are you so short-tempered today? Haven't you been sleeping well?'

The guvnor glared at Petleigh: it seemed like the inspector was provoking him.

'I'm short-tempered because we've just discovered fourteen children's skulls and three corpses,' said the guvnor through clenched teeth, 'and this family are being ruined by somebody. My Lord, you're a cold fish, Petleigh. Where's your damn heart?'

'I keep it at home when I'm called to a murder. Otherwise I couldn't do this—'

'At home!' barked the guvnor, stiffening. His damp brow drew down over his eyes, his swollen nose flushed with blood. 'With your wife who you told us you were divorcing?'

I took the guvnor's arm to calm him. 'What will you do now, Inspector?' I asked.

Petleigh continued to hold the guvnor's eye. 'Investigations, Norman.' He turned to Belasco. 'I need you to come to the station, sir. I understand this is the first time you've ever deserted the boat.'

'I got coshed last night,' protested Belasco, pointing at the bandage on his head. His eyes were still on the bodies. 'Knocked out cold.'

'Fetch the captain too. His nerves have the better of him at the moment, but he's going to have to start talking soon.'

'You want Suzie?'

Petleigh looked at her through the saloon window. He shook his head. 'I've already spoken to her.'

Belasco helped Moon up, then climbed off the boat with Petleigh. Arrowood fell onto a bench, his red face throbbing with heat and vexation. He pulled off his boots with a gasp, and we sat there with Suzie until the police wagon arrived, then watched as the coppers packed the ropes and skulls in canvas bags and carried away the bodies on three battered old gurneys. A crowd had gathered to watch, packed onto the pier and the Swan Stairs.

Suzie had one more look round, then locked the saloon, the wheelroom, the engine. She pulled on a simple brown bonnet and tied it under her chin. The piermaster stood by the gangway waiting for us.

'Terrible business, Suzie,' he said, a briar pipe hanging from his lips. Behind him, the crowd was following the coppers off the pier and up toward Thames Street. 'But they oughtn't to have left the boat here. I'll need this space later.'

'Sorry, Mr Wellersby,' she said. 'I'd have moved her if he'd let me.'

'Not your fault, my dear. And can you tell your father the fees are overdue?'

Suzie nodded, a great sigh drifting from her pale lips. I didn't think her grim face could have got any grimmer.

'You need anything?' asked the old fellow.

'A bit of luck is all.'

He shoved his hands in his pockets. 'You get some rest. I'll watch over her.'

We walked with Suzie to the bus stop by the Monument.

'D'you have any idea who those people might be?' asked the guvnor as we waited.

'No, sir. I never seen them.'

'The skulls were a message, and I think your father knows what they mean.'

She spun round, her eyes fierce. 'No, he don't! He'd have said if he did.'

'But he hasn't spoken more than a few words since Norman pulled them up, Suzie. Something's shaken him.'

''Course he's shaken! Someone's killed those people. 'Course he's blooming shaken up – his nerves is gone!'

'But yours haven't. Norman's haven't. Your father's been sitting there since this morning looking into the distance, his mind closed in on itself. That's what people do when they're remembering something difficult. What could it be, Suzie?'

Her brow was drawn low, her lips tight. 'Go after Polgreen,' she said.

'Was he being threatened by creditors?'

'We owed a bit, but they wouldn't do this, would they?'

'Did your father tell you of any other trouble he's had? Now or in the past?'

'He don't talk about his past. Never has done. Ma didn't neither.'

'What about his work? Did he tell you about what he did before the *Gravesend Queen*?'

'No, he never talks about it.'

'Didn't you ever ask?'

'Don't keep going on with the same question, Mr Arrowood. I don't know, but you got to see Polgreen again. He'll be back about seven tonight. It's him that's behind it. He's a bad heart. A nasty and evil heart.'

The bus arrived and we watched Suzie as she was swallowed by the press of people climbing aboard.

Chapter Twelve

Upper Thames Street was crowded out with carts and trollies and sweaty nags pulling rickety wagons to and from the warehouses. Little groups of kiddies dashed here and there, begging and nicking from the carts as they rattled along the road. Servants on errands pushed their way through the bustle, glad to get out of the house for a few hours, while dawdlers dawdled, chatting to neighbours and getting in every bugger's way. The first pub we reached was the King's Head and Lamb. Inside, the porters from Billingsgate were shouting and swearing, drinking hard with their white coats hanging open and their wooden hats by their feet. I got us each a mug of porter and a pot of eel jelly while the guvnor took a space by the door.

'No spoon?' he asked.

'None left.' I took a long swig. Once the beer hit my belly I felt the weariness come over me and remembered I'd only had an hour or so's sleep since yesterday. I lit a fag; the guvnor got his pipe going.

'I'm worried about that girl,' he said as he blew out a long cloud of silver smoke. 'If they'll kill two women they'll just as easily kill her.'

I finished my porter and held out my hand. Sighing, he

dropped me a sixpence, then looked back in his little cotton purse. He gave it a jiggle and cursed under his breath.

I went and got us two more.

'Change, please!' he barked before I even had a chance to put the mugs down. When he'd put away the coppers, he took a swig. He burped. 'We need those fifty shillings Moon owes us. Ask him as soon as he returns.'

'Petleigh's on the case now. The captain doesn't need us any more.'

'You know Petleigh won't solve it without our help.'

'And you know Moon can't pay us.'

With his pipe in one hand, the guvnor put the pot of eel jelly between his knees and dug in his fingers. He scooped the mess into his mouth, dropping a gobbet on his shirt front.

'Well, we can't just leave it,' he said with his mouth still full. 'Moon and Suzie might be next. Oh Lord, we can't keep working without payment, Norman. Not with my sister and the baby.' He wiped the gobbet off his shirt and licked it from his grimy finger. 'Petleigh was acting suspiciously just now. I'm more and more convinced the baby's hers. She's ashamed, why else would she refuse to tell me? But she doesn't seem to have an instinct for child-rearing, that's what puzzles me. She stiffens when she picks it up.' He puffed on his pipe and pondered. He shook his head. 'Perhaps it is an orphan after all. But why she wouldn't tell me that, I do not know.'

'Maybe she thinks you'll make her take it back.'

'She knows I can never make her do anything she doesn't want to do. She's just bloody-minded, Barnett. She makes a decision and that's it. Never changes her mind.'

'That's not true, William.'

We sat for a while thinking about it. We both understood that if it really was hers, then Petleigh had to be the father. He'd visited her so many times, brought gifts, played cards. It was that possibility that vexed the guvnor more than anything.

He cleared his throat. 'Could you ask her, Norman? There's too much anger between us for her to tell me. I think she trusts you.'

'It isn't really my place.'

'Your place? What does that mean?'

'You know what it means. I work for you.'

'I don't like it when you talk like that, Norman. We're bonded, you and me.'

'Maybe so, but we can't change where we're from. You may be a fallen man now, but you and Ettie came from a better place.'

'You're too sensitive,' he said quietly. 'You're too caught up in your childhood.'

'Look at me, William. I've a tear in my britches. A patch on my jacket. You really think I've left it behind?'

'It won't always be like that.'

'I'm useful to you because of where I'm from, and you need to remember that.'

He frowned. 'Anyway, I'm not a fallen man. I'm good at what I do. If any of our cases had been recognized half as much as that charlatan Holmes then—'

'Look at how you live. You've lost almost everything you had when you left the newspaper. Your clothes are almost as shabby as mine. You always owe somebody.'

'One of these days they'll report our cases properly,' he said. 'We'll start to get paid what we deserve.'

'And then we wouldn't be able to help folk like Moon and his daughter.'

'We'd do both.'

I dropped my fag and ground it under my heel. 'We can't ask Moon for the money.'

He sighed. 'No, you're right. He's already in debt.'

'Didn't Holmes pay you?' I asked, suddenly remembering where he'd gone the night before.

His raddled eyes shut for a moment. He took a big draught of his porter, then spooned the rest of the eel jelly in his mouth. As he chewed, he picked up a paper from the floor and opened it.

'Aren't you going to tell me what happened, William?'

'He wasn't there,' he said at last.

A laugh fell out my mouth afore I'd a chance to catch it.

'Where was he?'

'I don't know!' he barked, his fearsome nose-holes flaring. 'The hotel said he hadn't been there at all. I waited till morning and got the first train back. Four bob it cost me.'

'You haven't heard from him since?'

'Not even a blooming note of apology. I've sent him a telegraph.'

I watched the side of his face for some time, the blood sausage nose, the fleshy ears etched with soot, the thin, greasy hair curled over his balding crown. He took another lug of porter.

'Stop watching me!' he hissed.

I put out my fag and stood.

'I need a kip. You want me this afternoon?'

'There's nothing we can do until Polgreen returns at seven. Meet me then.'

I was just leaving when his hand reached out and gripped my thigh. 'I shouldn't have left you there last night, Norman,' he said, his eyes cast down to the paper on his knee. 'But you know I can't think straight when it comes to that charlatan.'

I was tuckered out when I reached my room. The building was quiet, and I was glad I'd told Lilly to go. The door stuck a bit so I gave it a kick, no patience left in me for care. It jerked open and there she was, laid out on her belly on my mattress. The air was thick with heat, wet with her catarrh. I looked to the floor: the chamber pot was still full, still there by the foot of the bed, and now there was a jar beside it, half-full itself.

Her face was pressed against the grey sheet. She opened one eye.

'Hello, Norm, darling,' she mumbled. 'I kept it warm for you.'

I threw open the window to the street.

'You said you'd leave.'

'I know, but where am I to go? And don't we have a laugh together?' She raised herself on her elbows and looked at me. Her stringy hair fell over her face. It was a face I liked well enough, it just wasn't the one I wanted to see. 'You didn't come home last night,' she said, covering her mouth as she yawned. 'I missed you, mate.'

'I was working.'

'You look knackered.' She patted the bed beside her. 'Get your boots off. Come on. I'll look after you.'

The anger had already left me, and all that was left was the tiredness. So off came the boots, the shirt, the britches. The mattress was a blessed relief, and even the sense of her body

86

next to me was a comfort of some kind. I should have fallen straight off to sleep, so tired was I, but as my head sunk into the pillow I thought of the little dead woman, her head resting on the belly of the bigger one. What were the two of them to each other? And what was the man to them? I felt the greasy rope in my hands, the ache in my arms as I hauled up the chain of bodies. Their faces came before me again, wet and streaming. They were playing with me, stirring my brain. I gave a grunt of rage; I'd be up again in a few hours and needed to get some sleep. I tried to stop thinking, to listen instead to the noises of the street outside. I turned my mind to the fingers working their way under my vest, stroking the black hair of my belly, and the slow breathing in my ear.

Chapter Thirteen

Arrowood was already at the pier when I arrived that evening. Next to the *Gravesend Queen*, a big paddle steamer, the *Clacton Belle*, had just docked and her passengers were getting off. The guvnor stood at the side, waiting for them to climb the stairs up to Swan Lane. Among them moved the gang of dippers: the lad in the mourning suit, the little girl in the ragged dress, the boy with the stained white britches. I nudged the guvnor as they lifted a watch and chain off a city gent then disappeared like pipe smoke.

It was low water, and Polgreen's boat was idling over by the barges, waiting for the *Clacton Belle* to give up its mooring. His decks were packed out with passengers, whose shouts and laughter came over the water: a good day for him with Moon's boat out of action. We climbed aboard the *Gravesend Queen* and found Belasco in the engine room. His hands were dark with grease and oil; his face shone with sweat. He told us Moon was still at the police station.

'Is he any better?' asked the guvnor.

'They let me go soon as I'd answered their questions so I reckon maybe he ain't talking yet.' He sighed and looked over at the *Clacton Belle*, at its shiny paddle box, the brass railings glinting in the evening sun. An African sweeping the deck shouted out a greeting. Belasco raised his hand and cried,

'Aye aye!' He dropped his voice again. 'It's hit him hard. Suzie gone home, has she?'

'About midday,' I said.

He nodded. 'I'm going to keep a watch here till morning. Just hope that the inspector lets us take the boat out tomorrow.'

'How much money does the captain owe, Belasco?' asked the guvnor.

The deckhand scratched his tattoo. 'Well, he owes the piermaster, and Suzie says they're behind on rent. I ain't been paid in a month neither. But it's more than that. We had a visit a week or so since from a couple of bad types. Money lenders, I reckon. Came on the boat looking it over like he'd borrowed on it.'

'Names?' I asked.

Belasco shook his head. 'Captain made me get off the boat when they come. One of them was big, bigger than you, Norm. Cauliflower ear, long moustache, bald. The other was a short fellow, built like a bull terrier. I didn't hear what they said, but it weren't friendly.'

'Does Miss Moon know?' asked the guvnor, turning to look up Swan Lane.

'She weren't there. Captain's not the type to worry her neither.'

Arrowood nodded. 'We'll keep watch with you tonight.'

'You don't have to, sir,' said Belasco. 'Reckon the Old Bill's looking into it now.'

'I wouldn't expect too much from Inspector Petleigh,' said the guvnor, looking up Swan Lane again. He frowned. 'You'd have thought he'd be here to interview Polgreen when he disembarks. Apparently he has more important things to do.'

Half an hour later, the *Clacton Belle* moved off to a great cheer from the crowd on Polgreen's boat. When it took its place at the pier, his son jumped off and tied the ropes, while Mrs Polgreen let down the gangway. We waited till all the passengers had cleared off, then made to board the ship.

'You stay where you are,' said Polgreen, appearing on the deck next to his wife. He wore a loose checked shirt, a black bowler, his battered face handsome enough for an older bloke. His fists gripped the handrail.

'We need to talk to you for a moment, Captain,' said the guvnor. 'It's important.'

'You can talk from there.'

'D'you know who tied those people to the *Gravesend Queen*?'

'No, and you're a bloody fool if you think I'd risk murder just to get this route.'

His son sat down on the bollard, the rope in his hand. He was a strong lad, clear-eyed and brown. He pulled an onion from his pocket and had a bite.

'Ah! So you *have* been intimidating him,' the guvnor declared as if Polgreen had so much as said it himself. It was one of his little ideas, that if you treat someone as having already confessed something they'd be more likely to admit it.

Polgreen let go of the handrail. He scratched his stiff whiskers. 'I did a few things to his boat, yeah. Smashed the windows. Threw some fish guts about. But it was his own fault, the miserable old prick.'

'How so?'

Mrs Polgreen took his arm. She was looking at me steady

like she knew me somehow. I was sure I'd never seen her before; I hadn't met more than a few Hindoos in my life.

'When we first started on the Gravesend run we didn't know how it were. He could have explained there weren't enough passengers for two boats. I'd have gone upriver. No skin off my nose. But he weren't like that, started up cursing and swearing, calling my wife the worst things, even my boy. I wouldn't stand for it.'

The guvnor looked over at Mrs Polgreen. 'I'm sorry to hear it, ma'am.'

'I don't need your sorry,' she said. Her accent was odd, like nothing I'd heard before. Wasn't Cornish, that was sure. Her cheeks were chubby, her black hair tied back tight on her head. 'I heard it many time.'

'I wouldn't take it,' said Polgreen. 'Made up my mind to drive him out. But I only did the guts and the windows, that's all. When I heard there'd been other damage I reckoned I didn't need to.'

'Wouldn't it have been easier just to leave him to his route?' asked the guvnor.

'I'm thinking that now.'

'That's what I say to him,' said Mrs Polgreen. 'He don't listen. Big bloody ape he is sometime.'

'Shut your face,' barked Polgreen.

'You shut your face,' she said, pulling her arm away and flicking him on the ear.

Their boy was listening to it all in silence. There was something angry in his eyes that unsettled me, something that seemed directed at his old man. This was a queer family, all right. But there was nothing unusual about that.

'I'd nothing to do with this morning, and you can tell the coppers that,' Polgreen went on. 'D'you know who those people were?'

'Do you?' asked the guvnor.

'Do I?' He was starting to get vexed again. 'Haven't I just told you it weren't me?'

'Cockles, mate?' asked a ragged woman coming along the pier. 'Winkles?' She showed us her bucket. 'Fresh as a daisy.'

'Fresh as a turd, you old teef,' said Mrs Polgreen from the boat.

'You shut your hole,' croaked the dirty woman.

'I'm up all night with those you sell last before. She's come out both me up and down.'

'Aw, why don't you learn to speak proper, Pocahontas?' The ragged woman turned back to us. 'What'll you have?'

'I don't think I will, thank you, madam,' said the guvnor.

She turned and showed me her bucket.

'Cockles, sir?' she asked me, shoving her finger up her nose. 'Winkles?'

I waved her away.

'I can see you're a reasonable man, Mr Polgreen,' said the guvnor, his voice now softer. 'Something evil's happened here. Wouldn't it be better just to start another route now? This feud has gone far enough. Rosherville Garden's dying anyway.'

Polgreen looked over at his wife for some time, exchanging whatever understandings or feelings passed between foreigners like them. He lifted his bowler and wiped his forehead. He nodded slow. 'Been thinking that's maybe best. Don't know what's going on with Moon and his old bucket, but I don't want nothing to do with it.'

'You're giving up the run?'

Polgreen nodded. 'I'm going down Windsor on Monday, see about getting a slot on one of them piers.'

I was watching his son as he spoke. For just a moment, the lad stopped chomping his onion. His eyes narrowed; a cloud passed over his face.

We watched the steamer push off. Its engines picked up and it moved away towards London Bridge.

'D'you believe him?' I asked.

'I'm not sure,' said the guvnor. 'I'm inclined to, but did you see his boy when he said he was giving up the route?'

'Something was up with him.'

'I felt a prickle go through me. Anger.'

I nodded. The guvnor believed emotions were contagious, and if you opened yourself you could sometimes feel what another person was feeling. It was something to do with magnetism, he said, some kind of invisible fluid passing between us all the time. I wasn't so sure about those fluids, but I thought maybe he was right about the emotions.

His belly made a low growl; he clutched himself. 'I saw a fellow selling trotters up there on Swan Lane. Go and get some, Barnett.'

After our supper, we took turns pacing the deck and sleeping badly on the floor of the saloon. By midnight it was raining. The guvnor had the only two blankets, yet still he complained about his rash and the rock of the boat, and when he did fall off he snored loud as the Prince of Wales. It was a long night, but no boat came close, no figure tried to climb aboard.

Suzie arrived at seven or so the next morning. The *Koh-i-Noor*, one of the bigger paddle steamers, was tied beside us, and a few deckhands busied themselves preparing her for the day ahead. Kate stood by her wherry, waiting for custom.

'Dad ain't here then?' asked Suzie.

'Must still be with the coppers,' said Belasco.

Her face darkened. 'Why're they keeping him so long?'

'He was too shook up to talk yesterday. Maybe he needed to sleep it off.'

She nodded, wanting to trust him.

'We'll go without him if he don't turn up,' said Belasco. 'We run her often enough when he's jiggered.'

'Right,' said Suzie, her bottom lip trembling as she said it. She was a girl on the edge of a woman, and she seemed to flip between the two like a turn in the breeze. I could see she was trying to be strong, but she was only fifteen. She breathed in deep, drew down her freckled brow, and set her face. 'Let's get her ready, then. I'll find Ken. See how many tickets he's sold.'

The three of us watched her as she crossed the pier and marched up the steps to the embankment. As she passed the crippled lad begging at the top, she gave his shoulder a quick rub, then disappeared into the throng.

'My Lord, I hope the Captain pulls himself together,' said the guvnor. 'This city eats girls like her.'

Belasco shook his head. 'You don't know Suzie too well, do you, Mr Arrowood?'

Chapter Fourteen

We were just leaving when Petleigh arrived. Behind him was another copper, a wide-faced fellow with a heavy trunk and legs too short for him. His eyes were eager, his moustache too thin.

'This is Inspector Girkin,' said Petleigh. 'A new detective with City Police. He'll be working on the case with me. Girkin, this is Mr Belasco, deckhand. Mr Arrowood and his assistant Mr Barnett. They're the private agents I was telling you about.'

'Inspector Petleigh's teaching you, is he?' asked the guvnor.

'He be guiding me, sir.' Girkin was a yokel of some kind. His speech was slow and furry, and he had that rabbity look of the fields about his face.

Petleigh gazed at him with disapproval. 'I told you the City Police managed to lose their two detectives at the same time. Well, Girkin was promoted only yesterday. A new generation.'

'Well, congratulations to you, young man,' said the guvnor.

'Appreciated,' said Girkin with a nod.

'We need have another look around the boat,' Petleigh said to Belasco. 'I've some more questions about the arson attack.'

'Why are you still keeping the Captain?' asked the guvnor.

'We let him go an hour ago. Couldn't shake him out of his daze. The surgeon says his nerves have gone, thought perhaps a day on the boat would snap him out of it. He's not here yet?'

The guvnor shook his head.

'What's that awful thing on your face?' asked Petleigh, peering at him.

'Erysipelas.'

'Looks frightful.' Petleigh took a bit of snuff. His clean white collar was buttoned tight to his neck, where a few shaving nicks dotted his smooth skin. His hair was oiled, combed down tight on his bonce; he still had a bit of that powder caked on his forehead.

'Perhaps Moon's gone home for a sleep,' said the guvnor. He looked at me. 'We'll go and find him.'

'If he's able to talk then send him back to us,' said Petleigh. 'You're not to start investigating yourself, understand?'

'Thank you for the advice, Inspector.'

'It's not advice, William. It's a command.'

'You haven't the power to command me. We're investigating a series of attacks on the boat until Captain Moon says we aren't.'

'The attacks are linked to our murder case. I'm asking you to desist, William.'

'And I'm refusing, Isaiah.'

Petleigh's neck had filled with blood. His sharp nose flared. He turned to the young detective. 'You see what I was telling you?'

'Do we arrest him, sir?' asked the young fellow, drawing a pair of wrist-irons from his pocket.

'Don't be a fool,' I said. 'He hasn't done anything yet.'

'What did you say?' demanded Girkin, stepping towards me.

'He hasn't done anything yet.'

'You call me a fool again and you'll regret it.'

'Easy, Girkin,' warned Petleigh, irritated by his apprentice's

96

manner. He looked back at the guvnor. 'Now, listen, William. If you interfere, if you withhold evidence—'

'I know, I know,' said the guvnor, already climbing down the gangway.

I got Moon's address off Belasco and we arranged to meet him back at the boat later. As we gained Upper Thames Street, I spied Ken in front of us in the crowd. You couldn't miss him: his britches too short, his waistcoat pink and green like a circus. He was taking money from a bloke stood before him. As we approached, Ken tucked the money into his pocket and tore a few tickets from his book.

'So that's ten o'clock just down there,' said Ken in his bold voice. 'Old Swan Pier. The *Rosherville Queen*.'

'You filthy swine!' roared the guvnor, grabbing Ken's arm from behind. The tout shrieked, his eyes wide.

'You're selling Polgreen's tickets, you little swizzler!'

'Mr Arrowood!' cried Ken. Then, with a jerk, he escaped the guvnor's grip and ran off into the crowd.

The area given over to slums on Jacob's Island was a good bit smaller than when I'd lived there as a boy, but the courts and alleys that remained hadn't changed much. The Moons lived on a filthy little street of broken-down buildings in the shadow of a tannery. Dogs and barefoot kids sat on the dark side of the street, keeping out of the sun and away from the bubbling, oozing sewer as ran down the other side. Flies were everywhere, swarming in a cloud over the filth, trying to land on our lips and in our eyes as we picked our way through the shells and bones and dog shit. Every window was boarded or smashed in. At the end was an old stables that matched the number Belasco'd given us.

The doors were gone, no doubt for firewood; we walked straight in. It was hot and unholy inside, heavy with a miasma of rottenness and waste. To our left were three horse pens, more flies, the floor a goo of decaying waste. In the first pen, two old men lay in a box on the floor. From the light coming in the door, I could see their shirts stained all down the front, their beards wild and greasy. Their mouths hung open, dark, toothless holes. As we approached they turned their pale eyes to us.

'You know where Captain Moon stays?' I asked them.

They just stared, a looked of tedium and terror in equal parts on both their faces. A mean-looking woman popped her head up from the next pen.

'Round the side,' she said. 'Stable at back.'

A load of kids ran past us.

'Oi!' barked the woman. 'You get that bread yet?'

She tried to swipe the first of them, a boy of eight or so. He dodged her, grabbed a knife from near her feet, and escaped.

We went back to the alley. At the end of the stable block was a thin dirt passage squeezed next to the tannery wall, and at the end of that was a black door. The guvnor pushed me ahead of him. Though the city was hot, that damp, dark alley got colder with every step we took. There were no windows, just sooty London brick, wet with moss, and that narrow I couldn't even raise my arms. The smell of sewage and damp got heavier.

'What a place to live,' murmured the guvnor from behind me.

At the end of the stable block we reached the door. I knocked; the wood was swollen and spongy.

There was no answer. I put my ear to the flaking black paint.

Inside I could just make out the sounds of movement, like a hoard of little scratching, twitching things.

'There's something in there,' I said. 'Maybe rats.'

I knocked again.

We waited. Still there was no answer.

'Captain Moon!' I yelled, knocking again.

Still there was no reply.

I tried the latch. It lifted. The guvnor stepped back a few paces while I pushed the door real slow in case a charge of vermin came at us.

The noise got louder as the door opened, but still we couldn't make out what it was. There was no light in there, just a dim glow from the part-opened door.

'Can you see?' whispered the guvnor.

A hot breath came out the stable door.

Then a bird shot out.

The guvnor yelled. I jerked as it just missed my face and turned upwards to the sliver of sky between the two buildings. The strange noise was clearer. It was like music somehow, flutes and chimes, laundry being shaken out. Rasping.

'What the hell is it?' asked the guvnor.

I pushed the door again, the sounds growing louder. Things were moving in there.

I pushed it all the way.

There was a sudden explosion of fluttering. Birds were everywhere, a frantic, moving tapestry of black and yellow, blue and red. The dust swirled amongst them; tiny, downy feathers fell like snow.

We froze. There was no window in the stable, just the dim light that seeped in from the narrow alley behind. Some more of the birds flew towards us and out, up into the sky and freedom. I stepped inside the storm, my eyes adjusting to the gloom. As I was getting out my matches, the guvnor gripped my shoulder.

'Norman,' he whispered.

At the back of the pen, we could just make out a wooden chair lying on its side on the floor. Next to it was a captain's cap. And above it, hanging by the neck from a rope, was Captain Moon.

Chapter Fifteen

I dashed over and righted the chair that lay below his feet.

'Get a knife!' I cried.

The guvnor scurried around the room while I climbed up and grabbed Moon's legs, pushing him up so the rope around his neck was slack. He was leaden and lifeless; his head lay on his shoulder like his neck was broke.

'Hurry!' I cried.

'Here!' The guvnor held out a breadknife. Quickly I sawed the rope. One . . . two . . . three . . . it gave suddenly and Moon's body dropped heavy to the floor, unbalancing me, the knife clattering on the stone just before I hit it myself. The birds screeched and flapped; more darted to the door and out into the light.

The captain lay there on the wet floor, his belly swollen in his dirty yellow shirt, each hand gripped into a fist. A look of fear coloured his popping eyeballs, foam dripped from his nose-holes, and out of his swollen lips poked a black tongue, thick and rigid like a stick.

'Oh, dear God, no!' the guvnor moaned, collecting the knife and sawing at the noose around his neck. I felt his wrist for a pulse.

Finally the guvnor cut through the rope, the knife slicing a gash in Moon's neck.

'He's dead,' I said.

The guvnor felt for a pulse too.

At last, he nodded.

We held each other's eyes.

'I'll find a copper,' I said, rising.

The guvnor stayed on his knees, looking down at the horrible grimace on Moon's face. 'How could you do this?' he hissed. 'What about your daughter? What's she going to do, you fool?'

'His nerves had gone,' I said. 'He couldn't think.'

'But Suzie!'

With the back of his hand be belted Moon across the face.

'Leave him alone,' I said, grabbing the guvnor and pulling him to his feet. There was something wild in his eyes, a mania I'd seen in him before. His hands were clenching and unclenching; he was biting his lips.

I righted the chair again and sat him down in it. Now that my eyes were used to the dark, I could see the room clearly. It was a poor enough place: a little table, a jug and washstand, three beams overhead, open to the roof tiles above. All was wood, and all unpainted. Two little beds stood next to each other, one on either side of a wooden fence that must have once kept horses in. Hanging from every space on the walls were birdcages, their little doors open, and perched on every surface, on the beams, the table, the little fence, were the birds. Starlings, blackbirds, goldfinch, linnets, titlarks, thrush – there must have been a hundred or more in there, and there was something queer about them. While half had their nervy black eyes on us, the others looked upwards, their tiny heads leaning to the side, and where their eyes should have been were what looked like tiny raisins, wrinkled and dried and dead.

'Go on then, Norman,' said the guvnor, getting hold of himself. He blew his nose. 'Get a constable for the damn fool.'

I found one eating an orange by Spa Road Station, listening to the Wesleyans holding an open-air hymn service. I brought back him to the stable, where the guvnor'd lit a paraffin lamp. Half of the birds were already gone, and only the blind ones now remained, all standing in their odd, head-upturned stance, only now they were singing, a maddening mix of tunes. A single, sighted blackbird stood proud on Moon's chest.

'Every time I chase it away it returns,' said the guvnor.

The copper, a roundish bloke, waved the bird away and put the lamp on the floor. He examined the body, writing a few notes in a little pad as we answered his questions. 'I'll have to get a detective,' he grunted, standing up. 'More blooming walking.'

'You'll need Inspector Petleigh, attached to the City Police,' said Arrowood. 'He's working on a case where this man's involved.'

The copper scribbled that down, then looked up. 'Now, gentlemen, I've deduced something already about this case. I follow Sherlock Holmes's methods, see. So you tell me if I'm right about this.' He paused for a moment, looking us each in the eye in turn. 'The wife's passed over, hasn't she?'

'How did you know that?' asked the guvnor.

'That's her,' said the copper, pointing at the blackbird as had just landed on Moon's chest again. 'Knew it soon as I saw her. Well, he'll be able to join her somehow.'

'That's hardly a deduction, constable,' said the guvnor.

'Am I wrong?'

'No, but—'

'Then I'm right, ain't I, sir?' said the copper, looking around the stable.

'That's not a deduction, that's—'

'What's up with all these birds?' interrupted the copper.

'Been blinded, most of them,' I said. 'Supposed to make them sing better.'

The copper frowned. 'Well here's another deduction: Captain Moon was in the Bird Fancy.'

'At least that one is a deduction,' mumbled the guvnor. 'Though they're probably the only ones who blind songbirds these days.'

'Either of you his family?'

'No,' said the guvnor. 'He's got a daughter.'

The copper sighed and shook his head. He scratched his bushy sideburns. 'Best if you tell her then.'

'That's your job, Constable.'

'No, sir, I ain't got time to wait around here till she gets back. We lost three PCs when they rearranged the beats last year, sir. You should see the distance I have to cover. Anyway, it'd be better coming from a friend. Now, any letter?'

The guvnor shrugged. 'I haven't seen one.'

The copper took our details and wrote them in his notepad.

'Right. I need to send a message to the station. Petleigh, you say?'

'That's it.'

'You two stay here,' he said, stepping out the door. 'Don't touch anything.'

There wasn't much to look through: a bucket with bowls, knives and spoons, a bag of coal next to the burner, a change of clothes for each of them. A few shoddy blankets, a sack of seed and close to a hundred cages. Seemed like they only spent money on the birds.

There was no suicide letter, but we found a wooden trunk hid under a sack. I got out my betty and worked open the lock. Inside were a couple of china dolls, chipped and stained brown, a christening dress, a bonnet with moth holes in it, a permit from the Thames Conservancy, a bible, and an embroidered shawl. Wrapped in a belcher were a bundle of letters.

The guvnor took up the lamp and began to read one. His face looked puzzled. He grunted. He opened another. He shook his head.

I picked up one and took it outside to the alley where the light was better.

My Dearest Love,

Where are you? You know I find the winter difficult, and she's harder when you dont say what your doing. I came to see you Friday last but there was nobody home. I know I ought not but I had to see you. Dont torment me, please dont. Come and visit. Soon as your home from wherever you been, come see me. I feel a little death every day that goes by.

Your faithful, eternal,

Feathers

I took it back into the room.

'They all from the same woman?' I asked.

'Mm,' he mumbled, taking up another. 'Irregular. Over the last ten years or so. The last one was a few months ago.'

'His lover?'

'It's hard to believe, but yes, a lover.'

The guvnor was just reading the last of them when the copper got back. He didn't like all those birds, so we agreed to wait with him on the lane till Petleigh arrived. Kids kept coming up, asking what was going on, but the copper only shooed them away.

It was after three when Petleigh stepped down from a cab with apprentice detective Girkin following behind. The PC hurried over and explained it all in half a minute. The kids and a few of the older folk swarmed around them, trying to listen in.

'Where's your carriage, Petleigh?' asked Arrowood when they'd done.

'They've taken them all back. Only for detective chief inspectors now.' He shook his head. 'It won't save any money: it's just going to be more expensive getting cabs.'

'What happened, mister?' asked a little lad with a shaved head.

'Go away!' barked Petleigh, making to give the lad a slap.

The kids jumped back, looking at each other. Then they laughed.

'Go away!' they shrieked, lunging at each other, slapping, giggling. 'Go away!'

'That be enough, kids,' said Girkin in his lazy country drawl.

'That be enough!' cried the shaved head boy, trying to do Girkin's yokel accent.

'Be that enough!' shrieked a girl, jumping up and down

while holding a scrawny kitten by its neck. The kids burst into laughter again.

'Enough that be!' cried a lad.

'Be be that!' screamed a little girl no more than five year, then shrieked with laughter as the others copied her. I couldn't help but laugh myself at those little monsters, but Girkin was vexed. He saw me smiling and scowled. He'd taken against me; I knew I shouldn't have called him a fool the first time we met him, but the young bloke really was a bit too full of his own importance.

'You think that's funny?' he asked, his head tilted back so he could look down his rabbity nose at me.

'You going to arrest me?'

'You want to watch yourself.'

'Did Moon say anything about the bodies?' asked the guvnor, raising his voice over the excited kids.

Petleigh loosened his tie. Trying to ignore the press of youngsters, he pulled his snuff box from his coat and had a toot. A girl of nine or ten tried to grab it.

'Leave off or I'll arrest you,' he hissed.

'I'll arrest you!' cried a younger lad, grabbing the girl's arm. Then they were all at it, grabbing and arresting each other and hooting with laughter.

Petleigh looked over the children's heads at us. There was something troubled about him today. 'Tell me exactly what you found when you arrived.'

'First tell me what Moon said about the bodies,' answered the guvnor.

'William!' snapped Petleigh. He brought out a perfectly ironed handkerchief and dabbed at his powdered brow. His black hair dye was starting to form a thin fringe below his hairline. One of the little girls shoved her hand in his coat pocket. 'Get off!' he cried, pushing her away.

'Come along, Isaiah, what did he say?' asked the guvnor again, this time in a more friendly way. He took Petleigh's arm, leading him away from the kiddies. 'What harm could it do?'

'He wouldn't answer any of our questions.'

'Why on earth did you release him? Didn't you see how melancholy he was?'

'Don't you dare suggest this is my responsibility. It's his own damn fault.'

'You should have thought. You should have kept him at the station.'

'He was a witness, not a criminal.' Petleigh's voice broke, and I could have sworn he was on the edge of tears. He turned away and blew his nose. Finally, with his back to us, he spoke again. 'Lead us inside, constable. And you, William, can tell me exactly what you saw when you arrived. Inspector Girkin, you ask around these people. See if anyone's seen anything.'

They pushed through the crowd as Girkin searched in his pockets for his notebook.

'Listen, mate,' I said, quiet as I could. 'We got off on the wrong foot the other day. I shouldn't have called you a fool in front of the inspector. I'd had a shock.'

'You want to watch yourself speaking to me like that,' he said. He didn't seem to understand that I was apologizing to him.

'I know. I'm sorry. Listen, Inspector, a bit of advice. I don't know how long you been in London, but if you want respect from your betters you need to stop talking like a yokel. It ain't

"That be enough". It's "That's enough". You don't use a "be" like that round here.'

'Who the hell d'you think you are?' he said through his teeth, his eyes tight with fury.

'You got to talk more like them if you want them to listen. It's just the way they are.'

He tried to grab my shirt front but I swung my arm, breaking his grip. His face reddened as he brought it up next to mine, but he didn't try to take hold of me again. The blacks of his eyes were like peppercorns. 'Think you're better than me, do you?' he growled.

'I'm the same as you. That's how I know.'

'You ain't the same. I'm a police detective. You be a bit of street rough. And you touch me again I'll have you up afore the beak.'

When Petleigh and Girkin had finished with their enquiries, they arranged for the police wagon to pick up Moon's body. Petleigh wanted to be sure it was suicide. We got a tram from Dockhead back to London Bridge and walked down to the pier. Barges and lighters were using it before the paddle steamers returned from their excursions, unloading hay and bricks and potatoes for wagons queued on Swan Lane. We were both silent, watching the men work in the thick, warm air, turning our heads eastwards now and then in case the *Gravesend Queen* should appear. Thick clouds had gathered above the city; a shipload of sorrow was coming Suzie's way, and there was nothing we could do to make it better.

The crippled lad we'd seen before sat at the entry to the steps, waiting for the day-trippers to return. The costers and wagon drivers carried their goods past him like he wasn't there, while he kept his eyes fixed on the tide, now beginning to surge upriver carrying a pack of black barges with it.

The guvnor walked over to the boy and dropped a ha'penny in his cap.

'How are you today, my dear?' he asked.

The lad turned his unsettling eyes up to us. He wore a brown smock, open to the belly, and his puny, crooked arms crossed his chest, the useless hands wilted like dead leaves. There was a nasty smell.

'Where d'you live, my friend?' asked the guvnor.

The lad gazed into the guvnor's eyes, his mouth open. His face was burnt by the sun, his lips blistered.

'You know what happened to that boat yesterday?'

The lad looked down at the pier, then to his left where a coster was carrying a heavy sack up to the street. He moved his bare foot over to the cap on the floor, picked out the guvnor's ha'penny with his toes, and stretched his leg out to the guvnor.

'No, lad, that's for you,' said Arrowood.

The boy shook his head, prodding the guvnor's hand with his foot.

'I want you to have it,' insisted the guvnor, stepping away.

'Let him give it back, sir,' I said.

The guvnor frowned. Then, with a sigh, he held open his hand. The boy dropped the coin into it and lowered his leg to the ground. As the guvnor stared at the money, the child shut his eyes, dropping his chin to his chest like he'd just gone to sleep.

I took the guvnor's arm and led him down to the pier. Under the arches of London Bridge, its funnel pumping out clouds of steam, came the *Gravesend Queen*.

Chapter Sixteen

Suzie stood by as the passengers stumbled off. What a crowd they were in their Sunday suits and dresses, shrieking and laughing, cock-eyed and unsteady, the children charging around their legs, pushing and fighting and crying. Suzie looked tuckered out, yet still she smiled at each as they stepped ashore, touching the women's hands, patting the nippers, giving a little hug here and there.

Finally they were all off.

'Almost a full boat,' she said as we walked over. 'Dad'll be pleased.'

Belasco climbed down the gangway, his hands black with coal, his face sooty.

'Can we go aboard, Suzie?' asked the guvnor, a warning in his voice.

'What is it, Mr Arrowood?'

'Let's sit down,' he said, taking her arm gently.

She shook off his hand, fear creeping into the corners of her eyes. 'What is it? Do they know who those people were?'

'Please, Suzie,' said the guvnor. 'Let's go aboard. We must talk.'

'Tell me what's happened!' she demanded, stamping her foot.

The guvnor took a deep breath. His voice was soft when

he finally spoke. 'It's your father, Suzie. I'm afraid he died. We found him this morning.'

She looked at Belasco, panic in her eyes.

'No,' she said. Her shoulders twitched. 'No, you didn't.' She brushed her hair back with her fingers. 'He was here.'

'We found his body this morning, in your home. He took his own life, Suzie. I'm so very sorry.'

'No,' she hissed, shaking her head wildly. 'He was here.'

Belasco was like a statue, his back straight, his head tilted. The gulls circling above the pier began to shriek, echoing themselves in the great, wide sky.

'That was yesterday,' said the guvnor. 'The police released him this morning. We found him a few hours ago.'

'No, you're wrong,' she said, throwing her arms in the air. She pushed between us and began striding toward the embankment. 'I have to go home and see him.'

'Suzie, come back,' the guvnor called after her. 'He's not there.'

She ran up the steps, dodging past the punters trying to get down. I started off after her, but Belasco pulled me back.

'I'll go,' he mumbled, his eyes dark and empty.

He gained the embankment just as she disappeared into the crowd.

The old piermaster came over to us. He didn't look too happy.

'They're coming back, are they?'

'I don't think so, mate,' I told him.

The old fellow scratched his head. His pipe hung from his mouth. 'Only we can't leave the boat there, eh? I got fourteen steamers arriving.'

I told him about Moon.

'I'm real sorry to hear it. Real sorry. Can't say I knew him very well, he weren't a chatty man, no he weren't, but he weren't a bad sort neither.' He tutted, his head falling. 'Poor Suzie, eh? She got other family?'

'I don't know,' I said.

'Tell me,' said the guvnor. 'Did you see anything out of the ordinary yesterday morning before the bodies were found? Anybody doing anything unusual? Any strangers?'

'Didn't see nothing and I told the Old Bill the same. Pier gets too busy on a Saturday. Folk everywhere, eh?'

'What about Friday night?'

'No, sir.' He waved his hand at me. 'Just your man there being left on the boat. That was the only thing unusual.'

The guvnor grunted and looked around the pier. The barge next to the *Gravesend Queen* finished unloading its hay and was casting off, moving out into the stream.

'I'll have to get a tug to move her,' said the piermaster.

'Is there anyone else who might have seen something?' said the guvnor.

'Try Katie,' answered the old bloke, pointing at the woman who ran the wherry.

'We asked her already,' I told him. 'Anyone else?'

The old fellow shook his head. 'Boat crews wouldn't notice. They're only here long enough to pick up and set down.'

'That boy on the stairs, what's his name?' asked the guvnor, pointing at the crippled lad.

'Monkey, they call him, but you won't get anything out of him. He'll talk to the young 'uns, but he ain't never said so much as a word to me.'

We walked back up the stairs.

'Hello, lad,' said the guvnor, his knees creaking as he squatted before him. 'You're Monkey, aren't you?'

The lad twitched his melting eyes at the guvnor, then looked away.

'You know Suzie and Captain Moon, do you, Monkey?' asked the guvnor. 'Of the *Gravesend Queen*? Well, we're trying to help them. I need to know if you saw anything odd yesterday morning? People who had no reason to be here?'

The boy turned his eyes to the guvnor again, nodding once at the ground.

The guvnor pulled out his purse and dropped a penny in the cap. The boy gripped the coin with his toes, raised his foot, and dropped it in the bag as hung from his shoulder.

'Well?' said the guvnor. 'What did you see?'

The boy's head turned away now, his gaze fixing on the river behind us. From where he sat, he could see right over the pier below. His paper-dry mouth started to move like he was chewing something.

'You want some food, Monkey?' asked the guvnor.

The boy's mouth went still. Though his gaze was fixed on the distance, you could see he was watching us out the corners of his eyes. His useless arms were covered in sores, the nails on his fingers long and curled. 'I'll give you a shilling if you'll help us,' said the guvnor. 'Please, Monkey. We're just trying to help Suzie and Captain Moon. Did you see anything yesterday morning or the night before?'

We waited for some time, but the boy just stared past us like we weren't there. After a few more goes, the guvnor gave up. He gasped as he tried to straighten; I took his arm and hauled him up, hearing his knees crunch.

'Well, it's good to make your acquaintance,' said Arrowood, reaching out to touch Monkey on the shoulder. The lad jerked his body away, leaving the guvnor's great sweaty paw hanging in the air. The guvnor's face fell. Without a word, he marched over to a cart standing outside Fishmongers' Hall, bought a bottle of ginger beer, and returned.

'You want this, lad?' he asked.

The lad frowned, confusion in his eyes. His mouth opened a bit then shut again.

'Yes? Shall I help you?' asked the guvnor as he moved it real slow to the lad's chin. He stopped with the bottle about six inches away.

For a few moments, the boy did nothing. Then his eyes turned to the left, the right. He opened his mouth, showing a row of brown stumps below and a couple of long canines above. The guvnor poured a little dribble inside. The lad's mouth closed and his eyes shut. He swallowed.

With his eyes still shut, he opened his lips again. The guvnor poured in another dribble.

Twice more he took the drink, then he shook his head. The guvnor put the bottle by his feet and took one more long look at the boy. Finally, we walked off to Swan Lane.

It was slow-going over London Bridge. Being Sunday, there were hundreds of walkers like us, and many more leaning against the wall watching the ships as the sun turned gold over St Paul's.

'He couldn't have seen who did it, sir,' I said as we trudged across. 'He isn't there at night. The ropes were tied on the far side, anyway. They would have been hid by the boat.'

'I know that, Barnett. That's not why I was asking. Those

bodies were put there to shock Moon, and shock him they did. I can't see any other reason.'

'To frighten him?'

'Or drive him mad.' He took a square of toffee out his pocket and bit off a piece, passing me the rest. 'Now, if you wanted to hurt a man so, and you'd placed a nasty surprise like that for him, where would you want to be when it was discovered?'

As we wandered along in the slow procession of bodies, I felt my lips break into a weary smile.

'Watching,' I said at last.

'Precisely, Barnett,' he said, pogging me in the belly. 'Precisely.'

Chapter Seventeen

Neddy was a lad we used now and then when someone needed watching or messages needed delivering. He lived in a basement room with his ma and sisters, down the dark end of Coin Street. They'd taken in a young girl to lodge with them a month or so back, the extra money meaning his ma could start on her gin earlier in the day. When we arrived that evening she was sat outside on the step, the youngest girl, Harriet, sitting coughing in the stairwell below. The girl was only four or so and couldn't use her legs too well seeing as one had a bend in it. She'd been slow to speak.

'Is Neddy in, mum?' asked the guvnor.

It took her a little while to focus her eyes through the fog of booze. Her face was burned from the sun and wet with sweat. Her hair rose wild and matted.

'Mr Arrowood!' she said, jerking up even as she swayed. 'Mr Barnett! You found me, then?'

'We're after Neddy, mum,' I said.

'Oh, am I pleased to see you,' she went on. She pulled herself up on the railings, but it was too much for her and she set herself down again. 'Yes, I was just sat here thinking we should have a little chat about your washing what you promised me, promised to let me have it, didn't you?'

'I did no such thing,' said the guvnor.

'Nor me, mum,' I said.

She squinted at us, her hand waving away a fly. 'Who you got doing it, 'cos I'll do it for less. Two shirts for a ha'penny. You won't get cheaper. Penny a bedsheet and they'll be cleaner than the Lambeth Palace. Anyone'll tell you how clean I can get a sheet. Ask anyone.'

'I don't think so,' said the guvnor. Neddy's ma was known all around for being the worst washerwoman in the area. She'd leave burn marks on your britches and blue stains on your whites, and things always seemed to go missing that she'd swear you never gave her in the first place. I could see from the look on Arrowood's glistening face that he was remembering the hole she'd somehow put in the belly of his fisherman's jumper, then insisted it was there when he gave it to her. It was a favourite of his, one that his wife Isabel'd given him one Christmas. The only folk let her have their washing nowadays were newcomers. 'We've a job for Neddy. Where is he?'

'Mama,' said the dirty little child in the stairwell. She held out her hand to us.

'Hello, my darling,' said the guvnor. 'It's very good to see you. Very, very good.'

'Arrow-oo,' she said, a very serious look on her face.

'Yes, Harriet!' he cried in delight. 'Yes, Harriett! I *am* Mr Arrowood, you clever girl.' He turned to me, the happiest I'd seen him all day. 'She said my name, Barnett. Did you hear?'

'Got a job for him?' squawked Neddy's ma. 'He's just off getting some medicine for me. Got this ache in me lungs. Pleurisy, I reckon. And that's on top of all the troubles I got. Some folk are cursed, I swear it though I do love this heat. Does a body good. You ask the Musulman in fourteen if I don't do a fine job, Mr Barnett. Looks like your shirt could do with a wash.' She started to hack, big bone-shaking coughs like her throat was full of gravel. Her eyes filled with tears; her face went even redder. The guvnor took her arm, stroked her back. She looked up at me and whispered, 'Oh, my dear, must be hard with your wife on the other side. Poor darling.' She turned back to the guvnor. 'The Musulman. The one lives with the coalman. You know him? You ask him. Thrilled with his bloomers. Spotless, they were, so they almost blinded you. You bring me yours tomorrow. Your bloomers, sir. Not just your bloomers, bring it all. I'll do it quick as you like. And cheap too.'

'Send Neddy over when he returns, ma'am,' said the guvnor, taking my arm.

'I'll send him over, sir. You mind you pay him well, though.' Her finger was wagging at us now, like we'd done something wrong. She clutched her chest again. 'I know the sort of jobs you send him on. Dangerous ones. You must pay him right for that.' Her hand felt behind her back on the stair, and I saw she had a little flagon there.

The pudding shop was at the other end of the street. We passed through the shop and down the back corridor to the dark of the guvnor's parlour. Upstairs we could hear Ettie moving about, while outside the small window hot rain began to fall. I put the kettle on and made tea, while the guvnor took off his shirt and wiped himself down at the scullery bucket. As we were sitting, Ettie appeared.

'She's asleep at last,' she said, pouring herself a cup of tea and taking a Garibaldi from the tin. 'Hello, Norman.'

'How are you, Ettie?'

'Exhausted,' she said, sitting in the chair by the window. 'The child isn't eating as she should. It feels like a war sometimes. I have to remind myself not to feel insulted, but it isn't easy.' She clenched and unclenched her fingers, looking at them. 'My hands always seem to be sticky these days. I can't understand where it's coming from. But what about you? What's your news?'

We filled her in on what had happened. She listened closely.

'Don't you think you should leave it to the police this time?' she asked when we'd finished. 'These people will kill you if you get in their way.'

'Petleigh's never going to solve this,' said the guvnor.

'You don't know that,' I said, wondering as I spoke why I was defending him. 'Petleigh's got his faults, but he's a better copper than you credit him.'

'Perhaps if there were some straightforward clues,' he said with a sigh. 'But there aren't any at all. It's up to us, Ettie. We must find out who's behind it before something happens to Suzie.'

'Who are the suspects?' she asked.

He shrugged. 'Polgreen. The men Moon was in debt to. Someone getting back at Belasco. But it doesn't add up: why would any one of them kill three people?'

'Doesn't the fact that Moon self-murdered suggest it's to do with him?' asked Ettie.

'He might just have given up. The river's full of people who've given up in this damned city.'

For some time, each of us sat with our thoughts. I remembered Uncle Norbert, drowned between two barges, and my pal Charlie who, at fourteen, sliced open his own gullet an hour after the doc told him his leg must come off. I caught

Ettie looking at me, a tired sadness on her face, and I wondered what it was she was thinking. We held each other's eyes for a moment, and I thought something bright was just dawning in her expression when her stomach gurgled. She clutched it, then reached out for another Garibaldi.

Finally, the guvnor put down his mug, collected the paper under his arm, and stood up the way he does when he's on a mission to the outhouse.

'I hope you left the lid down, Ettie. It was black with flies this morning.'

'I always put the lid down. It's you that leaves it up.'

As he stepped over to the door, he gave me the wink, pointing up at the ceiling where slept the baby. Then he was gone and we were alone for the first time since Ettie left for Birmingham. I looked into her weary grey eyes. She'd changed in the six months she'd been away and I was worried that the nameless thing we'd become to each other before she left was gone. It never looked like much: a touch here, a look there. A shape as could never be formed. We were too different for it to ever be more than that. Most of my life I'd lived in one room, with Ma in Bermondsey, then with Mrs B when we were first wed. We had a few good years when I was working for the law courts and could afford two, but when I lost my job and started working for the guvnor it was back to one room again. Mrs B never complained: it was where she came from too. But Ettie was different. She was the daughter of a troubled parson, educated, proper, fallen in rank, yes, but still the sort who could never be content in a single room in a house of single-room families. I was a child of the workhouse and the Jacob's Island slum, and I'd done things to keep Ma and me that I never wanted anyone to know. Ettie thought she saw me, but she only knew the outline. She didn't know how it had got into my soul, and working for Arrowood didn't help, either. Part of the reason he paid me was because of what I'd been, and though I'd changed some in all those years I spent working for the courts, working for him only made me rough again.

'He missed you,' I said.

She nodded, a cloud of impatience passing over her eyes. A baby noise came from above and we both looked up, tense for a moment.

'Ettie, can I ask you?' I said when it had passed.

Her lips tightened as she thought about it.

'Yes,' she answered at last. She smiled. 'You can.'

'Whose child is she?'

The smile weakened. She put her cup on the side table and finished off her biscuit. 'Don't judge me, Norman.'

'No.'

She nodded, looking me full in the face.

'She's mine.'

I wasn't expecting it to hurt, but it did, and I wondered what it was. Jealousy maybe, but I had no right to that. The discovery she wasn't perfect? I already knew that. No. It was more the way she said it, how blunt she was, as if it wouldn't touch me.

'Is Petleigh the father?' I asked.

A ruckus started up among the hens in the neighbour's garden, a frantic squawking and beating of wings. The cock cried out again and again, and through the window we heard the guvnor curse in his fly-blown stinkpit. Ettie looked up at the ceiling, tense. And then the hen fight was over and we were left with the rumble of London in the rain.

Still, the baby made no sound. She looked back at me. 'I can't tell you, Norman. I'm sorry. It's a complicated affair. The man has much to lose.'

'Why are you protecting him?'

'It was my decision to lie with the father, Norman.'

We looked at each other for some time. Finally, I got up and poured us more tea.

'Why won't you tell William? You know how he loves children.'

Ettie searched in the tin until she'd found a bourbon. She glanced at the door and dropped her voice. 'Did you know that Isabel had a stillborn about six months before she left him?'

I shook my head.

'It wasn't the first. She'd had one two years before.'

'I didn't know.'

'You two are so difficult, Norman; you didn't tell us about your wife dying either. Isabel wrote me once, after the second one. They were desperate for a child. She took it hard, but it sounds like he took it worse. It was back when he had his breakdown. You know he has the same weak nerves as our father.'

'Not as bad, Ettie.'

'I hope not.'

I'd only worked with him on one case when it happened. Through the 80s the guvnor was the main reporter on the Fenian situation for *Lloyd's Weekly*, and hearing about the plots and bombs and weapons shipments day in and day out had affected his nerves. He saw the danger signs everywhere, his fears about explosions in the underground and men with portmanteaus and poison in the water pipes. And then, as he was struggling with it all, a new editor started on the paper and gave him the boot.

It wasn't long after that I also lost my post at the law courts. Arrowood had started working as a private agent by then, and he asked me to join him. The first job we did together was the Betsy case, and we bungled that so bad a man was killed and a child lost his arm. That's what tipped him over, or so I thought. He wouldn't step outside the door, wouldn't leave the bottle or the chloridine alone, though Isabel was there all the while, kind and patient until she wasn't no more. His retreat from the world drove her away, leaving him with a hole in his heart and a queue of creditors at his door. They'd always seemed to fit together somehow, laughing at the same jokes and interested in what the other was thinking, so I was sure she'd come back once his nerves had mended. But she never did. Hid herself away in the country until she met this lawyer fellow in Cambridge and that was it. She made a new life for herself while he stayed in the ruins of theirs. But I never knew about the children. He never told me that.

Ettie went to the dresser and opened a drawer, from where she pulled a tiny woollen shawl. 'Sometimes I see him holding this, after he's had a few brandies. Isabel knitted it for the baby. And he always seems so angry.'

'He's angry with himself.'

'And with Isabel, and fate, and the Lord. And me. He thinks I'm restricting him by living here. That everything comes easy to me, though he's very wrong about that. He's always judged me.' Her eyes fell to the dusty floor, revealing the softer side she tried so often to keep hid. 'I just wanted him to love her before

I told him. You mustn't say, Norman. Promise me. I need to judge when the time's right. Do you promise?'

'Why make him wait more? It only vexes him.'

'You don't know how he still grieves for those lost children. He grieves for them as much as for Isabel. Just let him love the child, please, Norman. When he loves her I'll tell him.'

'I think he's better than that.'

Ettie looked thoughtful. 'Do you? He's not always in control of his emotions. I do worry he's getting like our father.' She took out her pipe, then realized she still had the biscuit in the other hand. She took a bite just as the door opened and the guvnor was back, a couple of flies drifting in behind him. He had a pained look on his face.

'Where's the Whelpton's?' he asked.

Chapter Eighteen

Neddy arrived shortly after. He wore a torn smock, a tray half full of broken and dusty muffins around his neck. His cap with its peak missing was too big, made for a grown man rather than a littleish eleven-year-old, and he'd taken to wearing a leather string round his neck as a tie. His hair looked like it'd been cut with a butter knife.

'Ah, there you are, my dear,' said the guvnor. 'But what happened to your eye?'

'Lant Street boys again, sir,' he said, resting his tray on the table. 'It don't hurt.'

The guvnor gave him a great hug, and dropped him on the floor. Ettie took him next. Seeing he was all squeezed out by then, I shook the lad's hand.

'Did you go to Sunday School this morning, Neddy?' asked Ettie.

'I couldn't, Miss Ettie. We hadn't nothing left for food.'

Ettie stroked his hair. 'Promise you'll go next week. Reverend Hebden wants to talk about Canada.'

'Yes, ma'am. I promise.'

'And take Abigail.'

'D'you hear about that girl in the Peabodys lays eggs?' he asked her.

'Lays eggs? What girl?'

'Ma says. She lays eggs like a hen. I even seen her.'

'You saw her lay eggs?'

'No, I saw her in the street. Ma showed me.'

'Oh, Neddy,' said Ettie, her eyes a-sparkle. 'I don't think she can really lay eggs. It's impossible.'

'She can. Everybody knows.'

'Did your mother take Abigail to the doctor?' asked the guvnor.

'Don't talk to me about Ma,' said Neddy, watching the orange cat as it rose and took a step towards his muffin tray. 'She's made us take a lady in and I got to share a bed with Harriet and Abigail and Harriet still wees herself. Sorry, Miss Arrowood, but she does. I'm the only one earns enough to pay the rent and I got to sleep with her weeing on me. It ain't fair.'

'No, it isn't, Neddy,' said the guvnor, trying to keep from smiling. 'I never enjoyed it when Ettie weed on me either.'

'I did not wee on you!' cried Ettie.

'Ma don't even try and earn enough,' said Neddy, his bottom lip stuck out. Normally he'd enjoy watching the guvnor tease Ettie, but he didn't seem to notice; what he was saying mattered a lot to him. 'I got to do it all. I want to work for you, Mr Arrowood, but I got to do the muffins too. Abigail don't hardly bring in nothing from the matches.'

'You're out of temper,' said the guvnor.

'Yes, sir. Sorry, sir.'

'Here, have one of these.' He held out a little poke of sweets to the boy.

Neddy took one, a dark green thing, and put it in his mouth. He chewed on it, his eyes pinching as he tried to understand the singular taste.

'It's a wine gum,' said the guvnor, tossing a couple in his mouth. He passed the poke to Ettie. 'A new type of sweetie.'

Ettie took a couple and passed the packet to me. 'I'll bet you're thirsty,' she said to Neddy.

'I am, Miss Ettie.'

She went through to the scullery.

'I need your help, lad,' said the guvnor as the orange cat leapt onto his lap.

''Course,' said Neddy, his eye on the poke as I handed it back to the guvnor. 'What is it?'

'I want you to go to Old Swan Pier first thing tomorrow morning. There's a crippled lad name of Monkey who begs at the top of the gangway. I want you to make friends with him. Then ask him about the bodies they found tied to the boat yesterday.'

'Is that your case, Mr Arrowood?' Neddy's little face was all concentration now. His eyes shone with excitement. 'Everyone's talking about it.'

'Yes, it is. I think Monkey might have seen something, but he won't talk to us. I've seen him talk to another boy about your age, so I want you to try. Ask about anything unusual the night before. Understand?'

Neddy nodded. You could see his little mind was turning it all over. Ettie came through and gave him a few digestives and a tumbler of cordial.

'And, most importantly, I want to know if anyone on the pier or the embankment was watching when the *Gravesend Queen* arrived that morning. That's the boat the bodies were tied to. People with no other reason to be there, who weren't boarding any of the boats. Can you remember that?'

Neddy drank down half the cordial as he listened. 'I got it, sir. How much you going to pay me?'

'I'll decide that when I hear what you've learned.'

'That's not fair,' said Ettie. 'Tell him now.'

'It's quite reasonable. What if he fails to get anything?'

'It won't be his fault,' she answered. 'You pay him for his time, just like you do with Norman.'

I didn't much like hearing myself being compared to an eleven-year-old, especially by Ettie. But she was right.

'Oh, all right,' groaned the guvnor as he tickled the orange cat. 'A penny.'

'Tuppence,' said Ettie.

'For goodness' sake.'

'Tuppence it is then, sir,' said Neddy, lifting his tray and hanging it back round his neck. He opened the door. 'What did you say those sweets were?'

There was nothing else to be done that day, so I took myself off. It was Sunday, the low clouds promising rain, the bells of St George the Martyr ringing out for evening service. I stopped in at the Old Tabard on Borough High Street and had a few pints and a bowl of oysters. I was tired, but as I approached my rooms on Adam's Place, I didn't feel ready to go home somehow. Lilly had promised she'd be gone but I wasn't so sure; that woman had a habit of staying and making me feel all right about it.

I turned back and wandered over to my brother-in-law Sidney's house, gave his wife a squeeze, kissed the kiddies, took him out for a few more pints. It was late by the time I pushed open the door of my building and climbed the squeaky stairs. No sound came from Mr Askell's rooms or the O'Learys', but the family in the attic were arguing again and old Noah was coughing in the room next to mine. There was something about the air outside my door that made me believe Lilly was gone, and now I found I half wished she wasn't. After a day like that, I didn't want to be alone. She gave me something after all, maybe just the rustle of her weight on the mattress, the sense a body gives the air of a musty room. Maybe it was crude as the movement of her hand on my thigh, but it was something I needed. Maybe I shouldn't have sent her away.

The door caught on the frame as I shoved it open. I could smell her straight away, and with the unwanted relief in my heart came a flash of anger.

She sat up in the bed as I stepped inside. On the floor I saw the chamber pot was still not emptied, and there were not one but two jars stood next to it. The window was open, a slight breeze coming in from the street. I took her arm and pulled her up.

'Norm,' she groaned. 'Leave off. That hurts.'

I made her get out of bed.

'Bloody hell,' she said as she stood there in just her drawers and vest. 'I was asleep. D'you have to be so rough?'

'You said you'd leave.'

She reached out to touch me. I stepped back.

'I got nowhere to go. Please, Norm. Don't make me go to the workhouse.'

'This ain't your home, Lilly. We ain't even known each other for a week. Where were you staying before?'

Her face darkened, the black bits in her eyes shrivelling. Her voice rose. 'Have a heart, will you? Don't put me on the street!'

'This ain't your home.'

'What's it to you? You ain't here most of the time, anyway.'

'You got to go.'

'No!'

'I told you now. Get out!'

She ducked down, pulling something from under the bed and lashing out at me. Something brushed my arm and I looked down, seeing nothing at first. Then a thin line of blood appeared. She held a clasp knife in her hand.

'Fuck,' I said. 'What've you done?'

The fury had left her face, her eyes wide with shock. 'Oh, Christ. I'm sorry. I'm sorry, Norm.'

The cut was about six inches long, from the inside of my wrist up to my elbow. Bright red blood was oozing out all along.

'You witch! Look what you've bloody done!'

She dropped the knife and grabbed my other shirt from the chair, pressing it to my arm, staunching the blood. 'We got to keep it there till it stops,' she said. There were tears in her eyes. 'Stop it getting infected. It won't bleed for long. It ain't deep, mate. Oh, I'm sorry. I just struck out. I'm scared to leave, Norm. I'm scared out of my wits. I'll make it up to you, you see if I don't. Here, let me hold it. You sit down.'

I wasn't in any mood to sit. I kicked the knife under the bed least she lost her temper again, then took her hand off my arm, keeping the shirt pressed down on the wound.

'I'm such a fool,' she said, her mouth downturned. She wiped her eyes. 'Does it hurt?'

I shook my head. 'Where were you staying before?'

'With a friend.'

'Why can't you go back there?'

She shook her head. Her stringy hair fell over her forehead. 'He won't have me back.'

'Because you slashed him?'

She smiled. 'You're my first slashing, Norm.'

'It was like this though, was it? Another bloke like me?'

She didn't answer.

'Ain't you got family?'

'No.' She stepped over to the window, pulling Mrs B's shawl from the chair and covering herself. Maybe it was because she stabbed me, but I didn't seem to mind this time. 'I ain't got family. Why does every bugger ask that? Some people got no family. Some people never had family. Why don't nobody see that? And no, I ain't got no friends, least none that can take me in. Don't you think I've tried all that? D'you think I wanted to come here with you who I never met afore, never leave the room for fear I wouldn't get back in? D'you think I'm living the life, Norm? Is that what you think?'

She turned her eyes to the window. Next to her, on the wall, hung the silhouettes of my missus and me we'd got done just after we were married.

We stood there in the dark for some time.

'You need to empty those pots,' I said at last.

She didn't turn to look at me. 'You'll lock me out.'

I went over to her, took her hand, and put a shilling in her palm. She looked at it. 'Oh, that's it, is it, Norm? The pay-off?'

I shook my head. 'There's a bloke on the corner selling fried fish. And get us a bottle of gin. We've got some talking to do.'

Chapter Nineteen

It was a dark, windy morning and the city was at work again. Suzie hadn't turned up at the pier, so we decided we'd best go find her. We crossed London Bridge, then made our way onto Tooley Street. Arrowood was vexed with me for not telling him what Ettie'd said about her baby.

'By why doesn't she want me to know? It's my damn house, for God's sake!'

'She will soon enough.'

His eyes narrowed like it pained him, and he muttered to himself as we passed Hay's Wharf. I didn't like it any more than he did; when Ettie insisted I keep quiet, I felt I must agree. But I didn't want to hold onto any more secrets than I already had, and the guvnor had more right to this one than me.

'Tell me, Barnett, for Christ's sake!' he suddenly demanded.

'I gave her my word, sir,' I said.

'Tell me, damn it! I'm your master, not her.'

I quickened my pace. He trotted along behind for a few minutes, then seized my arm and spun me around. With a growl, I lashed at him, breaking his hold on me.

'Listen, *master*,' I said, glaring at his swollen face. He was blinking away through his eyeglasses, the breaths coming in short jerks, his arms raised like he was about to have another go at me. 'I gave her my word. She demanded it of me. You wouldn't break your word, so why d'you think I would?'

His blooming red nose twitched. He made to speak then stopped himself. All around us the sour smell of the Courage Brewery filled the air, and I found myself feeling sorry for him.

'She told me you lost two children,' I said.

'We did.'

'I'm sorry. I didn't know.'

We were stopped outside the grammar school. He put his hands on the black railings; his shoulders fell. 'That was what drove us apart.'

'Have you heard from her?' I asked. When Isabel took up with the lawyer in Cambridge she'd asked the guvnor for a divorce, though he never got round to doing it. And then six months back the fellow died of belly cancer. He'd been waiting ever since.

'She doesn't reply. I know the lawyer's family reclaimed the house. She must have gone to her people in Norfolk.'

'D'you still think she'll come back?'

'She's had six months. If she was going to return, I think she'd have done it by now.' He sighed. 'If she's still silent by autumn I'm going up. Perhaps I can persuade her.'

'How are you going to do that?'

'I'll remind her how happy we were before . . . I'll show her I'm still that man.'

I put my hand on his hot shoulder. He turned to me.

'Ettie's going to tell me soon, then?' he asked softly.

'That's what she said.'

He nodded his great turnip head and began to walk. 'Let's get to work, Norman.'

The door was open when we reached the Moons' stable. Suzie was sweeping the dirt floor. She smiled when she saw us.

'I was hoping you'd come.' She put her foot on the broom head and held the handle upright over her belly. Her eyes were red. 'I got an idea about it.'

'How are you feeling, my dear?' asked the guvnor, looking around the dark stable. The mattresses were stood by the wall; the table was bare. More than half the cages hanging around the stable were empty. The others had sheets over them, and you could hear the little birds scratching and rustling inside. The birdshit was all cleared away, the feathers gone. The space on the floor where Moon's body had been was wet.

'Me?' She looked surprised. 'Oh, I'm just fine. Got a load on my mind, though. Lots to do. I'll put the kettle on, eh?'

We sat and watched her clump about the gloomy stable. She wasn't the most graceful on her feet before, but now she moved like her spirit was in a body it couldn't quite master. Her arms were jerky and each step crashed down that hard I felt she might jar her leg. She filled the kettle and put it on a hook over the fire, then noticed the fire wasn't lit and took it off again. She stared at the cold ashes in the grate. She picked up the coal scuttle, then put it down again. Her lip started to tremble, but she bit it hard and picked up the kettle again.

'It's too muggy for tea, Miss Moon,' said the guvnor. 'Did you sleep last night?'

'Too much to do, Mr Arrowood,' she said, pushing her wild hair from her freckled face. The kettle went back on its hook over the fire and she turned to us, folding her hands over her chest. 'You should have seen the mess this place was in. Listen, I been thinking how Polgreen did it. He paid that launch to crash into the wherry, then, while you was looking the other way, Mr Barnett, they use a skiff, row it out real quiet. That's got to be it. You just got to find the pilot of the launch.'

'Suzie,' said the guvnor softly. 'We'll talk about that later. Sit down. Where does your family live?'

'Southend,' she said as I took her arm, making her sit on a stool by the table. 'Whats that got to do with it?'

'You can't stay here alone,' said the guvnor. 'You must go to them.'

'I can't,' she said, standing again. She marched over to one of the mattresses leant against the wall and straightened it. 'I got to be here to look after the boat.'

'You don't, Suzie. Belasco can do that.'

'It's our boat. Dad and . . .' Her breath caught, and the quiver in her lip showed the first sign that she understood her old man was dead. 'I got to work.' She strode over to the open door, where the rain was starting to fall in the narrow alley.

'You can't stay here alone,' said the guvnor. 'Not until the fiend who killed those people is caught. We don't know what he'll do next. Go to your family, just until then.'

Suzie looked at him. She looked at me. She shook her head. 'I ain't going there. That's my ma's people. They were always nasty to him, wouldn't hardly speak to him. I won't go to them.'

'Is there anyone else? Any family friends?'

'It was just us,' she said.

Arrowood thought for a moment. 'Who's Feathers, Suzie?' he asked softly.

She shook her head. 'I don't know. Why?'

'We think she was a friend of your father's.'

'I never heard of her.'

'Have you sorted through his papers yet?'

She shook her head. The guvnor gave me the nod, and I went over to the trunk and dug out the bundle of letters. 'We found these when we were here last,' I said.

She opened the first one in the pile. A look of puzzlement and then disgust passed over her face as she read it. She opened the next. 'Are they all like this?'

'More or less,' said Arrowood. 'You must have some idea who it is.'

Suzie thought for some time as the rain rattled on the path outside. Then she shook her head. 'He never told me about her. They don't say his name, though, do they? *My Dearest Love*. Could be to anybody.'

'Then why would he keep them?'

She shrugged. 'If they were for him, why didn't he never tell me about her?'

'He wanted to spare your feelings, perhaps. Suzie, why wouldn't your mother's family speak to him? Do you think it had something to do with this Feathers?'

'They blamed him for Ma. She took her own life, see. Like him.' She took a sharp gasp as she said it, and I thought the tears were about to come. But they didn't; she only tied the letters back up, slowly, neatly. Finally she spoke again. 'They said it was him drove her to it but it weren't. She never got over it, them all dying like that.' Here Suzie paused. 'My brother and sisters.'

'Ah, there you are,' said a man who'd appeared in the door-way. He was a thin, straggle-haired bloke, his skin hanging down from his jaw, a pair of round eyeglasses on his nose. His suit was brown and wet.

'Mr Chitty,' said Suzie, wiping her eyes.

'Have you got it for me?' he demanded.

She shook her head.

'Right, then.' He stepped over to where a key hung from a hook on the wall, took it down, and put it in his pocket. 'You can take your clothes, but we're having the rest.'

'What's going on here?' asked the guvnor.

'Eviction,' said the bloke. 'No rent paid for four month.'

'But you can't! Her father's just passed away.'

'I'm real sorry to hear that, but I got another family coming in here this afternoon.' Mr Chitty bowed at Suzie. 'My condolences, Miss Moon. Now, get packing, eh, darling? I'll take the birds as part payment, and those mattresses.' He looked around. 'I'll take his clothes too. He won't be needing them.'

'Get out, you cur!' cried the guvnor.

'You get out, sir,' said the man, an ugly smile on his mug. 'This building's the property of Dr Kennard. You're trespassing.'

I took the man by the lappets and pushed him back to the door. 'Have a heart, mate,' I growled. 'You let her stay a while longer, just a few days to get herself together, eh?'

'Lads!' barked the man.

At once, two burly blokes appeared at the door, their shirts unbuttoned to the waist. One of them held a crowbar. The other was that wide he had to turn side on to get in.

I let go of Chitty and stepped forward. The both of them stared at me, their eyes cold and deadly.

'Listen, this ain't my decision,' said Chitty. 'I'm only the agent. Now, Boz, you get those mattresses and all the cages and load them up. Table as well.'

'Didn't you hear me?' demanded the guvnor. 'Her father's just died.'

The wide one lumbered over and picked up a mattress. As he pulled it towards the door, I wrenched it out of his hands. The very next moment I felt an explosion on my neck that had me stumbling across the floor, my legs weak, my ears ringing. I grabbed the table to keep upright, pain shooting from the crown of my head down to my fingers. When I looked up I saw the other rough stood before me, his crowbar raised in case I should move again. He needn't have bothered: the room was swaying too much to let go.

'Start packing, girlie,' hissed the agent. 'I won't tell you again. Get your clothes now or we'll take them too.'

There was no choice. The law was on their side and that one blow had drawn the fight out of me. The guvnor helped Suzie collect her clothes and papers and her old man's Sunday best and stuff it all into a feed sack, then the agents hustled us out, down the dark path to the alley, where a crowd had gathered in the rain to see what was going on. Already the two mattresses were on the agent's cart.

The guvnor held Suzie's sack over his shoulder. She stopped, taking one last look at her home, just as the two roughs came out the door carrying the table.

'Come,' said the guvnor. 'We'll get you to Southend, Suzie.'

She drew away from us. 'I told you I ain't going there. I'll sleep on the boat.'

'It's too dangerous,' I said. 'You don't know what they'll do next.'

'Belasco'll stay with me.'

The guvnor shook his head.

'You can stay with me and my sister,' he said. 'And I won't discuss it further.'

As we made our way through the crowd of punters in the pudding shop, busier today on account of the bakers' strike, the guvnor spotted a copy of *The Star* tucked under an old fellow's arm.

'Do you mind?' he asked, yanking it out.

'Help yourself, why don't you?' said the bloke, raising his eyes at the woman behind him as the guvnor scanned the columns.

He turned to the crime pages. 'Here it is. Now, let's see . . . they've identified two of the bodies. Actresses. Rachel Carroll and Gabriella Roughley, both of Archer Street, Soho.' He looked up. 'D'you know them, Suzie?'

Suzie shook her head.

'Someone reported them missing after seeing the story in the paper. An anonymous letter. They haven't identified the man yet.'

He gave the old bloke back his paper and we went through to the parlour. Neddy was sitting there alone, his cap on the table.

'Did he speak to you?' asked the guvnor the moment we stepped in the door.

'He reckons a lady and a gent were watching, sir. Came early, that's how he noticed them, before the day-trippers. They was standing right by him at the top of the stairs, watching the pier. Didn't give him any coin, neither. The gent said, "Here it is" when the *Gravesend Queen* came in to dock, so he knew they was watching out for her.'

'This is Miss Moon,' said the guvnor. 'She owns the boat.'

'Neddy, ma'am,' said Neddy with a nod, his face set and serious.

'What did they do next?' asked the guvnor.

'They watched a lady get off the boat, maybe that's you, Miss Moon. And you, Mr Barnett, Monkey saw you standing on the boat afore it came over to the pier. Least I think it must be you. When you both run back aboard the gent started laughing.'

'Did the woman laugh?' asked the guvnor.

'Not as Monkey heard. Just the gent.'

The guvnor pulled out his wine gums and offered them around.

'Then?'

'They watched till the coppers came, then they left. Didn't come back.'

'How did they look?'

'Proper, sir. The gent had a straw hat, red jacket, stripy pink shirt too, all clean and pressed. The lady was smart. Green dress, posh bonnet with a feather in it and boots tied with ribbons. A parasol with birds on it too, sir.'

'Birds?' The guvnor looked at me. I knew what he was thinking. Was this Feathers? Was all this horror the revenge of a lover? He shook his head, pondering, his eyes locked on mine. Then at last he turned back to Neddy. 'Hair?'

'She had yellow, sir. He didn't recall the gent's. Oh, and she had painted lips.'

'Height?'

Neddy shrugged. 'The gent had a belly. The lady was sort of thin. Not old and not young neither. Your sort of age, sir.'

'Did he hear them say anything else?'

'No, sir.'

'Good boy. You're going to make a fine detective one day.'

Neddy smiled wide. There was nothing he liked more than doing a good job for the guvnor. He never had a father himself, and the guvnor was the closest he got. Arrowood gave him another wine gum and turned to Suzie. 'You'll sleep with my sister. I'll show you up.'

'Aren't you going to Soho to ask about those two women?' asked Suzie.

'That's what we're doing now.'

'I'll come with you. Maybe I'll recognize someone.'

'You have other things to do, Suzie. Ettie will help you make the . . .' The guvnor paused. 'Well, you need to . . . make arrangements. For your father.'

Suzie looked at him blankly for a few moments, like she didn't know what he meant. Then her mouth fell open. The guvnor took her arm and guided her to the chair where she sat heavily.

'Put the kettle on, Barnett,' he said.

As I got the water boiling, Ettie came down the stairs with the baby in her arms. Its face was red, a rash over its plump legs.

The guvnor explained that Suzie would be staying. Though she looked like she hadn't slept for a week, Ettie smiled and took her hand.

'You're welcome here, Suzie,' she said. 'We're so glad to have you.'

Suzie looked at the little baby wearing only a thin cotton

dress, then up at Ettie's warm and earnest face, and she began to weep. Ettie passed the child to the guvnor and took Suzie in her arms, stroking her back as she gasped and choked, her shoulders convulsing, letting out all she'd been holding in since yesterday.

'Sorry,' she kept saying between sobs. 'Sorry.'

'You weep, my dear,' said Ettie. 'You just weep.'

I made the tea.

Neddy watched his feet.

The guvnor rocked the baby in his arms.

Suzie didn't let up until I'd got the five mugs filled and the biscuit tin on the table.

'How about a nice nap, my dear?' asked Ettie. 'You look like you need it.'

Suzie sniffed, wiping her eyes on her sleeve, then Ettie took her hand and led her upstairs. The three of us drank our tea. Ate some biscuits. Didn't speak. As he chewed a garibaldi, the guvnor paced the room, humming to the baby. She watched him with a curious expression, like she was at the zoo for the first time. The guvnor kissed her forehead; she chuckled. He beamed and kissed her again.

When Ettie finally came down, the child was asleep.

'Poor Suzie,' she said. 'She went right out. You'll have to sleep down here, William. Get that mattress back from Mrs Pudding.'

'I don't suppose Holmes has replied, has he?' he asked, putting the baby into the box on the table.

'No,' she said. 'There's been no mail at all.'

His face darkened. 'Right, Barnett, I think it's time we paid that hound a visit.'

Chapter Twenty

We took a slow bus to Oxford Circus and walked from there to Baker Street. It was early afternoon. The rain had stopped, and a steamed, tired feeling fell over the streets. People weren't talking; sweat prickled their red faces. The poor horses were foaming, their heads low as they pulled trams and buses and wagons loaded with all the gubbins the city needed to keep itself existing.

221B Baker Street was in the middle of a terrace of shops. Outside, two gents were talking by a brougham. The driver stood roasting by the open door, a green frock coat with gold brocade tied up to his chin, a matching topper. I shook my head and tried to catch his eye in sympathy, but he stared straight ahead like a Grenadier guard. Across the road, a shady, Russian-looking bloke was trying to look casual as he kept a watch on the building. When he saw us, he pulled his brown cap low over his face and shrank behind a growler parked by the lamppost. We looked up at the first-floor windows. Behind them, as everyone in London knew, were the rooms of Holmes and Watson. The guvnor nudged me, raising his arm to point at a silhouette you could see through the net curtains: the outline of a thin man sat side-on by the window, his chin prominent, his nose hawk-like. As we watched, the figure turned.

'It's him,' said the guvnor. 'I recognize that nose from all those damned pictures in *The Strand*. Let's see what he has to say for himself.'

He banged the door knocker. After a few moments we heard footsteps on the stairs and a wrinkled woman opened the door. She wore a black dress, a white pinny tied over it.

'We're here to see Mr Holmes, madam,' said the guvnor. 'I'm Mr Arrowood. This is Mr Barnett.'

'He's not in, sir,' she said. 'Would you like to leave your card?'

'Might we come in and wait?'

'I don't know how long he'll be, sir. Best leave a card.'

'I don't have a card.' The guvnor looked at her, his brow raised as if he'd just asked a question. But the woman was calm; she stood in silence, her eyes cool and confident. Eventually, he stepped back to the kerb and looked again at the silhouette in the window.

'Madam, we know he's in. He's sitting just there. We can see him.'

'Ah.' She leaned out the door and looked up and down the street. She whispered now: 'That's not him, sir.'

'It looks just like him.'

'But it isn't him, sir.'

'Who is it, then?'

'I can't tell you that. Would you like to leave a message?'

'Are you Mrs Hudson?'

'No, sir. I'm the char.'

'Well, listen to me. It's very important I see Mr Holmes. He requested my help on a case. It's urgent I speak to him. The case may depend on it.'

The woman raised her eyebrow but said nothing. The guvnor looked up at the window again.

'That *is* him up there, for goodness' sake!' He was moving from foot to foot now, his hands gripping the way they do when he's irritated. 'Don't deny it, madam. You must go up and tell him why we're calling. I'm sure he'll see us when he knows.'

'It isn't him, sir. Now, if there's nothing else, I need to get back to work.'

The guvnor quickly put his foot in the door. 'At least tell me where he is.'

'I never know where he is, and Mrs Hudson neither, sir. Everything's a secret with Mr Holmes. So, if you don't mind, take your boot away from the door or I'll call a constable.'

'Oh, what nonsense. I'll leave a note, then!' The guvnor scribbled something in his pad, ripped out the paper, and handed it to the woman. Only then did he pull his foot from the door. She shut it hard in our faces.

'Damn him!' hissed the guvnor, stepping back into the street without looking, right into the path of a horse. The horse tossed its head, rearing up and stumbling a few steps to the side.

'Idiot!' shrieked its well-dressed rider, raising his crop and whipping the guvnor across the neck. 'Look where you're going, you fat oaf!'

The guvnor backed away, covering his head as the toff tried to thrash him again. 'Get off!' he protested, while the horse skitted back and forth, its eyes wide with alarm. I stepped over quick and caught the bloke's stick, wrenching it out of his hand.

'Give that back!' the fellow cried as he tried to control his mount. I could see now he was no more than eighteen or nineteen year old.

I snapped the riding crop over my leg and tossed the pieces back at him.

'You'll pay for that!' he hissed, trying to kick me with his gleaming riding boot. I dodged it easy, slapping the horse's haunches and barking, 'Get on!' At once, the horse bolted down the road, the young fellow dropping foul curses as he fought to stay aboard.

'Thank you, Barnett,' said the guvnor, retrieving his spectacles from the road. 'What a bad-mannered fellow he was.'

He picked up an apple core from between two piles of dung and hurled it at the upper window. 'Holmes!' he yelled. 'Sherlock Holmes! It's Arrowood!'

Holmes didn't even move. Behind us, a tiny old woman approached a white horse shackled to a milk truck and gave it the biggest carrot I ever saw. As soon as it was in its mouth she pulled another from her basket and crossed the road to a grey shire horse standing wearily before a drayman's wagon. The guvnor snatched the carrot from the white horse's beak, snapped it in half, and returned the pointy bit to the bewildered nag's filthy teeth. He threw the other bit at the window. It bounced from the glass, falling back to the pavement.

'Holmes!' he shouted again. 'Open the window, Holmes! It's Arrowood!'

Still the dark figure behind the nets didn't move. The guvnor was getting wheezy now, his face damp and red. People had stopped on the pavement to see what he was shouting at, but he didn't seem to notice. He picked up the carrot from the road and hurled it again, harder this time. Too hard, it seemed, as it cracked one of the window panes.

'Holmes!' he yelled again. 'Sherlock Holmes!'

'That's enough of that!' yelled a constable from the other side of the street. He stepped across to us. 'You'll break that window.'

'The char won't let me in. She's pretending he isn't there!'

'You'd best move on then, sir.'

'But it's urgent I see him!' cried the guvnor, his hand still at the wound on his neck where the toff had thrashed him. Blood was trickling down onto his grimy collar. 'Look! He's sitting just there!'

'Happen he don't want to see you, sir. He's a very busy man, Mr Holmes. Now are you going to move on or shall I arrest you for causing a disturbance?'

'You can't blooming well arrest me for trying to attract a man's attention,' growled the guvnor, bending to pick up the bit of carrot once more.

'I can and I will,' said the PC, gripping the guvnor's arm and pulling him upright. 'Now drop that carrot.'

'We're just off, constable,' I said, taking the guvnor's other arm and yanking him back toward the Marylebone Road. 'Don't want to cause any trouble.'

'See you don't, then.'

'That damn cur,' muttered the guvnor as we walked. 'After all the trouble he put me to. Who the hell does he think he is? He was right there! All he had to do was come to the door for a minute, the arrogant swine.'

In a sudden wild fury, he thrashed his walking stick against a lamppost. It shattered, the bottom end spinning through the air and landing at the feet of a young bootblack.

'Now look at what he's done!' he bellowed.

I put my arm across his shoulder and led him away down the road. The poor old lump was close to tears.

Archer Street was a dark sort of place just behind the Lyric Theatre. The buildings were sooty and run-down, and though it wasn't yet tea-time, the judies were already stood in the doorways asking any half-decent man who passed if they were good-natured. The first one we approached pointed us to a building opposite.

The bloke who opened the door didn't know the two women were dead, but he didn't look surprised when we told him.

'So that's where they been,' he said. He scratched his belly through his checked shirt. His feet were bare. 'How was they done? A-strangling?'

'Stabbed,' said the guvnor. 'We're private enquiry agents, working alongside the police. I'm Mr Arrowood, this is Mr Barnett.'

'Mr Dunner,' said the bloke, giving us each a shake of the hand. 'They think it was Jack?'

'Jack's been gone near on ten year, mate,' I told him, noticing a woman lingering in the doorway down the dark corridor. I couldn't see her face, just an arm and the spread of her skirt. She was listening.

'I always said he'd be back.' He nodded at the judies across the dusty road. 'I told them girls that. I said he'd be back one day.'

'And you might be right, sir,' said the guvnor. 'He may well be out there, ready to strike. Are you the landlord here?'

'His agent. Me and the wife look after this building and one round the corner.'

'Ah. Just the man, then. Now, would you mind letting us see the ladies' rooms?'

The woman stepped out from the gloom. She wore a plain grey dress, a brown flannel scarf tied tight over her head.

'You bring the coppers back and we'll let you in,' she said, shuffling down to stand behind the man. Her eyes were narrow, her chin long and sharp. Her teeth were crooked and there were too many of them. She might have been bald too, as there was no sign of hair poking out from under her scarf. She looked the guvnor up and down, then over his shoulder at me. Her breath caught and, just for a moment, her eyes widened.

'Please, madam. It'll only take a minute'

The woman poked the bloke; he scowled at her.

'Tuppence?' said the guvnor with a sigh.

'Thruppence,' he demanded.

'Oh, very well,' he grumbled, fishing out his purse.

We followed him as he limped down the narrow corridor and up the stairs, the woman coming behind us. There was only one door on the first landing. The bloke unlocked it and stood aside. 'They got the whole floor.'

There were three rooms: a front parlour looking straight into the window of the building on the other side of the street, a kitchen no bigger than a privy, and a bedroom with a wide bed. It was done out nice, with thick curtains, foreign rugs, a newish couch and chairs. There was even a bit of green wallpaper up. It was a wealthier place than you'd think in such a dirty street.

'Did they have a private income?' asked the guvnor.

'You might say,' answered Mrs Dunner, her voice real quiet.

'It was a gent paid for the rooms,' said her husband. 'A Mr George. An uncle, so they said.'

'He weren't no uncle,' said the woman. There was a knock at the door below; the bloke left us and clumped down the stairs. I went over to the window to check it wasn't Petleigh, but it was a tinker with a grinding wheel.

'Why was he paying for the rooms, madam?' asked the guvnor.

'Why d'you think?' she asked sharply.

I went into the bedroom and opened the wardrobe door.

'You know where he lives?' I asked, looking through the clothes. There were seven or eight dresses hanging there, all fine. The hats had feathers. Two winter coats, a few shawls, a box of bows. A hook on the back of the door carried ribbons of every colour, while a little pile of bloomers lay in a corner.

The woman didn't answer.

'D'you know where we can find him?' asked the guvnor as I looked under the bed.

'We never had his particulars,' I heard her say from the next room. 'He sent the money regular every Friday till a couple of month ago. We ain't had a penny since. I'd been telling the young ladies we need the rent. They was going to talk to him.'

'We gave them two week more to pay,' said the man, clumping back just as I finished examining the bedroom. 'Then we'd have to turf them out.'

'D'you know if they had any friends?' asked the guvnor. 'Any family?'

'They kept to theirselves,' said Mrs Dunner. 'Close they were.'

'I see. And what does Mr George look like?'

'No whiskers, about your age,' she said, looking him up and down. 'Fat like you but not so ugly. Better dressed, of course.' She crunched up her face and peered at his cheek. 'That orange business ain't catchy, is it?'

'Erysipelas,' answered the guvnor, looking around the

parlour. 'I'd keep your cat away. What manner of hair did Mr George have?'

'Whiteish. We didn't see him again after that first time, but we're abed at nine. He did send a cab quite regular, pick them up, like.'

'And you don't know where we could find him?'

'There was one place they went dancing,' said the bloke. 'Nell Gwynn's on Greek Street. Maybe they know him.'

The guvnor quizzed them some more, but they couldn't tell us anything else about the man, and we could find nothing in the rooms that would help us: a few magazines, a whistle, some biscuits, a stack of penny dreadfuls and another of novels. We found a few coins in a box, which Mrs Dunner put in her pocket for the rent though I knew she'd be having the clothes soon as we were gone. There were no letters, no documents, no evidence that they knew anyone anywhere.

'Thank you for your help, Mr and Mrs Dunner,' said the guvnor as he followed me back onto the street. He gave a little bow, then suddenly a look of terror came over his face. 'Oh, my goodness!' he exclaimed, stepping towards the woman. 'Hold still, madam!'

'What is it?' she cried.

He snatched at her headscarf and whipped it off her head.

'No!' she cried out, clasping her head. 'Give that back!'

The guvnor jumped further into the street, shaking the scarf wildly.

'Give that back!' she demanded again, shrinking behind her husband.

'There, there, it's gone,' said the guvnor. 'No danger now. You didn't feel it, madam? No? It was a horsefly as big as an apple. Have you ever been bit by a horsefly? It's absolutely the most awful pain. I had it once. Couldn't sit down for a week.'

The woman darted at him, grabbing the cloth from his hand and quickly setting it back on her head, pulling it tight under her chin. But not before we'd seen the straggles of white hair plastered to her almost bald scalp. And not before we'd seen the bloody wound where her ear used to be.

Chapter Twenty-One

'Who did that to you?' asked the guvnor.

The woman pushed past her husband and stamped down the corridor.

'The doctor,' said Mr Dunner. 'It was infected.'

'Which doctor?' asked the guvnor as the woman turned into the back room and disappeared.

With a shake of the head, the man stepped back inside the house and shut the door.

Behind us, a dray stacked with barrels was rattling along the street, the drayman singing a hymn from his bench. I grabbed the guvnor's arm. Further up the street, Petleigh and Girkin were climbing from a cab.

'Get down,' I said, pulling him between the wagon and its great shire horse. Shielded from sight by the row of barrels, we crept along with it till it turned down Rupert Street and we were out of sight.

'How did you know about her ear?' I asked as we got back on the pavement and walked tall again.

'D'you remember you asked her a question from the bedroom? Well, she had no idea you'd spoken. I heard it clear enough and I was further away from you. She was standing in the parlour with the bedroom on her left. Now, when I asked the same question from her right side, she did hear.' We stepped off the pavement to get past a few folk watching a minstrel band. 'I was the one talking most, so keeping me on the right side would be a good strategy for someone with poor hearing on the left side. But tell me, Barnett, if you had a hearing defect on one side, would you tie a thick headscarf in such a way that it completely covered both ears in flannel?'

'Get on with it, sir.'

'It would make it even harder to hear. The only reason to do it would be if you wanted to hide something.'

'Could have been her baldness.'

'But you wouldn't cover the ears. I had a good look at her head as I climbed down the stairs after her, and it seemed to me the outline of her ear was clearer on the right side. I don't suppose you noticed.'

'No.'

'You must be more observant, Barnett. How many times have I told you?'

I looked away, tired of hearing him say the same thing whenever he'd noticed something that I hadn't. 'Very clever, sir.'

'I don't believe it was a doctor who cut it off. It's too much of a coincidence; I've never met a single soul in my life with a missing ear, and now we have two on this case and both connected to those two women. The chances are the same person cut hers off as severed the ears of the dead man.'

Greek Street was in the middle of Soho, only a short walk from Archer Street. The windows of Nell Gwynn's were covered in black boards, the door crimson, a great brass handle in the middle with a little peep-hole above it. Nobody answered when

I hammered on it. I wasn't surprised; it wasn't the sort of place to open till after dark.

'What now?' I asked as we stood on the busy pavement.

The guvnor pulled out his watch. For a moment he pondered.

'I think it's time we visited Gravesend, Barnett,' he said at last. 'See what that fellow Curtis can tell us.'

The train from Charing Cross was packed with commuters: there were no seats left. The guvnor was red-faced and sweaty from the walking, vexed at having to stand, and he had that look that said he needed to chew on a bit of mutton. I broke off a bit of toffee from my pocket and fed him as we lumbered out over the river and past London Bridge, the train stopping and starting, lurching and rocking. The guvnor, unsteady on his pins, held onto me as we made our way slow as a coster's cart through Spa Road, New Cross and Lewisham. Still, it was quicker than getting a boat.

At Blackheath the train emptied out and we got a seat. As we passed through Woolwich we saw glimpses of the river again, the great haze of masts and rigging, the long arms of the cranes rising above the rooftops. Then tunnels and deep cuttings green with leaves and white with chalk. Arrowood picked up a copy of *The Daily News* someone'd had left behind and had a read, grunting and sighing as he always did. 'They're sending the King's Rifles to Mashonaland,' he said. He looked at the other passengers and shook his head, then turned the page and peered through his eyeglasses again. Silence for a few more moments. 'Another murder,' he said, his eyes pinched up as he read the little writing. '*Kensington Outrage. Murder by a Madman.* Now, let's see . . .' I watched him as he studied the story, when suddenly his face changed. His hooter twitched in irritation; his brow wrinkled.

'Sherlock Holmes again, sir?' I asked.

'Lestrade's brought him in on *another* case! Good Lord, can't that policeman solve anything himself?' He read intently, his temples pulsing like at any moment parts of his mind might shoot out. 'The body was found on a doorstep. No identification, but a bust was stolen from the house and found broken further up the street . . . Well, well. It seems that a number of similar busts have been stolen or shattered over the last few days too. Holmes believes the killer must be a lunatic. He says there's no other explanation.' He peered up at me through his eyeglasses. 'No other explanation, Barnett. Poppycock! There are a thousand other explanations! How can he possibly rule them all out!' He threw the paper on the floor and fumbled furiously in his pocket for his pipe. 'He's no understanding of the heart. And damn well knows nothing of lunacy.'

'No, sir,' I answered, gathering up the sheets so as to have a read myself.

'Lunacy,' he muttered, lighting his pipe.

Gravesend's narrow High Street was busy, the weatherboarded buildings rising tall on either side. We walked along the riverfront gardens, past Bawley Bay, where boys were playing in the rusty water, past the Clarendon Hotel and on until we reached Terrace Pier. There we found the piermaster's office.

'Yes, gents,' he said, putting down his tankard and wiping his mouth on the back of his hand. A bit of bread and cheese lay on his desk. 'What are you after?'

'Did you know Captain Moon died?' asked the guvnor.

'Oh, bloody hell,' he said with a snort. 'He owes me two month, damn it!'

'We're assisting the police with some enquiries around the death,' said the guvnor. 'D'you know anyone who might have been damaging his boat?'

The piermaster shook his head.

'Someone he'd fallen out with, perhaps?'

'No, sir. Can't think of anyone.'

'I see. Well, is there anyone down here he was friendly with? Maybe one of the other captains?'

'He didn't give anyone the time of day. He'd let the passengers down and leave Belasco and Suzie on the boat while he went off to see his mate. Same every time.'

The guvnor frowned and scratched his chin. 'Tell me, sir, when you say his friend, do you mean Mr Curtis?'

'That's he, the bird seller. Got a little place on Princes Street opposite the churchyard.' The piermaster stepped out of his office and pointed at the spire as rose above the buildings. 'You can't miss it. You'll hear the singing anyhow.'

Princes Street ran along the side of the church. We heard the birdsong from a hundred yards away, and as we approached, a woman in black stepped out of the alley with a little girl swinging a cage. Inside, a goldfinch was clinging onto its perch for dear life as it knocked back and forth against her leg. At the end of the narrow alley was the thinnest house I'd ever seen, and from it came a riot of birdsong.

'Remember to clean the floor once a week, Ally,' called the man who stood in the door. 'And give him oats if he won't perform.'

He smiled at us. He was clean-shaved, his face like a pear,

with the wide jaws of a man who loves to laugh. He wore a clean white shirt with no collar, a pair of white boating trousers, and Chinese sandals on his feet. His hair was oiled and neat, combed in a long sweep from a side parting on one side and over his bald crown to the other.

'Mr Curtis?' said the guvnor, offering his hand. 'My name's Arrowood. This is Mr Barnett. I understand you're a friend of Captain Moon?'

The smile fell from the bloke's face. He swallowed.

'Why?' he asked, glancing over our shoulders to the empty road. He looked me up and down. 'What is it?'

'Could we come in, sir?' I said. 'We need to talk to you.'

'I don't think so. What is it?'

The building behind him had three tiny windows upstairs, with one more below crossed with iron bars.

'I'm afraid I have some bad news, sir,' said the guvnor. 'Captain Moon died two days ago. He took his own life.'

Curtis touched his belly with the tips of his fingers.

'Oh,' he said softly. He breathed out slow, staring at the guvnor's mouth, then let himself down gentle onto the step. As he sat there in silence, a confused look on his face, the birds in his house seemed to sing louder, like a wild, untrained choir.

'I'm so sorry,' murmured the guvnor at last. 'Barnett, go inside and see if you can make some tea.'

I stepped past Curtis and into the dark room. It was no more than eight foot wide, with a dry, biscuity smell and a tiny window obscured by a muslin cloth. Birdcages hung from hooks in the ceiling and stood on shelves as ran the length of the place. Canaries, linnet, tits and birds I didn't know the name of were standing around twitching, wondering what I was doing there. Two chairs sat next to a little writing desk, while a ladder led up to a hatch in the ceiling where his bed must have been. The whole place was spotless, the floor varnished and polished, the cages clean as a whistle. A little set of bookshelves held books on birds and the kings and queens, and proper novels bound in red and blue. *Uncle Tom's Cabin* lay face down upon a stool.

At the back was a tiny pantry with a small stove. On top, boiling away, was a pot full of little bones. I moved it and put the kettle on, then looked out the teapot and mugs. Outside I could hear the guvnor's soothing voice.

'He must have been a good friend,' he was saying when I brought out the tea.

Curtis nodded as I put his mug on the step.

'Did you know about his trouble with Polgreen?' asked the guvnor.

Curtis nodded again. He stared at the floor, his hands clasped together between his knees. 'He told me he'd hired you,' he said in a whisper. 'Did he leave a note?'

'No, sir.'

'He weren't one for writing.'

He covered his face with his hands, and we stood over him for a few minutes, drinking our tea and listening to the birds. When Curtis had control of himself again, the guvnor told him about the fourteen skulls and the corpses tied to the boat. 'I believe it was a message to him. I know it's difficult, sir, but I must ask if it means anything to you. The women's names were Rachel Carroll and Gabriella Roughley. Did he ever speak of them?'

Curtis shook his head slowly. 'I don't think so.'

'The children's skulls? Anything at all he might have told you?'

Curtis breathed out slowly, his arms trembling. A tear rolled down his cheek and dropped on the cobbles.

'The *Princess Grace*,' he whispered. Still he didn't look up.

'The *Princess Grace*? But what had he to do with that?'

Curtis gave a shudder. He squeezed his temples like he was trying to stop more tears coming. A couple of young boys walking past stopped to watch what was going on.

'Hook it, lads,' I said.

They moved on down the hill.

As we waited, I looked again at the house. Below the bottom window, on the sooty brick, was a great smear of whitewash, like someone had started something but never finished. The birds were quieting a bit now.

'Poor Solly,' said Curtis as last. He cleared his throat.

'What do you mean about the *Princess Grace*?' asked the guvnor softly. 'Please, Mr Curtis. It's important.'

Curtis finally looked up, wiping his face. His eyes were pink. 'Solly was the captain. He lived in Oxford then. He was the captain when she went down.'

'Good God,' said the guvnor. He looked at me. 'You remember the disaster, Barnett? It was about twenty years ago, wasn't it, Mr Curtis?'

'Sixteen.'

I remembered it. The *Princess Grace* was a paddle steamer up Oxford way. It crashed into a houseboat near Marlow, tore it in two. There was a child's birthday party aboard. It was in the papers for months.

'Fourteen children died,' said Curtis, each word soft and slow. 'The papers said he was drunk, but it weren't true. He never drank when he was working. There was a campaign. He was threatened in the street. Poison letters. They tried to set fire to his house. It got so bad they had to leave Oxford. He grew a beard, changed his name.' Curtis shook his head; his voice went quiet again. 'He thought he'd got away from all that, but they must have found out somehow.'

'What was his real name?' asked the guvnor.

'Buncher. Solomon Buncher.'

'Does Suzie know this?'

'She was only just born when it happened. He kept it from her.'

'But surely someone else must have told her? The family?'

He snorted. 'There's no family on his side, and his wife's . . . well, most of them won't even speak to him. The ones that do'd never talk about it. They see it as a disgrace.'

'D'you have any idea who was threatening him?'

'Must be the same ones.' Curtis suddenly took the guvnor's wrist, looking up at him. A fierce anger appeared in his eyes. 'I don't know who they were, but it's they who killed him. They're to blame. You must catch them, Mr Arrowood.'

'The police are working on the case now, Mr Curtis. They'll come and see you.'

'No!' cried Curtis, pushing himself to his feet. 'You mustn't give them my name. You tell them what I said. That's all I know. I can't help any more.'

'But why?'

'Trust me, I can't be involved with the police.' All his muscles were tense, his neck straining. His wide, heavy jawbone trembled. 'Promise me you won't. Promise me, sir.'

The guvnor frowned. 'But why, Mr Curtis?'

'Don't ask. Just promise me. Please, sir. I ain't a bad man, I swear it. But I can't have nothing to do with the police.'

The guvnor held his eye for a long time. 'Yes,' he said at last. 'Yes, Mr Curtis. I promise.'

Arrowood wanted to eat, so we walked down the hill to the riverbank and went in a pub called the Three Daws. I got ham and eggs, the guvnor brown shrimp and watercress, and we took our plates out to the riverside to eat. Across the calm water we could see Tilbury Docks and the low green fields of Essex. China clippers and Dutch galliots, steamboats and colliers were at anchor; skiffs and wherries moved between them carrying pilots and customs men and women selling food and ale. Bawleys were returning home from the estuary; hay-barges slid upriver on the tide, their copper sails high and full. We watched it all in silence, thinking about what had happened the last few days. Slowly, the sun began to set, turning the sky above Essex, the lazy water, even the drifting gulls a silvery pink. As I drank my porter and watched it happen before me, I thought there couldn't have been many more beautiful places on earth that night than Gravesend.

'Will *you* do it next time, Norman?' asked the guvnor, a green trickle of watercress juice oozing out the corners of his purple lips. He took a gurgle of porter from his tankard. Beside us on the table stood a little cage, and in it the blue canary he'd just bought from Curtis.

'Do what?'

'Break the bad news. Each time I do it I lose a bit of strength.'

I nodded. He patted me on the knee and had another mouthful of shrimp. A storm of laughter erupted from a table of men in yellow shirts who were dining just inside the open windows. When the noise had drifted away, he turned to me again.

'Norman . . . would you weep as Curtis did if I died?'

I studied him, his earnest, droopy eyes, his great bull's head framed in the pink sky, wondering what it was he was asking me with that question.

'No,' I said finally.

His lips tightened and he nodded.

'No,' he said with a sad smile.

When he finished his food he got us more porter. Then, one by one, he picked the empty shrimp skins from his plate, the heads and legs, and sucked the last goodness out of them. He spat each over the embankment wall then, when his plate was empty, brought it to his face and licked it clean.

'So that's why he never talked about his past,' he said with a burp old Sedley himself would've been proud of. 'And why he kept to himself around the other watermen. He didn't want to be found out.' He wiped his mouth on his sleeve, but only smeared the greasy green paste further across his face. 'At last we're getting somewhere, Norman. Now, I wonder . . .' He pulled out his watch. 'I wonder if we don't just have time for another plate of shrimp before the train goes.'

Chapter Twenty-Two

We arrived at Charing Cross at eleven and walked up to Trafalgar Square, where the gas lamps cast a hazy light on the sleeping figures laid out on the benches and steps. The fountains were dry, the lions dozing at the foot of the great column. Cabs and carriages passed around the edges, taking folk home from the theatres and dining rooms. The guvnor was limping, moaning about his boots as he went; he'd loaned them from his oldest friend Lewis back in the winter and they didn't fit him right. The guvnor was always having trouble with his feet.

Greek Street was restless with night life: colourful judies, their arms hooked with half-cut merchants; swell mobsmen with jewelled fingers and fat cigars; cocksure cousins escorting young ladies fresh up from the country. Among them wandered packs of moustachioed young bucks in lounge suits and bright ties, old generals and bankers with whiskers and toppers, moochers and dippers, palmers, bug-hunters, rampsmen and drinkers.

The door to Nell Gwynn's was open. A heavy-set bloke stood in the way, his arms crossed over his brown three-piece, the cloth too tight for his muscles.

He held up his hand as we made to enter, glancing at the bird cage in the guvnor's hand. 'Full up.'

On one side of his neck was a criss-cross of healed scars, thin white lines that ran from his collar up to his ear. He had no lips to speak of. We could see past him to the inside, all red curtains and mirrors, toffs laughing with young women in green and blue who coughed and drank. A few danced at the back, but it wasn't more than half full.

The guvnor held out a shilling. 'Our friends are inside already,' he said.

The bloke kept his arms crossed tight over his chest. The guvnor prised open the doorman's hand and inserted the coin, curling the fingers back over it. He patted his arm.

'So . . .'

'I'm sorry, sir, but we're still full,' said the bloke with a smile. Only now did I hear the Irish in his voice.

As he said it he moved aside. The guvnor took a step forward, but the bloke quickly put out his arm and stopped him. Two toffs in tails and starched white collars pushed past us and slid through, one of them patting the doorman on the shoulder and dropping something in his pocket.

'So that's the way, is it?' asked the guvnor.

'It ain't your place, sir,' said the doorman. 'But don't you take offence, now. It ain't my place either.'

'We're looking for some information about two women who used to come here, mate,' said I, just as the band started playing again inside the club. 'Miss Carroll and Miss Roughley. Rachel and Gabriella. They were fished out the river yesterday morning.'

He looked me in the eye and nodded. 'I knew them. And there was a bloke too, weren't there?'

'That's it. We're working for the captain of the boat they were tied to. You have any idea who might've done it?'

The doorman dropped his voice. 'I can't talk here. Meet me in the Twenty Grapes at one. Don't be late. I won't have long.'

As we walked back down the street, a couple of barefoot kiddies appeared out of an alley and asked us for a ha'penny. The older was a thin boy, about eight or nine, his face filthy with grime and soot, his head shaved a few weeks back and starting to sprout. One eye was swollen and bruised. He had no shirt, but wore a man's coat hanging down to his knees. The younger was a girl of five or six. Her grey dress had no sleeves, and looked like it was made by someone who didn't know how to make clothes. As I looked closer I realized it was a coal sack.

'Where are your parents?' asked the guvnor, fishing out a penny and handing it to the boy.

'Ma c-c-comin baa—' said the boy. He couldn't speak proper, the words all mashed up.

'Thank you, sir,' said the little girl.

'Your ma's coming back, did he say? Where is she?' I asked.

'She's coming back,' said the girl. Her voice was hoarse. She coughed as she peered at the little blue canary inside the guvnor's cage.

I nudged the guvnor, pointing at a pile of rags just inside the alley.

'How long have you been here, my darlings?' he asked.

The boy took his sister's hand and pulled her away from us.

'Go . . . wait. M-ma say.'

The guvnor looked at him for some time, then sighed. 'Well, you take care. I hope she comes soon.'

The Twenty Grapes was a noisy drinking den down an alley off Berwick Street, a place we did fit in. The floor was sticky, the air damp and hot, a little bloke banging away at a piano. There was nowhere to sit, so we stood in a corner and had a few pints, a few smokes, joining in the singing and watching the folk laughing and arguing in the hot basement. Just after one the doorman walked in. I got him a pint and brought him over to the guvnor.

'They was actresses,' he said. He took a swallow and rolled a fag. 'Not regular, but they'd been on at the Variety. They was waiting to hear about a farce coming up.'

'D'you know anyone who might have wanted them dead?' asked the guvnor.

'No,' he said, lighting up. 'Bit of fun, they were. Everyone reckons it's Jack. Had their guts ripped out, didn't they?'

'Jack never killed men,' said the guvnor.

'How d'you know?'

The guvnor nodded. 'I suppose I don't.'

'You find out who that bloke was they was with?'

'Not yet,' I answered. 'You ever hear of a Mr George?'

'Chelsea George? Sure, he owns Nell Gwynn's. But it weren't him. He wouldn't do that.'

'What was his relationship to the two women?' asked the guvnor, raising his voice to be heard over a new song just starting up on the piano.

'They'd have a drink together sometimes. I don't know no more than that.'

'Where can we find him?' asked the guvnor.

'He don't come to the club much these days. I don't know where he lives.'

The punters recognized the song on the piano was 'Daisy Bell' and gave a cheer.

'Does he own any other places?'

'I wouldn't know about any of that. I only do the door. Mind my own business.'

'Who runs the club for him?' I asked as half the punters started to sing.

'Nell Gwynn.'

'Can we talk to her?'

'She won't tell you nothing about him, you can take your davey on that. And I'll tell you something else: you keep asking about Chelsea George and you'll likely end up with broken legs. He's a man with a lot of friends.'

'Why are you talking to us, may I ask?' asked the guvnor.

The doorman drew deep on his fag.

'I liked them two. Bit of fun, like I said.'

The chorus of the song came round, and just about everyone in there started bawling:

> *'Daisy, Daisy,*
> *Give me your answer do,*
> *I'm half crazy*
> *Over the love of you*
> *It won't be a stylish marriage. . .'*

In the midst of the singing, a ruckus started up among a bunch of young navvies stood next to us and one of them was pushed onto the doorman, knocking his mug out of his hand.

'Sorry, mate,' said the young fellow as he tried to get back to his feet in the crowded room. He was no more than fifteen or sixteen.

The doorman grabbed his coat and hoiked him up. The Irish in his voice was thick now. 'You spilled my drink, you little prick.'

The lad's three mates tensed. They stepped forward, their

faces still grimy from work. They all wore loose brown caps, turned so the peaks were at the back.

'Don't come any closer, lads,' growled the doorman. He took hold of the young fellow's neck and squeezed.

'Leave off, mate,' croaked the lad as he struggled to get free. He was starting to panic. 'S-sorry. It was an accident.'

The doorman brought his face real close to the boy. 'You get us three pints. All right?'

The lad nodded, and the doorman gave him a shove towards the counter. The piano was still playing, but the crowd of drunken punters weren't singing any more. They'd moved back, leaving a space around us and the three navvies.

It was then I saw a knife in the doorman's hand. The navvies backed away, pushing into the crowd until they were on the other side of the room. The doorman slid the knife back in his pocket. Slowly, the other punters turned away, started talking again. Soon, the lad arrived with three pints.

'Did the ladies have any friends?' I asked when he'd gone to join his mates.

'They got on with everyone, but nobody especial, I don't think. They was always together.'

'When was the last time you saw them?' I asked.

He raised his eyes to the damp yellow ceiling. 'Would have been . . . three or four nights ago. Having a dance.'

'Did anything happen? Any arguments?'

'Not that I noticed.'

'Who were they with?'

'I don't know. I'm outside most of the time. They left alone, I know that.' He drained his mug and let out a monstrous burp.

'Look, I got to get back. I'll ask around for you. How can I find you if I hear anything?'

It was close to two when we walked back over Waterloo Bridge. The river was slumbering, just a few late barges taking the tide, the sound of the water lapping against the boats moored near the banks. Somerset House lay behind us like a great grey quarry, while, to the right, Big Ben rose in the moonlit sky. Ahead, the wharves and warehouses of Lambeth were dark, quiet but for a seagull barking forlornly as it drifted over the roofs. A young woman stood halfway along the bridge, looking out along the water.

'D'you need some help, miss?' asked the guvnor as we approached. He handed me the cage.

She was dressed simple, her hair tied up under a plain bonnet. A maid or a hotel girl, something like that.

'No, thank you, sir,' she said almost in a whisper. Her eyes flicked towards us, then turned back to the river.

'What are you doing here so late?'

'Just want to be alone, sir,' she said. She clasped her hands and strode away in the direction we'd just come.

When we reached the other side, we looked back. She'd crossed the road and was back in the middle of the bridge again, gazing out over the dark water.

'I hope that's not what it looks like,' said the guvnor. We watched the solitary figure for a few moments. 'I'm going back,' he said at last.

I took his arm and pointed. 'There's a copper coming over. He'll sort her out.'

We watched as the constable talked to her. He took her arm and led her towards Charing Cross.

'I've told you about Myer's ideas on the subliminal unconscious, haven't I?' said the guvnor as we walked down Stamford Street.

'Several times.'

'Much of the work the mind does on a case is when we're not trying to think about it. So let's go over what we've learnt to make sure it's all there on the table when the unconscious starts its work tonight.'

We stopped at the corner of Coin Street, where I was to take his leave. 'We know that Moon was probably being persecuted because of the *Princess Grace* deaths. The fourteen skulls represent the fourteen children who died. Whoever it was discovered his real identity, so we need to find out who that man and woman were who were watching on the pier when the bodies were found, and whether they had any connection to the accident.' He patted his belly thrice and pondered for a moment. 'We must dig out the newspaper reports on the tragedy. Now, what of the three poor souls tied to the boat? What have they to do with it all? Two actresses. An unidentified man.' He dragged the stick he'd lifted from the Twenty Grapes across the cobbles. A hansom trotted by, a couple arguing inside. 'Let's hope Petleigh's discovered the chap's name by now. And what of Mrs Dunner? It can't be a coincidence that both her and the dead man had their ears cut off, can it? If we can get her to talk, then we have a route to whoever tied those bodies to the boat.'

'I doubt she'll tell you.' I sighed. 'We need to finish this case quick, William. My money's running short. I need to earn.'

'I know,' he said softly. 'Norman, I'll understand if you have to find something else in the meantime. You know I can never leave a case once I've started, but I can't ask you to keep working for nothing.'

I looked at his face in the dark, wondering if he really thought I could walk away from Suzie. Until the killers were caught she might be in danger, and we both knew he couldn't do it himself. He needed me to keep him straight. And he surely needed me if things went curly, which they were going to do sooner or later.

'I'll pawn something,' I said at last. 'I want to help Suzie as much as you, William.'

My wife's shawl, her ring, her trunk. How many times had they been in and out of that pawnbrokers over the last year? I wondered if we'd ever get work stable enough that I didn't have to visit that little chiseller's shop no more.

He patted me on the rumple and took the cage back from my hand. 'Thank you, my friend. I took my portrait in this morning: I only had three shillings left.'

I bade him goodnight and made my way back to the Borough. I was dog-tired: it felt like it'd been the longest day of my life. My feet were raw, my legs so heavy that I was stumbling and tripping along the dusty paving, the last few pennies I had clinking in my pocket. I was glad Lilly'd be there when I got in, glad I'd told her she could stay with me a while longer. She wasn't a bad sort, really. Being down on your luck makes you stink a bit, that's all. Makes you desperate, and that never is a pretty look.

I climbed the stairs real slow, feeling there was no strength left in my bones. The door stuck; I put my elbow to it, relieved to be home at last.

The moonlight through the window gave enough light to see that the bed was empty. Lilly was gone.

Chapter Twenty-Three

When I woke next morning the room was dark and grey. Hunger scratched at my belly. I got on my britches, my boots, my shirt. As I went to the window, I noticed a little lightish patch on the wall where the silhouettes of me and Mrs B should have been. They were gone. I looked to the door. My winter coat and thick vest were missing. With anger rising in me, I searched the drawers and the trunk. My old darling's ring, her best dress, her ma's lavender brooch were gone too. Even her shawl, no doubt all of it already sold. I fell back on the bed, cursing. Lilly. And just when I'd promised I'd find her a place to stay too. Whatever happened to her now, she deserved it. The bloody street, the stinking strangers, the pizzle filling the jars. She deserved it.

With nothing to do with my anger, I rose again and went back to the window, watching the folk moving around below. The weather had broke and it was drizzling, the mud starting to form under the wheels and hooves. How stupid I'd been. Maybe Mrs B was punishing me for letting her stay. It'd only been a year after all. But no, I had to stop thinking she was watching me. My missus was dead, her body rotting in the Derby filth, her soul blown away like smoke. She was dead, and I was alone.

I reached the guvnor's rooms before lunch, wet from the light rain. Ettie was in the parlour washing the baby's clothes. Her face was pale and drawn. She'd worn the same frayed blouse every day for a week.

'He isn't here,' she said as I entered. She held a brush in her hand. 'He'll be in the Hog, no doubt.'

'He didn't arrive last night?'

She crossed her arms. 'He did arrive. The child has colic. I'd brought her down here so Suzie could sleep, poor girl. He came in, took one look, and went out again, leaving that damn thing.' She pointed at the cage on the table, the blue canary singing away like it was the happiest little creature in the world. She laughed and shook her head. 'The dear child was possessed.'

'We'd been working from morning till midnight.'

'I know.' She shook her head and sighed. 'It's going to be difficult with Suzie staying.'

I looked around the dingy room. Above the tiny fireplace was a big soot-free patch where the guvnor's portrait had been. A basket of nappies sat on the table next to the bucket. A thin straw mattress stood against the wall.

'How is she?'

'Quiet. Unhappy. Belasco came for her this morning. They're moving the boat back to St Saviour's Dock. Then he's taking her to arrange the funeral. Are you going to keep working on the case?'

I nodded. 'As long as there might be a danger to Suzie.'

'But you won't be paid again.'

'I know.'

She touched my arm and our eyes met. 'You're a good man, Norman.'

I felt my lips tighten. 'Not as good as you think, Ettie.'

Something happened in her tired grey eyes, a tiny flare of something, and I held her gaze as long as I could. When I looked away, she ungripped my arm and let her fingers trail down my coat sleeve, breaking her touch just as her thumb brushed my wrist.

'Norman, do you judge me for having a child?'

'My ma had me out of wedlock. Plenty of women did the same around where I lived, and plenty of people lived as married when they weren't. I don't judge you for that.'

'But you judge me for having relations.'

'I don't like the idea.'

'You think it's a sin.'

'No, Ettie. It's Petleigh. I don't like the idea of you having relations with him.' I cleared my throat. And I don't like how I misunderstood you, I thought. 'Is he supporting the child?'

She stepped over to the little window that looked onto the next building. 'I didn't say it was him.'

'He was courting you before you left. All those gifts he brought. The card evenings.'

'I told you I'm not going to answer your guesses.'

'Are you afraid William'll make trouble?'

'Perhaps. I don't know. I am afraid of trouble, though.'

We stood in the silence for some time.

'How's the baby now?' I asked.

'She's asleep, thank heavens. I'm going to pick up some Godfrey's from the chemist later. That should help. Norman, thank you for not condemning me. Most men would.'

'There are many kinds of men.'

She ran her hands across her hair, tied back tight on her head, parted in the middle. She smiled. 'And many kinds of women.'

We heard the door to the pudding shop open, then footsteps along the corridor. I was sure it was the guvnor, but when I opened the door a little fellow was standing there clutching his cap, his bald head wet with sweat, his moustache ragged over his dark lips. His grey shirt was grubby, the sleeves rolled up to his elbows.

'I got the deceased for you,' he said.

'What's that, mate?'

'The deceased. From the police surgeon.'

I looked back at Ettie.

'You've brought Captain Moon?' she asked.

He spoke to me instead of her. 'He's in the shop. Give me a hand to get him up, will you?'

'But this isn't his house,' said Ettie. 'We've got no space.'

Still the bloke spoke to me. 'I got instructions to bring him here for the viewing. Can't take him back. I can leave him in the shop if you prefer.'

'No, you can't do that.' Ettie looked at me. 'Did William mention this to you, Norman?'

I shook my head. She took a deep breath and had a think. Finally, she said: 'Well, I suppose there's nothing else for it. You'll have to bring him up.'

I followed the bloke down to the pudding shop, where a gurney lay on the floor. Moon's body was covered in a dark green canvas, flies beginning to collect around it. Some kids were standing there, hoping for a glimpse of the body.

'What the bloody hell is this, Norm?' called Mrs Pudding from the other side of the shop. 'Look at the bloody flies!'

'Sorry,' I said. 'We're taking him up.'

'Blooming liberty,' muttered Albert, wrapping up a spotted

dick. 'Bringing a blooming dead 'un in here while we're cooking.'

'Make us all ill, I shouldn't wonder,' said an old woman, taking the pudding.

'And you can take the bloody flies with you and all,' said Mrs Pudding.

The cartman and me lifted the gurney, and I led the way down the narrow corridor, stepping around the sacks of flour and sugar, and through the door to the parlour, where Ettie had cleared the table, all except for the birdcage where the little fellow still sang. On the mantel, not three foot away, sat the orange cat, watching it. We put down the gurney and lifted the body onto the table. It was heavy and rigid, and damp somehow.

'They already done the laying out,' said the bloke as he whipped off the canvas sheet.

There on the table lay Captain Moon, solid and calm, wearing the same black trousers and yellow shirt as when I lifted him from his noose. They'd tied a dark cravat round his neck so as to hide the rope burns, and managed to shove the rigid black tongue back in his gob and sew up his lips. His hair was combed, his whiskers trimmed, but the skin of his face was yellowish and waxy. His eyes stared up at the ceiling, and I wondered if he could hear that little bird from wherever he was. I lowered his eyelids while Ettie found her purse and put a penny on each eye. For a while we just stared at the horror of him. He smelt rancid.

The cartman cleared his throat. He had the gurney in one hand, the cloth under his arm.

'You need anything else?'

'No, thank you,' said Ettie.

Still he didn't move.

'Oh,' she said at last, fishing in her purse for a coin. Only when he had it did he turn to leave.

We were still stood there looking at Moon lying on the dining table when Reverend Hebden appeared in the doorway holding his topper in both hands.

'Good day, Miss Arrowood, Mr Barn—' He stopped as he caught sight of the body. 'Oh . . . I didn't know. This is . . .?'

'Captain Moon,' I told him. 'One of our cases. His daughter's staying here.'

'Oh, dear.' Hebden stepped over and laid his hand on Moon's arm. Shutting his eyes, he whispered a prayer. Then his eyes snapped open, the hand jerked off the dead arm. 'I've only got a few minutes. I just wondered if you'd thought any more about my offer, Ettie?'

The Hog was half full, a few sailors, a party of women, loud and already pickled though it was only just after midday. Old Loyle, the ex-magistrate, stood in a corner, his suit clean and creased, his four Pomeranians at his feet, while the Lascar Hamba polished his knife. Beverley Bright sat on a bench facing the door, her hands on her knees, a pipe in her mouth. Seeing the new barmaid wasn't there, I went behind the counter and down the back corridor to Betts' room.

'Busy!' she yelled when I knocked.

I gave it a minute or two, then knocked again. There was some rummaging inside, then,

'I said busy for fuck's sake! Piss off!'

'It's Norm,' I said through the door. 'You got the guvnor in there?'

A few seconds later, the door opened. Betts stood there wearing a meat porter's apron and nothing else. Her old skin shone with sweat.

'Try the tap room, darling,' she growled. Behind her on the stained bed a naked bloke of half her age stared at me, his hand stroking his privates. 'And tell him to leave my half a crown afore he goes.'

I went back through to the tap room and pushed open the door, hearing vermin scurry away in the darkness. The air in there was cold and dank, a heavy stink of old ale. I found a candle and lit it. Barrels were stacked on shelves on one side; on the other were flagons of gin and wine. The stone floor was wet, the walls green with slime and white with mould. And there he was behind the door, fast asleep on the floor, his head resting on what looked the most filthy mop in London.

'Up!' I said, taking his arm and pulling.

He groaned. He mumbled.

'Get up. It's time to go.' I put my hands under his oxters and pulled him to a sit.

'Let me alone,' he grumbled, his eyes still closed.

I had to turn my head away; even over the stink of stale ale and mould, his breath was enough to make a hangman swoon. His shirt was gone and his tits hung over folds of belly fat, the curly black hairs making his whiteness a horror. I stood on his boots and yanked him up quick. He let out a cry of pain but remained standing, his eyes still closed, his mouth open like he was about to be sick. His hair left a sheen of oil on his forehead, while great purple pockets puffed out beneath his eyes.

I took his arm and pulled him out to the pub, where Hamba

began to applaud. Old Loyle joined in, though we all knew he couldn't see more than a foot or two.

'Betts said to make sure he leaves her half a crown,' said the new barmaid.

I fished in his pocket and found the money. She handed me his shirt and coat. They were wet.

'He fell over in the pisser,' she said. 'I give them a dunk in the bucket.'

'Jesus Christ,' I muttered to myself. I propped him against the counter and grit my teeth as I dressed him in the wet clothes. He was unsteady, and I wanted to tip him over and land my boot in his belly. I often wondered if me rescuing him just made him worse. I often wondered how much longer I could do it.

'Sleep,' he said, his eyes opening a slit. They were yellow, laced with threads of blood, dull with guilt and discomfort.

'Help me, you fool,' I growled as I tried to get his arms through the sleeves. 'We got work to do.'

'I need some chloridine, Norman,' he moaned. 'My heart's beating in my head.'

I poured the chloridine I'd brought down his throat. I got him an ale and poured that down too. They hadn't any bread, so I bought a bit of cheese and made him eat. Then, when he was steady enough to walk, we said our goodbyes and went out to face the day.

I marched him up to Bankside. There we found a coffeehouse where I got him a bowl of porridge. Then another nip of chloridine. A mug of coffee. When we'd finished, his face still looked like fishguts, but at least he'd stopped moaning about his head.

'I had to get out of the house,' he said. 'The baby was down-stairs crying and crying. Ettie hasn't the first idea of how to mother it. I was at the end of my reason. I had to get out.' He looked at me with his guilty pig-eyes. 'Thank you for coming to get me, Norman.'

'I won't rescue you forever, William,' I said, but even as I spoke I didn't know if it was true. Perhaps I would. My future was like a thick, London fog. I had no way to think about it except I had to get up each day, had to keep earning. I felt stuck to him, and I didn't even know if I wanted to get free.

For some time we didn't speak. 'They brought Moon's body from the mortuary,' I said at last. 'He's on your table.'

'What?' he groaned. 'I'll never get to sleep now!'

I laughed.

'I've never liked corpses in the house, Norman.'

'It's better for Suzie. At least she can have a viewing.'

'I know, I know.'

'Did you tell her what Curtis said? About the *Princess Grace*?'

'I want to wait until we've pieced it all together. She's enough to come to terms with at the moment.' He drained his coffee, rubbed his temples. 'I didn't mean to make a night of it. I was just going to see if I could sleep in Betts' room. That's all I intended to do, but then . . . Hamba was there, and, well, he kept buying more brandy . . . and then I began to think about those three bodies. About what to do next. And then, thank the Lord, Dr Wu arrived . . . I had a bit of his special pipe and then, well, you remember how we prepared the facts for our unconscious last night? Well. It was as if a plan just dropped from the heavens. Now, listen carefully, Norman . . .'

Chapter Twenty-Four

I hammered on the door at Archer Street. As it opened, I gave it a great shove, leaving the guvnor to barge inside afore Mr Dunner knew what was happening.

'Here!' he cried. 'What's this?'

'We need another look at the rooms,' said the guvnor, already lumbering toward the stairs. 'It's very important.'

'Get out!' exclaimed the man, his voice crackly and weak. 'You ain't police. You got no right!'

Mrs Dunner stood in her dark doorway just past the stairs. She wore the same tight scarf over head as before. The guvnor paused and looked at the woman.

'We must know who did that to your ear, madam. It's a matter of life and death. If you don't help us you might be charged as an accomplice to murder.'

'The doctor did it, we told you,' said she, looking him up and down, at the hair stuck down on his grimy head, the grit on his damp, stained collar, the purple balloons beneath his eyes. 'Now get out or we'll call for the police.'

'We're working with the police, madam.'

'No, you ain't,' said the man. His feet were bare, his arms thin as straw. 'The police came, said you weren't nothing to do with them. Told us not to talk to you. So you get out now or there'll be trouble.'

'Who came exactly?'

'The two detectives. Just after you.'

'Names!' yelled the guvnor, come over a fury. 'Quick, man. What were their names?'

'I don't remember,' said the bloke. 'But that—'

'One tall, excessively neat, keeps fiddling with his moustache?' the guvnor interrupted. 'The other much younger. Solid build. A countryman?'

'That's them.'

The guvnor collapsed on the stairs with a groan, looking very gloomy, his elbows resting on his knees. 'This is very bad, Mr Barnett.'

'They might have killed them already, sir,' I said.

'Killed?' asked the woman, her eyes wide in alarm. 'Killed who?'

'You didn't tell them anything, did you?' I asked.

''Course we did,' said the man.

'You fools,' whispered the guvnor, shaking his heavy head. 'Tell me, were they wearing uniforms?'

'They was detectives. Plain clothes.'

'Did they have a police carriage?'

'Well, no—'

'Did you ask to see their identification?'

Dunner looked at his wife. 'Did we?'

'Oh, my Lord,' whispered the guvnor, his tangled eyebrows raised in horror. 'I just hope they're not already dead.'

'Who's not already dead?' cried Mrs Dunner.

'Those two are the murderers!' snapped the guvnor, getting to his feet. He was talking urgent now. 'And you've helped them in their crimes. Quick. There might just be time to save the other woman. Let us in Miss Roughley and Miss Carroll's rooms. We must retrieve the carbuncle.'

'The what?' she asked.

'Now!' exploded the guvnor.

She climbed the stairs, the two of us following, her husband limping behind. Her hand shook as she opened the lock. 'We weren't to know,' she said as the door swung open. 'You surely can't blame us for it? We didn't know!'

The guvnor darted over to the little table in the parlour and opened the drawer.

'Where is it?' he cried.

'What?' asked Mrs Dunner.

'The carbuncle! What have you done with it?'

I watched from the doorway, enjoying it all. This was his skill, his genius, the way he worked on folk. This was what made him a good detective.

'I don't know anything about a carbuncle,' she said, a look of fear in her eyes.

'We never heard of a carbuncle,' said the bloke, standing in the hall.

'It was here! It was right here in the drawer! For God's sake, you didn't let those two in here, did you?'

'Well, yes,' said the bloke, 'they searched the place, but—'

'They've got it,' said the guvnor, looking at me. 'Who knows what they'll do now. Oh, my Lord.' He fell to his knees on the rug, clasping his hands in prayer. His eyes rose to the ceiling. 'Please help us, Lord. I pray you forgive these two for what they've done. Please help us get there in time. Save that poor, defenceless woman.'

'You can pray on the way, sir,' I said, helping him up. 'We've got to get to the family. We've got to get to those poor kiddies before they find them.'

The woman stood open-mouthed.

'But we didn't know!' cried the bloke, his whole frame twisted and tight. 'We're not to blame!'

The guvnor strode to the door. 'That's not good enough, sir,' he barked. 'You've aided two murderers. Heaven help you if they strike again.'

'Maybe it was these two as took the carbuncle,' I said in a whisper loud enough for the couple to hear. 'Worth a pretty penny. Maybe they already pawned it, sir.'

Arrowood stopped for a moment at the stairhead. 'You could be right, Barnett. And I wonder what else they've taken.' He turned to the Dunners. 'We must search your rooms.'

'No, sir!' cried Mr Dunner. 'We don't even know what a carbuncle is!'

'It was the murderers!' cried Mrs Dunner. 'They must have took it!'

The guvnor rose his finger and pointed at them. 'We'll be back. You stay here. Do not leave this house until we return. Not even for milk. If we find you've stolen anything you'll be up before the beak. Let's just hope you haven't also been accomplice to a murder.' He began to climb down the stairs with me behind him. The couple came after us, arguing, pleading. Just as we were leaving the house, he turned and spoke quick: 'There's one thing might save them, and that's if we can find the other villain. So tell us who cut your ear off, madam. Do it now and save yourself.'

She hesitated.

'Hurry!'

'But she'll kill us!' wailed the woman.

'We'd never give your name,' snapped the guvnor. 'Who do you think we are?'

'We don't know who you are!' spluttered the bloke. 'That's the thing!'

'I told you. I'm Mr Arrowood. This is Mr Barnett. We're assisting the real Inspector Petleigh.'

Still they couldn't overcome their fear. They looked at each other, but neither could decide.

'We're private agents,' said the guvnor. 'We work with Sherlock Holmes. I've just returned from one of his cases in Coventry.'

'You're working with Mr Holmes?' asked the bloke.

The guvnor nodded.

'I've read all his cases. I don't remember you.'

'I don't enjoy publicity as Mr Holmes does.'

'Well,' said the bloke, looking at his wife, 'I'm sure Sherlock Holmes would keep us safe. He never lets people down.'

'No,' she said real quiet. 'He never does.'

'So tell me,' whispered the guvnor.

'It was Foulpipe Annie,' she said at last, her eyes white with fear. 'But you got to swear you won't tell her it was us said so else she'll have the other one as well. She said she would. Please, sir. I know we done wrong but you must promise not to tell her.'

'I give you my word.' The guvnor took the woman's hand. 'Now, tell me, madam. Why did she do it?'

Her head fell and she gave a deep sigh. Her husband lowered himself and sat on the staircase, its black paint chipped and scuffed.

'She came a fortnight past with a dirty fellow.' Her voice and body were limp, defeated somehow.

'Describe him.'

'Just a fellow, nothing special,' said the bloke. He nodded at me. 'About your height, dark hair, moustache. They wanted to talk to Miss Rachel and Miss Gabriella but they weren't in so they pushed their way into our parlour there.' He nodded at a dark green door by the stairs. 'They was rough, shouting and such. Wanted to know about the new bloke they was seeing.'

'Mr George?' asked the guvnor.

'No,' said the woman. 'They had a new bloke.'

'You're sure they didn't mean Mr George?'

'No,' she answered. 'He'd stopped paying the rent by then. Must have ditched them. They'd been seeing this new one since two month, I'd say. We didn't know his name or anything. Used to pick them up in his carriage. I told her that but she wouldn't have it. Just keep on at me, shouting in my face, "*Give me the name! Give me the name!*" but I didn't know his name.'

'I tried to get them out,' said her husband, his voice a-tremble. 'But the bloke knocked me onto the floor. A fighter he was. Had me in a hold, I couldn't get up.'

'That's when she did it. She held a knife to my throat.'

'A great long foreign one,' added Mr Dunner. 'Curly, it was.'

'Said she'd cut me if I didn't tell her.' Mrs Dunner was getting worked up now, talking faster, her hands gripping each other. 'Thought I was telling her porkies, see, but I weren't. I didn't know. Then she . . .' She made a cutting movement by her head.

'I couldn't get up to stop it,' said her husband. 'He had me on the floor.'

'I never had so much pain. I fought her off but she's like

a wild beast. It wouldn't come off . . .' She stopped, her eyes brimming. She gasped. The guvnor took her shoulder.

'Would you like to sit down, madam?'

She shook him off and stepped away. 'She gave it a yank but it wouldn't . . .'

'You don't need to tell us this,' said the guvnor. 'I can see the pain in you still.'

'I keep dreaming about it,' she said, the tears flowing proper now. She was gasping, choking as she spoke. 'Going th-through it again. I . . . I feel the pain too. Wake in terror, thinking it's happening . . . again. I d-don't like to go to sleep no more. I been through it once, that's enough. Why . . . wh-why do I have to be tortured over . . . and over? Why's that right?' She swallowed, wiped her nose with her hand, clutched her forehead. 'I sit up at night trying not to sleep. I can't bear it, sir. I can't bear it.'

'It's cruelty,' said her husband, standing from his seat on the stairs and taking his wife in his arms. She buried her face in his shoulder. 'It's bad enough to live in a world where people could do such a thing, but what kind of a God would make a person have to go through it again and again, night after night? It don't make sense. She ain't done nothing. Why do the mind work like that? Why make it like that? It don't make no sense.'

'No,' said the guvnor. 'There's no sense to it.'

'You mustn't tell her we told you,' said the husband, looking over his wife's shoulder as he held her to him. 'Promise us that.'

The guvnor nodded. 'I give you my word. Thank you for telling us the truth. We'll do everything we can to bring Foulpipe Annie to justice, but I'm afraid I must ask you a couple more questions. Are you strong enough?'

The bloke nodded.

'Why did she want to know who this new man was?'

'We don't know, sir. She just came out of the blue. She was looking for him, that's all we know.'

'You say you saw him. What did he look like?'

'Only the once. He was bald, a bit of a belly on him. No whiskers. He was wealthy, high-born like.'

'Clothes?'

'A lounge suit, newish. Wore eyeglasses too.'

'Hat?'

'Derby, I think.'

His wife nodded, her back to us, her head still on his shoulder.

'His nose? His mouth?' asked the guvnor.

'Just the usual, sir.'

'And you never heard his name?'

He shook his head. We shut the door and left the Dunners in each other's arms at the bottom of the stairs.

Chapter Twenty-Five

Foulpipe Annie was a ratcatcher, one of the last of those supplying vermin to the ratting pubs in the city, and it was in the sewers she caught them. She'd been in and out of prison all her life on account of the persecution she suffered from the police, who had some kind of prejudice against those who robbed drunks and cut up people for folk who didn't want to do it themselves. Not many'd seen her, but everybody in London'd heard of her. There were all manner of stories about her doings, all manner of warnings. *'Foulpipe Annie'll put you in her rat cage and eat you if you don't shut your face,'* whispered the mother to her beloved kiddies. *'And they'll eat your face too,'* whispered the old grandma, wishing again that she was dead. South London born and bred, she was, and a legend almost as horrible as Jack himself.

We went straight to my brother-in-law Sidney's cab yard in Bermondsey. Sidney liked to help us out on occasion: he got a thrill out of it. Most days he gambled, and that caused a lot of problems between him and his missus. Cock-fighting, bare knuckle, horses – he did it all. If anyone knew where ratting was going on, it'd be him.

Willoughby, the mongol who worked in the stables, ran over to us when we arrived.

'You come for me?' he asked, his smile wide as a scythe. 'We going to the pub today?'

'We need to ask Sidney something, mate,' I told him, pulling out of the hug he'd got me in. The rain had stopped, but the yard was wet and covered in black mud.

'Got a new horse, Mr Arrowood,' he said, taking the guvnor's hand and pulling him. 'Chestnut. Eighteen hands, he is. Good with the four-wheelers. You want to see him?'

'Not just now, my friend,' said the guvnor. 'Did you have that tooth pulled?'

Willoughby opened his mouth to show us – there was a new space in the row of brown stumps.

'Hello, gents,' said Sidney, striding over the cobbles, his bare chest bushy as a privet hedge. He ran his hand through his wavy grey hair. 'Is it him or me you want?'

We shook hands as the guvnor explained what we'd come for.

'There's only three places left do ratting,' he said. 'Cross Keys in Seven Dials and the Blue Anchor on Bunhill Row, both tonight. Then there's the Rainbow in Limehouse tomorrow. I'll come along. Ain't been for a while.'

'I was hoping you would,' said the guvnor. 'We're looking for Foulpipe Annie. D'you think she'll be there?'

His eyes narrowed. 'What d'you want with her?'

'She might have killed those three we pulled out of the river the other day.'

'You need to watch your step with her, Mr Arrowood. She's no good.'

The guvnor clapped him on the back. 'That's why I'm glad

you're coming along. But we'll explain everything tonight. Meet us at the Dials at seven.'

The warm rain started to fall again as we walked back along the Waterloo Road. The guvnor was panting, the sweat soaking through his jacket; his long night was catching up with him. We bought some boiled eggs and told Neddy's ma to send him over when he got back. When we reached Coin Street, Ettie was asleep on a chair next to the body, a half-eaten onion in her hand. The parlour was dark, a muslin cloth hanging over the window, the looking glass turned to the wall. The clock had been stopped.

Moon now lay in his Sunday best in a rough coffin on the table, still and heavy like a slab of putrefying beef. Two candles burned proud on either side. The stitches securing his lips had been torn out so it looked almost like he was smiling. One of the pennies had slipped from his eye, as if he'd twitched somehow, and it balanced on the ridge of his cheek. Flies pecked at his lips and crawled along his britches. I waved them away, but seconds later they were back, drawn like magnets to his silence. On the table next to Moon was the birdcage, and the little blue canary was singing away like a baby angel, only it didn't seem so blue today.

The stink had got worse, so the guvnor sprayed his cologne around the room. It helped a bit, but it didn't cover the sour smell as seemed to clog your nose and throat each time you took a breath. We stood in the little scullery eating our lunch as quiet as we could; it was only when I made the tea Ettie awoke. She seemed confused.

'What time is it?' she asked, straightening her skirt. She

looked at the onion like she didn't know where it had come from.

'Almost three,' I told her.

'Where's . . .' She looked at the window, frowning. There must have been three or four dozen flies drifting in circles in the centre of the room. 'We need fly-paper, William. And food. Is there any money left from the pawnbroker or did you drink it all away last night?'

'I'll get it later,' he grunted as he lit his pipe. 'How long's the Captain staying there?'

'The funeral's at St Giles's burial ground at ten tomorrow. You must brush your suit.'

'I'll have to sleep upstairs with you tonight.'

'No, William. Not with Suzie there.'

'She can sleep down here.'

'With her father's corpse? For goodness' sake, do you want to make her suffer even more?'

'Oh, Ettie. Plenty of people do it. That's right isn't it, Barnett? There's no choice if you've only one room to live in.'

It was true: I'd had my dead ma with me for three days. It was that or the public mortuary, and I wasn't having her there. Wasn't easy, though.

'Don't be cruel,' said Ettie, shaking her head. 'It's only one night. You're not afraid, are you, brother?'

'Of course not,' he muttered. His nose-holes had widened. He glanced at Moon. 'But these flies . . .'

Ettie bit from her onion.

'Get the fly-paper.'

He was looking at the birdcage, a puzzle on his brow. 'Is that canary becoming yellow?'

Ettie snorted. 'It's been dyed, you fool. It was always yellow.'

He chewed his baggy lip, his eyes a little sad. 'Is the child asleep?' he asked at last.

'Suzie's taken her out: I insisted she get some air. She's been up and down all day. It'll be better when we've got tomorrow over with.'

'Is it a pauper's funeral?'

'He'd been paying into a burial club.'

'Well, that's the first bit of luck she's had.' He puffed away for a moment, his thinking face on. 'So he kept up his funeral payments while he was falling behind on the pier fees and the rent. Well . . .' He frowned, then shook his head, rising from the chair. 'No, I cannot think. My mind's over tired. I'm going upstairs to sleep before the baby returns.'

We watched him lumber up the stairs, then the squeak of the floorboards above and the creak of the bed. The canary'd gone quiet, gnawing on a bit of something white in its cage. Through the open window we could hear the next-door hens clucking and a woman shouting somewhere up the street. I poured Ettie some tea, and she had it with the rest of her onion. We sat there in silence, comfortable with each other. Now and then I watched her; as she ate and drank her face softened, her shoulders fell. A gentle smile formed around her eyes.

'How are you, Norman?' she asked.

'Tired,' I said. 'This case is turning out hard, and it's likely to get harder still.'

'Did you tell my brother?'

'I told you I wouldn't,' I said. Maybe it was the heat, but it sounded harsher than I meant it. She looked at me for some time.

'May I ask you something?' she said at last.

'Of course.'

'Are you jealous at all?'

Our eyes met. Her pupils were small and dark. I felt it was a test.

'A bit,' I said. 'Though I've no right to be.'

She leant toward me, taking my hand.

'Then why do you never speak?'

'It's impossible, Ettie. You know that.'

Her sticky hand held my fingers as she looked into my eyes, pondering. Sometimes it felt as she treated things as a puzzle to be solved, as no more than stimulation for her restless mind, and that's what I saw in her face then. She bit her lip and withdrew her hand.

'It does seem so,' she said, lighting the guvnor's pipe which he'd left on the table. 'Now tell me before Suzie gets back with the baby, what happened in Gravesend?'

Gravesend. Already it seemed a long time since then. I told her about Curtis and what he told us about Moon's past. She listened real careful, having a puff now and then, asking questions. I was just about to tell her about Foulpipe Annie when we heard footsteps approaching outside in the corridor.

'They're back,' said Ettie, rising at once to get the door. It was only then I realized she'd been anxious about the baby being away so long.

But it wasn't Suzie. It was a couple of sixty or so, a woman tall as me with slope shoulders and a pale, clear face, a man with a bent back and a yellow wart on his lip. They both wore black.

'Is Suzie here, ma'am?' asked the old fellow. 'We come to see the Captain.'

Ettie brought them in, and they stood by the table for a few moments, examining Moon's still corpse, the man holding his bowler against his chest and nodding on and on as if it confirmed something he knew about life. The woman held a vial of Crown Lavender to her nose as she peered at it.

'Don't he look handsome,' she said at last.

'He always did,' he answered with some more nodding.

'Are you relatives?' asked Ettie.

'I'm Suzie's second cousin,' said the woman. Without being asked, she sat by the table. She pointed at the other chair. 'Sit down, Arthur.'

He sat, just as a little head from outside the window poked itself under the drape. It was a dirty-faced girl, no more than six or seven, her hair tied back in two ponytails. I recognized her as one of the kids that played out in the street.

'We come to pay our respects, sir,' she said.

I lifted the window cloth to have a look at her. She wore a little grey dress and mismatched shoes, and next to her in the dingy side alley stood a boy of maybe five year. Holding his hand was an even littler girl.

'Neddy says you got a dead,' said the tiny thing.

Ettie stepped over.

'Who are you, darling?' she asked softly.

'Pollyann Painter, ma'am,' said the leader, 'and these is my cousins. We come to pay our respects.'

'Did you know him?'

'We live down the road,' she said as if it explained everything.

'Can we see it?' asked the boy. He was a head shorter than the girl, no shoes on his feet.

Ettie looked at me. The tiredness that had of late clouded her eyes had gone, and the sparkle of delight that always warmed me was, at least for now, returned.

'Only for a moment, children,' she said.

One by one, I helped them climb over the sill. They were all too short to see into the coffin, so the older girl pulled the stool over to the table and climbed aboard. When she saw the body her face dropped.

'What is it?' asked the boy, trying to climb up too, though she wouldn't move to let him.

'It's only an old man.' She turned to Ettie. 'Ain't you got any dead children?'

'Why no, my dear,' said Ettie. 'Did you think it was a child?'

'We didn't know,' said the girl. She shoved the little fellow out of the way and climbed down. 'Let's go,' she said to her cousins. 'It's only an old bloke.'

The couple watched them in silence as they marched to the door.

'Sorry on your death, ma'am,' said the girl as they left.

'Sorry on your death, ma'am,' said the little boy with a bow.

The littlest one did a curtsy, and they were gone. Ettie shut the door, still smiling.

I was making the tea in the scullery just off the parlour when there was another knock at the front door. I heard it open, and for a moment there was silence.

Thinking it might be danger, I stepped back into the room and found myself frozen. For there she stood in the doorway, a carpet bag at her feet, her eyes dark and tired.

'Isabel,' said Ettie at last. She stepped forward and embraced her.

Isabel. The guvnor's wife had changed in the year and a half she'd been gone. Her face had filled out a bit, her chin losing its shape, while a few grey strands threaded through the black hair tucked under her bonnet. Last time I saw her was the day afore she walked out on him. A bad day that was. The guvnor in the clink, her cat sold, their cooking pots pawned and only me there to try and explain it to her.

'Ettie,' said Isabel as they embraced. 'It's so good to see you.' Only now did she see Moon's body on the table. A look of fear passed quick over her face and disappeared when she realized it was nobody she knew. 'Who's this?'

'A man who'd hired us for a case,' I said stepping forward.

'Norman,' she said, a smile breaking across her careworn face. She gave me her hand. 'I'm so sorry for what I said last time. I know it wasn't your fault.'

'I've had worse. William's asleep. Shall I wake him?'

'Not just yet.' She looked over at the coffin again. 'Poor man. What's his name?'

'Captain Moon. Owned a paddle steamer. They had nowhere else to put him out for the viewing.'

'Oh, dear.' She turned back to Ettie and smiled. 'How are you, Ettie?'

'Well . . . I suppose there's a lot to tell you, but let's have some tea first, shall we? You must be parched.'

Isabel took Ettie's hand. 'I've got something to tell you myself, but there are a few things in the shop I need to bring through first.' She turned back to me. 'Would you mind helping me, Norman?'

While Ettie set about getting the tea together, I followed Isabel through to the shop, thinking how pleased the guvnor'd be to see her. He'd been waiting, hoping she'd come back ever since the lawyer she'd been living with died at the start of the year. It was what he'd been hoping for more than anything else.

They'd put in some tables and benches in the shop over the last week, something I'd been telling them to do for years, and folk were queuing at the counter. Albert was wrapping pies and handing them over, while Mrs Pudding was taking the money. Their two lads were pulling trays from the ovens, sweat rolling down their bright red faces.

It was a squeeze to get to the front of the shop, where Isabel's luggage stood by the door. Neddy was sitting on her battered old trunk, his arm resting on the handle of a perambulator. And sleeping inside it was a baby.

Chapter Twenty-Six

'Yes, he's mine,' said Isabel, her eyes soft as she looked on the sleeping child. He wore a thin white dress, each hand lying by each ear, the tiny red fingers clenched. 'Leopold, after his father.'

We stood aside to let an old fellow into the shop.

'The lawyer?' I asked.

She nodded.

'I'm sorry about what happened to him.'

'Thank you, Norman.'

I looked at Neddy. 'Give us a hand with this pram, will you?'

We wheeled it through the shop, then lifted it high enough so we could get it over the sacks as lined the corridor. Isabel followed. We put it down again in the parlour, where Ettie stood open-mouthed. Before Isabel had a chance to explain, we went back for the trunk. Just as we were lifting that, Suzie returned with Ettie's child, so we carried the other baby carriage through to the parlour as well, then went back again for the trunk.

'They better give us some biscuits for all this lifting, Neddy,' I said as we reached the door.

'And they better be Peek Freans and all, Mr Barnett.'

The parlour was pretty well packed out now, and we had to move one of the prams to get the trunk in. Isabel, just inside the door, stood peering down at Ettie's child in the rickety old pram, while Ettie peered down at Isabel's in the new. Moon lay dead on the table, where Suzie stood talking to the old couple, their voices low.

'Does William know?' asked Ettie, straightening.

'He's about to find out,' said Isabel. 'Does yours sleep?'

'Not much, least not when she should. And yours?'

'Much the same.'

'I haven't decided on a name yet.'

'There's no hurry, I suppose.'

'Are you back to stay, Isabel?'

'I believe I am, Ettie.' The corners of Isabel's pale eyes crinkled just enough to tell you it wasn't an easy choice. 'I hope you'll stay, though. I don't mean to push you out.'

Ettie smiled. They looked at each other in silence for a moment.

'Are the others coming?' Suzie asked her second cousin.

'They couldn't get off work,' answered the old woman. 'I'm real sorry, love. They wanted to.'

'None of them? Not even Granny Sue?'

'She's abed with her legs again.'

Suzie snorted. 'They was always evil to him.'

'It ain't like that. They never got over your ma, that's all.'

'That weren't his fault.' Suzie winced; her hand went to her belly.

'I know, darling. But we're here. We're here for him.'

Suzie bent over and gave the woman a quick hug. As she did so, a little groan came out her mouth. She stood back up and looked at her old man, his penny eyes, his lips starting to draw back from the teeth, the orange and grey beard all smart and trimmed now. She touched his curled fingers.

'We'll get the boat out this weekend, Dad, don't you worry about that,' she said, then hurried through to the outhouse.

Leopold started to grunt, then screwed his face up like sweetmeat, kicked his legs in the air, and began to howl. Within seconds, the little girl screwed her own little face up, kicked up her legs and joined in too. Ettie and Isabel picked their babies up and jiggled the noisy little buggers, while Neddy clapped his hands over his ears. The couple looked on, no expression on their faces. It was a terrible row, and in the middle of it all lay Captain Moon, silent and serene and stinking like a slaughterhouse ditch. Isabel began to laugh. Ettie smiled, caught her eye, and began to laugh as well.

Over the woeful cries of the infants and the laugh of the two mothers, we heard the guvnor upstairs, the creak of the bed, the squeak of the floorboards.

'Ettie!' came the roar from above. 'I need to sleep!'

Ettie looked at Isabel and winked.

'Ettie!'

His bare feet appeared at the top of the stairs, then his dusty trouser legs. When he saw the scene below he stopped still, a look of astonishment on his face.

'Isabel?'

'Hello, William,' she said, pacing up and down with her unhappy child.

He descended fully, looking from her child to Ettie's.

'That's . . .' he said, his voice weak. 'Is that . . .'

'There, there,' whispered Isabel to her baby. 'Are you hungry again?'

The guvnor caught sight of her trunk.

'Are you . . .' he murmured, wrinkling his great swollen hooter.

'Why don't you feed him upstairs, Isabel?' said Ettie, patting her baby's back. 'I'll join you.'

'Are you back to stay?' the guvnor finally managed to say.

'Yes, William,' said Isabel. 'I am.'

'But the . . .' He pointed at the baby in her arms, unable to say the word.

'His name's Leopold.' She kissed the baby's head, then looked back at the guvnor. 'My son.'

And they were away up the stairs to feed the babies, leaving the guvnor staring after them. He gripped the edge of the table, his face pale. The old couple rose as Suzie returned.

'We'll see you tomorrow, sweetie,' said the woman, squeezing Suzie's hand. She stepped over to the coffin and said a silent prayer. 'Come along, Arthur.'

Suzie took them out, leaving Neddy, the guvnor and me listening to the sounds upstairs. The floorboards, the crying, the squeak of the beds. First one child went silent, then the other, until all that was left was the noise of the next-door hens.

'What did she say, Barnett?' asked the guvnor at last, his face a knot of confusion. He lowered himself to his chair, the cat launching itself from the mantel onto his lap as soon as he was seated.

'The lawyer's the father. She named the baby after him.'

His head seemed to wave. His eyes were fixed on Neddy, who looked uncomfortable with the guvnor's queer gaze. 'What kind of a name's Leopold, anyway? German?'

'I don't know, sir. She didn't say anything else.'

He nodded. With a shaking hand, he picked up his pipe, then put it down again. He cleared his throat. He smoothed his greasy hair over his bald patch.

'Well . . .' he said. 'Well, so she's . . .'

'She's back.'

It was what he'd wanted more than anything this last couple of years. But now he didn't look so sure.

'She's back,' he murmured. He shut his eyes. His belly groaned. He took out his watch and checked it. His voice was low, the strength gone. 'I need to stay here and find out what this is all about. You two can call on Harold at *The Star*. Get him to dig out the reports on the *Princess Grace* inquest. We need a list of the victims. Neddy, you bring it back to me. Barnett, you should have some rest. This might be another long night. I'll meet you at seven in the Cross Keys at Seven Dials.'

I looked at him sat there, his hands twitching in confusion.

'This might be good, William,' I said, putting on my boater. 'But it'll take time. You must be patient.'

He held my eye. He had the look of a man who had lost control of his fate.

Harold was out on a story when we reached *The Star*'s offices in Fleet Street. I scribbled a note and gave it to Neddy, telling him to wait and to take the list back to Coin Street soon as he had it. Then I walked home alone across Blackfriars Bridge, hungry and tired. My room was hot and empty. I opened the window, then went down to the privy to empty the chamber pot and jars Lilly'd collected. As I put them back under the bed, I found the knife she'd used on me back in the furthest corner where I'd kicked it. It wasn't a bad one, long-bladed like one of them they use at Billingsgate to gut herring. That was the only thing she'd forgotten to take. I put it in my pocket, picked up the shirt she'd used to staunch my wound and my last blanket, and went down to the pawnshop on Borough High Street. With fourpence warm in my hand, I got a pot of eel bits from the mute woman on the corner, then stopped in the pub for a mug of porter. When my belly was full, I went back to my room to get a few hours' kip.

Sidney was already at the Cross Keys when I arrived that evening, a mug of gin and water in his hand, a pile of cockleshells on the table afore him. The pub was packed out with men and dogs. The windows were boarded over, the only light coming from the open door. I got us drinks and was just sitting when the guvnor tipped up. He didn't look any more rested than he had when I'd left him.

'Neddy brought the list,' he said, lowering himself to the bench with a groan. He passed me a bit of paper.

'What did Isabel say?' I asked before opening it.

He nodded, taking a few moments before replying. 'The lawyer's family made her leave his house. That's why she's back. You know she owns our rooms, don't you?'

'I know.'

'Well, that's why she's back.'

'She still wants a divorce?'

'I didn't ask, Norman. I couldn't bear to. I told her how happy I was to see her, but there was no happiness in her face. She says she's forgiven me, but we cannot be again what we were before my . . .' he paused, swallowed, 'my difficulty. I hope that'll change when she sees I'm back on my feet. She'll remember how she felt.' He smiled at me, at Sidney. 'How we used to get on.'

I could tell by the look on his face that he wasn't as convinced as his words suggested. He'd put her through a lot, and I wasn't sure he'd changed as much as he thought. Much as I'd always liked Isabel, I was worried she wanted those rooms back for herself.

'Now, have a look at that list,' he said.

The paper had the names of all those killed in the houseboat disaster. Two on the *Princess Grace*, the steam launch Moon was driving, the rest on the houseboat *Marigold*. I looked down the names.

PRINCESS GRACE
Major Julian Klyberg
Catherine Pilkington

MARIGOLD
Henry Hurley
Catherine Donovan
John Harris
Johannes Schenke (child)
Catherine McGann (child)
Clara Harris (child)
Samuel Lipsky (child)
Jennifer Annaline (child)

The landlord opened a door at the back leading to a staircase. The noise in the pub grew as folk began to stand.

'Fourteen children were killed,' said the guvnor. 'Fourteen skulls.' He finished my drink as I read on.

Florence Gleeson (child)
Marie Courvoisier (child)
Lawrence Glyde (child)

Edward George (child)
Sophia van Essen (child)
Oliver Gilliver (child)
Lawrence Gold (child)
John Stokes (child)
David Du Pont (child)

I passed it to Sidney, and as he read I swallowed down his gin. I was shaken. A ghostly voice from long ago had whispered in my ear, a voice I wished I could forget. As I rolled a smoke, I couldn't stop my fingers trembling.

'Edward George,' whispered the guvnor, glancing around least anyone was listening. 'What are the odds that's the son of Chelsea George?'

'Maybe it's time to tell Petleigh,' I said.

'Maybe it is,' he said slowly. 'But will he solve the case, Barnett? I doubt it. That man couldn't solve a cup of tea.'

The last few men were rising from their benches and climbing the stairs. Dogs were sniffing the air, straining at their ropes to get up where the rats were.

I took the list from Sidney and looked again at the name there I recognized: Clara Harris. It couldn't be the same one. No family could have that much ill fortune.

'Come along, Norm,' said Sidney, slapping me on the back.

I folded the paper and followed them up the stairs. The landlord, a tiny fellow with curly orange hair, stood at the top, watching each person who passed through. In the middle of the room was a wooden pen about waist height. The windows were boarded shut like below, two oil lamps lighting the space. Stacked against the back wall were cages crawling with rats.

The dogs were excited, their owners holding them back while the punters milled about. An older woman sat alone in a chair by the pen's gate. She wore no head-covering, her long grey hair loose down her back, her chin soft with half a beard.

'We're looking for Foulpipe Annie, sir,' said the guvnor, pointing at the woman. 'Is that her?'

The landlord laughed, loud and booming, a laugh that didn't seem should come from such a tiny frame. 'Foulpipe Annie, you say?' he cried between his guffaws. 'That's the wife!'

'I do apologize, sir,' said the guvnor. 'I've never seen Foulpipe Annie.'

'Don't apologize!' cried the little fellow, his eyes bright. 'You made my day. That's the best thing I heard all year!'

'D'you know where we can find her?'

'No idea, mate. But she might still supply the Blue Anchor.'

It was too far to walk before closing, so we took a tram. Foulpipe Annie didn't supply their rats either and the landlady didn't know where we could find her. A wasted night. In the darkness we walked back over the river, both of us deep in our own thoughts. Clara Harris. That name had shook me, I tell you. It took me back to a place I wanted to forget.

Chapter Twenty-Seven

The money from the burial club was enough to pay for the coffin, nameplate and plot, but that was it. Sidney brought over the landau from his cab-yard, hitched up to two whitish nags, old dears with hairy, heavy legs and slack eyes. Both were due to be sent to the knacker's yard themselves next week, though they didn't seem troubled by it. The old couple from Southend were back, him in a brown suit and black tie, she in an old black dress and grey bonnet. Belasco's wife was there too, and their two kiddies, each with a black ribbon tied round their neck. Ettie and Isabel had their babies knotted into shawls tied across their chests, there being no room for the prams in the carriage.

I nailed the lid of the coffin over poor old Moon, sending him into darkness for the last time. The casket was short and heavy, and we felt his body slide about as we carried it through the pudding shop to the carriage. It made me remember my old Mrs B, and how I only managed a few steps before I couldn't bear the feel of her dead weight moving around in the box on my shoulder. I ducked away that day, my last and most shameful betrayal, leaving Sidney and the others to carry her out to the hole in the ground where she's lain ever since. A bad year, that'd been; it was only our work and the kindness of Ettie and the guvnor as got me through.

We got the landau's hood down and lowered in the coffin.

There wasn't enough room to lay it flat, so it was propped half upright, sticking up over the top of the rear bench.

'You any closer to knowing who did it?' asked Belasco. His hair, normally standing up on his head, was oiled and combed down flat, though already it was trying to rise again. His wife was next to him, his kids sitting on the kerb.

'We know Polgreen did some of the early damage, but I'm convinced he wasn't behind the corpses or the fire,' said the guvnor. 'Tell me, d'you know about a lady friend of the Captain's called Feathers? We found letters from her in his home.'

He shook his head. 'Maybe it was before my time.'

'You don't know of any lady friends?'

'I never saw any sign of that.'

As we waited for Suzie to come out, life went slowly on. Flies annoyed the old horses who twitched and blinked and flicked their hair; customers drifted in and out of the pudding shop; a milk cart stopped to collect an urn.

At last, the women appeared, the old couple following behind. Suzie went to Belasco, wiped a tear from his cheek and hugged him quick. She climbed aboard and sat next to the coffin, Ettie squeezing in next to her. When she was settled, Suzie put her arm around the baby, rested her head on Ettie's shoulder, and shut her eyes. Ettie kissed her forehead.

I helped the old couple onto the bench opposite, while Isabel climbed up to the box next to Sidney. He whipped on the horses and they began to walk, the rest of us following behind. Along the way people stopped talking to watch us pass, men doffed their caps, women bit their lips. We walked as far as Elephant and Castle, where we waited for a tram while the landau went on ahead. When we arrived at the burial ground on Forest Hill

Road, the coffin was already on the floor at the far end. The others stood with the parson, a young fellow from Bermondsey. Next to the coffin was a hole and a pile of dirt, a tarp weighted down with bricks covering it. A hundred yards away, under a rowan tree, stood Curtis, his head bowed, his hands clasped on his belt. The sun was blazing but the wind had picked up and was gusting, whipping around the women's skirts.

The guvnor went to stand by Isabel as we waited for the parson to begin. I don't know if it was the dusty wind or something else, but her eyes were moist, and she kept blinking and dabbing at them as if to stop herself weeping at the funeral of a man she'd never met. He laid his hand on her shoulder and murmured something. She twisted her body away, and I watched as he clenched his sad hand and let it fall to his side. When he spoke again, she looked down at her child, stroking his back, sad but not wanting to show it, vexed by her husband's presence, and I could see from the disappointment on his face that he knew it. Finally, he put his hands behind his back and turned his attention to the coffin.

It was a sad affair. All of us felt for Suzie, who stood clutching Ettie's arm the whole way through as the wind raged around them. Her bonnet was tied tight on her head, her face down. Fifteen, I thought over and over, wondering what life would hold for her now. Service, perhaps. A life in service, her spirit tamed.

The parson said a few words about Moon, a few prayers, a psalm. For man walketh in a vain shadow and so on. The coffin was lowered. Suzie sprinkled some dirt. Then it was over.

As we stood by the grave waiting for Suzie to look up, a coach with two fine black horses turned into the burial ground. Its body was dark green, its wheels crimson. It stopped outside the chapel, side on to us, and the curtain moved back slightly. Moments later, the coachman gee-ed on the horses and it began to move back down the drive.

The guvnor stepped over and took my arm. 'It could be those two who were watching the bodies come up,' he hissed. 'Get after them!'

I set off over the grass, but, seeing me coming, the driver whipped on the horses to a trot. I had no hope of catching them, and the carriage turned onto the road before I was halfway there. Shaking my head, I walked back between the graves to join the others. Some minutes later, Ettie led Suzie away.

As we made our way back to the landau, Suzie left the path, marching through the gravestones to where Curtis still stood under the rowan tree. The guvnor and I followed.

'Are you Mr Curtis?' she asked with a sniff.

'Yes.' He looked like he hadn't slept for days. His eyes were sunk in deep grey sockets, his nose was red, the skin broken. He'd shaved but was cut all over his neck and chin. 'And you're Suzie. He was so very proud of you.'

She nodded.

The guvnor caught my eye, a puzzled look on his face.

'Your father was a good man,' Curtis went on, his body stiff and upright. 'How are—'

'Didn't you never want to meet me?' interrupted Suzie, her words starting angry but ending unsure.

Curtis shifted on his feet. He wore a dark suit, a black scarf tucked into his collar. A teardrop appeared in the corner of one eye.

'Always,' he whispered, then hastily wiped away the tear. A quiet sob shook his body.

Suzie looked steady at him, comfortable watching a man cry.

'You was his only friend.'

Curtis took her hand.

'And he was m—' He stopped, looking helplessly at her. 'He was mine.'

Suzie stiffened and her eyes darkened. Then, just as quick, her shoulders fell and sadness returned to her face. She pulled away from him, picked up her skirts, and marched back to the carriage.

Curtis watched her go, his face a confusion of words unspoken, things not done.

'Is it true you've never met?' asked the guvnor, examining him carefully through his eyeglasses.

'Solly always made her look after the boat when they come to Gravesend.' His voice was soft and tired. 'It was because I was from the life he'd left behind. I wanted to meet her, but he was stubborn as a mule. Listen, Mr Arrowood, I want you to find who was after him. I can pay.'

The guvnor breathed in slow and rocked back and forth. He tapped his boot with his new stick. 'We can, Mr Curtis, but you know they can't be prosecuted for his death? He killed himself.'

'They killed those other three, though.'

The guvnor poked me on the arm and pulled out his pipe, stepping away to the other side of the tree.

'It's twenty shillings a day, sir,' I said. 'Plus expenses. We'd need three days in advance.' I looked back to check the others weren't watching us. It didn't seem right to ask for payment at a funeral.

'I only got five shillings,' he murmured. 'I can get you the rest tomorrow. You can trust me.'

'Mind you do, sir. We can't waste time coming to find you.'

As he was pulling the money out of his purse, he paused.

'You have done this sort of thing before?'

'Of course,' said the guvnor from the other side of the tree. He was digging at the ground with his stick, flicking stones and clods of turf over a crumbling headstone laid flat on the earth.

'We're the best in London,' I said, taking the money and stuffing it in my pocket.

'Give over, mate. Everyone knows Sherlock Holmes is the best. I'm only asking if you can catch them.'

'There are no certainties in crime,' said Arrowood, clutching his bowler to his head against the wind. 'But we're the best chance you've got, sir. And frankly, Mr Holmes isn't as good as they say he is. He has a chronicler, that's all. When you read the cases you notice mistakes. Much of his success is luck.'

'I don't give a damn about Sherlock Holmes,' snapped Curtis, turning away so as not to see the gravedigger, who'd started shovelling the dirt back into the grave. 'Tell me what you found about Solly so far.'

The guvnor went through all we'd learnt about the two dead women, Chelsea George and Foulpipe Annie. He got out the list of victims of the *Princess Grace* disaster, but Curtis didn't recognize any of the names.

'We need to discover if Chelsea George is related to the dead child on the list, and if Foulpipe Annie's been working for him,' said the guvnor.

'You done more than I realized,' he said, a new respect in his eyes. 'Why don't you take it all to the police?'

'Inspector Petleigh's in charge of the case. He works more slowly than a dray horse, and we're worried they'll come after Suzie. These villains need to be caught, and quick.'

'Why would they come after Suzie?'

'If we're right and this is about revenge for the death of a child, then killing Moon's daughter might be the final act.'

'What good would that do them? Solly's not around to suffer any more.'

'Revenge isn't just about making the victim suffer, Mr Curtis. It's about equalizing things in the person's mind. It started with the death of those children, and the death of another might be the only thing that'll finish it. Tell me, did Suzie really know nothing of the *Princess Grace* disaster?'

'He hid it from her.'

'So she doesn't even know her real name?'

'They worried she'd tell someone and then it'd all come out again.'

'Did her mother's family also hide it from her?'

'Her mum made them promise not to let on. Suzie was to be told eventually, when they was sure it was safe.'

The women were back in the carriage now, the old couple sitting where the coffin had been. Sidney was walking toward us.

'One more question, sir,' said Arrowood. 'We found some letters in his home from a woman called Feathers. A sweetheart. Can you tell us where we can find her?'

Curtis shook his head.

'But you knew of her?'

'Solly was full of secrets.'

'I got to get on,' said Sidney. 'The landau's booked for later.'

Curtis held out his hand. 'I'll get the money to you tomorrow, but you must promise to tell me soon as you find out anything new. Anything at all. Agreed?'

We watched as he hurried away across the windy burial ground.

Chapter Twenty-Eight

We met Sidney in Limehouse at seven. The Rainbow was in Medland Street, just behind Regent's Canal Dock. It seemed at first no more than a single room with a small hatch in the back wall. A couple of old women sat on stools, mugs of gin in their hands, while four thin dogs lay on the sticky, ash-strewn floor, looking up at us without lifting their chins. We could hear the noise of more dogs below. Through a narrow door and down some dodgy steps we reached the basement. It was dark, full of sound and movement. The smell of mould and smoke soaked whatever little air there was, and on top of it was a tinge of peppermint. Around the dripping walls hung dim paraffin lamps and stuffed dogs' heads mounted on painted boards.

A crowd stood pressed against the low pen in the middle of the room, watching the bout within. Over their shouts could be heard the snarling and growling, the terrified cries of the rats, the crunch of bones and the scurrying feet. We moved closer, until we saw inside the pen. There, surrounded by a squirming, shrieking cloud of brown rats, stood a frenzied bull terrier, shaking its stone head and crunching down on the bones of two rodents clenched in its bloody jaw. In an instant, it tossed aside the dead ones and leapt forward, catching another in its jaw, holding it down with its feet and tearing off the poor soul's head. Without stopping for breath, it plunged into another pile of vermin in the corner who were trying to climb out of the pen. The crowd brayed and gurned: men, women, young and old, Cockneys, Jews, Irish, Africans, Welsh, Chinamen, toffs in toppers, navvies in torn cloth caps, the whole bloody lot of them screaming at the dog.

'Good Christ,' muttered the guvnor.

'You ain't seen it afore?' asked Sidney.

Arrowood shook his head. He was staring at the fight, twitching with each act of savagery, grunting with each crunch of bone and tear of cartilage. He couldn't seem to take his eyes off it: I looked around the crowd, trying to spot Foulpipe Annie, but it was no use. The place was dark and crowded and it seemed every other woman in there could have cut off a bloke's ear.

Suddenly the bout was over. The owner pulled the dog out by its neck as a bloke in a spotted shirt counted the dead rats. A boy of seven or eight years with hands and legs encased in leather jumped into the ring and threw the corpses into a bucket, kicking away any live ones as got in his way. The floor of the pit was painted white, smeared with blood and rat shit, hair and gobs of torn flesh. The guvnor took it all in, his brow knit in concentration. A wild thrill lit up his eyes. Though he was afraid of it, violence sometimes touched something in him I could not understand.

The boy gathered the ones lying on the floor but still twitching. He brought them to a little table by the door and laid them out in a circle. The fat bloke took out his watch and watched them for a minute or two.

'Thirty-three!' he announced at last.

A few punters went over to a thin fellow in checked kicksies and took their winnings. A bald bloke brought over the next dog, a white and brown fox terrier on a leather strap. The crowd moved around it, poking its legs, examining its teeth, then formed a line by the bookie, who took their money and wrote their bets in a little book, a fat cigar stuck to his lips. Sidney had a look and put down a few bob.

'You having a punt, Norm?' he asked me.

I shook my head.

'How about you, Mr Arrowood?'

As the guvnor was about to answer, a strong girl came around with two heavy jugs of beer, filling mugs and collecting coins.

'Is Annie in tonight, miss?' he asked.

'Over there,' she said, nodding at the other side of the room where the rat cages were piled high against the wall.

Through the crowd we saw her. Foulpipe Annie. She was crouched on the floor, her leather-bound fist inside a cage, doing something to the vermin within. Though the cellar was packed out, people had left a space around her, like they didn't want to catch something. Her hair was long and thin, with two curls on each side of her face. She wore a man's canvas shirt, its sleeves rolled up to her elbows, and thick leather britches. Her shoulders were broad, her neck thick as a bull. She closed the cage and stood. Spread across her face was a wide, flat nose. Her eyes were tiny, shaded by her low, bony brow.

I watched her, stunned. It was like seeing Queen Victoria or Hercules or somesuch. By the time I'd got myself going again the guvnor was already over there with Sidney behind. He said something to her as I pushed through a little cabal of warty Germans.

'What is it you want?' she answered. Her teeth were short

and stubby and brown, each with an inch gap before the next one. Her voice was a surprise: light and soft, gentle somehow.

'Just some information, madam,' the guvnor was saying. 'About a fellow you killed.'

Her face didn't change.

'What makes you think I killed a fellow?'

'He was found by London Bridge, tied to a boat. You cut his ear off.'

'I did, did I?' She put a finger on one of her nose-holes and blew a gobbet of snot out the other. It landed in the pit. 'And who may you be?'

'Rats, Annie!' barked a dirty woman across the pen.

Annie took a couple of cages from the pile and tipped them into the pen. The rats fell in a squirming mass, then found their feet and ran around the edge of the arena, scrabbling at the wooden barrier. She went back and opened another cage, pulling out more of the beasts and dropping them in the other side. She stood and watched them, her hands gripping the wall.

'Kelpie!' announced the dirty woman.

The bald bloke picked up his fox terrier and held him over the pen. The rats formed towers in three corners of the arena, climbing over each other to escape. Pools of piss were seeping out from the piles of rats, easing towards the middle of the white floor. The fat bloke pulled out a watch and called: 'Three, two, one, begin!'

The dog was dropped into the pit and at once sprung into a pile of the terrified vermin. Shouts arose all around us. The pit seemed to boil: the white floor was a blur of movement as the dog tore into the creatures, crushing their necks and dropping them to the side. Some of the braver rats fought back, attaching to its legs with their teeth. One jumped at its eye and held on, the dog yelping, shaking its head. Again, the guvnor was hypnotized: his wet mouth hung open, his bulging eyes shot back and forth as the dog darted this way and that. He jerked and ducked as it plunged its snout into them, as it severed their spines and tore off their heads.

Foulpipe Annie beckoned us over. I pulled the guvnor away from the killing and we walked round the back of the crowd to where she stood alone by the pit, the press of folk preferring to watch four or five deep than stand next to her.

'I just want the name,' said the guvnor.

She straightened up to face him. 'And what else d'you want to know?'

'Who paid you?'

Annie scratched her tit and sniffed. She was a head taller than him, just short of me, and you got a feeling that whatever you did she'd stay on her feet. She squeezed her little eyes even smaller and peered at his face. 'What's that you got?'

'Erysipelas,' he said. A roar went up around the pen as the dog did something they liked.

'Catchy?' she asked, her wide, snot-clogged nose opening a bit.

'Only from cats.'

As he spoke, she laid her hands on his chest and gave him a great shove. He toppled backwards with a cry, tipping over the low barrier and landing on the floor of the pen. The punters cheered. The rats scattered. The terrier forgot its job for a moment and stood amazed, two shaking rats hanging from its bloody jaw. The guvnor scrambled up, but the white floor was slick with blood and piss. His knee shot from under him and he fell on his belly again. Half the rats were in piles in the corners, climbing on each other, leaping at the walls. The others were holding their ground, hissing, squealing. Everything was wet. As the guvnor tried to sweep them away, one shot forward, sinking its teeth into his ear. He shrieked, raising his hand to its hanging body, while two more went for him, one biting into his hand, the other his neck. Me and Sidney stretched over the barrier, trying to get hold of him, but he was just out of reach.

The dog started to bark furiously. Then it pounced, its front paws trapping a huge black rat. In a second it had torn the creature's body open then, without pausing, it clamped the rat's head between its jaws and began to shake it, sending the rat's body and tail lashing from side to side. At the same moment, the guvnor slipped again, crashing on his side to the floor and bellowing out in pain. The dog shook its head more wildly now, the rat's innards loosening, beginning to detach from the body cavity and flying around the pen, showering everything with blood and meat and tube and yellow bile, spraying the guvnor's face, and falling into his open mouth.

The crowd laughed, they cheered, they roared him on. The guvnor's eyes looked like they'd burst from his head: he couldn't seem to spit the stuff out. He was choking, ramming his fingers between his lips, while the dog's owner began to beat him on the back with a stick. I climbed over the wall, my boots in a pool of vermin, and hauled the guvnor up just as he managed to cough the bloody rat's guts out his gob. He retched, his feet slipping on the mush as he did so, pulling me across the pen. Feeling my boot crush something, I yanked the rat off his ear. The guvnor howled, and at the same moment the owner's stick landed on me. Sidney darted over to the bloke, wrenched the stick from his hand and swung it down hard on his bald, sweaty head, where it made a hollow thud. The bloke broke into an odd smile the moment it hit him, then cried out in pain.

I helped the guvnor out the ring as the mayhem continued. When we were finally safe and putting up with the backslaps and jokes of the punters at the ring-side, I looked around for Foulpipe Annie.

She was gone.

Sidney was gone too. The guvnor was pale, his hands a-tremble. I took him by the arm and led him out of the basement and into the street. He walked slow, like every step was his last.

'It's over, William,' I said. 'All done now.'

He nodded, then pulled his arm from me and puked over his boots.

'Oi!' called a bloke from down the road. There were no streetlights and the moon was buried in a thick bed of cloud, but we could see he was scurrying toward us. When he got close I recognized him. He was the twitchy bloke who used to sell matches outside a pub called the Barrel of Beef, a pub we had a lot to do with a while back. He had St Vitus' Dance, they said, and couldn't control his limbs proper so that they'd jerk and twist and kick out without warning. A bad affliction to have on the streets of London, and he had the scars and broken bones to prove it.

He came to a stop before us.

'You were asking about a man she'd killed, the w-w – one in the river,' he said, trying to catch his breath. His suit was finely tailored but hadn't seen a washtub for years. His hair was long and black, his face so pale it almost shone in the night-time street. He looked back up the alley: there was nobody else there.

'You know anything about that?' I asked when it was clear the guvnor was still out of sorts.

'Ten b-b-bob for the name.'

'A shilling.'

He sighed.

'Five b—'

'A shilling,' I said again.

His shoulder gave a sudden jerk. He held his arm down with his other hand. 'Put it in my pocket.'

I took out the guvnor's purse and put one of Curtis's coins in the bloke's jacket pocket.

'Emile Butterga-ga-grass. Buttuttergrass. Mother's butter! S-sorry.'

'Emile Buttergrass?'

'Yeah.' His shoulder jerked up again; he wrestled his arm down with this hand, his face a painful contortion.

'Who paid her to do it?'

'Th-that's all I know. Just overheard some blokes in the crowd. People think I can't hear. S-stupid. And no, they aren't in there. They left. N-n-never seen them before. D-don't tell her I said.'

'Trust us,' I said.

'I do. I watched you on the crim, the crim, on the, the C-C-Cream job.'

He looked at Arrowood, maybe expecting him to say something. But what a mess the guvnor was: wet and stinking, bites on his hands, his ear bloody, puke on his shoes, the knees of his britches saggy and dark. Strands of greasy hair fell over his forehead, his bald patch smeared with blood and filth. But it was worse: it was like something inside him had snapped.

'Thank you, sir,' he whispered, holding out his hand. But the bloke was still trying to control one arm with the other. He nodded and was gone, slipping away down a side alley.

Sidney's cab was still there, so I helped the guvnor up and waited in the street, hoping Sidney'd gone to the pisser and not got himself into trouble with Foulpipe Annie or her friends. He was back five minutes later.

'Where've you been?' I asked, relieved to see he was all right.

He passed me a bit of paper. 'I followed her. Think that's where she lives. It's just round the corner.'

I clapped him on the back. 'You might have just made all this worthwhile, mate,' I said.

He gave me the wink and climbed up to the box.

The guvnor didn't talk all the way back to Coin Street; I was worried that his nerves had gone, so we made sure he was back in his rooms and wasn't going to drink away his misery in the Hog. There was nobody in the parlour. I made his bed for him on the floor and helped him out of his jacket.

'New boots?' I noticed as I pulled them off. He said nothing. I brought a bucket and cloth from the scullery and gave him a wash, then put him to bed.

'Thank you, Norman,' he said, his head on the pillow, his eyes dark and troubled.

'You go to sleep, William. I'll call for you tomorrow.'

I was about to blow out the candle when one of the babies started to cry in the room above. There was movement on the floorboards, and moments later the other baby began to cry too.

I looked at Sidney, who shook his head.

'Lord help me,' whispered the guvnor.

We shut the door and fled.

Chapter Twenty-Nine

I called for him at ten next morning. His face was droopy, his eyes rimmed red, the scars on his ear and neck dabbed with Elliman's Universal. He was wearing his other suit, the yellow one, and his other shirt too. The babies lay in two boxes on the table.

'They've gone to the apothecary,' he said, his voice a little brighter than when I'd left him the night before. 'Left me with the little devils.'

I was relieved to see him up with a mug of tea in his hand. Twice before his nerves had gone, once after the Betsy case and the other when Isabel left him, and each time it took him weeks to get back on his feet. The way he was last night reminded me of those times, and that scared me more than anything. Like his old man who lived out his last years in an asylum, Arrowood had a problem with his emotions, and he walked a line that none of us could control. It had always been part of my job to keep him on the right side of that line, to pull him back, to stop him hurting himself more. Most of the time I could do it, but there was some darkness I couldn't fight, and I always had a sense of something trying to draw him down into the bog, a faint whistle from the lantern man, or his father.

'Any pain?' I asked, handing him the newspaper. I picked

up the vial of laudanum as stood on the floor by his chair. It was empty.

'Just the usual.' He quickly turned the pages, looking for news of Petleigh's investigation. There was nothing. 'Ettie had me wash my mouth with peppermint oil. I think my blooming gout's coming back.' He was silent for a few moments. 'Isabel plans to become a doctor,' he said eventually.

'A doctor? But how?'

'My wife has always had a workmanlike approach to the body. Hers and mine.'

I shuddered, thinking of his phlegms and gases, his monstrous gouty feet, his rashes and piles, each one of his imperfections revealed in gasps and groans as he lumbered through the lady London.

He frowned. 'There's a scholarship to create more women doctors. She's put in her papers.'

'How is it between you?'

'Oh, Norman. I've wanted her back so long, but she's come at the very worst time. We seem like strangers, and I've no time to get reacquainted with her, not until this case is over. There's no intimacy, not with my sister's great feet lodged under the table.' He worried about this in silence for some moments. 'Oscar Wilde said women love us for our defects. D'you think it's true?'

'I don't know, William.'

'I'm thinking of getting new teeth. D'you think that'd help?'

'I don't know.'

'I caught her weeping after the funeral. She said she'd been overwhelmed at the graveside thinking that Leopold would never meet his father, but I can't help wondering if it's because of returning here. She won't accept even the slightest comfort from me. At the moment it seems she'd rather live with Ettie.'

'It must go hard on you.'

'I don't blame her. This damn case is consuming me. I've no time to make it right.' He sighed. 'The baby's exhausting her, of course.'

'How is he?'

He gazed at little Leopold asleep in his box. A smile crept over his chops.

'Last month I was childless. Now I seem to have two. But, my goodness, can this one cry. I think that's the lawyer in him. Thank goodness I never met the fellow; I'd hate to see that hound's face in this little devil.'

'Have you a plan, William?' I asked, looking at Ettie's baby, wondering if I could see Petleigh's face there. 'This case doesn't seem to be solving itself.'

'Well, thanks to Sidney we've got Annie's address. We'll go this evening. If she's out, we'll get in and have a look for evidence. Something that links her to Chelsea George or the victims.'

It was then I noticed the empty birdcage sat on the floor in the corner. He saw me looking and sighed. 'The cat. And I only had him out for a few minutes.'

There was a hammering at the door. I rose to answer, but before I even took a step, it burst open and in marched Inspector Girkin with two constables behind him. He blinked like he wasn't expecting to see me, then an ugly smile came over his face.

'Norman Barnett,' he said in his yokel voice. 'I come to arrest you. Hold out your hands.'

The two constables stepped past him, one of them holding a pair of irons.

'What for?' I asked, backing into the room.

'Murder.'

'Murder?' barked the guvnor, getting to his feet. 'What are you talking about, man?'

The bigger copper grabbed my arm. I tried to pull away but the other belted me hard on the thigh with his truncheon. My legs buckled, and, as I fell, they got both my arms together behind my back and the wrist-irons on me.

'He hasn't murdered anybody!' cried the guvnor. 'Let him go!'

Girkin was stooping over, looking into my face. He smelt of liver. 'Who be the fool now, Barnett? Maybe you thought as I were a new detective you'd have some fun, eh? Well, you ain't having fun now, are you? Won't be much fun when you hang by your neck, I don't think.'

'It wasn't him, inspector,' insisted the guvnor as they hauled me to my feet.

'You be wrong there, Mr Arrowood,' said Girkin, a weasely smile under his thin moustache. 'He murdered those two ladies we pulled out the river and we got all the evidence to put him on the gallows. Question be, were you in on it too?'

'You haven't any evidence, you blithering oaf!' spluttered the guvnor. 'Where's Petleigh, for pity's sake? He'll set you straight.'

'We got plenty of evidence, don't you bother about that.'

'What evidence?' demanded the guvnor.

Girkin shook his head. 'All in good time, sir.'

'Oh, where's Petleigh?' said the guvnor again with a wave of his hand. 'You don't know what you're doing.'

'Inspector Petleigh's back with Southwark Police now. This be my case.'

'He left you alone? But you're not trained!'

Girkin's smile turned to a frown. 'You watch how you talk to me else I'll bring you in too.'

'I never murdered anyone, Inspector,' I said, trying to cool things down. 'You got to believe me. What evidence are you on about?'

Girkin opened his mouth to speak then hesitated, looking at the guvnor's wild face. He turned and walked out the door.

'Bring him to the van, constables,' he said over his shoulder.

They wouldn't answer any of my questions on the way to Old Jewry. There they measured me and emptied my pockets, while Girkin filled in the charge sheet. They had me strip, then wrote another form, noting my hair (brown and black), my eyes (blue), my scars (left thigh, lower back, right shoulder, neck), and lastly my tattoo (a heart for Mrs B).

I was thrown in a cell with three other miserable blokes who sat on a bench that ran around the walls. I lowered myself into a corner and shut my eyes. It didn't make any sense. How could they have any evidence? The only thing as tied me to the women's deaths was me being on the boat the night they were put in the water. It wasn't enough for a trial. Girkin couldn't be that ignorant. They must have something else. But what the hell could it be?

After some time I stood. I needed a bloody smoke, but they'd taken my baccy off me. I went to the door. There, a barred hole looked out at the cell door across the way. Framed in its own little window was a grey-bearded African face. The bloke gave me the nod.

We lingered there in silence for a couple of hours, until two other coppers led us upstairs, through the police office to the court waiting room. I was assigned a constable and there we sat as one prisoner after another was taken in.

No talk was permitted in that gloomy room, and in the silence we could just hear what was going on in the court next door. A copper presented the evidence, a witness or two was called, the prisoner was allowed to say something, and it was over. They were minor crimes, each taking no more than five minutes: theft of a loaf and two apples – four days' hard labour; throwing a soldier's boots in the river – ten bob fine and a pair of new boots; using obscene language on the highway – fourteen days without hard labour. It went on. Finally, the constable took me through.

The guvnor leapt up when he saw me.

'Norman!' He tried to take my arm, but the copper pushed him away. 'Have they told you anything?'

'Nothing. Did you find Petleigh?'

'I've left him messages all over,' he said, following us down the front.

The usher blocked his way. 'Sit down, sir. No more talking to the prisoner.'

'They've no case, Norman,' he called after me as the constable led me to the dock.

The magistrate sat on the bench at the front, under the royal arms. He was a hunched old fellow, a yellowed wig over his pink head, not anyone I recognized from my days working in the central criminal courts. A few reporters sat on the other side of the room. An old woman slumped on a bench at the back, her chin on her breast, asleep maybe. A younger woman was next to her with a boy about ten year old. At the end of their bench was a lawyer, a copy of the *Daily News* open in his lap.

The main doors opened and Girkin appeared. The guvnor rose to speak to him, but the copper shook him off and went to sit with a constable on the other side. He'd smartened himself up: his Sunday best, his trousers pressed, his collar starched. Over lunch he'd had a proper shave and his hair was cut and oiled so he didn't look so rabbity. He didn't so much as glance at me.

The magistrate peered through his thick eyeglasses at his ledger, his face screwed up. Finally, he raised a finger.

'Norman Barnett, sir,' said the clerk.

'Proceed with the charges,' said the magistrate, his voice like a cat in a bottle.

Girkin rose and opened his notebook. 'Murder of Miss Gabriella Roughley and Miss Rachel Carroll on or around July third.'

A cold silence fell over the court room, and I found myself breathing quick and short: I was being charged with murder.

'How do you plead, Mr Barnett?' asked the old fellow.

'Not guilty, sir. I never did it. I never even met them.'

The magistrate scribbled away; the clerk scribbled away.

'What's the evidence, Inspector?' asked the old bloke, looking up.

'Them bodies were found on the morning of July fourth tied to a boat off London Bridge, your honour. Boat called the *Gravesend Queen*.' Girkin's eyes were fixed on his notebook. His voice trembled. 'They weren't there at six the night afore.

That's when Mr Barnett took charge of the boat. He was on it all night, nobody else come aboard. He was the only one could have put them there.'

'Hold on—' I started to say.

'Silence!' ordered the magistrate. 'Continue, Inspector.'

'When owners arrived next morning, they found them two ladies and a gentleman in the water, tied by a rope to the gunwale. We don't know who the man be. There be a witness saw Mr Barnett with both the women the evening before.'

'What!' cried the guvnor, jumping up. 'What witness?'

'Sit down, sir!' said the magistrate. 'If you speak again you'll be removed.'

The guvnor lowered himself onto his bench.

I felt sick. I looked around the court, trying to make sense of it.

'And the witness will testify, inspector?' asked the magistrate.

'Yes, sir.'

'But I never even met them!' I said.

'Other evidence?' asked the magistrate.

Girkin turned the page of his notebook. I looked back at the guvnor, helpless. A terrible cloud was swallowing me. Only now did Girkin look at me. He was starting to enjoy it.

'We searched Mr Barnett's rooms just this afternoon. Found hidden under the mattress Miss Roughley's locket. We knew it be hers as there's her initials inscribed on it.'

'No!' I cried. 'You never found a locket in my room!'

'You'll get your chance to argue the evidence at the Old Bailey, Mr Barnett,' snapped the magistrate. 'For now be silent.'

'But someone must have put it there, sir. It wasn't me.' I

gasped as the constable prodded me hard in the ribs with his truncheon.

'Has the locket been identified?' asked the magistrate.

'Yes, sir. Mrs Dunner, the lady's rent collector, she knows it. And some of the women who go to a dancing place they used to go to. Nell Gwynn's, Greek Street.'

The magistrate scribbled in his ledger. He raised his heavy head.

'Do you understand the evidence, Mr Barnett?'

'None of it's true, your honour.'

'You will stand trial at the Old Bailey at the next available date. Given the seriousness of the charges I am persuaded that you present a sufficient threat to the public that I should remand you in custody. Take him down.'

He banged his gavel.

The constable led me out in a daze, tripping and stumbling over the floor, my feet like they weren't mine somehow. The guvnor tried to speak to me but they held him back. I was dizzy; all my strength, my fight, had gone. They walked me through the waiting room to a tiny, dark cell. An hour later they marched me out to the street where a Black Maria was waiting. They were taking me to Newgate Prison.

Chapter Thirty

They photographed and measured me, then led me into a hot, wet room. There I bathed in a great lead tub with four other men, two of them with skin so filthy and scabby a haze seemed to grow around them as they stripped off their clothes. The water was brown like mutton stew, and on its surface a carbolic scum specked with lice and fleas formed a queasy, sloshing blanket. Thus purified we were marched naked down the corridor to be inspected by the medical officer.

My cell was seven or eight foot wide, twelve or thirteen long, a grey asphalt floor, the whitewashed walls mouldy and flaking, marked with years and smears of human filth. The smell in there was unholy; I retched into the blocked toilet pan soon as the door slammed shut.

'Charming,' said the mangy wretch who lay on a plank board fixed to the wall. He wore no shirt. A raw, weeping burn ran up one arm to his neck and down, across his chest. The skin was gone, the flesh yellow, pink. Black. I could see from his twisted face he was in pain; in his mouth he clenched the handle of a wooden spoon. He held a blanket between his thighs, his britches rolled up to his knees. One of his legs was stripped of its skin, a film of yellowish pus spread over it.

'Fuck off,' I told him. The cell was made for one person. One hard board for sleeping, one stool, one small table. A couple of shelves with a scrubbing brush, a mug, a bowl. A bible. A high, barred window looked onto the block opposite. Fixed to the wall above a copper basin was a tap with a pipe leading to the toilet. I turned it on to wash away my puke.

Nothing came out.

'Don't work,' said the bloke. He rubbed at a gash across his forehead, scratched his wild, grizzled beard. There were only two types of prisoner in Newgate: those awaiting trial and those awaiting the gallows. Like me, he was still in his own clothes, so I guessed he hadn't been tried yet.

The bog was clogged with excrement, upon which five or six flies went about their business. As I looked around, the studded iron door opened and the warder hurled in a blanket, a wooden mug, a bowl and spoon.

'The tap don't work,' I said, pointing at the bog.

'So?' grunted the warder. He was Welsh, about my age, sweating in a thick blue uniform, a wooden club in his mutton hand. His moustache was thick as oakum.

'I need to send a message,' I said.

'They'll give you a lawyer.'

'When?'

'You'll get one, don't worry.'

'I need to send a message right away.'

'Watch out for him,' he said, pointing at my cell mate with his club. 'He's a molly.' And he slammed that heavy door so hard it felt as my head had been struck by a hammer.

'They do that every time,' said my cell mate, taking the spoon from between his lips.

'A molly, are you?'

'Now *you* can fuck off.'

'Look, it don't matter to me.'

He winced and bit down hard on the spoon. The pain passed after a few moments and he looked at me again with tired, red eyes. He nodded and took the spoon out his mouth.

'Dan's the name.'

'Norman. You in pain, Dan?'

'I'm burnt pretty bad.'

'Sorry to hear it.'

He shrugged, putting the spoon handle back in his mouth.

'Tell me, mate, how do I get a message out?'

'Ask your lawyer,' he mumbled, shutting his eyes and turning back to the wall. 'They'll get you one today or tomorrow.'

I didn't feel like talking either. The dread lay heavy in my heart. I knew from the years I worked in the law courts that Girkin's evidence was enough to convict me before a jury. And it had to be Lilly who'd put that locket in my room. She'd taken me for a mug, the thieving little cow. And to think I was warming to her. Whoever was behind the murders was setting me up, and Lilly must have been in it from the start.

I stared at my hands, listening to a distant drip somewhere behind the walls. My mind was wild and troubled, and it kept returning to that name on the list of those killed in the *Princess Grace* disaster: Clara Harris. Before I started working in the law courts I'd done a lot of things I was ashamed of, and I'd hid them all from Arrowood. I'd tried for years to leave the man I was behind, but Eustace Harris, Clara's old man, was what I was really grown from. Eustace Harris was the germ in my heart, the stone in my soul. Maybe now I was being paid back for what I did, but to us lads of the court, anyone with a weakness was game. I never told the guvnor; in spite of his sympathies for the wretched of this cruel city, he was a man of his own class. There were times I thought he'd understand if I told him; though he often lost control of his emotions, he knew his flaws and was loyal to the bone. But he was a man of many sides, and other times I saw that he was a prisoner of his own past just as I was a prisoner of mine. I never quite trusted him to understand what it does to a person to live the way I lived. Survival was everything on Jacob's Island. Shame, remorse, anything that made you weak was the same as giving up, and giving up was no choice at all.

'What are you in for, Dan?' I asked, not wanting to know his story but needing to escape my thoughts. My eyes fell on the hideous burns that covered him.

He turned to me. 'Fire-setting.' His face contorted; he bit down on his spoon again, agony colouring his eyes. Soon it passed and he breathed long and slow. 'Someone died, so, well . . . Trial's tomorrow. You?'

'Murder.'

He didn't react, just watched me like he'd given up. Someone was shouting curses in a cell down the landing. We heard a door unlocked, a beating, the guards growling. The door locked again. The dripping.

'How long you been here?' I asked.

'Four day.' The spoon handle was gnawed down to two rough prongs, and drool coated his orange whiskers. 'Keep your voice down, will you? You'll get a beating if they hear you.'

I rolled up my blanket and sat on it by the great black door. In the cells all around were men waiting to be put to death. You could feel it in the air. It was too thin to fill your lungs up proper somehow, and I felt short of breath. Panic rose in me.

I needed to do something. I stood and stretched my muscles. I thought about ramming my head against the wall, punching the door. I thought about screaming. I sat back down on the floor and held my head in my hands.

I couldn't eat the hard bread and soup when it came, couldn't swallow the cold tinful of tea. Dan didn't try to speak to me again for the rest of the day, but he chewed away on the spoon, moaning from time to time, his body spasming from the livid burns covering half his body. When night fell and the cell went dim, I rolled myself in the blanket and fell asleep on the floor, dreaming of rutting with my poor old missus, with Ettie, with the chandler's wife, waking, sleeping again, dreaming of sitting on a horse, waking, dreaming of nothing.

Next morning, as I lay on the hard asphalt staring up at the mouldy ceiling, the guard opened the door. In stepped Inspector Petleigh and the guvnor.

'Norman,' he said, helping me to my feet. He hugged me tight. 'How are you? How is it?'

'Get me out of here.'

'Shall I stay, sir?' asked the warder.

'No need,' said Petleigh, opening his snuff box and having a toot. 'We'll ring when we're ready to leave.'

The warder shut the door, softly this time.

'What the hell have you been up to?' asked Petleigh, turning to me.

'What have I been up to? It's you as put me here! You know I didn't do this.'

'It wasn't Petleigh,' said the guvnor, pulling a packet of food from his pocket. 'He's been moved back to Southwark. And if it wasn't for him I wouldn't have got in to see you at all.'

'Girkin put the case together,' said Petleigh. 'I didn't know about any of this evidence.'

Arrowood unwrapped the packet: cold beef and potatoes. I shook my head.

'Take it.'

'I can't eat.'

'I'll have it,' said my cell mate, sitting up. Arrowood handed it over.

'I went to see Girkin yesterday, as soon as William told me,' said Petleigh, sitting on the little stool. He was observing Dan eat the grub, his arms crossed tight over his spotless tan coat. 'The evidence is in order. They have two witnesses. Mrs Dunner says a man who looked like you picked up the two women from their rooms the evening before they were discovered in the river.'

'I was on the boat!' I cried.

'She's lying, Norman,' said the guvnor.

'And Lord Selby saw you leave Nell Gwynn's with the women later that night,' continued Petleigh.

'But I've never been in there!' I said. 'And I've never heard of Lord Selby. How can he know who I am?'

'He identified you to Girkin,' said Petleigh.

'But how?'

'I don't know. He pointed you out somewhere. Perhaps Girkin took him to the pier. I have to tell you Girkin's not going to let this go. It's his first murder case and he's an ambitious fellow. He's got something against you; you shouldn't have insulted him.' Petleigh paused for a moment. 'Tell us how that locket got in your room, Norman.'

He was avoiding my eye, and I realized then that he wasn't as sure of my innocence as the guvnor. I looked at him, so prim, so careful in the way he carried himself. If I didn't hate him for the way he'd treated Ettie, I hated him now.

The door opened again.

'Time to go, molly,' said the gaoler. Dan shoved the last spud into his mouth and stood. He held out his arms, groaning as the gaoler locked his wrists.

'Hope I don't see you again, Norm,' he said as he stepped out the cell.

'Hope you get justice, Dan.'

'Please don't say that, mate.'

The door shut quietly; the key turned. The three of us remained.

'Lilly,' I said. 'I met her in a gin palace the other day. Had a do with her. She stayed in my room for a few nights. Left yesterday. Stole a few things as a thank you.'

'You never told me about her,' said the guvnor.

'She'd nowhere else to go, she said. The lying bitch.'

'But how would she have got the locket?' asked Petleigh.

'I don't know, but she's in on it, that's for sure. She put it there.'

'Chelsea George is the father of the boy who died in the *Princess Grace* disaster, Norman,' said the guvnor. 'Petleigh's men have confirmed it.'

'And you should have damn well told me days ago,' said Petleigh, flattening his oily moustache with a finger. 'If this has nothing to do with you, then look at all the extra work you've caused!'

'*If* this has nothing to do with him?' cried the guvnor. '*If*? You know Norman didn't do it, Petleigh! They're setting him up because he was alone on the boat that night.'

'The two of you are fools. I told you to stop working on this case. Now look what you've blundered into! They could hang you, damn it!'

I knew it, but hearing it said like that knocked the wind out of me. I shook my head, trying to catch my breath. The guvnor took my arm, put his hand on my back.

'Norman, we'll get you out.'

'I talked to Scotland Yard,' Petleigh went on. 'Chelsea George is well known to them. He owns pubs and doss-houses all around Soho and St Giles. Cabs as well. He's involved in a gambling circuit they've been trying to crack for years. They suspect it's behind some beatings and a couple of deaths, but they haven't been able to get the evidence. No one will speak, even the victims. An Irish chap called MacNamara is his right-hand man.'

'Probably the doorman,' said the guvnor. 'Chelsea George must be behind it all. He was getting revenge on Captain Moon, tormenting him with those fourteen children's skulls so he'd know his real identity had been discovered. He was also paying the dead women's rent, and I'll bet he was the gentleman that Monkey saw laughing when the bodies were pulled out of the water. It's got to be him, and Foulpipe Annie and whoever else he has working for him.'

I nodded. It had to be Chelsea George, but somehow I couldn't stop thinking about that other name on the list of dead children: Clara Harris. But it couldn't be the same one. There must be thousands with that name in London.

'What is it, Norman?' asked the guvnor, eyeing me curiously.

I shut my eyes. 'Nothing.'

'What is it? Do you know something else?'

I shook my head. No. It had to be Chelsea George.

'We don't have much time, Norman,' said Petleigh, placing his hand on my shoulder. It was the first time he'd ever touched me. 'The trial could be within a week. The evidence is bad for you. Very bad. You could hang. If you know anything else you must tell us now.'

'No, inspector,' I said at last. 'I'm not thinking straight.'

'Right,' said Petleigh. 'Now where can we find this Lilly?'

I shook my head. 'She'll be long gone.'

'Her last name?'

'I don't know. She's about five five, dark hair, cut shortish. Strange eyes, blue and green and sort of black round the edge. Cracked lips. London accent with a bit of Scottish behind it.'

'Where does she live?' asked Petleigh as the both of them wrote in their notebooks.

'She said she's got no home. I met her in the gin shop in Falcon Court.'

Petleigh glanced at the guvnor and nodded. He turned and pulled the gong for the guard.

Some hours later, Dan returned. He was pale, his shoulders down. I didn't need to ask what had happened: his head was shaved, his beard gone. His burnt and ragged clothes were no more; instead, he was wearing the thick grey uniform of the condemned. He sat on the board, his arms resting on his knees, his head hanging down.

It was a noisy evening – a bloke in the cell next door wept for about an hour, his sobs deep and long like a table being dragged across the floor. Gongs were rung. Guards yelled and slammed doors. Someone sang a hymn. But from our cell no noise came. Dan barely moved. I gave him his tea and bread when it arrived. He drank the tea in one, then sat with the bread in one hand, his chewed-up spoon in the other, staring at the floor.

'I'm sorry, mate,' I said at last.

He nodded, put the spoon handle between his teeth, then turned on his side facing the wall. The bread had fallen to the floor. His breathing was slow, like his body had moved to a different clock. Then suddenly he spasmed and I heard him begin to chew the spoon handle again, manically, like he was possessed somehow. Like his life depended on it.

I sat on the floor trying to imagine my way out of there, but Dan's suffering was overpowering. It filled the cell until I could feel nothing else. What was he thinking? Was he thinking? If it was me I'd hope I could shut it all down, all the chatter, the sense of becoming nothing more than a body they did something to, a meal for their great, overbearing power. It was only a shame your heart didn't explode just thinking about it.

In the cell that night, I knew Arrowood's idea that emotions can be contagious was true. Dan's despair drifted through the air and filled me, his mute anger, his sorrow for himself. I didn't want to know who died in his fire, why he lit it, what happened, but I felt sad for him, the pure sadness of a man's death.

Dark fell and slowly the noise of Newgate faded. Poor old Dan still chewed away at the wooden spoon. I lay down on the hard floor, wrapped in the blanket, clutching myself. I turned again and again but found no comfort. It seemed like hours, but at last I felt myself drift off, grateful to escape the thick horror of our little cell.

The noise of guards clattering the doors with their clubs woke me. For seconds I felt the peace that sleep had brought, then, seeing the mouldy white wall at my side, remembered why I was there. The stench filled my nose, scraped down my throat. The slow drip still dripped. I shut my eyes again, trying to get back to sleep, to claim just a few more moments of peace, but a terrible battering at the door awoke me again.

'Up and about,' shouted the gaoler through the hatch in the door. 'Washroom in five minutes.'

I sat upright. My blanket was soaked. The floor was wet: I'd been sleeping in a slick of dark blood. I looked over at Dan lying on his back on the platform. His face was white as bone. His mouth was open, blood smeared all around his lips, his eyes gazing at the ceiling. One corner of his blanket hung off the platform, dripping onto to the floor. His arm lay at his side, the wrist gouged and torn and chewed. And jammed in the wound, levered under a clutch of open veins, was the splintered handle of his wooden spoon.

Chapter Thirty-One

I realized straight away what he'd done. He hadn't just been chewing the spoon handle to help him cope with the pain, he'd been making it into a tool with two rough spikes. As I lay asleep last night, he'd opened his wrist somehow, chewed it with his teeth, gouged it with the prongs, levered the veins out and worked at them until the blood began to flow. I turned away, squeezing shut my eyes. I couldn't bear to imagine his suffering. I had to get him out. A sudden bone-shaking shudder wrenched my body.

I leapt to my feet and pulled the gong over and over, until eventually the guard opened the peep hole. Moments later the door opened.

'He killed himself,' I said.

It was a different guard to the day before. He looked fifty or so, with long arms, his face brown and sweaty. Behind him was a young fellow with a hare lip. They stayed outside, holding clubs before them like I might pounce. After a quick look at Dan's body they shut the door, locked it again. I heard them unlock the next cell and take the prisoner to the washroom. Five minutes later they came back and let out the next one. And the next one. On it went, down the landing as I stood pressed against the wall, staring at poor Dan.

Food was now being delivered to the cells. One by one the

traps were opened, the porridge doled out, the tins of tea. Then mine opened.

'They going to take away this body, mate?' I asked the prisoner on food duty. The hatch was about chest height, and I had to stoop to see out.

His brown eyes appeared. 'Oh, Lord,' he said. 'Poor bloke.'

'I told them already but they just left him there.'

'I'll ask them, but he's a molly, ain't he?'

'What's that got to do with it?'

'Don't get curly with me, mate. That's how screws on this wing treat them. This is the only cell with no mattress, you know? Now, you want your grub?'

'Just the tea.'

He passed me a can of piss-warm tea and took another look at Dan. Then he shut the hatch and moved on.

I drank it standing, staring at the black door. Through the high, barred window the sun crept in; the heat was building. I thought of the many famous souls had passed through that accursed prison: Captain Kidd and William Penn, Casanova and Moll Cutpurse, Amelia Dyer, the Tichborne Claimant, Daniel Defoe. It was only last year Oscar Wilde was here. I wondered if they treated him as bad as old Dan. Maybe not; he was a toff, after all. I heard the cells open and close on the landing below, the murmurs of the prisoners, the sharp voices of the screws. Old Dan smelt bad already, the blood curdling, the shit in his blanket starting to lure more flies through the little ventilation holes as didn't seem to let in any air. I wouldn't look at him again. I kept my eyes up, at the door, the window. I brushed a fly from my lips.

After maybe an hour, I heard steps pounding up the stairs.

The key went in the lock, the door squealed open. I stepped aside, my back against the wall. The young fellow from before charged in, his club raised, and struck me on the side of the head. I cried out, just as the older bloke shunted me in the belly, making me double up, gasping for breath as their clubs rained on my back. I wanted to fall to the floor, but knew it'd be worse if I did that, so I covered my head, wrapping my fingers in my hair and pulling tight so I could feel a different pain, my own pain, a tiny strength somehow as each blow landed. Through it, I began to hear prisoners around the block cursing the warders, banging on the doors, the noise rising over the grunts of the screws and the thud of the clubs on my flesh. I was trapped inside a wild storm of pain and shock, juddered with each crack, no use blocking my tears as I fought to breathe and suffered even as I did. And then it was over. They left in silence just as they'd arrived, slamming the door shut with such force it was like a final explosion echoing in my battered head.

Only then did I fall to the floor. The other prisoners were quiet, like I was dead. Minutes passed, hours. I drifted in and out of consciousness, of pain. I thought I heard Dan whispering 'Mate' next to me. I felt the guvnor's hand on my back. I smelt the food coming again, heard my trap open.

'You all right, cocko?' said the prisoner on food duty. 'Want lunch?'

I moaned.

Other footsteps, doors crashing. More fights. The food came again as evening fell. My trap opened. I didn't look up, not caring if it was real or a dream.

'For now I am happy,' came a gruff voice. 'Not because you were made sorry, but because your sorrow leads to repentance.'

'I do repent,' I whispered.

'Then God will forgive your sins.'

As darkness fell I pushed myself upright. I had a blinding headache, my back felt raw and burnt, my hands were swollen, bruised, cut. The only place that didn't hurt was my face. My left side was damp where I'd lain in Dan's fluid. And there he was, there he still was, silent, flies crawling over his lips, in his mouth, burrowing into his nose-holes, licking his eyes. I realized they were everywhere – at my hands, hovering over the slick floor, drifting in circles above us.

I crawled over and pulled his cold, stiff corpse from the platform onto the floor, each movement I made like another blow. He landed rigid, heavy. Uncomplaining. He was thinner, his skin sunken, the bones of his neck and skull standing out. I wrenched the blanket from under him and wiped the board he'd been sleeping on, getting as much of the blood and filth off as I could. Then I wrapped him tight in the putrid shroud and pushed him underneath. I laid out my blanket on top of the board. It was my bed now.

Sleep came in short waves, followed by longer times when I was only aware of pain. I couldn't find a position that didn't hurt, and all night the flies buzzed. I wrapped my head in my blanket to stop them landing on my face, but the stink and damp of it was worse somehow. At last the cell became light, and sometime later I heard the screw banging doors, shouting, 'Washroom!' They missed me out, but soon after a prisoner came with the food. When he opened the hatch a cloud of flies escaped.

'Buggers!' he cried. It was the same voice who'd told me to repent the night before. He peered in, his eyes bright and old.

I got up, made myself eat the porridge, brushing the flies from the bowl, my spoon, my face. I had a raging thirst. I drank the tea down in one. He passed me another tin.

'When are they going to take the body?' I asked him. It sounded like someone else's voice; I coughed, trying to shift the bit of coal I was sure was lodged in my throat.

'Couldn't tell you, brother.' His accent was mixed, half-common London, half-rising in class, just the same as me. There were many of us around town, brought out of poverty by Irish priests and varsity parsons, Jewish schools and campaigning women, or raised by sex and crime. Whatever our route, we always knew each other, knew the secret codes and manners that made up our hybrid class.

As he took back the tin he grasped my hand through the hatch. His were bony and freckled, the nails split and brown. In a whisper, he added: 'Pray to God to bestow his grace and mercy upon you whilst you live.'

'Have a heart, mate.' I pulled my hand away, wondering what this holy man had done to get into Newgate. 'I haven't even been convicted yet.'

He shut the trap.

I lay in that buzzing hell all morning, my body a blur of pain. Outside, I could hear the corridors being swept. Later the doors were opened one by one and the prisoners taken out for chapel. Only the guards talked, and then only to deliver orders. The lunch duty never stopped at my door this time. I watched the shadow move across the room as afternoon passed. A crow landed on the ledge outside the high window and looked in. There was movement everywhere, little blurs of black, little whispers in my ear. For the first time that day my breath came short again, my heart raced. I slowly stood, pain running up my back, my stomach cramping. I rang the gong.

'Dead man!' I cried. 'Dead man!'

I banged the door, my back pulsing with pain. I cried out again.

I couldn't hear anybody coming, so I rang the gong over and over. Soon other prisoners joined in, banging their doors, crying for the guard, and somehow we ended up banging in rhythm, chanting in one voice, *Dead man. Dead man.*

At last, I heard footsteps coming up the iron stairs. They reached my landing and approached. The door was unlocked and two prisoners stepped in with a gurney. The Welsh screw from my first day there stood behind them in the corridor, with the young lad next to him. There was so much space outside on the landing, so much empty space. My heart seemed to open and hope flooded in, though all the cell doors were locked, the landings, stairs, the ground floor below empty.

'It isn't right you leaving him like that,' I said.

'Tell the governor,' said the Welsh bloke. 'Maybe we'll tell him you stuck that spoon in his arm.'

The prisoners loaded poor old Dan onto the gurney, wrapped still in his filthy blanket. Flies followed them out, scattering into the great central atrium of the prison block, while I picked up my blanket and waved out as many of the others as I could.

Another prisoner stepped in with a huge tin pail and tipped the water onto the floor.

'Thanks, mate,' I said. 'Can you empty the bog?'

The door slammed shut, the key turned in the lock, the hope fled from my heart. For the first time in that hellish gaol, I was alone.

Chapter Thirty-Two

Time moved fast and slow. I listened to the sounds of boots, the slamming of doors, a poor wretch protesting as he was dragged to the dark cells. I stood on the stool, looking out the high window at the clouds assemble and empty themselves over the prison yard. As it rained I felt the first comfort I'd had since arriving in that place of filth and despair. The food came again, but this time the prisoner said nothing. I drank the tea down, never happier for anything in my life. I killed many flies, examining their crushed bodies, their ooze between my fingers. After dark, I lay down on the board, my body still tender, my hands swollen and bruised. My thoughts raced. I had to get out of there. The guvnor'd never solve the case alone, and if he didn't track down the killers they'd hang me. For hours I tried to think how I could escape, but I was no Jack Shepherd. As dawn began to creep through the window, I finally drifted into a half-sleep.

I was awoke by the warder hammering on my door with his club. The key went in the lock and there he was, the Welsh bloke, and behind him the young fellow.

'Solicitor's room,' he said, taking off his idiot cap and wiping his blotchy brow.

A groan came out my mouth as I sat up: my back was giving me hell. I limped between them, out of the cell and into the bright light from the high glass ceiling, along the landing, past door after door, all the same black iron. We climbed down the stairs to the ground floor, then through more corridors, more iron doors, up some stairs and along a bridge over the exercise yard. Below were about twenty prisoners, some in ordinary clothes, some in grey prison uniform. The condemned. They walked in a circle, about three foot from each other, in silence. Then through another locked door into another corridor filled with the smells of the kitchen. Halfway along, the wall turned into glass panelling looking into a room. When I saw who it was in there my legs went weak, and I had to hold myself up on the window frame so as to keep walking. It was Ettie, dressed smart in the black skirt and jacket she wore to church, her hair brushed and put away under her most respectable bonnet. Behind her was a solicitor, a black suit and high collar. His face was half covered with a bloody handkerchief he held against his cheek. The perambulator stood next to him.

The warders let me inside.

'You've one hour,' said the Welsh bloke, then locked us in. He took a seat in the corridor on the other side of the glass while the young fellow disappeared back to the cell block.

For moments we said nothing. As Ettie stepped toward me I edged back, shaking my head, remembering the filth my shirt and britches were soaked in.

'No,' she said. 'Stay where you are.' She put herself in front of me, so my body hid her from the warder on the other side of the window. I needed to put my arms round her, but, seeing me about to move, she shook her head. A wretched emptiness in me cried out. I wanted to squeeze her body tight to mine, to pull her inside me, to fill myself with something else, something that wasn't me.

'You poor dear,' she whispered. 'Now listen, Norman. Do exactly what we tell you.'

Still hidden from the warder, she drew something from her mouth, turned, and passed it to the solicitor stood behind her.

'Sidney!' I whispered, only realizing when he took the cloth from his face it was my brother-in-law. He was dressed in lawyer's clothes: a black tail coat, a high collar, a silk topper. His silver hair was dyed brownish and he'd shaved off his whiskers, leaving just a moustache and a week's worth of stubble. Just like I wore it. There was fear in his eyes. Ettie moved away from me. She picked up her baby from the perambulator and began to scream.

The warder jumped up from his seat in the corridor and stared through the window. Ettie raced to the door, banging on it wildly.

'Open up!' she cried. 'The baby's dying! Quick, warder! The baby's dying!'

The warder fumbled with his keys.

'Hurry!' she shouted as he opened the door. 'She swallowed a pin. She's going blue! Help us, sir! The doctor! The doctor!'

'Yes, miss,' said the warder, standing aside as she ran out. 'In the medical wing.'

The warder locked the door behind them, and we watched as they hurried away down the corridor.

Without a word, Sidney made a quick movement across my face. I felt a scratch, then a sharp pain. He'd slashed me with a blade.

'Quick, get your clothes off,' he said, putting the blade in his pocket and undressing.

Moments later we'd exchanged clothes. I saw then that though his cheek was wet with blood there was no wound. He wiped it clean and handed me the bloody handkerchief.

'Hold it to your cheek. Make sure you cover half your face. And pray they don't realize.'

The blood was dripping from my cheek onto the white shirt I'd just put on. I staunched it with the hankie while Sidney took a bit of coal from the pocket of the jacket and rubbed it on his own face, smudging it with the sleeve of my checked shirt that he was now wearing. He did the same with his neck, his arms, his hands. He rubbed the coal all over his hair then scruffed it up so it rose in tufts and curls. Just like mine.

'But how will you get out?' I asked.

'Arrowood's thought about all that. They'll tell you later.'

The coal went back in the lawyer's jacket which I now wore, and he pulled out a flask of hair oil and a comb. He rubbed the oil into my hair and combed it flat with a side parting. Then from another pocket he drew out a wet rag and washed my face, my neck, my hands. Another came out and he did it again. Finally, he plopped the topper on my bonce.

'Now, quick. Turn your back to the window. When they get back, you say I've fallen asleep.'

He pulled out a chair and sat on it with his back to the corridor window, then slumped over on the table, his head buried in his arms. It was smart. From the back you could never tell it wasn't me.

I stood with my back to the window. Moments later Ettie and the warder ran along the corridor. The door unlocked.

'We have to get to the hospital,' said Ettie, her voice choking. At a pace, she put the baby in the perambulator and hurried back to the door. 'I wouldn't trust that doctor with my cat.'

'I'll accompany you,' I said in my best lawyer's voice. I didn't turn to face them. 'This bloody ape's gone to sleep. Curse him for wasting my time. He can swing.'

With the handkerchief to my face and bowing my head, I followed her out the door. The warder locked it with Sidney slumped inside and we ran along two more corridors, through three more iron doors. By the visitors' entrance I noticed my hand was still dirty; I thrust it in Sidney's jacket pocket, jabbing my finger on the little blade he'd put there. I jerked my hand out in surprise, realizing when it was too late that the blade had come out stuck to me. It fell, tinkling on the floor.

The warder turned, his eyes sweeping the ground. The tiny thing, a jeweller's knife or something, lay by his boot. He grunted as he bent to collect it. Ettie caught my eye. If we didn't have the pram we could have made a dash for it to the street. But there was no way.

He held the blade up to the light and examined it. Then he looked me in the eye. 'What did you say your name was, sir?' he asked.

Ettie gave the tiniest shake of her head.

'I'll come back tomorrow,' I said. 'I just hope he's more able to communicate.'

'Yes, sir.' He looked again at the blade. 'What did you say your name was?'

'Oh, you found it!' exclaimed Ettie, taking the blade and stepping between him and me. 'Thank the Lord she didn't swallow it. I was so worried. But you know how women can be. A hint of danger and the instinct just comes flooding out and heaven help you if you get in the way. I suppose your wife's the same.'

'Happen she is, ma'am.'

'You're a hero finding it. Imagine what they would have done to the dear child trying to get it out of her. But where was it?'

'It just fell, ma'am. Must have been stuck to one of you. It ain't a pin though is it?'

Ettie hesitated for just a second. Then she answered him cool as you like.

'We call it a pin. It's a jeweller's tool. It's got a sharp blade but also a little point. I was using it to mend that old pram. A very useful little fellow.' She reached up her hand and gave his ear a tug. 'Just like you, warder.'

A frightened smile appeared on his face, and, as he wondered about what had just happened, I opened the door and helped Ettie lift the pram down the steps to the street.

'Good day!' she said in her brightest voice. 'And thank you so much for finding this. You've no doubt saved us a great deal of wailing.'

He tipped his cap to her, then closed the door.

We hurried south, where we found a growler awaiting a fare. With a bit of pushing and shoving we got the perambulator in, me and Ettie squeezing side-by-side on the faded leather seat. The cabman gee-ed on the horses. As we made our way down Old Bailey, I kept a watch out the window, expecting guards to coming running out after us. Ettie gripped my arm. It was only when we reached Blackfriars Bridge I sat back.

I was free.

Chapter Thirty-Three

'How did you get in?' My voice shook, dislodged from my throat by the jump of the cab.

'We told them Sidney was your solicitor and I was his clerk. They had to let us in.'

'They believed you were his clerk?'

'I got the idea from a woman at my suffrage meetings. She's got a degree in law from the University of London, but since they won't allow women to practice she works as a clerk. There's a few of them, so she says, and the prisons have to let the clerk in with the solicitor. Anyway, didn't Elizabeth Fry and her women almost run Newgate at one time?'

'But how did you get the baby in?'

'We said we'd just come from a hearing next door, that she was a ward of court we were taking to her new guardian. The officer wasn't sure about it, but Sidney became furious. He's quite the actor, you know. He said we'd have to leave the baby with the poor chap for an hour or so. That changed his mind.'

'You shouldn't have done it, Ettie. What's going to happen to Sid?'

'William's sure they'll be lenient when we prove who really killed those three.'

I breathed in deep and looked at her long face, the thrill of what she'd done still bright in her eyes. 'They'll come looking for you. You could go to prison.'

'I'll be fine, Norman. Trust me.'

The growler made its way across the bridge, the Thames below thick with barges and tugs. It was hot in the cab; Ettie undid a few buttons, absorbed in herself. I watched her lips, her hands, trying to understand how she could have risked so much for me. Sensing something, I looked down at myself wearing the uniform of her class: the black lawyer's suit, the stiff white collar. I touched the silk topper, feeling changed, and when our eyes met again the space between our stations seemed smaller. I don't know who moved first, but, in some moment of mystery, our lips met.

The baby chuckled, and I felt Ettie's smile break out on my mouth. We broke our kiss and looked at the child. She was watching us as she laughed, her face a picture of delight. Then we laughed too, a little chorus of three, and in an instant, as if we'd stolen her merriment, the baby's face melted into a look of such despair.

She began to wail. Ettie stopped the cab and we lifted out the pram. As soon as the wheels touched the paving, the baby fell silent again.

'It's Reverend Hebden,' said Ettie as she pushed the pram along the side of the road, avoiding the press of people heading towards the bridge. She looked straight ahead. 'Her father, I mean.'

It wasn't a good path; the sweepers had formed little piles of dung at intervals, and she kept having to move out into the stream of horses and wagons. When we got to the steps, I took the front and we carried the pram down to Park Street.

'It's Reverend Hebden,' she said again, glancing at me.

'Yes.'

I tried to take in what she'd told me as we walked. Hebden. Not Petleigh. The bloody reverend. The holy man. Well, she spent that long at the mission, at meetings, teaching in the Sunday school. He must have been watching her, gaining her trust. Hebden, leader of the mission, vigorous and ambitious with that fine, straight back, that silky hair. A man to take advantage of any opportunity the Lord might send. A snake.

'Say something,' she said.

'The bloody hypocrite,' I cursed, a taste of acid in my mouth.

'Don't, Norman. It was me as much as him.'

'I take it you're not going to marry?'

She shook her head, striding just ahead of me, her fists tight on the pram handle.

'But how?'

'How? Norman, please.'

'But did he . . .'

'We both wanted it. And both regretted it.'

'But why Hebden, Ettie? Why him?'

'Because he was there. And he was clean.' She allowed herself a quick smile. 'It's a positive quality.'

I knew she was trying to make light of it, but it felt like an insult, and we didn't speak again as we made our way to Lewis's shop on Bankside. There the guvnor and his oldest friend sat outside on a bench eating fried fish from a greasy paper.

'Norman, thank God,' said Arrowood, shoving the last bit of fish in his gob and stepping over to me. He was dressed as a parson, with a wide-brimmed hat, a dog collar, a long black coat; his eyes were a-twinkle with tears of relief. It was the first time

I'd ever seen him with no whiskers, and for once his hair was cut short and straight. I pushed him away as he tried to embrace me.

'What the hell have you got Sidney into?'

'He's in no danger.'

'He's in Newgate! Far as they know he's helped a murderer escape. You shouldn't have asked him to do it, you damn fool!'

'Sidney insisted, Norman,' said Ettie.

'But it was your scheme, wasn't it, William?' As I glared at him, a shifty-looking fellow with a parcel stuffed in his pocket approached and scurried into the shop.

Lewis rose, wiping his hands on his britches, and followed the bloke inside the dark cave.

'They'll let him out when we find the murderer,' said Arrowood.

'And what if we don't?'

'We stand a better chance together, Norman. What if I couldn't do it alone? You'd be hung.'

'Why do you think you're not worth saving, Norman?' asked Ettie, moving the pram into the shade. I ignored her; after what she'd just told me, she had no right to ask a question like that.

The scruffy bloke came out the shop without his parcel. Lewis followed, lighting a cigar. The wind picked up, throwing dust in our faces.

'How's Suzie?' I asked, trying to control my anger.

'She's staying with Lewis,' said the guvnor. 'She and Belasco took the boat out this weekend. You won't credit it, but Polgreen was back. And after he swore to us he'd move on! I tell you, this damn city never fails to disappoint me.'

'Did you find Lilly?' It only struck me then that Arrowood must have told Ettie about Lilly. That she knew about her when we'd kissed and she'd kissed me just the same. I glanced at her, confused, but she was fiddling with the baby's binding, unconcerned.

'Sidney and I went to that gin shop twice,' said the guvnor. 'Nobody knew a Lilly; nobody recognized that description. We've been in all the pubs around Falcon Court.' He paused as a gang of kids ran past. 'Oh, and Mr Curtis called on me yesterday. His lip was all puffed out, blood in his eye. Said he'd fallen out the train trying to get off, but I'm quite certain he'd been beaten. I pressed him but he wouldn't explain.'

'You think it had something to do with Moon?'

'Could be.'

'Did he pay you?'

'Just as he said.' He pulled out his purse and handed me a twenty-shilling note.

'He paid me actually,' said Ettie, looking up from the baby. 'William left the room.'

'Have the police confirmed the dead man was Buttergrass?' I asked.

'His wife identified him,' said the guvnor, holding out a little packet of tobacco to me. 'He was reported missing the day you found the bodies. Didn't come home the night before. Thank Petleigh for this, by the way. And he sent his men to check the graves of those fourteen children killed in the *Princess Grace* accident. None of them were disturbed. They must have dug up the skulls from a graveyard somewhere else.'

Nobody spoke for a few moments.

'Oh, and I went to see Nolan yesterday,' said the guvnor. 'He promised to see what he could find out about Chelsea George.'

'It's got be him, hasn't it?' I said. 'I mean, no question?'

Arrowood nodded his great potato head. The fish grease shone on his lips. 'He's connected to both the fourteen skulls and the three corpses. He was slowly driving Moon out of his wits in revenge for the death of his son. And he was paying the two dead women's rent until a couple of months ago.'

'What about Buttergrass?'

'Foulpipe Annie's a hired assassin. If our twitching friend is right about her killing him, somebody hired her. It could have been George.'

'But why?'

'I don't know. Perhaps for the same reason he stopped paying the two women's rent. We need to find out what happened between them.'

'And how are we going to do that?'

He shrugged. He swallowed. There was something wrong. Something that didn't fit. I blew out a gust of smoke and looked at each of them in turn. 'Girkin must see George's got more motive than me,' I said.

'A motive means nothing without evidence. We need to get to the bottom of it quickly. The police'll be everywhere looking for you. You mustn't go anywhere near your room, or Coin Street or Sidney's place. Or any pub you're known at. Ettie will go into hiding at the women's sanctuary.'

I looked at her. 'The mission?'

'Reverend Hebden and Reverend Jebb have agreed to help,' she said.

'Hebden's become quite the outlaw, hasn't he?' I said, holding her eye.

'Reverend Jebb takes charge of the sanctuary. He's the only man there.'

'There's something else,' said the guvnor. He glanced at Ettie. 'The police had an anonymous tip-off. You pawned some clothes the other day, didn't you?'

I nodded.

'Including a shirt and a blanket?'

I nodded again, despair filling my belly.

Ettie put her hand on me.

'There were bloodstains on the shirt,' he said.

'Lilly,' I muttered, my voice hollow, seeing it all now.

He bit his lip. 'And there was a knife.'

Chapter Thirty-Four

I turned away, wanting to hide my face as the turmoil churned inside me. The warehouses rose all around us, the lifting bars, the windows, the weatherboard. A cart full of tea crates approached, pulled by a piebald horse with a great bloated belly. Its eyes were rimmed with pink tears, its long nose streaming. A Chinaman in a long, shiny jerkin held the reins. The wind picked up and I felt hollowed out, like I'd lost something I couldn't get on without. How could Lilly do that to me? After all we'd shared that last night together, how could she?

'D'you want some tea, Norman?' asked the guvnor after some time.

I shook my head.

'Have some tea. You'll feel better.'

'You have some bloody tea!' I barked, spinning round. In a fury, I kicked out at a broken doll's head as lay in the gutter and at once felt shame-faced. There was something busting to get out of me. Lewis took my arm, and I let him lead me into the shop. It was dark in there, a stink of damp and old cigar butts, but I felt old Lewis a comfort of some kind.

'We need to get you changed,' he said softly, sitting me down on a barrel.

'They shouldn't have done it,' I said.

'They seem to think you're worth saving, my friend, even

if you don't. William's been beside himself with worry these last few days. He hasn't slept. He's been to see everybody he could think of, pleading your case. And Ettie too. They'd have done anything to save you.' He looked down on me with his sad, brown eyes. He laid his hand on my cheek. 'They love you, Norman.'

I blinked and looked away. In silence, among the boxes of bullets and gunpowder, the knives and rifles hanging from the walls, Lewis shaved off my whiskers and gave my hair a skin cut. When he was done, he had me get out of my solicitor's clothes and put on a soldier's uniform. I don't know what regiment it was, but the britches were dark blue and the coat had an upright collar and a golden twirl stitched onto the wrist. A row of brass buttons marched down in a line from my neck to my ballocks. A white belt went outside the coat, a boxy cap on my bonce, and a lead-tipped neddy in my pocket. He looked me over, then opened a drawer and pulled out a little swagger stick. I appeared to be a sergeant.

The blood had stopped flowing from the slash in my cheek but it stung like blue hell, so Ettie cleaned it up and smeared on a bit of Elliman's to help it set. I ate the pudding they'd saved, then the guvnor and me, the parson and the soldier, set out for Whitechapel, stopping at each street corner to check for coppers ahead. Though the disguises were good, I knew that the cut on my face might give me away.

Nolan was an East End fence and a small-time thief, a pal of mine from back in the old days. We often went to him if there was anything we needed to know about the shady side of London. He knew a lot of people who knew a lot of things, and was the type of bloke who'd help you out long as you sent him a salmon or a chicken every now and then in return. He lived on the third floor of a crooked house just behind Cable Street.

'They got you out then?' he asked, gripping my hand. He peered at me and the guvnor, nodding at our disguises. 'Blimey, what are the two of yous like, eh?'

'It's good to see you, mate.' My voice was cracked and dry; though I'd only just finished off a pint, I had the thirst of the devil.

'And who gave you that?' he asked, nodding at the cut on my face.

'Sidney.'

His brow lifted but he didn't ask more. 'Well, you watch yourself. Sounds like you been fitted up proper.'

He took us through to the back kitchen and poured out three mugs of ale. His chairs had gone, so we stood around the table. Stacked by the wall were about fifty copper pots.

'I spoke to a few mates from town,' said Nolan. 'Seems that Chelsea George is well known in Soho. He came over here from Belgium as a young man. Udolf van Oor he was back then. Built hisself up from nothing. They say he's a proud prick. Flies into a rage if he thinks anyone's trying to get the better of him. Never does anything nasty hisself, though. He uses Foulpipe Annie for the rough stuff, but he's got others. Brings them in when he needs them.' He paused to light the fag that was lodged behind his ear. 'Used to be a ganger on the Royal Albert Dock, had a big contract with a few hundred navvies working for him. That's where he made his money first. He'd only pay the men in tickets and the only place you could spend them was in his own tommy shop where two shillings'd buy you what one shilling would get you anywhere else. Short weights, higher prices, rank food, you know the story. Anyone who challenged him got the boot.'

'We campaigned against the tommy system at *Lloyd's Weekly*,' said the guvnor.

Nolan finished his beer and poured us more. 'I know you did. Now, just afore the contract ended he disappeared with all their wages. Most of them navvies got by on tick from month to month. So when they came home with no jobs and no wages for the month there was trouble. Plenty were evicted. Whole families out on the street. Grandparents, babies, and the only place for them to go was the workhouse. The men went out on the tramp, trying to get work on the railroads and such. Our friend Mr George, or van Oor, as he was then, left London and was never charged. I'd heard the stories, only I didn't know it was the same fellow. He's changed his name to George by the time he comes back, see.'

'When was this?'

'He disappeared seventeen, eighteen year back. I tell you, William, there's a lot of Irish'd like to see him paid back for that.'

The guvnor looked up at the ceiling and thought about it. The plaster had fallen off from half of it, and you could see the floorboards of the room above through the lathes. 'A few years before the *Princess Grace* disaster,' he said at last.

Nolan had a drink. 'He came back five year later and set hisself up in Soho.'

'Not Chelsea?'

'They call him Chelsea George on account of him always wearing a red jacket, like the Chelsea Pensioners.'

'He's no links to Chelsea?'

269

'Not as I know.'

'Does he have family?'

'Couldn't tell you. But running off with those wages was the start of it all for him. Used the money to build up gambling lines. He'd loan money to fools who couldn't stop theirselves until they owed so much there was no way out. That's how he come by a string of doss-houses and pubs. All owned by folk who couldn't pay their debts. Nell Gwynn's was one. Her old man was that deep in debt to George. Dead now of course. Drank hisself into the grave.' Nolan stubbed out his fag in a can and poured us more beer. 'He'll get a tip-off from one of his bookies or gaming rooms about a fellow who can't seem to stop. So he's there to lend him a bit here and there, and he don't mind too much when the bloke don't pay back on time. It's all pally. They have a drink together. A sandwich. And he'll loan a bit more each time as they try and win back enough to pay what they owe. He tells the house to let them win now and then, keep their hopes up. It goes on, month after month. Then, when they've no hope of paying it back he turns on them. Makes them sign promissory notes saying they'll pay it all back on a certain day else they forfeit some of their property. Usually a house or a business, those are the folk he's looking for. He likes to own a man, William. And he's clever.'

The guvnor shook his head, putting his hand on his belly like he was sick. 'He's clever all right,' he said softly, looking at me. 'He's got the police convinced Norman killed those women.'

'I'm sorry for you, mate,' said Nolan, pouring more ale. A cloud had come over our little social, but we drank it down anyway. 'Oh, and he lives on his own in a big house Kennington,' he said, getting up. 'I got this for you.'

He took a bit of greasy brown paper from the shelf and passed it to the guvnor.

Arrowood opened it and smiled. 'Is this his address?'

Nolan winked. He filled our mugs again and raised his for a toast.

'To justice,' he said.

Chapter Thirty-Five

It was late afternoon when we reached Archer Street. Opposite the house, the children were leaving school, the judies watching them from doorways. A couple of working men lingered on the corner of Great Windmill Street, waiting for the kids to leave afore approaching.

It was the missus opened the door.

'Yes?' she asked.

'We'd like a quick word with you, madam,' said the guvnor. It was then she recognized us and tried to shut the door, but I had my foot in the way and we pushed through, backing her up the dark corridor.

'Mr Dunner ain't here,' she protested. 'And we told you all we know, didn't we?'

'We know he's not here,' said the guvnor. 'He's where we left him.'

'What? What've you done with him?'

'All in good time, Mrs Dunner. All in good time.'

'Leave me alone, please, sirs.' She had her hands up in front like we were about to set upon her. Her pale face wore a frightened grimace, a jumble of crooked teeth staring out at us from her open mouth. She wore the same plain dress, the head-wrapping, a stained pinny tied loose at her back.

'You told the police the two women left with my friend here the night before their bodies were found,' said the guvnor.

In a flash she darted into the front room and slammed the door. I put my shoulder against it and gave it a great shove, hearing the woman yelp and fall to the floor. The guvnor stepped into the room.

She lay on her side on the linoleum, her hands covering her face, sobbing. There was an old brown couch in there covered with a tartan rug, a rocking chair with one arm, a few prints of Venice on the wall.

'There, there,' he said, kneeling by her. 'We just need to ask you a few questions, that's all. Now, let's sit you up.' He put his hand under her arm and helped her over to the couch. When she was sat, he brushed the floor dust from her pinny, put a cushion behind her back, then sat himself in the rocking chair.

'Can we make you some tea, madam?' he asked with a smile.

She shook her head, wiping her thin eyes.

'Well, just say if you change your mind. Now, you told the police my friend here left with your two tenants.'

'You said they weren't police.'

'Ah, yes. That was a ruse, I'm afraid, to get you to tell us who mutilated you. Sometimes we must play a little trick, but it's only to see justice done. But I do apologize, Mrs Dunner. I really do. So tell me, why didn't you tell us you'd seen my assistant before when we were last here?'

'We was scared you'd . . .' Her voice was like a little mouse under the floor. 'You'd do us . . . in.'

'But we told you we were with the police, madam.'

'We weren't sure if you was or not.'

'Then who did you think we were with?'

'We didn't know,' she said, her voice suddenly strong. As she touched her tight grey headscarf, her hand shook wildly. 'How could we know? We just did what you told us. We didn't know anything about a carbuncle neither. Oh, where's Mr Dunner? What've you done with him?'

'Your husband's quite safe, I assure you. But I can't guarantee that he'll remain safe.' Arrowood stood and went to the window. He pulled back a bit of the net curtain and looked out. Then he turned back to the room, giving me the slightest nod.

I knew what he wanted, so, as he packed his pipe, I placed myself by the window, watching out in case her man returned. The woman watched all this, her eyes wide with fear, her fists clenched in her lap.

'Where is he?'

'What I don't understand, madam,' whispered the guvnor, 'is that you can't have seen Mr Barnett here leave with the two women.'

'I'll tell the coppers we didn't see him! I'll tell them, and Gerry'll tell them too. You got my word, sir. I'll tell them soon as you're gone.'

There was no sign of her husband down towards Great Windmill Street, so I turned to check the other end. Four young women were going in the stage door of the Lyric. And there on Rupert Street was Mr Dunner, a basket in one hand and a sack in the other. He paused at the corner to put down his load, wiping his forehead with a sleeve.

I cleared my throat, signalling to the guvnor as he lit his pipe.

'That's good, madam.' He spoke quicker now. 'In fact I'll

go with you to the station to make sure you do. That's all we need, then you and your husband will be safe. But, of course, if you change your story again later, then Miss Foulpipe Annie will likely pay you a visit.'

'Yes, sir,' she said, rising from the couch. Out the window, I could see Dunner still on the corner, now talking to a bloke in a striped suit.

The guvnor lifted his hand. 'Not yet, madam. What I can't understand, and perhaps I'm being very slow, but what I can't fathom is how you saw Mr. Barnett at all.'

'Gerry let him in, that's how.'

'Gerry let him in. I see. But how did you see him?'

'I was watching from there.' She pointed to the doorway of the front room. 'I always do. I saw them go out the door, the three of them.'

'Mr Barnett, here?'

'That's it. With his boater and the patch on that coat he had before he got that soldier's clobber. That's how I knew it were him.'

'Are you sure it was the same boater?' asked the guvnor.

'With the green and yellow band. And you can't miss that patch, neither. It's the wrong colour.'

Mr. Dunner was on his own now. He picked up his basket, his sack.

'But I was in the cab,' I said, telling her just what the guvnor'd told me to say. 'I never got out.'

She started, like she didn't think I could speak.

'The cabman knocked on the door, I told him to,' I went on. 'You couldn't have seen me.'

'But . . .' Her head was drawn back like she had a double

chin. Her little eyes stretched open. 'No . . . but . . .' She looked at the guvnor, then back at me. I turned to the window. Dunner was walking towards the house.

'That's what we don't understand,' said the guvnor, his voice severe.

'We'll tell the coppers that, if you want,' she said. 'Anything.'

'But why did you say you saw him? Just tell us, madam. That's all we want to know. Why say you saw him?'

'Because we did!' she wailed, the tears rolling down her face. 'We did see him and he did come into the house, but we'll tell it the other way, I swear we will. We'll tell it the way you say it was. I must've remembered it wrong. Yes, it's coming back to me now. It was the way you say. It was the cabman. I never saw him. He never got out the cab.'

Her husband was now passing the house next door. The guvnor's eyes were flicking from her to me, his face red. I pointed to the door.

'You've been most helpful, ma'am,' he said, rising from the sofa with a grunt. 'I'm sorry for alarming you. Your husband was never in any danger. We didn't in fact speak to him. Another ruse, I'm afraid.'

We heard the door open. The women leapt up and ran out the room. 'They're here!' she cried.

She was behind Mr Dunner when we gained the corridor. It took him a moment to see through our disguises, then a look of fear came over his face.

'Don't be alarmed, sir,' said the guvnor. 'We're leaving. Just one more thing. What time was it you saw my assistant?'

'We never saw him!' said the woman. 'He was in the cab!'

'Eh?' said her husband.

'You shut your face!' she cried at him.

'But what time did the ladies leave?' asked the guvnor.

'About ten,' she answered.

The guvnor looked up and down the dark corridor. 'You've never put gas lamps in?'

She shook her head.

'And there are no streetlamps out there?'

'No, sir.'

The guvnor filled his chest with air. 'Right, time to go! Come, Barnett. Plenty to do.'

They pressed themselves to the wall as we passed and stepped out to the street.

'We'll go direct to the coppers, I promise,' said the woman.

'No, no, don't bother with that,' said the guvnor with a smile. 'There's really no need. You've told me everything I needed to know.'

'What's—' started Mr Dunner.

'I said shut your face!' cried his missus, slamming shut the door.

There were no coppers around so we hurried away, checking again at the corner. My back was aching and the slash in my face stung, so I popped into an apothecary and bought a box of Black Drop, swallowing three as we walked down the road.

'So now we know,' said the guvnor when we reached Charing Cross Road. 'Now we know.' He had that contented look on his mush that he always had when he'd done something clever, and he was waiting for me to ask so's he could boast about it. He nodded, gazing at the many windows of the Palace Theatre, his eyes creased into a thousand folds as he savoured whatever little triumph he thought he'd won.

'God bless you, Reverend,' said a woman carrying a tray of posies. She did a little curtsy.

The guvnor touched the rim of hat. 'Peace be with you, my darling.'

She scurried away. We crossed the traffic of Cambridge Circus, all the while checking for coppers, and made our way along Shaftesbury Avenue.

'Go on, then,' I said finally. 'Explain it.'

'They really did see you,' he said, lighting his pipe. 'At least, someone they thought was you. Someone with the same hat band and the same singular patch.'

'But you know Chelsea George made them say it.'

'That's what I thought, but I needed to test her. She was prepared to tell the same story in front of you, that says something. And then, when confronted with your story where you admitted to picking the women up but claim she couldn't have seen you, she appeared confused. I felt it myself. Did you?'

'No, I didn't feel it, but I saw it in her.'

'Right. Now, if she'd been telling a falsity, then your story wouldn't have confused her. She'd know you were right, and that lying was useless so she'd either tell us she was being coerced, or she'd make up something else. Or stop talking. But her first reaction was to insist she did see you, and she did it with passion and what seemed to me like certainty. It was only after that she pretended to remember your version.'

'But she didn't see me.'

'She saw someone she thought was you. The fact is, whoever it was didn't have to look much like you as it was so dark. Similar hair, moustache, same build, that all was needed. And Chelsea George did one very clever thing: he found the two most distinctive details of your appearance and had this man mimic them. Once they'd seen the hat band and a similar coat with a patch that was the wrong shade, that'd be enough. It's the way the eyes work, my friend. You read your William James. It's all in there. The eyes only do part of the seeing; the mind and memory make up the rest. So, Barnett, now we know that the murderer had someone pretend to be you, what's the next question?'

'Just get on with it, sir.'

'How did they know you'd be alone on the boat?'

He said nothing for a while as we wandered through the crowds of Long Acre. Strangers tipped their hats and nodded as they passed. He didn't notice; he was in a world of his own, muttering to himself, pondering the problem. Just as we reached Drury Lane, he spun round.

'Good God!' he cried. 'He managed the whole thing! He knew that the boat was always moored in the stream on Friday night for the Saturday trip to Gravesend. That was the best place to do it because it was away from the wharves where someone might see them tying on the ropes. That's why he staged the arson attack on the Thursday. Moon had to put a guard on the boat after that.'

'But how did he know it'd be me?'

'George could easily have hired someone to give Belasco a beating to keep him away.' He sighed and thought for a moment. 'And it seems that telegraph asking me to go urgently to Coventry might have been a ruse to get me away from London. Nothing to do with Holmes at all. Good heavens, what must that charlatan think of me now, attacking his house the way I did?'

'Lucky the Moons were away at their wedding party. Moon'd never have left the boat after the arson.'

The guvnor shook his head. 'George must have known about that. It wouldn't have been hard if he had his men hanging about. Suzie was very excited about that party. I heard her tell Ken and the piermaster. And several of the customers.'

'Why'd they choose me?' I asked. 'Why not Belasco?'

'Good question. It would have been easier to set him up. Well . . .' He thought for a moment. 'Perhaps George has Belasco in his pocket. Anyway, I think we—' With no warning, he grabbed my arm and pulled me quick into a milliner's shop. 'Police,' he hissed.

I edged behind a display of hats, peeking out through them at the street. The guvnor went to the corner of the shop, his back to the window, pretending to try on straw boaters from a rack. Soon enough, the young PC came into view. He stopped at the shop window and looked in, cupping his hand around his eyes to shield them from the sun. I pulled back further behind the display.

It wasn't clear he could see inside too well, but the shop girl, an orange-skinned creature with a mouth as wide as a panama hat, seemed to know him. She waved. He squinted a bit, then smiled. He pointed at his watch and held up eight fingers.

'Never say die!' she yelled, then laughed like a fowl.

He winked and pootled off.

'That's you, sir,' she said, coming from behind the glass counter to stand by the guvnor. 'I never saw that colour suit anyone better.' The hat he wore had a purple band as matched his nose.

He tilted his head as he inspected himself in the long glass upon the wall.

'It does suit me, miss,' he said. 'I cannot deny it.'

'You've got the bone structure too, sir. A noble chin, a full nose. Like one of Lord Darbly's sons.'

'I have been compared to Moses,' he said, tilting his head. 'By an artist.'

'Most parsons can't carry a boater. It's like a tray on their head. But you, sir, it's like you were born to wear it.'

The guvnor smiled. He tilted his head to the other side; he fingered the rim. 'Mmm.' He practised tipping it and bowing. He spun it on his finger. 'Good weight too.'

'Make them in Henley, sir. An old family business. All the gentlemen wear their boaters at the regatta.'

He put it back upon his head, turned side-on to the looking glass and looked again. He seemed to blow himself a kiss. 'The regatta, eh? What's the price?'

When he'd paid up, we returned to the street again. I asked him what we were to do next.

'Another visit to Nell Gwynn's, I think,' he said, his new hat swinging from his finger in a box tied up with a bit of string. 'But it won't be open for hours. We'll have a rest until then. You look like you need it.'

We couldn't go anywhere near our rooms while the coppers were looking for me, so we found a doss-house near Lincoln's Inn Fields, the sort of place you can hire a bed for eight hours at a time. The manager, a one-legged fellow who talked like he had a mouth full of peas, took fourpence from the guvnor then led us up to the first floor and into a small back room with plaster falling off the walls and bare floorboards underfoot.

Four coffin-sized boxes lay on the floor next to each other, three of them with sleeping men. He gave one of them a hard poke with his crutch. 'Shake a leg, mate,' he growled. 'It's after six. I give you an extra half-hour as it is.' He poked the bloke again. 'Come along. I got a reverend and his sergeant needs their sleep.'

I held out my hand to give the old fellow a help up. His face and neck were crusted with grey mud, and he was wearing three shirts, each past ever being clean again. There was a smell of piss coming off him. He stepped straight into his boots, which had no laces and no tongues. Held his back. 'Oh, my Lord,' he muttered. 'My sweet Lord.'

'Go down and get yourself a cuppa,' said the manager.

The man nodded and shuffled out the door. The guvnor looked at the manager. 'You'll wake us at two?'

'Will do,' said the bloke, clumping back out to the stairs.

'That's yours,' said the guvnor, pointing at the box the old bloke had just got out of. 'Get some sleep. We've a lot of work to do later. I've got to meet Flatnose down the road, but I'll be here when you wake.'

I was too tired and sore to ask him what he was doing. As he left the little room, I climbed into the bed on the floor. The box was only just wide enough, the mattress a bit damp, but it didn't bother me. Not after where I'd been these last few days. Tonight I was grateful to be breathing in the foetid air of the last of the St Giles slum.

Chapter Thirty-Six

We reached Greek Street just after three. Outside Nell Gwynn's, the doorman was talking to a couple of toffs. Four carriages waited in the road, their horses silent and glum while the drivers stood smoking in a huddle. The guvnor pulled me round the corner onto Little Compton Street and out of sight. He took out his watch and held it under the streetlamp, the hat box dangling from his wrist.

'Do we wait for one of the women to come out?' I asked him.

'Ettie'll be out any minute,' he said. 'And before you start complaining again, no, I didn't tell you. You'd only make a fuss. We couldn't go in, you know that. The doorman'd recognize us from fifty yards.'

'But—'

'No, Norman. She suggested it. There's nothing you can do. She's in there. She's been in for at least an hour. And actually, who better to try and get information from the women who dance in there but another woman?'

'I hope she's not doing her Cockney accent,' I said at last.

'I forbade her.'

He edged to the corner of the street so he could keep an eye on the door. It was about a hundred yards further up, and we could just hear the sound of the dance band. It was early Tuesday morning, and the club didn't seem busy.

'You got a beating in gaol, didn't you?' he asked as he watched. 'I mean not just your face. You're limping.'

'Only blisters.'

He grunted. I suppose we didn't look so queer, just a parson and a soldier hiding round a corner. I swatted a few pigeons away from our feet with my swagger stick, wondering what Ettie was doing in there. They wouldn't like her asking questions, and I didn't know if she was careful enough to keep herself out of danger. She had a faith in the Lord that made her blind to the little things as made a difference in that sort of world.

A couple of fellows in frock coats and silk toppers came out and climbed into one of the carriages. The horses were whipped on, and it clattered off towards Oxford Street.

The bells of St Mary's rang half three.

'She's late,' muttered the guvnor, his eyes fixed on the street ahead.

'She'll be out soon.'

He pulled out his watch again. 'We need to be at the Hog at four for Flatnose.'

Flatnose Fisher was a cracksman, a friend of Nolan's. He was a solitary bloke, lived alone in a basement off the Old Kent Road. A queer one, was Flatnose. Not the type you'd want to spend an evening with, that was sure.

'He should be in Chelsea George's study in Kennington right now,' said the guvnor, taking a quick look at me. 'I've been puzzling over Lord Selby, you see. He's the only witness the police have of you talking to the two women in Nell Gwynn's. Why nobody else? Not the waiting girls, not the whores, not the barmen. Only him. It would suggest that Selby's lying. That the fellow pretending to be you wasn't in the club with the women that night at all. But why not? It would be perfect – a room full of witnesses. So why didn't they get him to go there after the Dunners? The only explanation I can think of is that this mystery man was known at Nell Gwynn's. If that's the case, it would be too risky for him to go there with the women. There'd be too many people who'd know who he really was and wouldn't misidentify him as you. So, what if we say that Lord Selby's simply lying? Then why?

'Perhaps he was part of the conspiracy to get revenge on Captain Moon. Now, I checked the list of victims of the *Princess Grace* disaster, but I couldn't see anyone obviously related to him. I did find out a little about him from an old friend who writes the society pages at the *Gazette*, however. Selby comes from a colonial family, most of their money from sugar. A fervent Christian and one of the founding subscribers of the mission at Spitalfields Tabernacle. But that was years ago. It's an open secret he's a gambler and has debts. So how about this? What if George asked him to say he saw you there? He'd be the perfect person to give false testimony; the word of a Lord's worth ten from the rest of us, so the chances are the court wouldn't need any other witnesses. And that means that George either paid him or has some hold over him. Given what we know of both men, the most obvious explanation is that Selby's in debt to George.'

'So you've asked Flatnose—'

'—to find George's IOUs and promissory notes and bring them to us.'

'You've been busy, William.'

'I couldn't bear to lose you, my friend,' he said, and in the dim gaslight a little sparkled tear appeared in his eye. He bit his lip in a worried smile and let out a timid fart as a cat might do. A dog barked somewhere in the Soho night.

He patted my rumple and turned back to watch Nell Gwynn's. It was then we saw Foulpipe Annie appear from a side street just up from us. She pushed her way through a group of pickled lads and crossed the road to the alley opposite, no more than fifty yards from where we hid.

'Down,' whispered the guvnor, sinking to his knees on the pavement so we were peering through a set of black railings. I got to a squat behind him.

'Annie! Annie!' came the sound of children's voices. And then they appeared too, the little kiddies who'd begged from us the other night as they waited for their ma. The boy and his younger sister rushed to the big ratcatcher and pulled at her legs and danced around her. Foulpipe Annie bent to give each a big hug, the boy pretending to suffocate, his little sister giggling. The lad wore the same ragged shorts but his chest was bare. The little girl carried a broken bottle in her hand.

'Oh, my lovelies,' said the woman in a kindly voice. She looked at the boy. 'What happened to your shirt, Davey?'

'Bullies.'

She stroked his head. 'I got to learn you to fight, ain't I? Now, what have I got for you two lovelies, then?'

The girl dropped her bottle and clapped her hands. Annie had a rummage in her shoulder sack.

'I hope it's not rats,' whispered the guvnor, shifting to get himself more comfortable. He grunted. 'My damn knees.'

First she pulled out a couple of blankets and gave them one each. The boy draped it around his shoulder like a cape. The girl watched him careful, then she did it too. Annie drew out a bottle next and gave it them.

'Lemonade, lemonade!' cried the girl, popping the lid off and holding it to her mouth. The boy snatched it away as Annie brought out a loaf and a wrap of cheese.

'Now, you share that. No fighting. Did you see your ma?'

'Ma say wait,' said the boy.

'I know, but did you see her, Davey?'

'We waiting.'

'We didn't see her,' said the girl, who was better with her words than her brother. 'She never come back.'

'Then you must come with me now, Flossie,' said Annie. 'You been here long enough. Your ma ain't coming back.'

The boy took his sister's hand, the loaf and cheese under his arm, the bottle gripped in his other fist. 'We go wait,' he said.

'Don't be silly. Come to my house. They'll put you in an orphanage if they catch you.'

'Annie!' the doorman barked from up the road.

She stood up and looked over. Then she turned back to the kids. 'I'll give you one day more, but if she don't come back then you're coming home with me. You understand?'

The girl nodded; the boy just looked at her. Foulpipe Annie bent down and grabbed his arm hard. He squealed. 'Understand?'

Finally, he nodded.

'Keep out of sight till morning. Go to sleep. It's no good you being about so late.'

She went across to the doorman and spoke to him. He disappeared inside the dancing rooms, while she lumbered down the street and stood in the doorway of an apothecary, away from the glow of the streetlamps. Soon, two blokes stepped out the club, looked up and down the street, and walked down towards Annie. Without speaking to her, one stopped and stood crow by the shop before the apothecary, the other stopping outside the shop after. They crossed their arms, their faces hard.

'Protection, sir,' I whispered. 'George must be afraid of her.'

They waited like that in silence for five minutes or so before another man came out. We knew it was Chelsea George the moment he gained the street: he wore a lounge suit red as ox blood, a cravat, his walking stick and boots clicking on the pavers. He was hatless, his white hair cropped close to his head. We pulled back against the wall, watching through the railings.

George handed Annie something. She put it in her sack. They whispered for a minute or two, him using his stick to point down towards the river, then Annie went off towards Oxford Street. The two bullies watched her go, then joined the boss. The doorman walked down from the club. They whispered.

'Keep an eye on them,' muttered the guvnor. 'My legs can't take any more.' He crawled out of sight around the corner, then used the railings to stand up, his knees clicking as he rose.

'You need to lose some weight,' I whispered.

'Please, Barnett. Ettie's had me taking tapeworms. They're playing havoc with my guts.'

A gentleman in a topper and frock coat came out of the club with a young woman on his arm. The kiddies raced over from the alley, their hands out. But just as the old fellow was about to hand them some money, George approached them.

'If you don't mind, sir,' he said, 'we're trying to stop them begging here. It only encourages them.'

'Well,' said the old fellow, his voice like pastry crust. 'If you think it's best.' He put the money back in his pocket and helped the young woman into one of the cabs. As it moved off, George went over to one of the other cabbies and took the fellow's whip. Then he spun round to the children and, in a blur of red, brought the whip down hard across Davey's face. The little boy screamed in pain, and, while the awful sound echoed in the street, George thrashed him again, this time across the thin arms he'd raised to protect himself. The blanket fell to the floor.

The guvnor rushed past me. I pulled him back as we heard the whip whistle down on the lad again. There was another cry, and the girl was shrieking too. The guvnor fought to get free, but I hauled him round the corner. We heard the whip crack against the lad's skin again, another scream, the girl wailing in terror.

'Let me go, damn you!' he barked as he fought me.

'You can't go,' I hissed in his ear.

'We have to help!'

'There's four of them. You show your face and we're dead.'

But now there was silence. I peeked out: Chelsea George was gone, though his bullies remained, stood outside the door of the club. One of the cabbies was with the lad, who lay on the floor, sobbing. He was giving him a drink from a flask.

The doorman moved from the doorway and there was Ettie, her arm linked with a younger woman wearing a hat with silk feathers in its band. And linked to this other woman's arm was a fellow dressed in a bang-up jacket and cowboy heels: a swell mobsman, clear as day. The three of them stopped outside the club and laughed. Ettie wore a summer bonnet with flowers, a ribbon tied round her chin. She unlinked her arm and gave the woman a kiss. She swung her parasol. The fellow tried to take her back inside but she pulled away, laughing, and was about to make her way down the road when the doorman stepped over and took her arm.

I felt the guvnor stiffen beside me. Then, before I knew what he was doing, he was off, striding down the street. I had no choice but to follow.

The doorman seemed to be holding her tight as she tried to pull away. His voice was low and firm.

'No,' I heard her say.

A bloke appeared in the doorway of the club and lurched forward, followed by a woman. The doorman let go of Ettie and caught the bloke, who was in his cups, swaying and jabbering, the lady laughing like a drain.

'I'll get you in the cab, sir,' he said, and gave a whistle. One of the drivers crossed the street.

Ettie took her chance and made off towards us. The doorman, still holding up the fellow looked after her. And saw us.

'Run, Ettie!' cried the guvnor.

With one hand clutching her bonnet and the other her parasol, Ettie flew towards us. We turned up Old Compton Street and ran on, the guvnor limping and groaning as we went. When we were halfway to Cambridge Circus, I looked back. The doorman was nowhere to be seen.

Chapter Thirty-Seven

Down Charing Cross Road we fled, the guvnor waddling and stumbling, his hat box swinging from his wrist.

'Curse these boots,' he muttered. 'There's stitching right on the heel!'

'Serves you right,' said Ettie. 'Stealing boots off a dead man.'

'I swapped them, for goodness' sake. He owed us money.'

'Suzie could have sold them.'

'Keep your voice down, Ettie, for heaven's sake. We don't want to draw attention to ourselves.'

Ettie shook her head. A few cabs were about, but not much else. When we reached the National Gallery, we saw a copper up ahead, turfing the sleepers off the steps of Trafalgar Square. We ducked across the road to St Martin's and crossed the Strand, then on down to the river.

'Well, that was quite a beano,' said Ettie when we were safely on the footbridge and sure there was nobody tracking us. She had a swagger about her, and watching her enjoying the adventure was almost a joy. She nudged me in the back. 'Did he tell you that it probably wasn't Sherlock Holmes who sent him the telegraph?'

'What did you discover in the club, Ettie?' snapped the guvnor.

She caught my eye and smiled before answering. 'I talked to a couple of the women who work there. Also actresses.'

'Have you been drinking?' interrupted the guvnor. 'I can smell it on your breath.'

'Of course I've been drinking, you fool. What else was I supposed to do?'

'Not become drunk.'

'Be quiet, William. They told me Rachel and Gabriella fell out with Mr George a couple of months ago. They felt he belittled them when he had an audience. They'd warned him to stop but he didn't, so they cut him off. He was furious. They stayed away a month or so, then returned to the club with a new admirer. Emile Buttergrass.'

'Didn't they know what type of man George is?'

'Oh, they knew. But they wanted to show him up in front of his customers. One of the ladies I spoke to warned them to stay away, but they wouldn't listen. Said they were scared of nothing.'

'What was their relation to Buttergrass?'

She shook her head. 'He treated them, that's all they know.'

'And what else did you learn?'

'Nothing. It took me a long time to get that. I had to pretend I was after a man.'

She turned her head to me. The guvnor was walking ahead, his body rocking as he hobbled along the bridge. We were in the middle of the river now, looking out towards Lion's Brewery and Waterloo Station beyond. It was almost four, and the rising sun was starting to pale the sky over St Thomas's.

'We need to meet a fellow in the Hog,' said her brother. 'We'll get you a cab, Ettie.'

'I'll come with you. I need a brandy.'

'What about the child? You need to feed it surely?'

'One of the young mothers in the sanctuary is feeding it. You're paying her for that, by the way, William.'

'What? And deprive her own baby of the milk? Why didn't you ask one of the ladies who hadn't a child?'

We'd reached the other side of the river and were climbing down the stairs. Ettie said nothing for a while.

'How d'you think wet-nursing happens, William?' she asked at last.

'Well, I don't know . . . rubbing the breast or somesuch?'

'Rubbing the breast! You can only wet-nurse if you've had a baby yourself, William. Don't you kn—'

She went silent, realizing she'd given something away she hadn't meant to.

The guvnor raised his hand to his whiskers and scratched them, realizing also. 'So . . .' he said, a confusion in his face. 'Hmm . . . So you mean . . .' He shook his head.

'Yes.' She pulled him to a stop in the empty street. 'It means the baby's mine, William. You are her uncle.'

He looked at me, stared at me, his eyes tunnelling into my head as if it was impossible to engage with her. Then a great gust of air came out his mouth, his shoulders fell, and a little grin appeared on his lips.

'I'm her uncle,' he whispered. 'That little thing that loves me.'

'It wasn't Petleigh,' she said, kissing him on the cheek and stepping back. 'And I'm not going to tell you who it was. And why are you carrying a hat box?'

As we made our way through the dusty South London streets, the dark slowly lifting, the guvnor tried again and again to make her tell, but she remained steadfast. I could see him wrestling with his emotions, trying to be angry with her but unable to overcome his joy at discovering himself an uncle. It was in this fashion we entered the Hog.

Hamba was playing cards with another Lascar in a corner; on a bench sat a couple of porters filling up with ale before the market opened. We ordered a couple of pints of porter and a brandy and hot water for Ettie, and were halfway through our drinks when Flatnose walked in, all kitted out in the house-breaker's uniform: dark suit, black cap with a long peak, black boots. He hurried across the greasy wooden floor, his feet stuck out sideways, a thin portmanteau under his arm that he dumped on the table in front of Arrowood.

'You got my money?' he asked.

'Did you find them?'

Flatnose looked around the pub, checking nobody was listening. He nodded and dropped his voice. 'Took a bit longer than I wanted. Top safe, it was, but I found what you was after. Found a ledger with the repayments too. He's going to miss that soon enough, so you just keep my name out of it. I don't want Chelsea George knowing it was me.'

'Of course,' answered the guvnor, handing him an envelope.

Flatnose shoved it in his pocket, tipped his cap to Ettie, and stepped over to the counter, where he asked for a couple of pickled eggs. The guvnor heaved himself up. 'Just one more thing, Flatnose,' he said, lumbering over.

They spoke quietly as the cracksman paid up and put the eggs in his jacket, then the both of them went outside onto the street. Moments later the guvnor was back.

'What was that about?' I asked him.

'A bit of insurance,' he said. 'Now let's see what he's brought.' He opened the bag and pulled out two small piles of papers tied round by a ribbon. One he handed to Ettie. 'Have a look through that. Barnett, we need more drinks.'

Ettie finished off her brandy and pulled her stool closer to the table. I ordered more liquid and a bowl of pork rinds, and brought another candle over to the table. The guvnor snatched one of the rinds from the bowl and chewed it as he opened a much-used ledger. He polished his eyeglasses, lit his pipe with his mouth still full, and set to work.

I sat with my mug of porter, happy to let them get on with it. A couple of tired bargees had come in and were sitting with gin jars in their hand, staring at the murky window as the early morning light seeped in. Hamba and the card player had fallen asleep on the bench. The barmaid sat on a stool, her head rested on her arms spread over the counter, the mop on the floor aside her. The Hog was one of the few places around South London that never shut. That was how Betts liked it.

The first pile held more than two dozen IOUs signed by Lord Selby, stretching back three or four years. The amounts started at a pound or two, then increased. The last one, dated three month before, was for a hundred and fifty quid. The guvnor found them listed in the ledger along with the repayments, not that there were many of those. Putting it all together, Lord Selby now owed Chelsea George £617 4s 6d. It was a bloody fortune.

Ettie undid the ribbon of the second, smaller pile. It held three promissory notes, all signed by Selby. She read the first and passed it over. It was dated 1893, made out for the total of the IOUs for that year minus the amount Selby'd paid back, which wasn't much. It gave a further date when the money was due, and set out a 'fee' of half the total to be added each six months the money wasn't repaid. The second, dated 1894, was the same, with the money from the year before added.

'Good heavens,' said Ettie as she read the third note. She pulled the candle closer and read the note again, shaking her head. At last, she pushed it over the table. 'Read that one,' she said, holding my eye.

It was dated 1895, the same form as the other two, but this one set out a forfeit. If the sums were not paid back within six months, Chelsea George had the right to claim ownership of the property at 15 Brompton Crescent. But that wasn't all. The final sentence, just before Selby's shaky signature, said: 'The debtor will in addition willingly and without prejudice sacrifice one ear.'

A great, tired grin broke over the guvnor's washed-out face. 'He's made his first mistake,' he whispered.

Chapter Thirty-Eight

Though it was only six, Scrapes was up having his sausages when we reached his house on Waterloo Road. It seemed the guvnor'd already explained things to him, as he took us direct into the parlour where a document lay on his writing table. He took up his pen.

'The amount?' he asked. His voice was dull, the lids low over his eyes like he was sick. He wore a yellow cravat tucked into a silk lounge coat.

'It's £617 4s 6d,' said the guvnor.

Scrapes looked up. His thin, nobbled nose gave a low whistle. He took out a spotted handkerchief and tried to give it a good hard blow, his eyes watering with the effort. It was quite bunged.

'Good Lord,' he said at last, stuffing the hankie back in his jacket. 'And you're sure this is the only way? Chelsea George isn't a man to play with.'

'Please, Reggie. Norman's life's at stake.'

He grunted but didn't look at my direction. Scrapes had something against me; I didn't know what. Apart from the first time we met, he'd never spoken to me direct. He was really the guvnor's man.

'There's the signature,' said Arrowood, unfolding one of the promissory notes from the portmanteau and putting it on the desk.

Scrapes nodded. He wrote the figure about halfway down the document he'd prepared, then held a magnifying glass over Chelsea George's signature and copied it slow as you like onto the bottom of the page. He was a tall fellow, and had to bend low over the table to see it right. 'You owe me a favour, William,' he said as he wrote. 'And I will ask you to repay it. But don't you dare tell anyone it was I as did this. Where does Selby live?'

'Fifteen Brompton Crescent.'

When it was blotted and dry, Scrapes handed the document to the guvnor. 'I just hope it works,' he said, picking up the newspaper from a side table. 'D'you fancy coming to the races at Gatwick this weekend? Silver Ring's running. Just you, William. Not your sister again. Her views rather spoil the occasion.'

The guvnor picked up his bag. 'Wouldn't miss it, Reggie. As long as we're not in prison.'

'Or dead,' I said just to lighten things.

Scrapes said nothing as his bony finger traced down the list of the day's races. 'You can let yourself out,' he said.

It was only just seven and we were on the street again. Waterloo Road was busy with buses and trams and folk hurrying to get to work. The guvnor explained what he wanted me to do when we met Lord Selby.

'What if he recognizes us?' I asked, finding it hard to follow. I was tuckered out, weak from the few days I'd been in prison and washed out from working all night.

'He's only seen you once, and we don't know how far away he was. I'm hoping he won't have much of a memory of your features, probably only your height, your shape, your hair and moustache. The upper classes don't see the common people

298

in any detail, anyway. Not in passing. They're much better at recognizing their own.'

I thought about that for a while as we made our way up the road. 'You think it goes the other way too?'

'I don't know. Anyway, we've changed our hair and lost our whiskers, and that soldier's uniform will help.'

'You think it'll be enough?'

'William James says our attention's like a spotlight. What we know of a person depends on where we direct that spotlight. It's the same principle I used in your gaol-break. Selby should notice our uniforms first, and immediately begin to form an impression of who we are based on his understanding of parsons and sergeants. He'll certainly notice your scar as well, which you didn't have before. I'm fairly sure he won't have the first idea you're the ape he identified to Girkin.'

'Ape?'

'I'm seeing it from his point of view, Barnett. Don't be so thin-skinned.'

Since we needed to catch Lord Selby before he left the house, the guvnor hailed a hansom. I was asleep almost before my arse touched the bench.

The next thing I knew the cabman was shaking my arm. 'We're here, mate.'

The guvnor was also fast asleep, his hat on his knees, his mouth hanging open. I roused him, we paid, and there we were on Brompton Crescent. On one side of the road were private gardens; facing them was a curved row of tall white houses, with black railings along the pavement. Polished horses shackled to gleaming carriages stood waiting outside half of them, coachmen sitting proud on their boxes waiting for their masters or mistresses to go somewhere just as nice. A valet or something came up from the basement steps of the house we stood outside, a basket on his arm, and hurried away down the road. A horse pissed long and strong two houses down.

It was a butler opened the door. He was young and already bald. A thick moustache hung from his nose like a bat.

'We must see Lord Selby at once, my man,' said the guvnor. 'It's urgent.'

The butler looked us up and down, seeing a fat parson and a soldier with a wounded cheek, quite possibly from the South African campaign. 'What name, sir?'

'Reverend Locksher. Tell him Mr George sent us. He'll see us.'

The fellow allowed us entry. Inside was air and marble everywhere: the floor, the tables, the urns as stood at equal spaces along the wall. Ahead was a wide set of stairs with a thick red carpet held down with brass rods. He took us into a parlour and left us there, closing the door behind him.

A rhino's head stared at us in astonishment from its mount on the purple wall, beneath it a globe where every Christian country was coloured golden. In a corner stood an almost naked African girl, also staring at us, with little gems in her wooden eyes as seemed to be trying to explain something she knew we wouldn't understand. The guvnor inspected the books as we waited. I stood by the window, watching the horses standing outside, worrying that Lord Selby would recognize me.

Five minutes or so later he came in. He had short legs and a long, barrel-chested trunk, a huge, shiny forehead and a small downturned mouth. He looked from me to the guvnor. He didn't seem to know us at all.

'Yes, what is it?' he asked in the dominating tone of a man used to ordering people of a lower station.

The guvnor stepped forward and held out his hand. 'I'm Reverend Locksher. This is Sergeant Stone of the Eighteenth Hussars.'

He didn't take the guvnor's hand. 'You said Mr George?'

'Let me explain, my Lord,' answered the guvnor. 'My Christian mission, and that of my associate here, is debt. We have a passion for it.'

'You have a passion for debt?'

'Yes, sir. For helping people manage their loans and their debts. It's our mission, you see.'

'You mean you do this as Christian work?' asked Selby. He didn't seem to be getting any less confused by the guvnor's explanation.

'Indeed yes. For the glory of God, praise His name.'

'Halleluiah!' I cried, overcome by an urge to play my part.

Lord Selby gave a start.

'The Sergeant here is the numbers man,' said the guvnor as if in explanation. 'As the good book says, it's Christian work to help the debtor and the creditor. Two in one and sinners both.' He was convincing, I had to give it to him. I suppose it was in his blood. His old man was a parson, before he was committed to the asylum, that is, though I suppose he was still a parson even when tied to his chair.

'I don't understand.' Selby wore a tight, starched collar, a sandy lounge suit. His brown hair was thinning. 'Is there a message from Mr George?'

The guvnor reached inside his coat, took out Scrapes's document and Selby's IOUs and promissory notes, and handed them all over. 'We own your debt, Lord Selby. All six hundred and seventeen pounds, four shillings and sixpence.'

His Lordship took a pince-nez from the bureau and examined the paper, his little round nose screwing up, his top lip lifting over his blunted teeth. He wiped his little hand across the broad beach of his forehead. He crossed the room and sat on a high-backed chair, reading the document again.

Finally, he looked up. 'Mr George has sold my debt to you?'

'Bravo, your eminence!' cried the guvnor with a clap. His eyes were bright, his smile a delight. 'We own your debt and you are now a member of our organization. We prefer *member* to *debtor* at the mission. We're in this together, see? *Debtor* is rather judgemental and of course only the Lord Himself, praise his name—'

'Halleluiah!' I rejoiced.

Selby flitched again. The man was a bag of nerves.

'— can judge,' the guvnor concluded.

'But why did he sell it to you?' asked Selby.

'I believe he needed money quickly. It's quite common. We try and be there at those moments, take the credit notes from the hands of Satan and deliver them into the light. Your worries are over, sir. We're here to help you.' The guvnor stopped and pointed at a cigar box on the mantel. 'Might I?'

Lord Selby jumped to his feet and offered the box to the guvnor, then to me.

'Oh, sir,' he said, blinking with gratitude. 'Oh, thank you, sir. I was at my wit's end. Haven't slept for months. Mr George has been tormenting me. He's a hard man, a cruel fiend, sir; it was like being in the claws of a bear.' He lit our cigars. 'But you've saved me. Oh, Reverend, thank you. Thank the Lord for your ministry.'

He took the guvnor's free hand in his and knelt before him, kissing his signet ring. 'My salvation,' he whispered, and began to weep.

The guvnor patted him on the head and helped him stand. 'There, there, my dear chap. That's what we're here for. So Mr George has made life difficult for you, has he?'

Lord Selby took out a silk handkerchief the size of a jib and wiped his face. Blew his stubby nose. 'He made such threats, Reverend. Such awful threats. He was counting down the days. And he made me. . .'

'Made you what?' asked the guvnor in his gentlest voice. He took a blast of his cigar and puffed it out lovingly over the man's shiny forehead.

'It's of no matter.'

'I feel it is of matter, Lord Selby. Indeed, I must know. My business is to rescue decent men like you, but to do that I need to know what manner of man is the creditor. What trouble he might have got his debtors into. We'll no doubt come across Mr George again and we need to know all his tricks. We're His soldiers, don't you see, sir? The sergeant and I are fighting a war for the almighty Lord Jesus, praise His name.'

'Halleluiah!'

'The risen Christ has chosen to help you, now you must choose to help Him.'

Lord Selby took a cigar for himself and lit it up. His hand trembled. He strode to the window, inspected the roadway, then paced back to the fireplace. 'I cannot tell you, Reverend. You'd understand if you knew.'

'Shame,' said the guvnor. 'Well, the decision is yours.'

'You'll have tea?' said Selby with a ring of the bell. 'And some crumpets?'

'Anything that makes you happy,' said the guvnor, collapsing onto a leather sofa just as the butler opened the door. After making his order, Lord Selby also sat. I remained by the window.

'What church did you say you were from?' asked Selby. 'Or is it a mission?'

The guvnor looked at him for some time, his eyes soft, a kindly smile on his face. Selby tried to smile, but it didn't come off. He glanced at me. He shifted in his seat.

'I didn't say,' answered the guvnor at last. 'And I'd be grateful if you said nothing about this to anyone. It's very important. You can imagine that if we advertised ourselves there would be queues of debtors begging our services, and we would have to turn most of them away. Our resources are limited. We can only help those whose creditors have an urgent need to sell their loans, and even then the members we help are carefully selected for their faith and their discretion. I can trust your discretion, sir, as a good Christian?'

'Why of course.'

'So tell me, sir. What are we to do? What are we to do?' The guvnor held out his hand to me. 'The promissory note, Mr Barnett.'

I found the note in the portmanteau Flatnose had nicked and handed it over. The guvnor passed it on to Selby.

As he looked at the note, Selby went pale, starting from the long, globed forehead, down to his button nose, his jutting jaw. His hand trembled. He swallowed. 'Where are those crumpets?' he suddenly barked.

'Now, let's see . . .' said the guvnor slowly. 'It says there that if you don't pay the debt by the end of this month, then this house will be seized.'

Selby nodded, puffing hard on his smoke.

'And an ear?' added the guvnor.

Selby rang his bell impatiently.

'Well, your worship, if you feel you cannot work with us, we have no choice but to recover the debt. We'll have the money at the end of the month.'

'What? But I can't pay, that's the problem!'

The guvnor's face fell. 'Oh no, no. I don't want to take the house! Lord Selby, don't make me do that.'

'No!' cried Selby in alarm. 'Not the house! All my capital's in it! You said you'd help me. Where will my family go if I lose my home?'

'I could recommend you a very economical place in St Giles, sir,' I said. 'They've a kitchen and all.'

Selby looked at me aghast. He puffed and puffed again, the ash falling on his barrel chest, the smoke hazing the air. He stood and paced to the globe, then returned.

'But how else can we solve it, Lord Selby?' asked the guvnor. 'Our mission can only do its work if our members co-operate, but you won't tell us the first thing about Mr George.'

'Can't you give me more time?'

The guvnor looked at me. 'What d'you think, Sergeant Stone?'

'Well, we might extend the time,' I said slowly. 'If there were a small payment to show good faith. But Lord Selby has no money.'

'I do have money for day-to-day, just not the six hundred,' said the fellow. He stood on the tiger-skin rug, his cigar butt smouldering between his fingers.

'Give us five pounds,' I said.

'Yes, I can manage that.'

'But I think the Lord would require something else,' said the guvnor, rising and stepping over to the bookshelves where he'd noticed a small statue of Jesus having his feet washed by a judy. He breathed in deep and laid a finger on the son of God's pretty head. 'He'd want you to help us with our work.'

'You want me to tell you what Mr George had me do?' asked Selby, jamming his cigar into a heavy glass ashtray.

'It would help us assist future gentlemen.'

Selby nodded. 'There's a murder case, the three bodies dragged out of the river by London Bridge. You've heard of it?'

The guvnor nodded.

'Well, he had me say I'd seen a man with one of the women in his club. He had me identify the chap to the police.'

I kept my eye on him. The guvnor said nothing. Selby shifted uneasily, then looked over at me. Something changed in his face; his eyes sharpened. It wasn't that he recognized me, I don't think, rather that something inside him made the connection but didn't tell him.

'That's a criminal offence,' said the guvnor.

'I had no choice!'

'Why did he ask you to do it?'

'He didn't tell me.'

'Had you ever seen this chap before?'

'No, Reverend.'

'Then how could you identify him?'

'Mr George came with the police inspector and I to a burial ground where the chap was at a funeral. We were in Mr George's carriage. He'd told me beforehand what the fellow looked like.'

'Didn't you realize the man might be hung?'

'Mine wasn't the only evidence against him.'

'Well, Lord Selby, did you ever wonder why George insisted

you make this identification if the other evidence was good enough? Didn't it seem unnecessary?'

Lord Selby stared at the guvnor as he thought it over. 'Oh, my Lord,' he said at last. 'I didn't think of that.'

'Even a criminal doesn't falsify evidence if he doesn't have to. It suggests that perhaps the other evidence is also false, don't you think? Which means you might have sent an innocent man to the gallows.'

Lord Selby's eyes fell; he swallowed.

'Now, which inspector was it?' asked Arrowood.

'Inspector Girkin, of Old Jewry.'

'I know him. A young fellow, wet behind the ears. Hmm. If you confess to him, there's a danger he'll go directly to Mr George and question him, which puts you in danger. No, we'll go to a friend of mine. Inspector Petleigh. You'll retract your statement and identification and explain that you were threatened by Mr George. Give him all those IOUs and promissory notes. Now, this is important. You must insist that Petleigh does not give this information to Girkin for twenty-four hours. He respects the privileges of your station, so he'll do as you ask. You don't need to know why: we're going to fix this mess for you. But listen. You must make no contact with Mr George from now on. If he tries to speak to you, do not respond. This is very important. Do you understand?'

Selby nodded. 'I'm afraid he'll kill me.'

'You're now on the Lord's team, my friend,' said the guvnor. 'Have faith and accept his protection. There's a case building against your Mr George.'

Chapter Thirty-Nine

When we'd had our tea and crumpets, we checked the street for coppers, then climbed aboard Selby's coach for the short trip to Blackman Street. The driver pulled up a few corners before the police station. Selby was silent, his face grave. Arrowood took his hand.

'Don't be afraid, my Lord,' he said. 'You're doing the right thing. Now remember, you mustn't mention us. Say you've had an attack of conscience, and refuse to go into town to see Girkin. Say you're due in the House or somesuch.'

When Selby had gone, I sat in the carriage, the curtain down, while the guvnor went to the chandlers. He came back with a bottle of Vin Mariani and *The Standard*.

'You're on page three,' he said as he climbed back inside and crashed onto the bench. 'Let's see . . . suspected of the murders of three people found by Old Swan Pier . . . Two accomplices, a man and a woman with a baby. Ah, Sidney's named . . . Here's how they're describing you: *Wound on the cheek, brown/black hair, moustache, patchy beard, eyes far apart, six foot or above, solid build, heart tattoo on right arm.*'

'It's the left.'

'And they have you wearing the solicitor's outfit. That's good. Thank the Lord Lewis thought of getting that soldier's uniform.'

He turned the page and took a swallow of the tonic. I lit a

smoke, peeking out a corner of the window at the folk walking along outside. There was a bit of wind blowing, weak sunshine. I wondered how long it would be before I could walk along the street as myself again.

'Ah!' he cried suddenly. He shifted his great hocks on the bench and took a long suck at the bottle. 'You remember that murder in Kensington? Where all those Napoleon busts were being stolen?'

'The Sherlock Holmes case?'

'Yes. Remember how Holmes said it could only be the work of a madman? Well, it seems it was no such thing: it was a few villains looking for the Borgia pearl.' He read on a little, then looked up. 'They knew the pearl was hidden in one of a certain batch of busts, but they didn't know which, so they were trying to track down every one sold from a particular shop. I told you he was wrong about it, didn't I?'

'Yes, sir.'

'Ha! The great genius. I told you, didn't I, Barnett?'

'Yes, sir.'

He held my eye in the queer way he does sometimes when he's had a big plate of beef. He winked.

'I think he's beginning to lose his sparkle, that fellow.'

He opened the curtain on his side and watched out the window for a while, smiling to himself, stroking his belly.

'What are we going to do, sir?' I asked him. 'Selby only gets us part of the way. What about the Dunners and the evidence Lilly planted?'

He nodded, his face turning serious again. 'I've been puzzling over her role in all this. Tell me, when did you say you met her?'

'The night before Moon and Suzie came to see us.'

He pondered for a moment. 'Well, either she just happened to be in your room when they came to plant evidence and they compelled her to help them. Or she was in it from the start. Tell me, the night you first met, was it you who talked to her or did she approach you?'

'She spilt my beer. Offered to buy me another.'

'And that was it? You spent the rest of the evening with her?'

I nodded. She clung to me from five minutes in. She clung to me, and I liked it. Maybe she saw the need in me. Facing another night in my empty room that I wanted so to fill with a different kind of memory, I was easy meat.

'If she was in on it from the start, then Moon coming to us for help was no accident either.' He took another swallow and passed the bottle to me. 'We need to find out why Moon chose us. And we need to find Lilly. Should we go around the pubs again? Sidney and I might have missed her.'

'We'll never find her that way. There's a pub or more in every street in the Borough. Anyway, the coppers'll be all over the place looking for me.'

The guvnor twisted the handle and pushed open the little door. Lord Selby climbed aboard.

'It's done,' said he, wiping the sweat from his face with his hankie.

'He agreed not to tell Girkin for twenty-four hours?' asked the guvnor.

'He did. I gave him the notes.'

'Good fellow.' Arrowood patted the gent on the knee. 'Is there anywhere you can take your family for a few days until this has blown over?'

'My brother lives in High Wycombe.'

'Good. Now, we need to borrow your carriage and driver for a day or two. You don't mind, old chap?'

'Well . . .'

'We'll drop you at home. You can take your family to the station in a cab.'

'I must trust you, mustn't I, Reverend?' said Selby, his bulging eyes tired. I did feel sorry for the little Lord. 'I'll instruct Donoghue to take you wherever you wish. But tell me, sir, what is it you're going to do?'

The guvnor bit his lip and dropped his voice to a whisper. 'We're going to make sure Mr George cannot harm you, that's all I can say for the moment. You must trust us. And trust in Him, sir.'

We arrived at St Saviour's Dock just in time to see the *Gravesend Queen* puffing away into the river, its paddles churning the greasy brown water. The inlet was crowded and busy, the air a clamour of groaning beams, wheels crunching cinders, workers shouting and laughing.

Suzie stood still as a post, watching her boat take the current and run more quickly down toward Tower Bridge. Her old togs were gone and now she wore the uniform of the CSJ, the women's sanctuary connected to the mission: a plain bonnet tied tight to the skull, a long brown skirt, a yellow blouse buttoned high. In her hand was a document. Belasco stood by her side, his fists tight by his belt.

'Suzie, what's happened?' asked the guvnor, coming by her side. 'Who's driving your boat?'

'They took her,' she said, not taking her eyes off the little steamer as it passed a line of clippers at anchor in the Pool.

'Bailiffs,' said Belasco. He'd had his hair cut and it didn't look good.

'We was just polishing the windows and they came aboard.' Her eyes were full and shining, her mouth downturned in the saddest way. 'Dad borrowed on her, and now they're selling her to pay the debt. '

'Oh, Suzie,' murmured the guvnor.

She shook her head. 'I got nothing now.' Then, in a moment, she took hold of herself. She straightened, breathed in deep. 'I'm sorry about this, Belasco. What'll you do?'

'Don't you worry about me, mate. I'll get work on another boat. And you must too. You're born to the river, Suzie. You remember that.' Belasco looked at me. 'She ain't made for service. It'd kill her.'

I kept my mouth shut. A lot of people who aren't made for service go into service, that was the way of it. Sometimes it's the only choice you got.

Suzie crossed her arms over her shirt. 'Ain't you supposed to be in prison, Mr Barnett?'

'Supposed to be,' I said.

'Well, you better take care. Coppers were here this morning looking for you.'

'You joined up then?' asked Belasco, shoving his finger down behind my white belt and giving it a tug. 'What is it, Bengal Lancers?'

'Get your dirty fingers off,' I said, swatting at him with my swagger stick. He tried to catch it but missed.

'Sergeant, are you?' he asked, nodding at my stripes. 'Getting arrested for murder's worked well for you, ain't it?'

'I wouldn't recommend it, mate.'

'You found anything else out, Mr Arrowood?' asked Suzie.

She tried listening as the guvnor filled her in on some of the things we'd discovered about Selby and Chelsea George and how Lilly had set me up, but her mind was on her boat. Every shout, every groan of rope and slap of oar made her look about. She still didn't know about her old man and the dead children on the *Princess Grace*, and he didn't tell her, not just then.

'We need to know something, Suzie,' he said when he'd finished. 'How did your father get my name? Why did he come to me?'

'Belasco told him about you.'

The deckhand stepped off the path to let past a boy rolling a barrel. A cold anger rose in me as I watched him, and I knew I'd kill him if he was in on it.

The guvnor turned to him, his eyes ablaze. 'Why did you recommend me?'

'A bloke in the beer shop was telling me about you,' said Belasco. 'About how you caught them salt thieves in Deptford.'

'That wasn't our case!' barked the guvnor.

Belasco tensed.

'Tell us who put you up to it,' I growled, stepping up to him.

'Nobody put me up to it,' said Belasco, low and steady. 'A bloke in the bleeding boozer told me about you and the salt thieves. It's him as got it wrong, so don't you go threatening me, you mug.'

'Which bloke?' I demanded. 'Which boozer?'

'The one down the road from my gaff. I'd never seen him in there before.'

'Who was he with?'

'He was on his tod.'

'Did you speak to him first?' asked Arrowood.

'He spilt my beer. Offered to buy another. We got talking.'

The guvnor looked at me, his fury gone. 'Sounds familiar, Barnett.'

I nodded.

'When did this happen?' he asked.

'Couple of days afore the Captain came to you,' answered Belasco. 'Afore they destroyed the awning.'

'Did you ever see him again?'

Belasco shook his head. 'He ain't been back.'

'Describe him.'

'Short hair, good suit, maybe Irish. I wasn't sure. Had these scars on his neck.'

'The doorman at Nell Gwynn's,' said the guvnor. 'Good Lord. That means that they picked us out before the murders, Barnett.' He turned back to Belasco: 'Would you recognize him again?'

'Reckon so.'

'Good. We need you to come and look at someone.'

After dropping Suzie at the women's sanctuary, we went to Willows' coffeehouse. All the way there I'd been thinking about Clara Harris. I knew I should tell the guvnor, but still I hesitated. It'd destroy his faith in me. And I feared Ettie's judgement even worse than his. By the time we arrived I was wet with sweat, overheated. My head was beating, my body aching from the battering I'd taken.

The guvnor and Belasco went in to check there were no coppers about, while Selby's coachman climbed down for a smoke. I swallowed a couple of Black Drop and washed it down with the last of the Mariani wine.

'We're grateful you taking us around town like this, mate,' I told him, careful not to raise the curtain too high.

'Better 'n doing nowt,' he grunted.

'We'll be inside a few hour. We'll send you out some grub.'

When the guvnor gave me the signal, I jumped down from the carriage and hurried through the busy shop to Rena's back room, a little place she kept for private meetings. There was a table, a few chairs, sacks of flour and stacks of crates. Looked like it hadn't been cleaned since the eighties, and it was hotter than an oven in there. I tried the window to the yard but it was painted shut.

'I been thinking about what you told us back at the dock,' said Belasco. He slumped on a stool in the corner, his arms crossed over his brown chest. 'But I can't see what it's all got to do with the Captain. Was one of the women Feathers? Or is Polgreen in with Chelsea George?'

'We don't know all of it yet,' answered the guvnor, tapping out his pipe onto the floor. 'But there's something I didn't tell Suzie. Before getting the *Gravesend Queen*, Captain Moon ran a boat from Oxford. The *Princess Grace*.'

Belasco sat up. 'Not the one in the accident?'

The guvnor nodded. 'He was blamed for it in the papers. There was a petition. They drove him out of Oxford.'

'That was him?'

'His real name's Solomon Buncher. He changed it to Moon to escape the harassment.'

Belasco nodded. He itched hard at his tight hair. 'So that's why he'd never speak about his past, is it? I thought it was because of his wife and kids.'

'We think the fourteen skulls represent the children who

died. It turns out that Chelsea George lost a son in the accident. We think it was him behind the attacks on the boat. He was tormenting Moon.'

'Why didn't he just kill him?'

'I suspect he might have done eventually. He wanted him to suffer first.'

'So those three dead bodies . . . were they involved in the *Princess Grace*?'

Arrowood shrugged. 'We don't know yet. Chelsea George had some sort of relationship with the two women which went sour. Mr Buttergrass was involved somehow. But we need to get to the bottom of this quickly. Every hour Norman's on the street there's more chance someone will recognize him, and we must get Sidney out of gaol. That's why we need to find out if the person who gave you our name is connected to Chelsea George.'

Belasco looked over at me.

I nodded. 'We've got to work it all out quick, mate. Else they'll string me up.'

'Don't tell Suzie about her father, will you, Belasco?' asked the guvnor. 'Not just yet. She's had enough to deal with without discovering she's not who she thinks she is. We'll tell her when the case is over, when she's had a bit of time to grieve.'

Rena came in and put down three big mugs of coffee and a bowl of porridge for each of us. She smelt strong of sweat. 'I read about you in the paper, Norm,' she said. 'You got to be careful.'

'I know, mate,' I said. My voice was weak, my belly all-overish from knowing what I needed to do.

'You know that fellow Buttergrass who was killed?' she went on. 'You see the reward his aunt's put out?'

The guvnor came to life. 'What reward?'

'You didn't see it?' She pointed at a pile of old newspapers in the corner. 'It's in *The Times*, in there somewhere. Thursday or Friday, I think it was. A hundred quid.'

The guvnor was already scrabbling through the papers. He pulled one out, jammed the eyeglasses on his nose, and found the notices, his eyes jerking and flicking. 'Not there,' he said, tossing it over his shoulder.

'Oi! Don't mess up the place,' cried Rena.

He found another and rifled through that. 'Ah! Mrs Emilia Ewart. *For information leading to the capture of the murderer of Mr Emile Buttergrass, whose body was found at Old Swan Pier, 4 July, a sum of £100.*' He looked up. 'D'you hear that, Barnett? A hundred pounds!'

'Yes, sir.'

'That'll get our name about. What'll Sherlock Holmes think when we win that, eh?'

'Won't he try to solve it himself, William?' asked Rena.

Arrowood's face dropped. 'Of course he will, damn it. He's always sniffing out a reward, the money-grubbing scurf. Oh, Lord, he'll be looking for you already, Barnett. But no matter. We'll get there before him. We'll either be dead or heroes by this time tomorrow. I just hope he doesn't get in our way. What do you think of that hat he wears, Rena?'

'Quite handsome, actually, Willy.'

He scowled. 'And all the other detectives in London'll be on the case as well, I shouldn't wonder. Pollaky, Field, Pinkerton's. Half the retired parsnips in the country'll be solving it from their studies, no doubt. Well, we're far ahead of all of them.'

'I need to tell you something, William,' I said.

He sipped his coffee and took a bite of porridge with his mouth still full. 'What is it?'

'It might not just be Moon they were out to get. It might be me too.'

'I know that.'

'I mean, it might not just be Chelsea George behind it. See, there was another name on the list of dead kids, Clara Harris. I knew someone called that when I was younger. Her family had good reason to want me dead.'

He'd stopped eating, his head frozen over the bowl. 'You mean the family might be in on this with George? To get at you?'

'The sister's the only one left now, far as I know. She could easily have met George after the accident. There were campaigns and petitions about the *Princess Grace* disaster. All the families came together against the Thames Conservators and the steam-ship company and such.'

'But why you?'

'I did something to Clara Harris's father when I was younger that I've been ashamed about my whole life. It's not important what it was, but it was bad enough for the sister to want to see me go down.'

'What did you do, Norman?'

'It's not important. Trust me, William.'

'I won't judge you, if that's what you're worried about. What you've done before doesn't matter to me, but I need all the information. Your life's at risk.'

'All you need to solve this case is their names,' I said, my hands around the hot mug of coffee, my eyes fixed on the wall. 'Don't try and persuade me as I won't say. It won't help you solve this case.'

'Tell me, damn it!' he cried, throwing his spoon to the table. His eyes were wide, his neck clenched. He leapt from his seat and took my arms. 'God's teeth, are you stupid? Spit it out!'

'No, William,' I said, ready for anything he'd throw at me. 'You think you'll understand but you won't. You'll never understand what a person'll do living in a place like Jacob's Island.'

'Tell me!'

'No.'

'Leave him alone, William,' said Rena. 'He's got his reasons.'

The guvnor looked at her, back at me, at Belasco. He shook his head. He let go of my arms, stepped back, pulled out his pipe and turned away, plugging it with shag from his pouch. Muttering to himself, he went to the filthy little window and lit his pipe. Finally he turned back.

'Give me her name. This sister.'

'She was Valeria Harris back then; I don't know if she married since. And I don't know where she is now.'

The guvnor stood by the window, smoking and thinking. Time passed. When it was clear he had more thinking to do, I picked up the *Daily Chronicle* and tried to have a read. Belasco didn't touch the papers, probably never learnt his letters. Soon, in the close heat, he fell asleep.

Chapter Forty

We picked up Neddy about nine that night. As we made our way over Waterloo Bridge, I watched the lad enjoying the carriage. He stroked the leather, opened and shut the silk curtains, looked inside the polished brass lamps. There was a little cabinet between the seats; he opened it and took out a champagne glass, pretending to sip from it.

'Cheers,' he said to Belasco.

'Cheers, son.'

'Whose is it, Mr Arrowood?' Neddy'd lost his shoes somehow, and wore a child's sailor's cap he hadn't had before. He was small for his age; I sometimes feared he'd already stopped growing.

'We're borrowing it from Lord Selby.'

Neddy's eyes widened in surprise. 'This is Lord Selby's?'

'You know him?' I asked.

'No,' he said, like I'd accused him of something foul.

As we spoke, the guvnor tore out a leaf from his notebook and wrote on it. He handed it to me. *Police were here*, it said. *Seen at pier. Witness. V*

'This is for George. If it was he and Valeria Harris at the pier when the bodies came up, then he'll go to her, even if he doesn't recognize the handwriting.' He took the note from me and gave it to Neddy. 'Now listen very carefully, my dear. There's a man in a brown suit guarding the door of the dancing rooms we're going to. Scars on his neck. You're to walk up to him and drop this note at his feet as you pass. Keep walking for two shops, then turn back and shout: *'There's a note on the floor for Mr George!'* Exactly that. Don't add any of your own words and shout it twice. If he doesn't pick it up, keep shouting. As soon as he's got it, you turn and run as fast as you can down the street opposite. Keep running until Charing Cross Road and go straight home. We'll see you tomorrow. Now tell me what I just told you.'

Neddy did it, getting the words exact. 'Again,' said the guvnor.

'I just did it.'

'Again.'

'I remember!'

'Neddy!' snapped the guvnor.

The lad hopped off the bench so he was standing between our legs, holding onto the guvnor's knee against the toss and tumble of the road. He cleared his throat, held his arm out in the air like a music hall singer, and shouted his lines as loud as he could. It was the funniest thing I'd seen in a while. When we'd stopped laughing, the guvnor gave him a hug.

'How much?' asked the boy.

'Tuppence.'

'You give me three last time.'

'No, I didn't.'

'It is dangerous,' I said.

'Three sounds about right,' said Belasco, smiling at me.

I gave him a wink.

The guvnor wrinkled his nose. 'Oh, I suppose,' he said at

last. 'Go on then, you little chiseller. Now tell me, what have you been up to?'

'I had a meeting with Reverend Hebden just now, sir, about going to Canada. He says they want boys like me to build the country.'

Something that looked like fear came over the guvnor's face. He blinked and swallowed, then asked: 'Does your mother want to go to Canada?'

'It's just for the boys.'

'But what about your sisters?'

'I can send my wages back to them. Reverend reckons they'll be better off.'

'But you're only eleven. You can't go all that way alone.'

'And I'll get a farm when I'm older, everyone does. Then they can come live with me. It's more healthy, better air and all. There's all this land and nobody using it.'

'The native Indians own that land,' said the guvnor.

'Reverend says they ain't using it.' He glanced at Belasco. 'Are you an Indian, mister?'

'Spanish,' said Belasco. 'Born here though.'

'Don't you want to work for me any more, Neddy?' Arrowood's voice was soft. 'I thought you wanted to be a detective?'

'I do,' said Neddy, getting less sure of himself the more he was questioned. 'I want to, but Reverend Hebden says it ain't a proper job. It's the new world, Mr Arrowood. Crying out for young lads like me, they are. And it don't rain.'

The guvnor watched Neddy steadily. 'Let's talk about this after I've had a chance to speak to the Reverend.'

'Are you cross with me?'

'Of course not. I'm cross with Reverend Hebden for wanting to take you away from your family. But I'm not cross with you, Neddy. Here.' The guvnor pulled out a punnet of gobstoppers from his pocket and gave one to the lad. He had two himself and passed them to Belasco.

We were still sucking on our sweets when we reached Greek Street, where we pulled over about ten shops down from Nell Gwynn's. It was about half nine. The club wasn't open yet, but the pubs all around were noisy and gay. Punters were lounging in the street, laughing, shouting, shrieking. The sun was almost down and all was coloured with golden light.

The little begging girl we'd seen before appeared from the alley and approached a couple of unsteady clerks. One of them dropped her a coin and she scampered back. Soon she returned, singing 'There Is a Happy Land' as a couple of judies passed by arm in arm. They ignored her. The child looked so small beside them with their wide skirts and parasols. She hardly even came up to their waists.

The guvnor opened the carriage door and beckoned her over.

'I won't get in,' she said, moving her head to peer in at the four of us inside. We must have looked a sight: a parson, a soldier, a dirty boy with no shoes, and Belasco, who looked like he'd been put together out of parts from different bodies.

'You're Flossie, aren't you, darling?' asked the guvnor. 'Davey's your brother?'

She stared at him, her little fingers plucking her coal sack dress. 'He's sick, sir,' she said at last.

'Did your mother come back?'

The girl's mouth turned down. She didn't answer.

'Where is Davey, Flossie? Is he near?'

'He's sick.'

He turned to Neddy. 'Go and see if there's a boy in that alley, will you, lad?'

Neddy hopped out. The girl stood there on the cobbles, looking up at us. She swallowed. Though it was too hot for it, Foulpipe Annie's blanket was over her shoulders like a shawl.

Neddy returned in moments. 'He's all red and sweating, sir. He needs a doc.'

The guvnor climbed out of the carriage and was back moments later with the older brother in his arms. He passed the little body to me and I set him on the bench. The boy had a raging fever: his lips were dry, his eyes shut, his thin arms and legs floppy. The guvnor knelt before the girl. 'We're going to take him to the doctor, my darling. You must come too.'

'Ma said we got to stay here.'

'I'm sorry, but I don't think your ma's going to come back, Flossie. Now, your brother might die if he doesn't get some help. You must come with us.'

The girl looked at each of our faces in turn. Her eyes were big and blue, her face sooty, her nose small as a bean. She wasn't crying, but I could see she wanted to.

'We'll take you to Annie,' I said. 'She's our friend.'

'Annie?' asked the girl.

Neddy climbed down from the carriage and took her hand. 'Come on, mate. These gents are my friends. You can trust them.'

Finally, she nodded. Neddy helped her get aboard, and she squeezed onto the bench next to her brother. Arrowood fell in beside her with a grunt. 'Look at his back,' he said to me.

The boy's face was bruised and cut from where he'd been

thrashed by Chelsea George the night before. I turned his thin, fevered body and saw the three livid lines on his back where the flesh was sliced open. One wound was full of yellow pus, the skin around it a furious, swollen purple. He was infected bad.

No sooner had we shut the carriage door than Nell Gwynn's opened and the doorman came out. He looked long and hard up the street towards Soho Square, then down towards us. I thought maybe he'd recognize Lord Selby's carriage and maybe he did, but he didn't bother with it. I nudged Belasco and pointed at the doorman. 'Is that the bloke told you about Mr Arrowood?'

He peered out the window. 'That's him. I'd recognize that ugly fuck anywheres.'

'Belasco!' cried the guvnor. 'The children!'

'Oh, sorry kids,' said Belasco, sitting back on his seat. The coach was only made for four, and with the boy half laid out on the bench, it was a hot squeeze. 'Looks like someone's sharpened their knife on his neck.'

'That's Chelsea George's man,' I told him.

'I didn't know that. He just bought me a few drinks. Seemed friendly, said he'd seen my old man fight.'

'You weren't to know. They'd planned it all out.'

'Right, Neddy,' said the guvnor. 'You go now. Remember: run as soon as he picks it up. Don't try and do anything else to help us. I'll be very cross if you do.' He patted the lad on the back and opened the door. 'Go straight home. We'll see you tomorrow.'

Neddy climbed out and ran barefoot down the street, leaping over the piles of horse dung here and there, swerving round a couple holding hands, a soldier, an old woman selling cockles.

As he passed the doorman, he hopped onto the pavement, and we saw the folded paper flutter to the floor. A wagon stacked high with bricks, pulled by a strong grey horse, passed us as we watched Neddy stop two shops further up. Just as Arrowood told him.

Neddy was cupping his hand by his mouth when there was a loud crack and the wagon tipped on its side, one wheel breaking away. The bricks shot off, crashing over a bill-sticker crouching on the pavement with a bucket. The poor bloke was knocked clean over, buried up to the waist under the whole wagonload of bricks.

Everyone in the street stopped what they were doing. Neddy shouted out, but the doorman was facing the other way, watching the screaming bill-sticker. The carter ran over to dig the fellow out. Neddy shouted again, but still the doorman didn't turn.

Now that the wagon was tilted with two wheels off the ground, the horse couldn't get its balance. It skittered back and forth, whinnying, trying to stand upright, until finally it went too, its back legs crumpling, falling with a mighty whack on the street. A little boy passing the club cried in fright, his mum pulling him away and kicking the letter into the middle of the street as she did so.

'Oh Lord,' muttered the guvnor, opening the door again and climbing to the ground. I jumped out after him.

Neddy made a dash for it, running into the road to collect the note and pushing it into the doorman's coat pocket, who frowned, catching Neddy by the sleeve.

Neddy tried to pull free, but the doorman held tight. With his other hand, the bloke reached into his pocket for the note, then opened it and brought it up to his face, squinting in the half-light as Neddy tugged and twisted. I picked up one of the bricks and chucked it over the heads of the cabbies who were trying to dig out the bill-sticker. For a few seconds, as it flew through the gaslit night, my breath caught in my throat.

It struck Neddy on the side, then landed with a small explosion by the doorman's feet. In his surprise, he let loose his grip on the lad, who jerked his arm away and was off, hurtling up towards Soho Square. The doorman looked to see who'd chucked the brick, but I'd dropped to my knees behind the cabbies, out of sight in the mêlée.

The doorman read the note again, turned and disappeared into the club.

We got the bricks off the bill-sticker, but his leg was smashed up bad: a bone stuck out from his britches just below the knee. Seeing it, the fellow started to scream again. The guvnor hobbled over to the frantic bloke and offered him a vial of laudanum. The man stopped screaming long enough to tip the liquid down his throat, his eyes wide as a halibut, then clutched the guvnor's hand, moaning and trembling. The cabbies lifted him to one foot and helped him hop into a cab. I followed Arrowood back to the coach.

The guvnor gave Belasco Doc Lorrimore's address. 'Get a cab there. When the doctor's seen the boy, take them both to my wife at the pudding shop on Coin Street.' He opened his purse and gave Belasco a few bob. 'Wait until we return. If anyone calls, don't let Mrs Arrowood answer the door.'

Belasco climbed down. I passed the boy to him.

'Now, little Missy,' said the guvnor to Flossie. 'You do what Mr Belasco says. He's taking your brother to the doctor, and then to my home to rest.'

'You said Miss Annie,' she said.

'I'll take you there when I get back, darling. Mr Barnett and I have some work to do first.'

'No!' she said, her voice tiny but firm. 'You said Miss Annie.'

'Well, well. You're a strong little thing. Your mother would be proud of you. But you must trust somebody now. Davey's very ill. The doctor'll give him something and then he'll need to sleep. Here.' He pulled out the gobstoppers and popped one in her hand. 'It's very important you have this. Do you understand?'

She looked at the sweetie for a little while, and nodded. Then she climbed down from the carriage and followed Belasco along the road.

A few minutes later, Chelsea George came out the club. The doorman and one of his roughs were with him. From up the road came the green carriage with crimson wheels we'd seen at the funeral, stopping to allow George and his two men to climb aboard. Our coachman Donoghue got the horses going and we followed them down to Piccadilly, then along the side of Green Park to Knightsbridge. On we went, past Harrods, the Albert Hall, the Royal Palace Hotel.

The streets got emptier the further from the West End we travelled. Past St Mary's and the West London Hospital to Hammersmith Broadway, where George's carriage stopped. We pulled over behind a cabbie's coffee stand and watched as the doorman helped George to the ground, where he walked over to the urinal and relieved himself. Fastening his red jacket, he got back in the carriage and they were off again.

All the shops of King Street were shut, a bit of candle light in some of the upstairs windows. We passed a copper on his beat, poking his stick at a few poor wretches asleep in the doorway of the Home and Colonial. On we went to Chiswick where, just after the Packhorse and Talbot, they pulled over again. The bells from some nearby church rang eleven. The three men got down and walked to the door of a shop, where George took a key from his pocket and let them in.

The shop was dark, but in the streetlights we could see shelves in the window displaying bottles and jars, and illustrations of beautiful women with big eyes and outstretched hands. Above it was a sign, black with golden writing:

Forever Young, Forever Lovely

The glow of a candle appeared in the window above, then, moments later, a gas lamp was lit in the shop below.

'Go and have a look,' said the guvnor.

The high street was mostly deserted except for a few dogs nosing about and the odd bloke stumbling home from the pub. George's driver was sitting on the box smoking, his back to us. I crept over to the bicycle shop next door and poked my head round the wall. Through the rows of tubs and bottles displayed in the window, I saw George's two men near the door, their backs to me. George himself was sitting on a barber's chair, looking into a glass and talking. He wore a shiny black bowler over his bright white hair, his pale face etched with deep lines. And there, arranging a display of ostrich feathers on the counter, was Valeria Harris. I pulled back my head quick as I could, my heart beating wild from the shock of seeing her again. She'd put twenty years or so on her face and a little weariness on her shoulder, but it was her all right.

I took a few slow breaths until the floating feeling in my

head was gone, then looked back. George was standing now, his hand on the back of the barber's chair, talking loud and fast, while Miss Harris was trying to get a word in. She clutched a tartan shawl to her neck, and was so caught up in what they were saying she didn't see my face at the edge of the window. As they argued, a door behind the counter opened and a woman backed in holding a tea tray. She wore a black dress, the white ribbons of a pinny tied round her waist. As the door swung shut, she turned, and in that instant our eyes met. It was Lilly.

Chapter Forty-One

I knew I should duck back and run, but there was something in her face that held me, something I only saw that last night she was with me. George and Miss Harris still argued, the two bullies still stood by the door, waiting. One word from her and they'd be out the door and onto me. Everything in my mind was telling me to get away, but our eyes seemed locked together. Lilly was changed: her face was clean, her hair glossy and combed back, her bearing upright and sure. She'd acted her part well and I felt a mug. Then, as she laid the tea tray on the counter with her eyes still on me, she gave the slightest shake of her head and the spell was broke.

I turned and ran down the road, signalling for Donoghue to follow. The horses began to trot; soon they caught up and I climbed aboard.

'So they're all in it together,' said the guvnor. He passed me a pint of brandy. 'The only one we haven't identified is the fellow the Dunners and Polgreen say looks like you.' With his walking stick he rapped on the side of the cabin. 'Coin Street, Mr Donoghue!'

When I'd had a couple of swallows and lit a smoke, he spoke again. 'What did you do to Valeria Harris's father?'

I took a big breath and fixed my eyes on the floor. 'Eustace Harris,' I said. I drank again. 'When I was seventeen I put the bite on him. He dropped himself off Waterloo Bridge a couple of nights later. Wasn't fished out till he reached the Isle of Sheppey. He had two daughters: Valeria and Clara. His wife was already dead.'

'So you knew Valeria?'

'I saw her once. I never met her.'

'And you think he killed himself because of you?'

'It was because of me.'

'And she knew you'd blackmailed him?'

'I didn't think so, but a few years back I heard some private agent was asking questions around the places I used to live. It never came to anything. I thought it was over, but she must have found out somehow. There's a few from Jacob's Island who'd talk for a ha'penny and a slice of onion.'

I flicked my eyes up at him sat on the seat opposite, the coach rattling and rolling through Hammersmith. His elbows were on his knees; his big face loomed in the dim light, creased and brown like an old boot. His eyes were fixed on me in a sympathetic silence. I looked away, out the window at the shops going past outside, signs covering the walls advertising Bovril and bikes and everything else as didn't matter just then. I knew what he was up to. It was his silent face, the one that made folk uncomfortable, that made them say more. I took another swig of the brandy, dropped my fag out the window. I rolled another.

His belly groaned. Still he said nothing, bathing me in his thick, unwanted kindness.

'Aren't you going to tell me what you blackmailed him about, Norman?' he asked at last.

'No, sir.'

'Don't be a damn fool.' The sympathy was gone. 'How can we end this case if you withhold that information?'

'We can solve it just as well without you knowing it. They were after me and Moon, that's all that's important.'

'You *must* tell me.'

'I won't. All you need to do is prove it was them. That's what Curtis is paying you for.'

'Don't tell me what he's paying me for! *I* employ *you*, remember. If it wasn't for me you'd be emptying privies.'

'Go fuck yourself. Sir.'

'You're impossible.' He snatched the brandy from my hand and drank long and hard. He wiped his mouth. 'When this case is over you don't work for me any more. I can do without your ingratitude.'

We rode in silence back to Coin Street, where we got down. Belasco had gone home, and Isabel was watching over Davey sleeping on the guvnor's mattress in the front room. Little Leopold was upstairs. Flossie lay with her head on the table, also asleep.

When the guvnor stepped towards Isabel, she moved away, towards the scullery door, and, as she passed the glow of the lamp, we could see her eyes were red.

'Isabel, what's the matter?' asked the guvnor. 'Have you been crying?'

She turned her head away. 'Nothing's the matter. I'm perfectly well.'

'Are you sure? You look like you've been crying.'

'Oh, William, please don't go on so.'

'I'm sorry I haven't been here more for you.'

'I told you I don't expect anything from you. But we do have to talk about our situation when your case is finished.'

For a quick moment he said nothing. Then he raised his eyes to the ceiling and asked: 'How's Leopold?'

'The police were here again,' she answered, rubbing her eye with a knuckle. Her skin was sallow, her lips thin. 'Will Ettie be home soon? I don't much like being here alone.'

'I hope so.' He did a sad little curtsy, touching his hat. 'Do you like me as a parson?'

She sniffed. 'I'm too tired to appreciate you, William.' She looked at me. 'You shouldn't be here, Norman. You'll be recognized, even dressed like that.'

'What did the doctor say?' asked the guvnor, kneeling to lay his hand on the lad's damp forehead.

'It's a blood infection,' she whispered, looking at the girl. 'There's nothing can be done. It'll be in his heart soon.' Above, the baby made a noise like a chuckle. Isabel's face fell. 'Oh no. Not again.'

The guvnor stroked the boy's wet hair. The little chap's breathing was weak, drops of sweat above his lip, his eyes shut. 'There's a woman they trust. I promised the girl I'd take them.'

'Let him rest, William,' said Isabel.

'You said you'd take us!' said the girl, raising her head suddenly. 'You said!'

Upstairs, Leopold began to bawl.

'Davey's not well, darling,' said Isabel.

The girl climbed down and stood facing us, her hands on her hips, her head no higher than the table. Her face was set. 'Annie'll look after us. She said she would. You can't break your word. You'll go straight to hell if you do.'

'He's too ill, Flossie,' said Isabel, putting her hand out to touch the girl's hair.

'I don't care!' said Flossie, jerking away. Her voice was rising now. 'We got to go. I'll smash your baby's face if you don't take us.'

'That's not nice, sweetie,' said Isabel, irked now. 'You mustn't say things like that.'

'I'll say what I bloody want!' The little five-year-old screwed her face up. '*Sweetie.*'

'I'll take you,' said Arrowood. 'Stop being nasty.'

'It's her being nasty,' said the girl. 'She's broke my day.'

'You can't move him, William!' declared Isabel.

'You've got your hands full. He'll be more at peace with Annie.'

'More at peace? He doesn't know where he is!'

'You don't know that.'

'It's cruel, William.' She dropped her voice. 'The poor soul's only just hanging on. It'll kill him.'

'I promised to take him.'

Isabel turned to me. 'Norman, tell him.'

'I'm sorry, ma'am,' I said.

I carried the boy to the carriage, the girl following, and soon we were on our way again.

The horses were tiring, so we stopped at Sidney's cab yard and got the nightwatchman to borrow us fresh ones. Davey didn't notice: he slept on, over bumps and corners, lurches and judders. All the while, the guvnor fussed about him, wiping his fevered brow, adjusting the blanket under his head. The address Sidney'd got us for Foulpipe Annie was a place in Limehouse called Black Bull Court, a broken-down row of dwellings on an unpaved alley, a sewer running right down the middle. We clambered down and rapped on the door. Moments later it opened and there she was, a snarl on her face and a club in her hand.

'Annie! Annie!' cried Flossie from the carriage door.

Annie dropped the club and rushed over, scooping the girl up in her arms. 'Hello, my darling. What you doing here?'

'The men brung me,' said the girl, her face buried in Annie's breast. Annie looked past her into the carriage, at Davey lying on the bench. She reached out and touched his cheek.

Gentle as a new mother, she put the girl on the ground and turned back to us. Before we knew what was happening, she'd shoved the guvnor against the wheel of the carriage with a knife at his gullet.

'Wait!' he spluttered, trying to pull her arms away. But the blade was pressing against his windpipe: a single nick would have sliced it open.

'Get back!' hissed Annie at me.

I stepped away. It was a curved Arab thing, its blade six inches. The guvnor was wheezing and gasping, his eyes wild with fright.

'What happened to him?' she demanded.

'He got a blood infection from a beating he took for begging in the street,' said I, remembering what the guvnor'd told me. 'It's going to his heart. We didn't know where else to bring him.'

'Who was it?' she barked, giving Arrowood a hard slap on his chops. Her voice was full of fury, her black eyes shining.

Arrowood tried to speak, but could only croak. She eased the pressure on his throat.

'We were down the street,' he said, gasping for breath. 'Too far away.'

'I should slice you.'

'Then it'd be me and you, Annie,' I said. 'And I'd like that.'

'You?' she snarled, looking over at me. 'You're a bit of fluff.'

Her eyes froze me, and I knew she was right. Violence was part of her, run through her flesh, pumped through her heart. For me it was just a thing I wore, like a muffler, a boater. Next to her I was a child.

'The children,' whispered the guvnor. 'Don't let them see this.'

She stared at me for some time more. Then in a flash she whipped the knife from his throat and stood away.

The guvnor clutched his neck. 'We need your help, Annie,' he gasped.

'Go to hell,' she said, lunging at him again just to make him start. 'I'm still deciding whether to do you in.'

It was after three in the morning when we rolled into Gravesend. The streets were empty and quiet; a summer rain had just started. When we reached the church, we climbed down. The place was black as the Queen's Tobacco Pipe. I let the guvnor take my arm, and I led him down the short alley, feeling my way by the wall. I rapped hard on the door.

No candle was lit. No sound within. I felt for the little window next to the door, hoping to have a look inside the tiny house, but a board had been nailed over it.

'Window's been broke,' I said.

I hammered hard on the door again.

A few moments later we heard floorboards squeak within.

'Who is it?' came Curtis's voice from behind the door.

'Arrowood,' I said.

A lock. A chain. A bolt. Another bolt. Another. A weak candle light showed as the door opened an inch. Curtis's eye appeared in the gap. Finally, he pulled open the door.

'What is it?' he asked. He wore a long nightgown, his feet bare. He hadn't shaved for some time. In his hand was a shotgun, its muzzle pointed at the floor. 'Is it Suzie?'

'Suzie's safe, but we have news,' said the guvnor as we stepped inside. The same cages hung from the walls and ceiling, the same two chairs sat there waiting, the same bookcase full of books. But the place was changed: it smelt dirty, like he hadn't cleaned out the birds for days, and cups and tankards and bowls cluttered the shelves and floor. No sound came from the cages, each covered in its own sacking shroud.

'Why so late?' asked Curtis, standing the gun real careful behind the door. He lit another couple of candles so we could see proper.

'You asked to be informed of every development, sir,' said the guvnor. 'We're playing the last hand. There's danger everywhere. If anything happens to us, you must tell everything I'm about to tell you to Inspector Petleigh of Southwark Police.'

Curtis looked from the guvnor to me. His face still showed the evidence of the beating the guvnor'd told me about: a bruise around one eye, his forehead scabbed, his bottom lip swollen. 'Of course,' he said at last. 'Sorry. I just woke. Let's have a brew. Take a seat.' He went to the back of the thin room and lit up the little paraffin stove; the guvnor sat on a chair, while I took the stool by the door. It was impossibly close, the three of us in there with all the sleeping birds, all breathing the same air. As the kettle boiled, the guvnor told him all as had happened. Curtis scribbled notes in a ledger, asking questions to make sure he understood everything: he took the addresses and descriptions of everyone, of the pubs, Nell Gwynn's, Forever Young, Forever Lovely; he asked about every event, what followed what, what each had said. We told him as much as we could remember.

'You've discovered plenty, Mr Arrowood,' he said when we'd finished. He took a couple of dirty mugs from the floor and poured out the tea without even rinsing them. He dumped a couple of sugars in each and handed them over. 'I'm sorry I doubted you.'

'You doubted me?' asked the guvnor, his mug halfway to his gob.

'I read about you in the papers in the new year. That business in Catford.'

'Then why did you hire us?'

'You'd already started, and Solly seemed to trust you. He was my closest friend, Mr Arrowood. I couldn't bear to explain it all to Sherlock Holmes or someone.'

'Holmes would never have taken the case.' The guvnor took a noisy swallow of his tea, spilling a few slurps down his parson's tunic in his agitation. 'Maybe if you'd lost a gemstone, or had a letter in secret code.' He had another gulp and looked at me from the corner of his eye. He was still vexed.

'We need two more days' payment, sir,' I said. 'Forty shillings.'

Curtis lifted the cloth from one of the cages, opened the little door and drew out a cigarette box. Two pound notes were in my hand moments later.

'You don't have a biscuit, Mr Curtis?' asked the guvnor.

Curtis shook his head.

'Nothing?' asked the guvnor, a look of disbelief on his face.

'I have an apple.'

'Thank you, sir.'

Curtis turned back to his cupboard and took the apple from a drawer. He handed it to the guvnor, who polished it on his shirt and took a munch out of it.

'Who beat you, Mr Curtis?' he asked, his mouth full.

'I fell. I told you that.'

'If this has something to do with the ca—'

'It has nothing to do with the case,' Curtis said sharply. 'Tell me, how are you going to bring Chelsea George to justice now?'

'I cannot tell you my plan, Mr Curtis,' said the guvnor, taking another big bite. 'But you must trust me.' He nodded as if to confirm it, but I saw beneath his expression that he had no plan, nor any notion how we were going to end this case.

Curtis sipped his tea, thinking it over. 'Whatever you think is best,' he said at last. He squeezed past my knees and opened the door. 'Well, gentlemen, I appreciate you coming but I need to get back to bed now. Tell me about anything else soon as you can, will you? Any time.'

He shook our hands hard as we left. He seemed bigger than before. More firm in himself. Before he'd been flattened by grief, but now there was something different about him.

Chapter Forty-Two

Day was breaking as we rolled out of Gravesend, a hazy pink light as made the fields and chalk pits of the Kent countryside like heavenly gardens. Lovely as it was, we both fell asleep, only waking when Donoghue banged on the door. It was six, and we were back on Chiswick High Road, parked outside Forever Young, Forever Lovely again. Already the wagons were trundling along, carrying their loads of milk and chickens, carrots and beans into town. Folk hurried along the pavements to their work in the breweries and brickyards and manufactories.

'How long this time?' asked the coachman. His voice was dull, his eyes red from the long drive.

'Have a sleep,' said the guvnor. 'We'll wake you.'

We crossed to the beauty shop. I pulled out my betty and got to work on the lock, while the guvnor stood shielding me. I had it open in a couple of minutes, but the door wouldn't budge.

'Break it,' said the guvnor.

One shove of my shoulder and the bolt carriage tore off the door frame, making no more noise than a coin falling to the floor. We went straight across the shop and through the door behind the counter, where we found a kitchen. There, on a little truckle bed by the back door, was Lilly. Hearing our footsteps, she sat up, clutching a blanket to her chin.

'You!' she growled, her voice rough with sleep. Her eyes were crusted, her lips cracked. 'Don't come near me, you bastard!'

'We need some answers, Lilly,' I said.

She reached under her bed and pulled out a cleaver. 'Get out of here right now. My mistress has a pistol. She'll come if I call.'

'There's no need for that, Miss Lilly,' said the guvnor, sitting himself down on a stool by the cooker. 'We just need to ask you a few questions, then we'll leave. We're not here to hurt you.'

'Is she upstairs?' I asked.

'Don't you talk to me!'

'Is she upstairs, Miss Lilly?' asked the guvnor.

She nodded at the back door. 'In the privy. She's got her pistol with her.'

'Does she take her pistol to the privy?'

Lilly scowled at him. 'Afraid of trouble, ain't she?'

I stepped over to the window and rubbed some of the grease away till I could just make out the outhouse in the corner of the yard. A pair of pink slippers poked out below the peeling door.

Lilly pushed the blanket aside and got to her feet, still holding the cleaver before her. She wore a yellowish nightshirt, threads hanging from the hem, moth holes and little smears of blood dotted across its sweep. She laughed; a bitter, nasty sort of laugh. 'You might hear her squeal in a minute. If you're really lucky she'll sing the "Old Piggy" song.'

'Norman might be executed because of what you've done,' said the guvnor, standing to face her.

'You back off!' she said sharply, raising the cleaver to her shoulder. The guvnor stepped away. 'What do I care if he's executed? He ain't nothing to me.'

'Just tell me who sent you to Norman and we'll leave you alone.'

'Time to go, mister. Get moving.'

'Please, miss. Tell us and we'll go. You can't send an innocent man to the gallows.'

'What do I care which man goes to the gallows? You're all the same.' She lurched at the guvnor; he backed further away. 'I'll chop your ballocks off, darling.'

I kept my eye on the privy door: one of the feet had gone back inside, the other now extended further out into the yard.

'Don't be like that,' said the guvnor. 'There's two of us. We'll take you to the police.'

'I'll do you some damage first, mate,' she snarled, waving the heavy cleaver at him. 'I'd love to slice one of them pink hands clean off. You want that?'

'No, thank you.'

'We ain't going to hurt you, mate,' I said. 'But they'll hang me if we don't do something.'

Her eyes flicked toward me, her lips softening. She swallowed.

'Whatever you think of him, Miss Lilly, he did enjoy you staying with him,' said the guvnor softly.

For a quick moment she looked surprised, then the anger came back. 'Shut your face! He kept trying to chuck me out. Every time he come back he tried to get rid of me.'

'I know, but not for the reason you think.'

'I said shut your face! Now I mean it, get out or I start swinging.'

He stood his ground, but still she didn't swing. She looked at me quick from the corners of her eyes, then back at him.

'His wife died last year,' said the guvnor. 'He can't get over it. He felt warm to you, he told me he did, but he was guilty. He thinks she's in the room, watching him. He was torn, you see. He wanted you there, but he couldn't allow himself, thinking she was watching, that he was causing her sorrow.'

She glanced at me, but just as our eyes met she looked away again.

'Now he'll be killed if we don't find out who sent you. Please, Miss Lilly. Was it Mr George?'

Suddenly she seemed to explode. 'I told you to leave! Get out!' She swung the cleaver at the guvnor: it whistled past his chest.

Arrowood shuffled round the table so it was between them. He spoke quick. 'You don't have to worry about Mr George or your mistress. The police are going to arrest them today. And they'll charge you as an accessory to three murders if you don't tell them the truth. You're facing prison, miss. Oakum. The crank. Five or six years, I'd say. I understand if you won't tell us, but if you tell the police who was behind what you did, it'll go easier on you. Turn Queen's evidence. If you don't, you'll be away for years.'

She looked at me quick, then back at the guvnor. The privy door was still shut, but we had to get out soon. Valeria Harris couldn't take much longer to do her soil.

'The police already know it was you who planted the evidence,' said he. 'This is the only way to save yourself.'

Lilly looked at the door to the courtyard again. She pouted her lips, had another think. Then she spoke quick. 'I was told to stay in his room till someone called to tell me what to do next. I had to do it. They're bad people.'

'Who?'

'Mr George and her in there. I couldn't say no. Then, after

I'd been in there a few days, this old witch throws something at the window and I see her down on the street.'

'Describe her.'

'Like a monster, she was. Tall and broad. Leather britches. Nose like a Berkshire.'

'Foulpipe Annie,' said the guvnor.

'She gives me the locket and a little knife and tells me I got to cut him through the shirt, make sure it gets blood on it and that I got to take it to the pawnshop.'

'She tell you to nick all my missus's clobber as well?' I asked.

'Shut it!' she hissed.

'Why'd they kill those three people, Lilly?' asked the guvnor.

'Mr George said the women betrayed him, and he blamed that other bloke for taking them away. He's a horrible temper. The last girl they had here, you should've seen what they done to her.'

A pigeon beat its wings just outside the window, and I noticed the slippered feet were gone. A nightcap appeared in the vent between the privy door and the lintel.

'She's finished,' I said.

'Don't say anything to your mistress,' said the guvnor. 'If you let on, she'll escape.'

'You think I'm stupid or something?'

'When we return with the police, you must tell them everything. Show them you're helping.'

'Get out, will you? She'll shoot you both.'

'Swear you'll tell the police.'

'I said get out!'

The privy door squeaked open.

We hurried through to the shop, shutting the kitchen door behind us. Moments later we were out on the street.

Chapter Forty-Three

Rain was falling as we rolled up Kensington High, the sky low and brown overhead.

'It's fortunate she still has a shine for you, Norman,' he said. He sneezed and wiped his great potato nose on his sleeve; it seemed seeing her anger had softened his own.

'How d'you reckon that?'

'I knew there was some conflict inside her when she didn't immediately raise the alarm. She could have. Her mistress was there, with a gun, so she says. But she held back, despite her fury at you. But it was the moment you called her "mate" that convinced me. It disarmed her, that little bit of affection from you. Did you see her mouth soften, the sudden glance at you to see what was on your face? She still holds a candle for you, that's why she was so angry. Not afraid we'd broken in. Angry. Seeing that, I thought there might just be a way to make her think again.'

'She's no right to be angry with me. I told her I'd help her the night before she disappeared. She was only there to do me over, anyway.'

'Oh, Norman. It's not about whether we have the right to feel something. We just do. Remember how you felt when you discovered she'd left your room. I'll bet you felt rejected. You wanted her out, you made that clear to her, and when she did leave, you felt rejected. You did, didn't you?'

I looked at him, not wanting to admit it.

'And at Lewis's shop when you discovered she'd wounded you in order to create evidence. I offered you tea and you roared at me?'

'I was angry, that was all.'

'It was more than that, Norman. I could see you were hurt. Even though you'd used her for your own comfort, you felt rejected.'

'It was different.'

'It was the same. We want others to want us, even when we don't return the compliment. We're wounded by rejection, even when we deserve it. It was the same with Lilly. Judging by the way she talked about all men being the same, we might suppose she'd been disappointed before. So, when you wanted her out of your room, you touched on something sensitive. You didn't know then she was a liar, yet you still wanted her out. And after you'd made love with her too. How would she feel about that?'

'Guilty, I hope. She was sending me to the gallows.'

'People are more complicated than that, Norman.'

I knew he was right. Though he sometimes misfired, he did know something about the psychology of the mind. And so he should, with all those books stacked up in the corner of his room. That was what made him a good investigator. I'd just rather he didn't use it on me.

'Why didn't we take her with us? She's a danger.'

'She knows too much. If she disappeared, Miss Harris would

be on the boat-train to France within an hour. We need more evidence before we upset things.'

'D'you think she'll testify?'

He shrugged. 'We won't know for sure until we get the police there. We need another witness to support her story, anyway. One who can place Harris and George at the scene.'

'Monkey?'

He nodded. 'If he can identify them we stand a chance. It puts them together when the bodies are brought up. No jury would believe that's a coincidence, not with Harris's connections to you and George's connections to Captain Moon and the two women. We'll take the boy to Petleigh and persuade him to arrange an identification.'

We got out the carriage on Swan Lane and walked down to the pier. It being Wednesday, there were no pleasure steamers about, just folk with bent backs lugging burdens to and from the barges in the steady rain. Monkey's spot was empty, and neither was the blind soldier there either. We approached the piermaster.

'D'you know where Monkey is, sir?' asked the guvnor.

It took the bloke a few moments to see who we were through our disguises, and when he did, his eyes flicked over to Fishmongers' Hall, no doubt wondering if maybe there was a copper could help him. Maybe he was thinking of the £100 reward; the whole of London must have known about my gaol-break by now.

'I didn't do it,' I told him.

'He didn't,' said Arrowood, 'but we know who did. It's urgent we talk to the boy.'

'He's only here at the weekend,' said the piermaster, looking at me steady as the rain fell all around him. 'He'll be up West End somewhere, earning his crust.'

'Where exactly?' asked the guvnor.

'Could be anywhere. You seen Suzie recently?'

The guvnor told him about the *Gravesend Queen* being seized.

'Poor darling. She's a river girl, she is. This is where she belongs.'

'Listen, d'you know where Monkey lives?' asked the guvnor. 'It's very important.'

The piermaster pulled his sou'wester tighter to his neck. Water ran down his front, dripping onto his boots. He wiped the rain from his face. 'Didn't your mate find you?'

'What mate?' I asked.

'The one who was here earlier asking about the boy.'

'What did he look like?'

'Like not much. Had a boater like you used to wear, Mr Barnett. Same build too.'

'Where does Monkey live?' I said.

'Up by Charing Cross. There's a couple of little nooks under the railway bridge this side of the river, about head height. Sleeps in one of them with his brother. One of them dippers. But he'll be begging somewhere now.'

I grabbed his arms and pulled him close. 'You even think about telling the coppers you seen me and I'll feed you to the gulls. Understand?'

The old fellow swallowed, nodded. The guvnor patted his back. 'Mr Barnett's innocent, sir. This reward business has upset him.'

We went direct to Charing Cross and got on the embankment path under the bridge. Above us in the girders were lines and lines of pigeons, the paving below crusted in their waste. Scattered everywhere were oyster shells and empty winkles, bones, greasy wrappings: it was a place for those poor souls who had nowhere else to sleep. Piles of newspaper and sacking were stashed here and there, their beds tidied away; all the residents of that hotel were elsewhere for the day.

The nook was about seven foot up in the brickwork, just under the arch. I had to climb on the guvnor's back, and from there was able to get my hands on the edge and a foot onto a sticking-out brick below it. I used that to hoist myself so my head was just high enough to peer into the little cavity. At first all I could see in the gloom was a pile of rags. I pulled myself further up until my knees were on the ledge.

There I waited for my eyes to adjust. The space was about four foot high, six long, the same wide. The pile of rags was crawling in flies. The smell caught my throat. Covering my nose, I reached out and pulled away the filthy top blanket.

Monkey's wretched body lay there, still and twisted, awash with blood. The wound in his neck was like he'd been ripped open by a wolf. As I stared at him, blinking away my tears, a train hurtled onto the bridge above my head, its deafening, thunderous clatter like hell itself was celebrating.

Chapter Forty-Four

We left Monkey alone in his nest beneath the railway bridge and drove to Southwark Police Station. The guvnor was grim, his eyes loose with sorrow, his body slumped on the bench.

'They're trying to cover their trail,' he murmured, one hand gripping the other in his lap. We both knew why. It was his note, the word 'witness'. Just one word. One word had got Monkey slaughtered.

'I should have thought,' I said at last.

'I wrote it, Barnett. It was me.'

We stopped just around the corner, where, for another shilling, the guvnor persuaded Donoghue to lend me his livery for the rest of the day. The coachman was relieved it was over and could return home to sleep; it'd been a hell of a night for him. When he was wearing my soldier clothes and I his coachman's uniform, we said goodbye, promising to return the carriage at the end of the day.

'If something happens to us the police will have it,' said the guvnor. 'Tell your master.'

Donoghue nodded. 'You'll be right, sir. I got a feeling about it.'

The guvnor gave him a miserable smile. I climbed onto the box wearing the coachman's wet clothes: white britches and knee-high boots, a topper with red trim, a thick rubber coat. The rain was still falling, the bench wet, the reins slick in my hands.

'Are you sure they won't recognize me?' I asked as the guvnor stood watching me from the street.

He shook his head. 'Don't let them see your face. As long as you stay up there on the box they should only notice the uniform.'

I drove the carriage round the corner and waited outside the police station. Five minutes later Petleigh came out with the guvnor, the bundle of notes that Flatnose'd taken from Chelsea George's house in his hand. The inspector didn't even look up as he climbed into the carriage.

'Old Jewry, driver,' said the guvnor, banging on the roof with his stick.

I flicked the horses and we pulled away.

'You're doing the right thing, William,' I heard Petleigh say in the cabin below. I kept it slow, straining to hear them over the grind of the wheels. 'And you think Norman will give himself up?'

'I think I can persuade him,' answered the guvnor.

'How can you be so sure he's innocent?'

'He's never been able to hide anything from me. And Selby's just admitted to you he lied about seeing him with the women. What did you make of those papers he brought?'

'I haven't had time to look at them.'

'You haven't had time! What the hell have you been doing?'

'This isn't my case, damn you! I've got a woman beaten half to death by her husband on the Old Kent Road last night and an arson at the hospital. Four patients dead. What d'you think I've been doing, reading the *Telegraph*?'

'Let me show you.' For some moments they didn't speak. Then, his voice calm, the guvnor said, 'Look, there's the promissory note. George had him sign to say he'd sacrifice his ear.'

Silence for a few moments, then Petleigh replied: 'Good Lord. Well, that certainly links George with Buttergrass. But what of all the other evidence against Norman?'

'Each point against him's bunkum.'

'It's Girkin you must persuade, not me. He's convinced Norman's his man. He's determined to see him hang.'

'Girkin's young and out to prove himself. Admitting he's wrong won't come easy. He needs a wiser man to guide him, and from what I saw before, he trusts you.'

I heard the inspector do some snuff. He cleared his throat. 'Girkin lacks an analytical instinct,' he said. 'He's only interested in evidence that supports his belief.'

'This is why he needs you, Petleigh.'

We crossed Southwark Bridge and climbed up Queen Street, the horses slowing, their hooves finding it harder on the wet wooden road. Still the rain fell, but, in the dry inside the carriage, Arrowood was explaining to Petleigh how they were to persuade Girkin. As it went on, an irritated tone grew in Petleigh's voice, until finally he exclaimed:

'Enough, William! I know how to deal with him.'

At Cheapside, we turned past Mercers' Hall, then turned again into Old Jewry where the two of them got down and went in the police station. I moved the coach around so my back'd be to them when they came out. I was nervy. Girkin hated me, and I was sure that amount of feeling'd see through my disguise at once. One glimpse of the scar on my face and I'd be back in Newgate in no time.

Ten minutes later they were out again with Girkin and two constables. Four of them climbed inside, while the younger constable stood on the footboard, holding tight to the rail. Again the guvnor tapped on the roof.

'Archer Street!' he cried.

The road to Soho was packed with unhappy horses pulling wagons, cabs, trams and buses. Seemed like half of London was on the road that day. We passed St Paul's and Christ's Hospital, crossed Holborn Viaduct and on down to Shaftesbury Avenue, stopping and starting all the way. Brollies were up, brown puddles covered the tarmacadam, downpipes spewed rain onto the pavements. Water was dripping off the rim of my topper, down my collar, dribbling into my shiny boots. I didn't look back at the copper on the footboard, but I was sure he wasn't too happy either.

'And Barnett don't know we're coming?' I heard Girkin ask in his slow, yokel voice.

'Of course not,' said the guvnor. 'He claims he's innocent. Seems to think I'll believe him.'

'We thought you be in on the gaol-break, Arrowood,' said Girkin.

'Never. He betrayed me and I'll never forgive him. Now, gentlemen, before we go any further we must discuss the reward from Buttergrass's aunt. It's only fair if I get the biggest share. Shall we say half, with a quarter each for you two?'

Petleigh spoke: 'Thirds. We won't bargain with you, William.'

'Thirds,' agreed the young detective.

The guvnor groaned. 'Well, it's not right, but I don't seem to have any choice. Tell me, Inspector Girkin, have you any notion why my man did it? I'm at a loss. I just cannot understand it.'

'Probably in his line,' answered the copper. 'A degenerate. I knows it from his face first time I see him. Resentful, spiteful. Quick with his fists too, I'll wager. Ain't that why you hired him as your strong man?'

'That does describe him rather well.'

'Here's my deduction,' Girkin went on. 'The oaf was in love with one of them women and she ditches him. He's drinking on the boat, mulling it over, like. Gets hisself into a jealous rage and decides to act. Hails a wherry and Bob's your uncle. Finds her with her pal and Buttergrass. Can't back down. Whoomp. Does them all in.'

'Of course,' said the guvnor, like it'd confirmed everything he'd always thought. 'He's always had a problem with drink. A weak head and a strong fist, that's him all over. Tell me, d'you think there's anyone else involved? Maybe someone's paid to have him hidden in Archer Street? He's not lacking food and drink in there.'

'I'd say so.'

'Now, there is another thing to complicate matters,' said Petleigh. 'Lord Selby came in to see me with some new evidence this morning. I told him to see you, Girkin, but he out and out refused to travel the extra miles to the City.' Petleigh told him about Selby's confession. 'I can't make head nor tail of it. And the other thing is that someone delivered these papers to the station. Anonymously. Here, let me show you. These are Selby's IOUs.' We were passing a mission group belting out 'Rock of Ages', and it drowned out their talk for a while. When we were away from them, I heard Petleigh again. 'And this is the promissory note.'

'Crikey,' exclaimed Girkin. 'Did you see this?'

'See what?' asked Petleigh.

'About the ear. Lord Selby's to sacrifice his ear if he don't pay!'

'His ear?' spluttered Petleigh.

'It's down here!' said Girkin. 'Didn't you see it? It says if he don't pay his debt he forfeits an ear.'

'But that's barbaric.'

'Forfeit an ear?' cried the guvnor like he'd only just caught up. 'It can't say that, here let me—'

'You leave it alone, Arrowood,' said Girkin. 'This be important.'

'Important?' said the guvnor. 'But why?'

'Don't you see?' Girkin went on. 'Buttergrass had his ear cut off. Can't be a coincidence, can it?'

'There must be a connection,' said Petleigh.

'You mean this Mr George had something to do with the murders, inspector?' asked the guvnor.

'I'd put money on it,' said the yokel. 'Could be him supplying food to Barnett, for wasn't it he paid the rent on the ladies' rooms? Those two who look after the place must be in on it too.'

'We knew there was something suspicious about them, didn't we?' said Petleigh.

'Just so, sir,' answered Girkin quickly.

'You were looking at her quite intensely as she talked.'

'Yes, sir. Seeing how she presented herself.'

'You mean the head scarf, Inspector Girkin?' asked the guvnor slowly, as if it was all just dawning on him. 'Yes, yes, now you mention it. I think you might be right about that.'

'Yes,' said Girkin, though he didn't sound too sure about it.

'I think he might be right, Petleigh,' said the guvnor.

'About what?' asked Petleigh.

'The headscarf.'

Silence for a few moments.

'Yes,' said Girkin at last. 'Say, what did you think about that headscarf, Arrowood?'

'Ha!' laughed the guvnor. 'You're testing me, Inspector.'

'I am, sir. So, what does your detective sense say?'

'He's awful, Petleigh,' said the guvnor with a chuckle. 'Isn't he awful?'

'Awful,' repeated Petleigh.

Despite my worry Girkin'd see me when we stopped, I appreciated Arrowood's performance. He was an actor, all right: the guvnor knew how to play a man.

'Well,' he went on, 'it's only now you say it that I realize there was something funny about that scarf. But are you really going to ask her to take it off?'

A moment's pause. 'She has to if we ask,' said Girkin.

'Well, if you're right, then the case is solved,' declared the guvnor. 'Top class.'

'Top class, Girkin,' said Petleigh.

'Thank you, sir.'

'Isn't he good, William?' added Petleigh. 'Didn't I tell you? He worships Sherlock Holmes, don't you, Girkin?'

'I'd give anything to do a case with him one day,' said the young fellow, his voice quickening in excitement.

I stayed on the box and pretended to fiddle with the brake so they wouldn't see my face as they got down onto Archer Street. The guvnor was right: not once did they even look up. The older constable rapped on the door. When they were inside, I jogged over to a potato man on the corner of Rupert Street and got myself a spud. I checked his paper as he put a bit of butter in it. They were still talking about my gaol-break, giving the same description of me in the lawyer's uniform. I was glad for Donoghue's livery: it made me part invisible at least. Keeping my hand over my cheek to hide the scar, I took down the drink bags for the two horses and gave them a swallow. When they'd finished, I moved the carriage down past the house, so I'd have my back to them when they came out again.

It was about fifteen minutes later that Arrowood and the coppers appeared again. I glanced over my shoulder to see Mrs Dunner stood in the door, her eyes red with tears. The headscarf was in one hand, the other cupped over her missing ear. Her husband stood behind. It was only when the men were back on coach did they talk again.

'You said Barnett would be there, William,' said Petleigh.

'He said they might move him, but he gave me another address in case,' answered the guvnor. He rapped on the roof. 'Chiswick High Road, coachman. Forever Young, Forever Lovely.'

'How did you know, Girkin?' asked Petleigh as I got the horses moving. 'About the poor woman's ear?'

'There was something about her, like you said,' said the young copper. 'When I read about the ear in Lord Selby's note, I just put it together.'

'I don't think they'd have given up Foulpipe Annie's name so easily to me,' said the guvnor. 'They must have trusted you.'

I nodded to myself. In a different situation I'd have enjoyed hearing him continue to work on Girkin, but Monkey's death weighed heavy on me. It was down to us and I knew it. Too many folk had died on this case. We had to bring Chelsea George to justice for all their sakes.

'So, now we have witnesses who'll say Annie was asking about Buttergrass just before he was murdered and that she cut off Mrs Dunner's ear,' said Petleigh. 'Can we trust them, d'you think?'

'I believe so,' said Arrowood. 'They were terrified of giving her name. Did you see her eyes darting about? It's just as Darwin said. And no wonder, given what Annie'll do to them if she finds out.'

'We need to arrest her straight away,' said Petleigh. I heard the sniff as he took a toot. 'But how to find her?'

'Barnett'll tell us,' said Girkin, his voice thick with venom. 'He's working with her. One way or another that villain'll talk. He better had be at the next place, Arrowood.'

Chapter Forty-Five

The beauty shop was open, a woman of fifty-odd sitting in the barber's chair with her hair dressed in a bright green ooze and a great pink sheet over her bulk. The five of them marched in, and I watched through the window as Girkin spoke to Valeria Harris. She shook her head. The older copper went up the stairs with Petleigh, Miss Harris climbing after them. Arrowood and the younger one followed Girkin through the door at the back. Moments later they returned to the shop with Lilly. She wore a sober dress, her hair in a bun, a white pinny over her front.

The copper came back down the stairs with Petleigh and Miss Harris. More words were spoke by Girkin. Miss Harris spoke next, her face tight with fury, while Girkin looked on with his great stupid mouth open. Petleigh stroked his moustache, nodding, looking cool-headed in his neatly pressed suit. The guvnor spoke; they all looked at him, then at Lilly. She nodded. Miss Harris shook her head, talking, pointing her finger. The guvnor spoke; again. Lilly began to talk now. Harris rushed over, striking her on the cheek, yelling. It was at that moment I knew that what the guvnor'd done when we were here last had worked: Lilly had confessed after all. As long as she'd told them everything, I was safe.

The younger copper took Miss Harris's arms and all the while the customer sat there under the pink sheet watching their reflection in the looking glass. Now Girkin was asking questions, his hands in his pockets, an excited look on his wide face: Lilly answered again and again. As it went on, the customer crept out of her chair, took off her sheet, and tiptoed out the door and down the street, her hat in her hand, the green gunk dripping down her back.

After a bit more talking, one of the constables put Valeria Harris's wrists in irons, while the other did Lilly's. They left the older copper there with the women while the rest came out and climbed back into the carriage. Not one of them looked up in my direction.

'You don't know where Barnett is, do you, Arrowood?' asked Girkin from inside.

'I'm sorry, Inspector. They must have changed their plans. But it wasn't wasted time. You've got two arrests already. Tell me, what d'you make of what that slavey said?'

'Another link to Mr George, that's the first thing. Second is that woman who give her the locket must be Foulpipe Annie, I reckon. Same description as the Dunners give us.'

'I tell you what I'm thinking,' the guvnor said. 'I'm thinking this Foulpipe Annie was Barnett in disguise. What d'you think of that?'

'In disguise?' cried Girkin. 'In disguise? You hear that, sir? He thinks he's in disguise!'

'Damn fool,' said Petleigh.

'Oh dear, dear. So he come to his own house in disguise and asks the slavey to plant evidence, do he? You're more a fool than I thought.'

'It's just a suggestion, Inspector,' said the guvnor.

'Think about it. He plants evidence to get hisself hung? Good grief, not even he's that stupid. No, that be Foulpipe Annie all right, and that slavey's evidence links her to the murders. We've enough on Annie to arrest her right now.'

'I see,' said the guvnor slowly. 'But what's Barnett's place in all this?'

'He been fitted up for the murders.'

'But the Dunners saw him pick up the two women.'

'You oughtn't to believe everyone in what they say, Arrowood, not if you want to be a detective. Selby says he was lying, remember? They maybe been made to say it too.'

'So Barnett's innocent?'

'Reckon so.'

My whole body loosened as he said it, and I realized how tensed up I'd been since we collected Girkin and his men. I didn't have to hide no more: I wasn't going to be hung for murder. Despite how impossible the guvnor'd been, I felt grateful to that dirty old bastard.

I flicked the reins. The horses had just started to move when a bloke ran past wearing a boater with a green and yellow band. It took me a blink to realize what I'd seen.

I pulled up the horses and leapt down to the road, landing in a missing cobble and twisting my ankle. Time seemed to slow as a woman took my arm to help me up. I hobbled back to the shop, my heart pounding, my feet not moving fast enough, and saw him through the window, standing over Lilly, her shackled hands out before her as he brought down a knife. He spun in surprise as I burst through the door, his knife dropping with a clatter. Before I could think he flew at me, knocking me off balance. By the time I'd found my feet, he was out the door and gone.

Lilly's face was blank, her eyes empty as she stared at me. Her hand was clutched to her side, blood running through her fingers. Already her pinny was soaked red from the wound in her hip. The constable was on his hands and knees, blood dripping down the side of his face and onto the floor. Valeria Harris stood by the counter, her face pale, staring at them. Only then did she turn to me, and for the first time our eyes met. I felt a nauseating judder inside me, like something heavy had crashed hard against my soul. It was hate, pure, cold hate, and I knew I deserved nothing less. For a sickening moment all was still, all sound gone, all movement frozen. Then I picked Lilly up in my arms and stumbled back onto the street. I stood there, looking left and right, not knowing what to do. She gripped my arm tighter and tighter, like she was trying to stop herself crying out. Her eyes were on my face, her mouth open. She was losing too much blood.

I struggled to the shop next door, a bicycle place. A woman jumped up from her stool as I entered.

'Lilly!' she cried. 'What's happened?'

'Stabbed,' I said. A bloke came through from the back. 'You, mister, get a doctor. And quick. And you, missus, get a towel and hold it hard on her hip. Stop the bleeding.'

Finally, Lilly seemed to see me proper. 'Thanks, mate,' she whispered, then gasped, squeezing her eyes tight shut. The woman was on her knees now, staunching the blood with a tablecloth.

I hobbled to the door, and, as I stepped onto the street, I heard Lilly again: 'I'm sorry, Norm.'

Arrowood poked his great turnip head out the window just as I reached the carriage. 'Where've you been, coachman?'

'I don't suppose you know where Annie is, do you, Arrowood?' asked Girkin from inside the coach as I climbed on the box and collected the reins.

Another rapping on the ceiling. 'Limehouse, coachman,' barked the guvnor.

Chapter Forty-Six

We rolled into Black Bull Court about midday. The constable hammered on the door. A dog started barking somewhere behind the buildings. He hammered again. The door wrenched open and there she stood, fearsome, thighs like oaks in her tight leather britches, her brow low and boney, her nose-holes clogged with black snot.

'What is it, coppers?' she shouted, holding her fist clenched by her shoulder, ready to let it fly at the first of them to speak.

The constable stepped back; Girkin shoved him forward again. The guvnor looked up at me on the driver's seat, jerking his head at a little path down the side of the building. Quiet as I could, I climbed down to the slimy mud that counted as a street, my boot crunching on a layer of shells and fishbones.

Annie reached behind the door and brought out a club. 'I said what is it?' she demanded again. It was then I noticed her eyes were red, her wide face smeared with grit. She stepped forward.

They were in a line, frozen. The constable, Girkin, Petleigh, and Arrowood at the back shielding himself. I took the chance and crept behind the horses to the path.

'We've come to arrest you for murder, Annie,' said Petleigh.

With one jab she floored the constable. Girkin and Petleigh backed out of range, the guvnor still behind them. And as the copper crawled away from her too, Flossie appeared in the door, peeking out from behind Annie's legs.

'Get back in the kitchen, darling,' said Annie in her gentler voice.

'I'm sad, Annie,' said the girl. She'd been dressed in a little pair of leather britches too, and her tangled hair was brushed straight and long, with two curls on either side of her little face.

'Come quietly, Annie,' said Petleigh. 'The game's up.'

'You stay back!' Annie bent down and brought her face near the little girl's. 'I know you're sad, Flossie. I know you are.' She hugged the girl, and as she did I stepped over to the path. It went between her building and the next, a dark alley where it seemed they dumped all the rubbish. I clambered through the tarry black puddles and piles of rotting refuse till I reached a wooden gate at the back of the house. There I burst the lock with my shoulder and found myself in a tiny courtyard.

The kitchen was unlocked. Inside was an old range, a deep, stained sink, piled with dirty pots and bowls, a ragged wing chair. And there, laid out on the kitchen table, was Davey. He was dressed in a Sunday suit, his face white, his thin body still. He was dead.

I took it all in, then, quiet as I could, stepped into the corridor. Ahead and with her back to me, framed in the doorway to the street, was Annie, Flossie still clutching her trouser leg. Petleigh was talking. She told him to fuck himself. I got my neddy out and slowly moved up behind her, placing each footstep so careful on the dusty boards. My heart was thudding in my chest; my fingers tingled. Girkin caught my eye from the street, and I knew he'd recognized me. The guvnor'd seen me too; he spoke out, trying to cover my movements.

'Mr George gave you up, Annie!' he yelled. 'He's in custody!'

'You think I'm simple or something?' she hissed.

'You're facing murder! Give yourself up now before it's too late!'

I was not three steps from her when I felt my boot sink on a loose board. A creak. Annie turned and launched herself at me, her fingers biting into my neck as she crashed down on top of me. I couldn't breathe. She dug hard into the gristle of my neck as we battled on the floor, her other hand shoving my chin back till it felt as my spine would snap.

'Norman!' came the guvnor's voice through the pain. Flossie was screaming like I never heard before, and there were shouts, feet. I twisted and jerked, knowing I had to get at Annie's hands, but my arms were pinned to the floor by her knees. My vision filled with colour. Then I heard nothing but ringing in my ears, and suddenly the pain was gone and I was floating, feeling warm and happy. I blacked out.

It must have been only seconds later that I came to, a roaring, painful breath being sucked into my lungs, a weight on my chest like a tombstone. I couldn't see anything at first as I twisted to get out from under her. Flossie screamed and screamed. Then my sight snapped back and I was staring into Annie's face and a dirty pair of hands as were gripping her hair, pulling her head back. Her eyes were red. Her tongue lolled over her blistered lip, warty and yellow. Out her mouth came a gurgle. Then I saw it was Girkin, sitting on her back, a savage look on his face as he tried to tear off her head. My neck was free, but they were crushing me. As I fought to catch my breath, the constable flew in the door and got one of Annie's wrists in irons. Girkin jumped off her and the constable raised his truncheon high, bringing it down hard on her leg. She jerked up, giving me enough space to squeeze out from under her just as the PC shackled her other wrist.

I rose. The room spun around me. I clutched the wall, bent over, heaving. The guvnor was next to me, his hand on my back.

'Breathe slowly,' he was saying, stroking me. 'Slowly.'

'Leave her alone!' wailed the girl from the doorway. She was gasping, weeping, her hands clenched tight by her side.

The guvnor turned to her, knelt, and took her hand. 'It's over, darling,' he said. 'Don't cry. The fighting's over.'

'Annie,' said Flossie between gulps of air. Her little chest was jerking, her face wet with confused tears. 'Annie.'

Girkin and the constable hauled Annie upright.

'Don't cry, sugar plum,' said the great ratcatcher, her hands cuffed behind her back. 'No need for that, eh? Annie's fine. Everything's all right. They'll look after you now.'

'I arrest you for murder, Annie,' said Girkin. His heavy chest was rising and falling as he moved from one foot to the other. 'There be two witnesses so don't you say it ain't so.'

'Shove it.'

Girkin turned to me, a sly smile appearing on his mug. 'Norman Barnett,' he said. 'I'm arresting you for gaol-breaking.'

'Don't be a fool, Girkin,' said Petleigh. 'We're in the middle of solving this case.'

Girkin's rabbity face twitched, then his lip curled. 'I ain't forgotten you, Barnett,' he said at last. He turned to the constable. 'Right, Hodge, you watch the prisoner. We'll search the rooms.'

There were only two doors: one at the back to the kitchen and another at the front next to us. Petleigh and Girkin went in there.

'Stay where you are, Arrowood,' said Petleigh over his shoulder. 'Don't touch anything.'

While they were rummaging in the front room, I caught the guvnor's eye and nodded at the kitchen door.

'Come back here, sir,' barked the constable as Arrowood squeezed past him. 'The inspector says not to touch anything!'

Annie stood on the front doorstep, her arms locked behind her back, while the constable held her shoulder. Flossie stood on the other side, gripping Annie's legs, her face wet and red. I looked through into the front room, where Petleigh and Girkin were searching. The window panes were covered with newspapers, and, stacked in piles around all the walls, were cages creeping and twitching with rats. It smelt no different than the sewers themselves, and in the middle of the floor, under a canopy of drifting flies, was a big mattress. There were no sheets, just a roll of blanket turned black with filth for a pillow.

I stepped back to let Girkin out. His hand was wrapped in a dirty cloth, and in it he held a watch.

'Where d'you get this?' he asked Annie.

'I never seen it before.'

'In a cigar box in one of your cages.'

'You bloody liar!' she said in a fury. 'You put it there yourself!'

He flipped open the case. 'The inscription gets you hanged, Annie. *Dearest Emile,*' he read. '*Fondest love, R & G.* Rachel and Gabriella, I'd wager.'

'You get that done yourself, did you?'

'We got you good, Annie.'

'I'll see you in hell then, wurzel.'

'You might as well tell us who be in it with you.'

'That ain't the way it works.'

'No jury in London'll let you off with this evidence. You'll hang for it, you will.'

'You lying toerag.'

'Spill it, Annie.'

'Spill your ballocks, copper.'

Girkin sighed. 'Take her to the carriage, Hodge.'

'Wait,' said the guvnor, coming through from the kitchen. 'There's something you should see first, Inspector.'

He led Petleigh and Girkin into the kitchen. I heard them whisper to each other, then Petleigh appeared in the doorway.

'I assume you wish to say your goodbyes to the boy, Annie.'

Her face softened.

With a calf leather glove, Petleigh brushed his jacket. 'Bring her down, Constable,' he said.

Annie stomped past me, the constable after her. Flossie tried to follow, but I took her arm. She was stunned, tired.

Through the doorway, I watched Annie go to the table, bend over, and kiss the boy's cheek. The bells of St James's rang out over the houses, and for a few minutes they let her alone.

'How did he die?' asked Petleigh at last.

'Blood infection,' said the guvnor. 'From wounds to his back caused by Mr George, owner of Nell Gwynne's. He beat the boy with a cabbie's whip for begging. We saw him do it, Annie.'

She turned to the doorway. 'Flossie?' she said, her voice a-quiver. 'Did you see the man who beat him?'

Flossie tried again to reach the kitchen but I held her back. She nodded. 'Davey was crying.'

'D'you know who the man was, darling?'

'He was the boss man. From the dancing club. The red one.'

Annie nodded. She turned back to the table and looked at Davey, the fight and fury gone from her face as she spoke. 'I'll give you one name. Nobody else. Just one, so don't you go asking me over and over. Chelsea George. He paid me six quid to do them in, those two women and the bloke. Two quid for each. He told me where they'd be. Set it all up. You get him and I'll testify. I'm turning Queen's evidence. But I ain't giving up no more names.'

'You're a murderer, Annie,' said Girkin. 'You'll swing.'

'Then he'll swing with me.'

I took Flossie to the street. As they stepped past us, the girl pulled away and grabbed Annie's hand, cuffed as it was behind her back.

'I want to go with you,' she pleaded.

'No, love. You can't come.'

'But you said, Annie. You said.'

'We'll find somewhere nice for you to live, Flossie,' said Arrowood.

'Till Annie comes back,' said Flossie, glowering at him. Then she looked up at Annie's sad face. 'You're coming back, right?'

Annie bent down. 'Give me a hug, darling.' Flossie put her arms round her neck. 'You be strong, darling. You promise? You got to be strong forever.'

The constable took Annie to the station in a cab, while the rest of us made our way to Kennington. Chelsea George's house was a five-storey, double-fronted affair, bright white, with chequered tiles running up the steps. Though it was early afternoon, all the curtains were shut, and nobody answered when Girkin knocked. We returned to the pavement and climbed down the stairwell to the basement door. A cook answered.

'Is your master in, mum?' demanded Girkin. 'City Police. It's an urgent matter.'

The woman rubbed her hands on her apron. 'Couldn't tell you, sir,' she said. 'I've just been down here in the kitchen. It's only me in today.'

'Can you take us up?'

She looked confused. She wiped her hands again.

'You must, mum. We're about to arrest him.'

Finally, she nodded and led us up the narrow servant stairs to a back corridor, then through to a wide, tiled hall lined with plants with great, shaggy leaves. A chandelier hung above, while a wide stairway curved to an open landing. She knocked on a white door, ten foot high and gleaming. There was no answer. She tried the handle, but it was locked. Impatient, Petleigh opened the door next to it and stepped inside. We followed.

The room was large, with a piano, a couple of sofas, several more chairs, a huge marble fireplace. Above the mantel hung a painting of an expedition somewhere in Africa. And on the carpet was a body.

Girkin marched over to the curtains and jerked them open. Chelsea George lay on his back in a pair of red silk pyjamas, his arms out straight by his side, one leg neatly crossed over the other. His white hair was gone, his forehead, his face naught but a ragged cavity of gristle and bone. The only feature left on his half-exploded skull was the prettiest pair of Belgian ears you could ever hope to see.

Chapter Forty-Seven

I slept from Wednesday afternoon to Friday. When I gained the streets, my feet heavy, my head in a fug, the story was in all the papers. Girkin had made sure of that. It was Girkin as solved it, Girkin as made the arrests, Girkin as worked out I was innocent. The guvnor wouldn't be happy about that, so I thought I'd keep clear of him least until Saturday. First thing I did was visit Sidney's place, where his wife Pearl told me he was still in stir for assisting my gaol-break but getting out next week. Not many blokes'd do what he did for me: he was a true friend, all right, and I'd make sure Arrowood gave him some of that reward money.

Petleigh'd persuaded Girkin to leave me be over the weekend as long as I handed myself in on Monday morning. I'd get a week or two hard labour for gaol-breaking. It didn't seem fair, but the law was the law or something like it at least. I could take it: it was a whole lot better than the gallows.

The case had been hard on me, but I had the weekend ahead and I was going to enjoy myself. I still had a few shilling in my britches, so I knocked up my old pal Nobber Sugg and joined him for his usual Friday afternoon trip to the races at Alexandra Park. We drank porter and ate oysters, lost a few bets and won a few others, and ran into a crowd of old faces from the Bermondsey days. I felt warm, pleased to be around blokes like myself for a change, happy to be lost in a great crowd, in the shouting and boozing, in the thrill of it all. It was good to be back in my old clothes again, mispatched or not.

On the way back, we stopped in his local where we met his old girl and a few of her friends. There was a thin woman in there banging away on a battered piano. We got a few pints of gin and had a right old jolly, singing and smoking and telling stories in that packed little pub. It was good to be free. Good to be alive.

I was as full as a tick by the time I climbed the stairs to my room around midnight. A note was shoved under my door. It was from the guvnor, asking me to meet him at Old Swan Pier at eleven next morning. I dropped onto the bed and fell asleep with all my clothes on.

It was Saturday, and it seemed as nothing had changed from that first day we waited on the pier for the *Gravesend Queen*. Queues of day-trippers coiled from the jetty up the stairs to the embankment, touts hawked them tickets, women sold parasols, fans, sweeties for the children. It was mid-July and the sun was out.

The guvnor stood at the top of the steps, in the spot where Monkey used to beg. He was washed, his hair cut, his whiskers trimmed. He wore his new boater and a striped river jacket I'd not seen before. It wasn't new: the elbows were worn down and one of the pockets was stitched with the wrong colour thread, but it almost fitted him. He looked a new man.

'It's good to see you looking yourself again, Norman,' he said, clutching my hand. He touched my cheek, where the scar was crusted over. 'Does it hurt?'

I shook my head.

'You've suffered on this case. I was afraid for you.'

'I'm fine now, William.'

'What I said before . . . I insulted you. I didn't mean it. I was worried. I was afraid.' Still holding my hand, he reached into his pocket and took out a five-pound note which he pressed into my palm.

'From Curtis?' I asked.

'No, he's coming to meet us this afternoon. Girkin called on Buttergrass's aunt on Thursday: she insisted he take the reward money then and there.'

I looked at the five-pound note in my hand. It'd been years since I'd had that much money, but I shook my head. 'The reward was a hundred quid.'

'Petleigh and Girkin took a third each, Norman.'

'So where's the rest of it?'

'There isn't any more.' As he spoke he caught sight of someone behind me and raised his hand. I turned and saw Ettie coming down from Lower Thames Street, pushing the perambulator through the crowds. Suzie was holding the crook of her arm, and they were laughing. Suzie whispered something in her ear, and they laughed again. Though the sun was out and strong, it seemed a special light shone on them as they moved through the day-trippers.

I pushed the fiver back in his pocket. 'That ain't nowhere near enough,' I whispered as the women arrived.

Suzie greeted us with the same bright smile that came so readily to her face before she lost her old man. It was good to see. She wore the long skirt and yellow blouse of the women's refuge. The tan was going from her face, the freckles less striking. Ettie looked rested, a bit red-faced and damp from the sun, but her smile disappeared when she looked at me. It was like I'd let her down somehow. Before today that would have troubled me, but I found I couldn't worry. I was going to gaol on Monday. I was alive. Those two facts were larger to me than anything else that day.

Suzie was examining the pier, her eyes sweeping over what used to be her life. The *Koh-i-Noor* was docked, and passengers were starting to board. Next to it the *Clacton Belle* was pulling out. The ticket seller Ken was standing in the middle of it all with a billboard round his neck advertising tickets for Margate. The lighterwoman lounged by her boat smoking a pipe, while the piermaster was having a go at the African fellow for using the wrong bollard.

'I do miss this,' said Suzie with a sigh. 'Reverend Jebb's very kind, but I don't know if I can stick a life inside.'

She stepped forward, her eyes narrowing as she caught sight of something on the river. Out in the current, coming under the arches of London Bridge, was a little paddle steamer. It was puffing out smoke like billy-o, which swirled and misted all round it, but you could just make out the red of its paddle boxes, the green of its funnel.

The guvnor was watching her, biting his lip. Ettie watched her too.

'Is that ...' said Suzie. She raised up on her toes to get a better look over the heads of the folk wandering down the steps. 'It is. Look! It's the *Queen*. What's she doing here?'

The boat went out of sight for a few moments as the *Clacton Belle* passed, then it approached the pier, coming in to dock at the space the bigger boat had left. There was nobody on deck.

Suzie ran down the stairs, dodging in and out of the crowd. I helped Ettie carry the pram down, and we joined her at the edge of the pier. As the boat touched the side, the door to the engine room opened and Belasco stepped out. He wore no shirt, his chest tanned and strong. He raked his fingers through his badly cut hair, smiling wider than I'd seen any man smile.

'You ain't bought her, have you, mate?' Suzie called up to him as she looped the ropes over the bollard.

'No, Suze,' said Belasco in his high-up voice. ''Fraid not.'

'So who owns her?'

Belasco scratched his tattoos. A tear came to his eye.

'You do,' said Arrowood.

Suzie turned to him. She turned back to Belasco. She turned back to Arrowood.

'We bought it back for you,' said the guvnor. 'From the reward money. It's yours.'

'But that's your money,' said Suzie as Belasco threw down the gangway and came to join us. 'You solved the case, Mr Arrowood.'

'It's your father's money. He employed us to work for him on solving the case, so the reward money's his. Those are the rules. This is your inheritance, Suzie.'

'I won't take it, Mr Arrowood. Really, I won't. You worked hard for that money. Norman almost got hisself killed.'

'You must, Suzie,' said Belasco, 'else I'm out of a job. You think your old man'd want to see you work as a servant? All day indoors? You think he'd want to see the *Gravesend Queen* in someone else's hands? Do it for him, girl.'

'The boat's paid for,' said the guvnor. 'I'll scuttle her if you won't agree. Believe me, I will.'

'You'll make a fine captain, Suzie,' said Ettie. 'You were born for it. Everybody knows it, even Reverend Jebb.'

The piermaster came up behind us. 'Can you move the boat, Miss Moon?' he said. 'I got another coming in.'

Belasco stepped back onto the gangway. 'Come see us in Wapping sometime, Norm. I want you to meet my cousin. I reckon you'd get along with her.' He held out his hand to Suzie. 'Get a move on then, girlie. We've work to do.'

Suzie looked at the guvnor, a tremble on her lip. The crowds moved around us, the gulls swooped above, while the dirty Thames flowed on, out to Gravesend and the sea. Then, at last, she took Belasco's hand. As she climbed the gangway, I shook my head, for both Ettie and her brother were weeping.

Chapter Forty-Eight

We sat in the parlour. Isabel and Ettie were at the table, the orange cat on the mantel, watching the door. The empty bird cage lay forlorn in a corner. Flossie was under the table, dressing a little dolly Mrs Pudding had found her. The guvnor sat in his chair, a baby in each arm, singing 'Daddy Wouldn't Buy Me A Bow-Wow'. Both little faces stared at him, listening careful as he droned on.

The window and back door were open, but there was still no breeze and we were suffering with the heat. The potboy'd just been, so I poured out mugs of ale and passed them round. Ettie didn't look up from her tract as she took hers. I was irked; she'd kissed me easy enough when I was a lawyer, but now I was back to what I was she'd turned cold. I reckoned that seeing me as one of hers before let her see the difference between us more clearly now. I shouldn't have been vexed; I always knew it was so, just maybe started to believe it wasn't.

Isabel was deep in *The Daily Chronicle*. The tin of biscuits was between them and they both crunched away as they read. It was a celebration of sorts, though a sad one for all the tragedy along the way. By the time Curtis arrived at half two we'd finished the ale and were all a little loose. I stood up to let him have my stool. He wore an open shirt with no jacket, a pair of mustard flannels, a straw boater. His face was clean-shaved but still a bit beaten: he looked tired.

The guvnor handed the babies to their mothers and poured us each a mug of brandy.

'The case is finished, Mr Curtis,' he said. There was no pleasure in his face.

Curtis was silent for a long time, as if wrestling with something inside. He stroked his heavy jaw. 'Thank you, Mr Arrowood,' he said finally. 'Tell me what happened.'

The guvnor explained how Chelsea George and Valeria Harris had colluded to get their revenge on Moon, and how they'd sent the letter pretending to be from Sherlock Holmes to get him out of London so I'd be alone on the boat that night. He told him how they used Lilly to set me up for the murder, how the coppers had arrested Foulpipe Annie, and how she'd given up George when she learned he was to blame for little Davey's death. I watched Curtis as he listened, the respect growing in his face as the guvnor described how he'd managed to bring the case to its end.

Finally, he told him what we'd found when we went to Kennington.

'The police say George was killed sometime on Wednesday morning,' the guvnor said slowly. 'He'd been dead about six hours. Someone discharged a shotgun twice into his face.'

Curtis swallowed his brandy, the twitch of a smile crossing his lips. Quickly, he wiped his mouth.

'The neighbours heard shots between six and seven that morning but didn't send for the police,' continued Arrowood, watching Curtis close as he spoke. 'It seems George had a habit of shooting pigeons from his loft. That would have been before the cook arrived. No sign of forced entry, so we can assume

George let the killer in himself. He doesn't have a butler, just the cook and a maid, but it was her day off.'

'Well, I can't say I'm sorry,' said Curtis. 'They have any idea who could have done it?'

Arrowood said nothing, just puffed on his pipe as he held the fellow's eye.

'Perhaps that one who looked like Mr Barnett?' suggested Curtis. 'You said he was probably working with Annie. Or maybe one of his debtors? I'm sure there were others had it in for him.'

Arrowood raised an eyebrow.

Curtis finished his mug. 'Were there any witnesses?'

'Nobody on the street saw anything.'

Curtis had another sip but his mug was empty. The guvnor poured him more. 'Tell me, Mr Arrowood, if the police hadn't found the watch, would Annie have been convicted?'

'Hard to say. She might have got off.'

'Stupid of her to keep it, wasn't it?'

The guvnor nodded and took a drink himself. He'd stopped scrutinizing Curtis, and it was then I understood something I sensed at the time but hadn't paid much attention to. Annie's reaction when they brought out the watch was real. She'd never seen that watch before.

The guvnor caught my eye and gave me the slightest nod.

Curtis stood. 'Could I use your privy? It's been a long journey.'

Isabel directed him. While the two mothers put their babies in the boxes, the guvnor filled us with brandy again.

'You gave Flatnose something in the Hog afore he left,' I said to him. 'Was it the watch?'

The guvnor looked at Ettie. She looked at Isabel.

'You all knew about this?'

'Norman, they were going to hang you!' said Ettie sharply, looking at me for the first time. 'We knew it was Annie. We had to make sure she was arrested.'

'But where did you get Buttergrass's watch?'

'It wasn't his watch,' said the guvnor. 'I bought it from Nolan when you were in Newgate. He had it engraved for me.'

'And you didn't tell me?'

'I forgot.'

'You forgot!'

'Good Christ, Norman, it was all moving so quickly. I was deciding each move as we went.'

I nodded. In truth, I was proud of him. He never really had a plan. Inside that pig-knuckle head he'd been thinking furiously, working it out one step at a time. I didn't know who else could have done it.

'Did you show him the letter?' Isabel asked him.

The guvnor began to plug his pipe, ignoring her.

'What letter?' I asked.

'William,' she said, a smile on her dark lips. 'Where's the letter?'

'I threw it away,' he muttered, not looking up.

Isabel rose and went to the bin in the corner. After a little rummage, she pulled out a crumpled bit of paper. I noticed Ettie grinning at her as she handed it to me. I opened it and read.

Baker Street, 16 July, 1896

Dear Mr Arrowood

Your letter of the fourth only reached me yesterday, having been absent from London on a case. Let me assure you that I did not summon you to Coventry, nor did I ask for your assistance. I cannot understand why you might think that.

I am told you cracked my parlour window while I was away. I request you send me 7/6 for repairs, which I will pass on to Mrs Hudson, my landlady. Please do so immediately as there is a draught.

Yours truly, Sherlock Holmes

PS. I read this morning that your assistant Mr Barnett helped Inspector Girkin apprehend Foulpipe Annie. I offer him my congratulations. She was a foul pest and London will be safer without her.

I looked up. The guvnor was dealing with his pipe. Isabel, her eyes alight, held her hand over her mouth.

'That's decent of him,' I said at last, a smile on my face I couldn't seem to shift.

'Seven and six for a plate of glass!' he grunted, his teeth clenched on the pipe stem. 'Damn swindler. It'll never cost that.'

'You did break it,' I said.

'Well, I'm not paying that. He's still saying he wasn't there when we saw him clear as day.'

'He didn't mention you helping Inspector Girkin, William,' said Ettie. 'Only Norman.'

'You've both already said that. Several times. It's become tiresome.'

Ettie and Isabel caught each other's eyes and laughed. There was a sudden fluttering and squawking from the hens next door.

'What's that?' cried Flossie from under the table.

'Probably just a cat got in again, darling,' said Ettie. 'Nothing to worry about.'

'So the coppers haven't any evidence on who killed Mr George?' asked Curtis, coming in from the yard.

'Not that I've heard,' said Arrowood. 'Some of those involved in this case are going to escape justice. Unless Annie talks, the fellow who they thought was Norman'll never be caught. He could be on a steamer to America by now. Unless . . .' The guvnor paused. We were all drinking quick now, relieved to be getting it all out, making sense out of it. 'Unless you want us to go after him, Mr Curtis?'

The birdman shook his head. 'I'm happy with what you done, Mr Arrowood. Tell me, did you find out anything else about Chelsea George?'

'He was a ganger some years back. Did a flit with his men's wages, disappeared for a few years and came back with a new identity.'

'He didn't completely disappear,' said Curtis. He had another gulp. Ettie rose and filled our mugs again. Sometimes the taste she had for brandy shocked me. 'He was living in Oxford, same time as Solly.'

'You knew him?'

'Not really. I was in Oxford then too. We used to go to the same club, but he weren't the sort you wanted to get too close to. He was vindictive.' He sighed and looked up at the ceiling.

'Solly shone bright back then. He made life good. It was after the accident he changed.'

'You didn't tell us that, Mr Curtis,' said the guvnor, blowing out a long train of smoke.

'It wouldn't have helped, would it?'

The guvnor shook his head, a fuddled pride remaining on his face from discussing how he'd reached the end of this most complicated case. I smiled to see him like that, tipsy myself from having not had any proper food that day.

'What about Polgreen?' asked Curtis. 'Was he in on it?'

'I don't think so,' answered the guvnor. 'There was a feud between the two of them. They both damaged each other's boats. Polgreen admitted to two incidents but not the rest, and I believed him. There were no signs of lying in his behaviour, no momentary changes of emotion, no inconsistent expressions of the face. And I think if he was involved he'd deny everything. George and Harris must have been behind the awnings and the fire. They wanted to hound the captain, and they needed to make it costly enough that it would drive him to hire us. If he hadn't killed himself, no doubt they'd have had Annie do it, but only after Norman was executed.'

'You didn't explain what Mr Barnett did to Valeria Harris to make her want him dead,' said Curtis, turning to me. 'Mr Arrowood said some trouble with her father?'

The question took me by surprise. I don't know why: it was the obvious thing he'd want to know, but in some way I felt I'd shut the door on it already. I looked at the guvnor, then at Ettie. She was relaxed from the brandy but still stiff with me somehow, and I felt even more vexed at her than before. Maybe it was the booze had loosened up my heart, but something wild rose in me: I wanted to shock her. I wanted to show her who I really was.

'I was sixteen or seventeen,' I said. 'Ma was sick, dying so it seems, and I was paying our way. We owed a few folk. It was hard. It was hard for everybody. A mate showed me a way to earn easy money in Wapping, helping out the sailors on shore leave.' I watched Ettie steady as I spoke. She was lighting her pipe, not looking at me. I took another swallow. 'They come ashore with their wages, want a bit of fun. We looked after them.'

The guvnor nodded, but I wasn't sure he knew what he was nodding to. Curtis watched me steady. I waited till Ettie was looking at me again. 'We'd have a drink with them. Give them a tickle if they wanted.' The tiredness in her grey eyes meant I couldn't read what was in them. Either she didn't know what I was talking about or she didn't want to. The guvnor had twigged, though, and the smile was gone from his face. 'There were a few of us lads took the road to Wapping Wall. It didn't do any harm. Anyways, there was this older boy in my court said I could get paid a lot more for doing less up St James's Park, where the gents had more money in their purses.' I took another swallow. 'Hogan, his name was. Lenny Hogan.'

Ettie was still none the wiser. The guvnor was shaking his head. 'Norman, you don't have to,' he said.

'I know I don't.' I swallowed half the mug down and felt the burn; the devil was in me now and they were going to know, whether they wanted or not. 'He took me up there one night, told me to walk over to this gent on a bench, tell him I could show him nine inches.' Still I held Ettie's eye, watching as she began to understand. 'It was Eustace Harris, Valeria's dad. He led me to the bushes. Took no more than five minutes, and there was a guinea in my pocket. The only problem was Hogan was waiting there for us when we came out, and he had another fellow with him. He held a knife up to Harris's throat and got his name, his address, his business. They said he'd to pay fifty quid or we'd swear sodomy against him. He was a tea merchant. They said they'd ruin him. Gave him two days to pay.'

'Norman, no,' whispered Ettie. 'And you didn't stop them?'

I poured myself more brandy. 'Two days later he'd thrown himself off Waterloo Bridge.'

The guvnor shook his head, his eyes sick with shock, cold with judgement. Isabel bit her lip. Ettie just stared. I'd appalled her, and it felt like a liberation.

'I'm guilty, simple as that. For five years everything I did to make money for Ma and me was against the law. That's just the way we were. But I've been ashamed every day since for what we did.'

'You're not that boy any more,' she said.

'Yes, I am. That's the point, Ettie.' She held my eye, and though it was painful, it felt like the most honest moment we'd ever had between us. 'I'm not the person you think I am. Not a lawyer, nor a soldier neither. What I've done is what I am. It's me, man and boy.'

We sat in silence for some time, flies buzzing in tight circles in the middle of the little room. Through the window, we could hear the hens clucking next door. A woman shouted. Isabel stood, came over to me and squeezed my hand.

'We can see you're suffering from it.'

'I am. But not for being a renter. I won't apologize for that.'

'If you ask Him, He forgives,' said Ettie softly.

I shook my head, wondering if she was deliberately missing what I was saying.

When nobody else spoke, I rose and went to the privy.

I stayed there for some time, my head in my hands. My arms and legs felt weak, my breath short. I'd dropped a burden I'd been carrying for years, and now I wished I hadn't. I sat there until I was sick of my thoughts, my memories, my worn-out emotions. When I came back, they were talking about the case again. The guvnor nodded at me, but there was no smile. I stood against the wall.

'And Suzie?' asked Curtis. 'How is she?'

'She's got the *Gravesend Queen* back,' said the guvnor. 'She's going to start the run again with Belasco.'

'Good,' said Curtis. 'Perhaps she'll visit me now.'

Ettie filled our mugs again. She fell back heavily on her chair.

'Do I owe you anything, Mr Barnett?' asked Curtis, his eyes fixed on his boots.

'No, sir,' I told him, my voice hollow. 'You paid us enough.'

'It was a kind thing you did for Suzie, William,' said Isabel, taking Ettie's mug and finishing off her brandy.

Despite the heavy atmosphere, the guvnor smiled and blinked through his eyeglasses, a little colour coming to his cheeks.

'But you should never have taken that poor boy out in the carriage,' she went on. 'It probably killed him. I don't care what Flossie wanted, you should never have done it.'

'I didn't want to,' he said, a true sadness in his eyes. 'I'd promised them. I thought once he knew he was with Annie he'd be at peace.'

'Tripe,' said Ettie. 'The boy was unconscious. I know why

you did it, brother. You were using him. You wanted Annie to see him die.'

'Ettie, please.'

'I know your tricks.'

'Ettie!'

'His last hours, and you put him in a bumpy carriage across London. Surely that wasn't necessary?'

The guvnor stood. He drained his mug and uncorked the brandy again, pouring himself a splash. He offered the bottle to Curtis, who shook his head. Ettie and Isabel had a splash. I stood by the door, unoffered.

'Chelsea George was going to get away scot-free,' he said. 'We had Annie, but her type never give up their accomplices. Monkey's dead, so no witnesses at the scene. They won't bring a murder conviction on the basis of the ear mentioned in Selby's promissory note. George would have hired the very best lawyers, and I'm afraid to say they would ruin Lilly. She's compromised by what she did with Norman: they'd use it to question her character. They'd put a case forward that she was in it with Annie and was blaming George and Harris to get herself off. It doesn't matter that she's no motive: they have her planting the evidence. So you tell me how we could have brought him to justice.'

'You'd better pray to the Lord for forgiveness, William,' said Ettie. Then she looked at me and opened her mouth to speak. But didn't. My story was too shocking, too far from home, and she didn't know what to do with it. Safer to argue with her brother.

'Doesn't the Lord decide who dies and when?' asked the guvnor. He wasn't arguing, wasn't irked. He was only asking.

'Who's to say the Lord didn't sacrifice little Davey? Who's to say the Lord didn't use me as a tool to bring that fiend to justice?'

'But you didn't bring him to justice. Someone with a shotgun did that.'

'There's no point discussing this, Ettie. You judge me. I did it. I don't regret it.'

'You mightn't be so certain, William,' said Ettie.

'Oh, leave him alone, Ettie,' said Isabel sharply.

Ettie twitched, a wounded look on her face, and silence fell over the room. Curtis turned from one to the other. The guvnor breathed heavily. You could see in that great, irksome face, that he was glad for Isabel's support.

'Anyway, you need to tell Suzie about the *Princess Grace* and her father's real name,' said Ettie at last. 'It isn't fair. She doesn't need to be protected from that.'

'I'll tell her,' said Curtis, standing up. 'I'll tell her everything. I'd like to get to know her better.'

He got the address of the refuge from Ettie, then said his goodbyes to her, and Isabel, and little Flossie under the table.

The guvnor rose. 'We'll walk you out,' he said.

We followed Curtis through the dark, cluttered corridor to the pudding shop, and pushed through the line of punters. As we stepped onto the street, the guvnor reached behind and squeezed my arm. I was hollowed out and headachey, and I confess that little gesture felt a comfort. I'd been afraid so long about him judging me, but it seemed that all along it was I who'd been judging him.

'Thank you for everything,' said Curtis as we made our way up Coin Street. They walked together, I trailing behind. 'You ain't got the reputation you deserve.'

'Thank you, sir,' said the guvnor.

'If you're ever in Gravesend, you must call on me, Mr Arrowood. As a friend.'

'That would be wonderful. Perhaps we can go for shrimps. But please, call me William.'

'And I'm Carl, William,' said the birdman, stopping at the corner of Stamford Street as if stunned by the press of people walking past. He turned and looked me in the eye. 'Carl Curtis, Mr Barnett.' The warmth had gone from his face, and, in the moment before he spoke again, I knew what he was about to say. He brought his lips up close to my ear. 'But you may call me Feathers.'

The guvnor held my arm as we watched him stride down Stamford Street, becoming less and less until he was lost in the crowd. And was gone.

Historical Notes and Sources

The Thames

The Thames was a busy working river in the 1890s. It was lined with docks and wharves where cargo to and from all over the world was loaded and unloaded. Fishing boats came as far as Billingsgate to sell their catch, lighters carried goods from larger ships to the wharves, and barges carried goods between London and other parts of the country. Day-tripping on paddle steamers was a well-established summer outing for families of all classes. The newer boats, such as *Glen Rosa* and *Koh-i-Noor*, were bigger and better-equipped than the older ones, offering entertainment and both first and second classes. These boats took day-trippers inland towards Maidenhead and Oxford as well as to the coastal towns of Essex, Kent, East Anglia and France. The older boats, such as the fictional *Gravesend Queen* of this book, were left in their wake, catering mainly for the working classes and travelling to nearer destinations such as Gravesend, Southend and the Medway towns.

Deaths from accidents and suicides were common on the Thames. The idea for Captain Moon's collision on the *Princess Grace* came from a 1878 disaster, in which the collier *Bywell Castle* hit the paddle steamer *Princess Alice* as it returned from Gravesend with a full boat of day-trippers. About 650 people died, the greatest loss of life of any accident on the Thames.

Homosexuality and the Law

Homosexual behaviour between men, but not women, was illegal in the Victorian era, and, while there were many who supported same-sex relationships, social attitudes were for the most part hostile. Some historians suggest that lesbian behaviour was not included in legislation because Queen Victoria did not believe it was possible, while others suggest legislators didn't want to alert women to the possibility. Although the death penalty for sodomy was abolished in 1861, men could still be arrested and given a life sentence for it. Section 11 of the Criminal Law Amendment Act 1885, proposed by the Liberal MP Henry Labouchère, made 'gross indecency' between men a crime, and it was used to prosecute gay men when sodomy could not be proven. This law was used against both Oscar Wilde and Alan Turing. Wilde is mentioned in the book as having been in Newgate: before being transferred to Reading Gaol, he was held at Newgate; Pentonville and then Wandsworth prisons.

As Peter Ackroyd reports in his book *Queer City*, men in the nineteenth century could have sex with each other in private residences, male brothels and in certain pubs, parks and alleys. However, blackmail for male homosexuality was common, and some men chose suicide rather than face exposure. Because no definitions were given in the 1885 Act for what counted as 'gross indecency', it became known as the 'The Blackmailer's Charter'. The legislation was only repealed in 1967.

Ratting and Bird Singing Contests

Both ratting and bird-singing competitions were held in working-class pubs in the Victorian period. According to Kellow Chesney's *The Victorian Underworld*, ratting involved putting a dog (usually a terrier) in a pen full of rats, the winner of the competition being the animal that killed the most rats in a set time. Gamblers of all classes would attend these events, and bookies were ever ready to take their bets. In London, ratting was popular around Southwark, St Giles and Spitalfields. Mid-century, ratting pubs might buy two to seven hundred rats a week from families who specialised in catching them. Although ratting became less popular towards the end of the century, there were still a few pubs doing it in the 1890s. The description in the book draws on Henry Mayhew's account in *London Labour and the London Poor*.

Bird-singing competitions were more respectable than ratting. Bird-keeping was an important aspect of working-class life in Victorian London, enthusiasts being known as the 'Bird Fancy', who would gather in places such as Hare Street in Brick Lane on a Sunday night to show and talk birds. Birds such as linnets and goldfinches took part in singing competitions, in which expert scorers would judge each bird's performance. Some owners believed blinding birds by pushing a hot wire into their eyes improved their performance, although this practice was frowned on by most and would have been rare by the 1890s.

Would Barnett write '-ize' or '-ise'?

A friendly reader pointed out that I was using the '-ize' spelling (e.g. organize) in previous books, rather than the more common current British '-ise' spelling. From my searches on the internet, it seems that, in England, the rules of spelling were quite loose in earlier historical times, with 'ize' and 'ise' both used for the same words. However, the '-ise' spelling began to dominate in

Victorian times. This post from author and editor Hannah Kate explains the history nicely: https://hannahkate.net/in-defence-of-ize/ Since I'd used 'ize' in the first two Arrowood books, and since 'ize' was still common in the Victorian period, we decided to stick to that for this book as well.

Sources
Many thanks to the British Library Newspaper Collection, the Thames River Police Museum and the London Docklands Museum. I've also relied on a number of books, articles and websites, the most useful of which are listed below.

Peter Ackroyd, *Queer City: Gay London from the Romans to the Present Day,* Chatto & Windus, 2017.

Ari Adut, 'A theory of scandal: Victorians, homosexuality, and the fall of Oscar Wilde', *American Journal of Sociology, 111*(1), 2005.

Walter Besant, *The Thames*, Adam & Charles Black, 1903.

Peter Box, *Paddle Steamers of the Thames*, Tempus, 2000.

Judith Flanders, *Victorian City*, Atlantic Books, 2012.

Ruth Goodman, *How to Be a Victorian*, Penguin, 2014.

Michelle Higgs, *Prison Life in Victorian England*, Tempus, 2007.

Lee Jackson, *Victorian London* website, https://www.victorianlondon.org

Chesney Kellow, *The Victorian Underworld*, Maurice Temple Smith Ltd, 1970.

James Lambie, *The Story of Your Life: A History of the Sporting Life Newspaper (1859-1998)*, Troubador Publishing, 2010.

Jack London, *The People of the Abyss*, Hesperus Press, 1903.

Henry Mayhew & John Binney. *The Criminal Prisons of London and Scenes From London Life*, 1862. Downloaded from https://www.victorianlondon.org/publications5/prisons.htm

Henry Mayhew, *London Labour and the London Poor*, Griffin Bohn, 1861.

Mortimer Menpes & Geraldine E. Mitten, *The Thames*, A & C Black, 1906.

Mick Sinclair, *The Thames: A Cultural History*, Oxford University Press, 2007.

Neil R. Storey, *Prisons and Prisoners in Victorian Britain*, The History Press, 2010.

Julie-Marie Strange, '"She cried a very little": death, grief and mourning in working-class culture', c. 1880-1914. *Social History*, 27 (2), 2002.

The Royal River: The Thames, From Source to Sea, Bloomsbury, 1885.

Henry Walker, *East London Sketches of Christian Work and Workers*, Religious Tract Society, 1896.

Oscar Wilde, *The Ballad of Reading Gaol*. Originally published 1898.

Acknowledgements

Thanks again to my friends Karen Johnston, Elizabeth Enfield and Vincent Wells for reading this story and helping me improve it. I'm also very grateful to my editor, Dominic Wakeford, for his careful reading and thoughtful guidance, and to my agent, Jo Unwin, for her enthusiasm and advice throughout.

ONE PLACE. MANY STORIES

Bold, innovative and
empowering publishing.

FOLLOW US ON:

@HQStories